GREAT LIVES:

THE AMERICAN FRONTIER

PATRICIA CALVERT

Atheneum Books for Young Readers

To my brother, John Dunlap,
affectionately

Atheneum Books for Young Readers
An imprint of Simon & Schuster Children's Publishing Division
1230 Avenue of the Americas
New York, New York 10020

Book design by Martin Zanfardino/ PIXEL PRESS

The text of this book is set in ITC Century Book.

First Edition

Printed in the United States of America

10 9 8 7 6 5 4 3 2 1

Library of Congress Cataloging-in-Publication Data
Calvert, Patricia.
Great lives : the American frontier / Patricia Calvert.—1st ed.
p.   cm.
Includes bibliographical references and index.
Summary: A collective biography of great figures in the history of the American frontier.
ISBN 0-689-80640-X
1. Pioneers—West (U.S.)—Biography—Juvenile literature. 2. Frontier and pioneer life—
West (U.S.)—Juvenile literature. 3. West (U.S.)—Biography—Juvenile literature.
[1. Pioneers. 2. Frontier and pioneer life—West (U.S.) 3. West (U.S.)—Biography.] I. Title.
F590.5.C35   1997
920.078—dc21
96-48519
CIP   AC

Contents

Foreword

*We could put Emerson's quote another
way: History has a human face. That's
true for most of history around the
world. It is men and women who put
events in motion, sometimes out of
necessity, sometimes out of free choice—
and that seems to be doubly true when
we think of the American frontier.*

We don't think of the frontier as an
invisible threshold that Americans
crossed at the direction of a government. Rather, we think of the individual
men and women who took it upon themselves to press beyond the safe limits of
what was known into the unknown. In
our mind's eye, we see Daniel Boone as
he steps out of the forest to lead his folk
down the newly carved Cumberland
Road, which opened Tennessee and
Kentucky for settlement. We watch as
Sacagawea beckons to Captain William
Clark and tells him she recognizes the
country the expedition is passing
through, that the "Great Water" of the
Pacific can't be far away. We observe
dashing General George Armstrong
Custer, resplendent in military garb,
heading deep into Indian territory along
the Little Bighorn River to keep his appointment with destiny and the Sioux.

Even though the western frontier is
still very much alive in our books,
music, and films, we might do well to
ask ourselves exactly *where* that frontier was located. Did it necessarily mean

Oregon or Texas? Did it always mean Dakota Territory or California?

In truth, "the West" was present in the minds of English colonists even before they arrived in the New World. As they stood on the docks of Liverpool, awaiting passage to America, emigrants turned their eyes westward. Almost from the moment the first settlements were made along the Atlantic coast they continued to do the same. That is, the ocean at their backs clearly marked the eastern edge of the settlers' world; exploration and colonization along the northern and southern coastline of the New World proceeded quickly, but always, always, the new inhabitants of America found themselves peering deep into the western forests and imagining what was *in* them or *beyond* them.

As the boundaries of the colonies were pressed outward, the West became more than one specific place. Once upon a time, Andrew Jackson, seventh president of the United States and a resident of Nashville, Tennessee, proudly called himself a "westerner." Eventually, the West also came to mean Pennsylvania, Ohio, and Indiana; later, it meant Illinois, Iowa, and Missouri (which we now call the Midwest); still later, it meant the vast "prairie ocean" of Kansas, Nebraska, and Dakota Territory. Nor did a quest for the West end once settlers reached the edge of the Pacific;

much later, Alaska and Hawaii were included in Americans' westward embrace—and we called the whole adventure our "Manifest Destiny."

Although nearly every nook and cranny of the United States from Boston on the Atlantic to the Baja on the Pacific has now been mapped and explored, we still experience the West as a place peopled by the brave men and hardy women we have become acquainted with through novels and movies. The West, therefore, essentially became a *place in the imagination* and remains a mythical domain even today.

In modern times, Americans find it necessary to challenge themselves with such dangerous sports as hang gliding, whitewater rafting, or leaping canyons on motorcycles—but those men and women who went west didn't need to invent adventures for themselves. Sometimes, merely staying alive was the most immediate challenge they experienced and was part of merely getting from one day to the next. In a sense, the ordinary often resulted in the extraordinary.

Although we know something of the hardships those early Americans faced, we persist in seeing the opening of the West in romantic terms: actors such as John Wayne made sure of that. It's no surprise, then, that we want to cover our ears to shut out the screams of Daniel Boone's sixteen-year-old son James as he was tortured to death in 1773 by Shawnees as the family headed toward the Cumberland Gap. We shrink from thinking too long about how Lewis and Clark and their men considered themselves lucky to be able to sit down to a feast of maggoty elk meat on Christmas Day, 1805, after they reached their destination along the Oregon coast. We are chilled to the bone when we read that on a cold, gray November afternoon in 1847, Marcus Whitman was tomahawked to death at his Oregon mission, and hours later his wife, Narcissa, was murdered as well, her body thrown ignominiously into the muddy yard beside that of her husband.

When people went "westering," as it was called back then, in small groups, or sometimes only a few men at a time, they left behind family, friends, and security, thereby giving birth to the passionate individualism of American society. Once in the West, such folk knew they must depend entirely upon themselves for building homes, providing food, raising children, and defending themselves against the ravages of weather or attacks by Native American tribes who understandably resented their relentless intrusion into tribal lands.

Yet it would be a mistake to view the extension of the frontier all the way to the Pacific as being accomplished in one smooth, well-ordered sweep. Rather, it proceeded in small increments

and was made by folk with distinctly different interests in the West. The likes of Daniel Boone and Davy Crockett and their kin sought cheaper, more readily available land for homesteads. Kit Carson and Jim Bridger—called "the mountain men"—went to harvest beaver fur from western rivers and creeks. Meriwether Lewis and William Clark intended to make maps, gather information about the native people who already inhabited the area, and collect samples of previously unknown plants, animals, and minerals. James J. Hill, a merchandising clerk, and John Deere, a blacksmith, came looking for jobs; Francis Parkman, George Bird Grinnell, and Frederic Remington wanted to preserve the magic of the "real" West before it vanished beneath the onrushing tide of settlement and civilization.

One of the most interesting things a reader will note in this volume is how frequently the paths of early westerners crossed—amazing when one considers that at the beginning of the nineteenth century the country west of the Mississippi was huge and mostly unpopulated by whites. Nevertheless:

- William Clark took part in the Battle of Fallen Timbers in 1794; it was also Sam Houston's first major military experience; General "Mad Anthony" Wayne commanded both young men and also befriended a moody, troubled fellow named Meriwether Lewis;

- Jim Bridger was wounded by a three-inch iron-tipped arrow during an attack by Blackfoot Indians and carried it buried painfully in his hip for several years—until a young missionary doctor named Marcus Whitman removed it at a rendezvous at the Green River in Wyoming in 1835;

- When Davy Crockett arrived at the Alamo in 1836, Jim Bowie—who was an acquaintance of Sam Houston—was already there; a month later, both would die, then would step onto the pages of history books and become immortal;

- Buffalo Bill Cody met George Custer as both entertained the grand duke Alexis of Russia on a hunting trip in 1872;

- George Bird Grinnell joined General Custer in an exploration of the Black Hills in 1874, and Mary Jane Cannary—better known as Calamity Jane—also went along;

- William Cody befriended Sitting Bull of the Sioux and in 1885 included him in his Wild West Show.

Did the individuals whose biographies are collected in this volume know they were marching straight into history, that two hundred years later we would still be compelled by their adventures? It is true they knew they were part of some-thing extraordinary, yet in the beginning their motives were as ordinary as yours or mine. James Jerome Hill got off the train in Minnesota to look for work—but likely never dreamed he'd accumulate one of the largest fortunes in America. After losing an election in Tennessee, Davy Crockett told his family he was "going to texes" (Texas) in search of cheaper land—but didn't plan to die defending the Alamo. Narcissa Whitman, a devout Methodist, earnestly desired to bring the word of God to the Indians of Oregon—not to perish at the hands of those whom she came to serve.

When Frederic Remington was selected to illustrate Francis Parkman's *Oregon Trail*, Parkman wrote in the preface of the book on September 16, 1892, "The Wild West is tamed and its savage charms have withered. If this book can help to keep their memory alive, it will have done its part. It has found a powerful helper in the pencil of Mr. Remington, whose pictures are as full of truth as of spirit, for they are the work of one who knew the prairies and the mountains before irresistible commonplace had subdued them."

The biographies in this volume will introduce readers to a few ordinary men and women—Indian and white alike—who led extraordinary lives in the West when it still possessed what Parkman called "its savage charms."

GREAT LIVES:

THE AMERICAN FRONTIER

Daniel Boone

1734–1820 Quaker backwoodsman, hunter, surveyor, guide. Fought in the French and Indian War, laid out the Wilderness Road, established Boonesborough in Kentucky. Explored more wilderness than any man of his time, but died without an acre of his own.

Daniel Boone came naturally by wanderlust. In 1717, at age fifty-one, his Quaker grandfather left Bradninch, England, and sailed to America to join his three oldest children, George, Sarah, and Squire, whom he'd sent ahead to assess opportunities in the New World. They settled in what is now Pennsylvania, where young Squire, a weaver like his father, married Sarah Morgan in 1720. The sixth of their eleven children, a boy born on November 2, 1734, was named Daniel, after Sarah's favorite brother.

Two early stories hint at Daniel's character. When a smallpox epidemic struck Oley Township, his mother kept her children indoors to protect them from the dread disease. Little Daniel loved the outdoors and chafed at such confinement. He decided the best way to solve the problem was to get the pox and be done with it. One night, he and his older sister Elizabeth sneaked away to a nearby farm, where they climbed into bed with children they knew were sick. Sure enough, they became infected, but lived to tell the tale. Family legend reports Daniel was scolded but not severely punished because, as his mother admitted years later, she "favored him above all" her other children.

If Sarah was easy on Daniel, his father was far sterner. When a misdeed required punishment, Squire switched his sons until they asked for mercy, whereupon he gladly put down the switch to reason with them. It worked with all the boys except Daniel; this son

1

refused to beg for mercy, preferring to silently endure the thrashing.

Between the ages of ten and sixteen, Daniel accompanied his mother each summer when she took her dairy herd to a pasture several miles from home. Nearby was a spring to keep milk and butter fresh, and Daniel's father built a rude cabin for shelter. Sarah made weekly trips home with butter and cheese she'd made, which could be sold or traded for materials such as nails, shoes, and seed corn. Soon, Daniel asked to stay behind. While keeping one eye on the cows, he perfected his aim on rabbits with a spearlike weapon he made from a sapling root. When he was twelve, his father gave him a rifle, and by the time the boy was fifteen, he was one of the best shots in the county and the family never lacked for fresh meat. These summers gave Daniel his profound love of the wilderness. Woods, streams, and fields would always be more congenial to him than the inside of any dwelling.

What little schooling Daniel got came from the wife of his older brother Samuel. When Daniel was thirteen, she taught him to read and to write "a common farmer's hand." Daniel's spelling was inventive rather than accurate, which led his father to comment, "Let the girls do the spelling. Dan'l will do the shooting."

Religious persecution had caused Daniel's grandfather to leave England, and a difference with Quaker doctrine in America caused the Boones to move once again. In 1742, Daniel's sister married a "worldling," a man not of the Quaker faith. To make matters worse in the minds of those who counted on their fingers, Sarah was pregnant at the time of her wedding and was required to make a "confession" to the congregation. Five years later, Daniel's older brother Israel also "married out." The Society of Friends instructed Daniel's father to publicly apologize for his failure to instruct his children properly; he refused, and the Boones left Pennsylvania in May 1750. Daniel was six months short of his sixteenth birthday.

The family traveled through the Cumberland Valley, then into the Shenandoah (one can trace their approximate route along U.S. Highways 422 and 322), and in October 1750, Daniel's father claimed 640 acres of land in the Yadkin River valley of North Carolina. For Daniel, the family's new home was heaven on earth: wild turkey, deer, and bear offered meat for a good marksman, and the boy once brought home thirty deer in a day's time. Bear Creek reportedly got its name because Daniel killed ninety-nine bears along its banks during a single season. Beaver, muskrat, and otter were easily trapped, providing extra income from the sale of furs.

For years, both England and France had pressed their claims to this area; England based its ownership on the Virginia Charter of 1609, while France cited the exploration of the Ohio River by René-Robert La Salle in 1669 as its right to the territory. French interests were mainly in the fur trade; the English regarded the vast raw materials of the area—timber, coal, and agricultural products—to be of primary importance in building a colonial empire. Both countries enlisted the help of Indians to assert their respective claims.

In the spring of 1755, General Edward Braddock arrived in Virginia to take charge of British as well as colonial troops in the struggle against the French and their Indian allies in what was called the French and Indian War. George Washington, a little-known major in the colonial militia, was attached to Braddock's staff. Even though colonists such as Washington were experienced Indian fighters, Braddock refused to take their advice, claiming they had "little courage and no good will." His arrogance would cost him dearly.

The Braddock expedition needed wagon drivers, and one of the volunteers was young Daniel Boone. Braddock's mission was to capture Fort Duquesne, the French outpost overlooking three great rivers—the Ohio, Allegheny, and Monongahela—near present-day Pittsburgh. Braddock practiced a traditional European style of warfare: troops were marched on the enemy in rigid columns in broad daylight. The Indians were amazed at the easy targets the British red coats made, and picked them off with ease. In three hours on July 9, 1755, 26 British officers, including Braddock himself, were killed, along with 714 enlisted men.

The wagoners had been ordered not to retreat, but when they saw the regulars flee past "like sheep before the hounds," in the words of George Washington, they realized their heavy wagons were a deadly liability. Boone and other wagoners such as John Findley cut the traces on their teams, then galloped to safety on the lead horses. Boone didn't see Findley again for fourteen years; when he did, their meeting would change his life.

Back home, Daniel renewed an interest in a girl he'd met two years earlier at his sister Mary's wedding to a Welsh Quaker. Rebecca Bryan, quiet and dark-haired, taller than most girls, now charmed him even more. Daniel himself was described as "five feet eight inches in height, with broad chest and shoulders . . . his hair moderately black; blue eyes arched with yellowish eyebrows; his lips thin . . . a nose a little on the Roman order."

The young couple were married on August 14, 1756, in a ceremony conducted by Daniel's father; Daniel was twenty-one, his bride seventeen. Rebecca became a mother almost overnight—because the two young sons of Boone's brother Israel, orphaned by the death of both their parents, came to live with the newlyweds. The couple's first child, James, was born in May 1757, and another son followed in 1759. By the time she was twenty, Rebecca was mothering four little boys.

The couple settled along Sugartree Creek on Rebecca's father's land. Daniel provided for his family by hunting, trapping, and "scratch" farming (raising only enough to provide for immediate needs). When attacks by the Cherokees became more common, however, the family moved to Culpeper County, Virginia.

But the staid life of a farmer was not for Daniel. Soon he was off on a long hunting trip, during which he carved the famous inscription on a tree in present-day Tennessee: "D. Boon cilled a Bar on tree in the year 1760," which documented the deed and also demonstrated his creative spelling.

When Daniel heard that operations against the Cherokees were about to commence, he enlisted in the militia commanded by Colonel Hugh Wadell. By late 1760, the Cherokees were ready to surrender, and Boone was present at the signing of a peace treaty on November 19. After the militia disbanded, Boone hunted through east Tennessee, then farther into Virginia, one of his companions being Nathaniel Gist, the son of George Washington's famous scout. When their hunting was finished, Boone returned to his old farm on Sugartree Creek, tended to crops, then fetched his family back from Virginia.

The area was becoming ever more settled, no doubt pleasing Rebecca, but taxing Daniel's patience. As game became scarcer, it was necessary for him to roam farther and farther to get meat. Soon, he was taking his oldest son with him. On severely cold nights, Daniel folded eight-year-old James into his deerskin jacket, cradling him against his own body to make sure the boy stayed warm.

In the summer of 1765, Boone joined Major John Field in an exploration of Florida, which had recently been ceded to Britain by Spain. The British were offering one hundred acres of free land to any Protestant settler, but during the five-hundred-mile journey the travelers discovered that game was scarce, that much of the country was swamp, that the creeks were full of alligators and the air full of mosquitoes. Daniel arrived home on December 25, 1765, giving his family the Christmas present they wanted most—himself. What he had acquired

This portrait of Daniel Boone hangs in the National Portrait Gallery. It was engraved by J. B. Longacre from a painting by C. Harding. ARCHIVE PHOTOS.

during his trip wasn't easy to show off; it was a deepened knowledge of the American frontier in all directions.

Boone once said that when he "could not fell a tree close enough to the door for firewood," it was time to move on, and during the next two years, the family moved three times—always westward. Just as he was wondering what he ought to do next, Daniel received a visitor: John Findley (sometimes spelled Finley), the friend from his days as a wagoner for General Braddock.

Findley had become a trader and was seeking to expand his business. He'd heard stories about a "Warrior's Path" used by the Cherokees to attack their enemies, the Shawnees, which took them through a gap in the mountains into a land reputed to be the finest a man could wish for. Findley needed a guide to help him find that passageway and was willing to pay a wage to such a man.

Until now, Daniel had never been able to provide more than a subsistence living for his wife and children. To make matters worse, he was being sued for nonpayment of several debts. Findley's offer couldn't have been presented at a better time.

On May 1, 1769, a party of six men left Boone's cabin, one of them John Stuart (also spelled Stewart), husband of Daniel's youngest sister, Hannah. Part of the expedition was financed by Judge Richard Henderson, who was prosecuting the debt cases against Boone, and who also was interested in acquiring land beyond the Cumberland. Boone's party intended to make up other expenses by trapping and hunting; the skin of a buck deer was worth a dollar—a tidy sum in those times; even today, we use the term "a buck" to mean a dollar.

Before long, Boone and Stuart separated from their companions and hunted as a team. After Indians stole all of their hides and furs, they agreed to split up and meet regularly once every two weeks. When Stuart failed to show up in February 1770, Daniel searched for him, but found only a cold campfire and the initials "J.S." cut into a nearby tree. Five years later, during the expedition to build the Wilderness Road, a man's bones were found inside a hollow sycamore tree, along with a powder horn bearing Stuart's initials. The bones of the skeleton's left arm indicated a bullet wound; it was surmised that Stuart had been wounded by Indians, had hidden himself inside the tree, then had bled to death.

When spring came, Daniel traveled alone throughout Kentucky—the Indians called the land Ken-ta-ke, meaning "place of fields"—and explored the Ohio Valley as far as present-day Louisville. A lone white man was easy prey, so in the event of danger, Boone headed for the canebrakes, dense masses of wild cane that stretched for miles in some places and grew as tall as thirty feet.

By 1771, there was strong talk of eventual war between the colonists, who grew more independent each year, and the British, who intended to keep them submissive. That was a distant worry to Boone, however, and in 1773, he again explored Kentucky with a few hunting companions. By now the routes into Kentucky were well traveled, causing Daniel to wonder if all the good land would be taken by the time he was able to settle there himself.

On one of his trips home, Boone stopped to rest in Castle's Woods, a tiny community of log cabins in western Virginia. There, Daniel met Captain William Russell, who, for his heroism in the French and Indian War, had been granted a sizable tract of land in Kentucky but had never gone to inspect it. After listening to Boone's glowing tales of the place, Russell hired him as a guide, his aim being to establish a settlement there.

Boone hurried home and told his family about these new prospects. His brother Squire agreed to make the trip too, as did five other families. Daniel's father had already died, and his mother judged herself too old for such a journey. She bade a tearful farewell to her favorite son and never saw him again.

At Castle's Woods, the Russell party joined Boone's, and the group, numbering about thirty persons, set off on September 25, 1773. There were no roads to travel on, so no wagons were taken; rather, packhorses were loaded with the travelers' possessions and crates of chickens; children too small to walk were perched on top of the load. Older children were responsible for keeping cattle and hogs from straying into the woods.

James Boone, Daniel's oldest son, was now sixteen. As the group was camped only a day's walk from the Cumberland Gap, it was attacked by a party of Shawnees. The two young Mendenhall brothers, whose parents had cast their lot with Boone, were killed outright. James Boone and Captain Russell's son, Henry, seventeen, suffered a far worse fate. They were captured alive, then tortured horribly before being clubbed to death. Rebecca gave her best linen sheets for the boys' shrouds, and they were buried in a single grave.

The journey to Kentucky, which had started with such high hearts, was abandoned; the other emigrants turned back for home. Daniel had no home to return to, but a log cabin at Castle's Woods was lent to him. The family remained there for the next two years, and in the spring of 1774, Daniel returned to James's

A sketch of Daniel Boone's settlement at Boonesborough, Kentucky. From Historical Sketches of Kentucky by Collins, published in 1848.

grave site, later describing the time as "the worst melancholy of my life."

On June 27, 1774, Daniel accepted a mission that must have taken his mind off his loss. The corrupt British governor of Virginia, Lord Dunmore, had sent a poorly armed survey team to the bluegrass region of present-day Lexington, with the aim of obtaining land for his own profit. Dunmore's greed had inflamed the Indians' hatred of whites, and the Shawnee and Mingo tribes had taken to the warpath.

Captain Russell, charged with rescuing the survey team, recommended Boone and Michael Stoner as "two of the best Hands I could think of." Stoner, a Pennsylvanian and fine marksman, had been with Boone on the fatal Kentucky expedition. The two men traveled by night to avoid detection by the Indians; it took two months to locate the surveyors and take them back to Castle's Woods for safety.

Once home, Boone and Stoner discovered most of the men at the settlement had joined the militia that had been called up by Lord Dunmore to deal with the worsening Indian crisis—now called Dunmore's War—and they were ordered to stay behind to protect the women and children. Three rude forts— Fort Russell, Fort Blackmore, and Moore's Fort—were built along the Clinch River, and Daniel was put in command of all of them. The final battle came on October 10, in what today is Virginia; heavy losses were incurred by whites and Indians. However, a much bigger war was just about to begin, the one between the colonists and the British Crown.

With the Revolutionary War about to commence, Daniel's former prosecutor, Judge Henderson, was finally ready to make his move into Kentucky. Henderson knew of Boone's firsthand knowledge of the area and offered Daniel an irresistible opportunity: If Boone would help negotiate with the Cherokees for twenty million acres and lead a road-building expedition into Kentucky, his reward would be two thousand acres of prime bluegrass land.

In the spring of 1775, Boone arranged for Henderson to meet with a thousand Cherokees for treaty talks. The Indians were beguiled with guns, shirts, blankets; there was plenty of food and rum to be enjoyed. At first, the Indians refused Henderson's offer, but a treaty granting Henderson ninety thousand square miles for fifty thousand dollars was finally signed on March 17. However, Dragging Canoe delivered a warning to the whites: "We have given you a fine land, but I believe you will have much trouble in settling it." He referred to a "dark cloud over that country," meaning the Shawnees. Daniel, who had lost James to them, didn't need to be reminded of their ferocity.

Boone wasn't present at the treaty signing; he'd left a week earlier with a party of thirty men, his brother Squire among them, to begin work on the project that would be called the Wilderness Road. Only a month later, on April 19, 1775, 130 Minutemen made their stand at Lexington, on the road to Concord, in Massachusetts. The American Revolution had commenced.

The Wilderness Road wound more than 250 miles from the Holston River in Tennessee, over the Cumberland Gap, into the heart of bluegrass country. Each road builder was promised pay enough to buy at least four hundred acres of land, but the project did not proceed smoothly. The crew camp was attacked on March 25, and two men were killed, causing some workers to quit immediately. Boone never considered giving up and sent a message back to Henderson: "If we give way to them [the Indians] now, it will ever be the case." When the settlement was built on the south side of the Kentucky River, it was named Boonesborough, and within a year, more than a hundred men were living there.

In June, Daniel returned home to collect his family and bring them to Kentucky. Rebecca was about to give birth to their ninth child, but the baby, a boy, soon died. When she was well enough to travel, the family set out: Israel, 16; Jemima, 13; Lavinia, 9; Rebecca, 7; Daniel, 6; Jesse, 2. Fifteen-year-old Susannah had recently married William Hayes, a member of the Wilderness crew, and was already living in Boonesborough. What did Rebecca Boone think when she looked down upon that rude settlement, three hundred miles from any church, store, or village? To Daniel it was another grand adventure; to her, it might have seemed more like a nightmare.

In the summer of 1776, the nightmare became real: Jemima Boone and two other girls were kidnapped by Indians. The trail was fresh because one of the girls, the only one wearing shoes, deliberately made deep indentations along the path wherever she could. After three days of tracking by Boone and several other men, the girls were found alive. Boone's men caught the captors by surprise and rescued the girls unharmed.

One of the most urgent needs of settlers along the frontier was for salt, which they used to preserve fresh meat. In January 1778, Daniel led a party of thirty men to salt springs located forty miles from Boonesborough. There, he and the men boiled down the briny water to render out the salt. It took 840 gallons to make one bushel of salt, yet more than three hundred bushels were sent back to the settlement.

One day, as Daniel was hunting for meat for the salt crew, he was captured by Indians and taken to the camp of their chief, Blackfish. There, Daniel was surprised to discover the Indians were fully equipped with British rifles and commanded by a handful of British soldiers. Daniel attempted to strike a deal with his captors: he would surrender his men at the salt camp, arguing that since the British would pay up to twenty pounds for each prisoner, the Indians would be better off to trade the prisoners for cash than to kill them.

The Indians voted among themselves, fifty-nine for death, sixty-one for life. Then the captured men were shown off by the Indians to their British allies at Fort Detroit, where Boone led Governor Hamilton to believe that the settlers had not yet made up their minds whether to support the colonists or the Crown. In appreciation for what the governor thought would be converts to the British cause, Boone was given a fine horse and a saddle, angering the other captives, who believed Boone was a traitor.

Some of the thirty men in Daniel's crew were, indeed, sold to the British, but Chief Blackfish decided to keep Daniel for himself, to adopt him as a son. In an elaborate ceremony, all the hair except a four-inch scalp lock was plucked from Daniel's head. He was stripped naked, then scrubbed with coarse sand in an ice-cold river to "take his white blood out." He was painted with tribal symbols, given a tomahawk and Indian clothing, and named Sheltowee, or "big turtle." He was even given an Indian wife.

During the next four months, Daniel carefully built up the confidence of Chief Blackfish. He joked with his captors and seemed relaxed in their presence. The other captives complained bitterly that he seemed to enjoy his new life, and later Boone admitted having "a great share in the affection of my new parents, brothers, sisters, and friends." Nevertheless, he was fully aware that his family was waiting back at the settlement. In preparation for escape, Daniel carefully hoarded bullets and dried meat. Then in June 1778, while the Indians were off on a hunt, he gathered up his supplies, mounted his horse, and fled.

The flight to Boonesborough, 160 miles away, took four days. His horse gave out after a day-and-night gallop, and forty-four-year-old Daniel finished the journey on foot. When he arrived at the fort, the settlers couldn't believe their eyes, but Rebecca was not among them. Assuming Daniel was dead, she had taken her younger children and returned to North Carolina.

Rather than follow her, Boone vowed to make a stand with the other settlers and quickly set about preparing the fort for the attack he knew would come soon from combined British and Indian forces. The walls of the fort were repaired; food was collected; water was gathered in barrels and buckets. The wait commenced.

The siege of Boonesborough lasted seven days, and the settlers survived it due largely to the shrewdness of Daniel Boone. Afterward, however, he was accused of being a British spy and was arrested in October 1778. His surrendering of the salt crew was given as evidence of his Loyalist sympathies. A trial was held, and Boone was declared innocent of all charges; in fact, he was promoted to the rank of major in the militia for saving Boonesborough from destruction.

Daniel immediately set out for North Carolina to bring Rebecca back to Kentucky. For a full year, she refused. In the autumn of 1779, Daniel packed up a wagon, gathered some friends and relatives together, and prepared for the trip to Kentucky. Only then did Rebecca acquiesce. But the Boonesborough they returned to was not the one they'd left: the town overflowed with emigrants; the settlement had just harvested its best crop; a school had been started.

For Daniel, Boonesborough's success was both a blessing and a curse: true, there was safety in numbers, but numbers caused game to become scarce, and once again Boone found himself

moving farther away, this time five miles away to a place he named "Boone's Station." The war for independence was a long way from over, however, and Indian raids continued. In 1780, while Daniel was hunting with his brother Ned, the two were surprised by Indians, and Ned was killed. Since Ned strongly resembled Daniel, the Indians believed they had killed "Old Boone," and they beheaded Ned to prove their deed to their fellow tribesmen.

A year after Ned's death, Boone was promoted to lieutenant colonel in the militia, and later acted as sheriff and surveyor of Fayette County. Kentucky now numbered twenty thousand white residents. In March 1781, Rebecca Boone, already a grandmother, added to the population by presenting Daniel with their tenth and last child, a boy named Nathan. They were soon to lose a son, however: in 1782, their second-born son, Israel, twenty-three years old, was shot by Wyandot Indians and died in Daniel's arms.

By 1786, Boone's land claims in Kentucky were said to total more than 100,000 acres and ought to have made him a rich man. However, surveys in those early days were haphazard. Claim boundaries overlapped other claims, and it wasn't unusual for a settler to clear land, plow it, plant it, then lose it to another settler in a court battle.

Boone admitted that he was "unac-quainted with the niceties of law," and "through my own ignorance [my lands] were swallowed up by better claims."

Ironically, one of the men who cheated him also made him famous. An eastern land speculator swindled Daniel out of ten thousand acres, then later recounted Daniel's life story to a school-teacher named John Filson, who wrote an account titled *The Adventures of Col. Daniel Boone*, published in 1784. It was reprinted in French and German editions, and although most Americans still knew nothing about their native son, he became a celebrated figure in Europe, where he was eulogized by poets such as Lord Byron. Later, James Fenimore Cooper immortalized Boone in *The Leatherstocking Tales*, while painters such as John James Audubon and George C. Bingham painted portraits of him that were based more on fancy than on fact.

Meanwhile, Daniel struggled as always to provide for his family. He tried running a tavern and surveying; he served in the Virginia Assembly; he bartered horses. At age sixty-four, he was forced to give up his last bit of land in Kentucky to settle old debts. Now he began to listen to his son Daniel, who was said to resemble him more than any of his children. Young Daniel had gone to explore country owned by the Spanish,

now known as Missouri Territory. Old Daniel was offered 850 acres if he would lead settlers into this country, and each family he induced to come along would be offered 400 acres. In 1799, the year of George Washington's death, Daniel started life afresh by heading for Missouri Territory, seven hundred miles away. Family legend says he walked every step of the way.

In 1803, Missouri Territory changed hands; Spain deeded the land back to France, then France sold 800,000 acres to the U.S. government in the Louisiana Purchase. The United States refused to recognize Daniel's land claim and confiscated every acre of it. In 1814, however, a special act of Congress awarded Boone 850 acres, but when his old debtors back in Kentucky heard the news, Daniel was forced to relinquish his property one final time. Not that he was homeless: his children had extensive holdings, and for seven years Daniel and Rebecca lived in a log cabin on the property of their son Nathan, the longest continuous time they'd ever spent together.

In March 1813, Rebecca, aged seventy-four, died after a brief illness and was buried in a family plot overlooking the Missouri River. After her death, family members observed that Daniel "was never contented" again. The old world was passing: three of his siblings also died, including his beloved brother Squire, who had shared so many adventures with him.

Anticipating the end, Daniel had a coffin of black cherry wood built and examined it often, claiming to have "taken many a nice nap in it." In the summer of 1820, nearly blind, Daniel became feverish while visiting his daughter Jemima. He insisted on returning to Nathan's home and made the trip against a doctor's advice. When he arrived, he asked that he be prepared for death by being shaved and having his hair cut. "I am going. My time has come," he said, and died on September 26, 1820, just shy of his eighty-sixth birthday.

Even in death, Daniel was prone to wanderlust. A dispute arose over whether he belonged in Kentucky or Missouri. His bones were disinterred and then reburied on a bluff overlooking the Kentucky state capital. However, a recent examination of the bones indicates they might not be Daniel's at all! Perhaps he's exploring still, eyes turned always to the west.

James Bowie

1796–1836 Frontiersman, adventurer. Left home at age eighteen to settle at Bayou Boeuf, Louisiana; joined the Long Expedition, an early attempt to achieve independence for Texas. Later became a Texas Ranger and fought at the Alamo. A frontier weapon, "the bowie knife," was named after him.

Before reading about the life of James Bowie, most people already know two facts about him: he died defending the Alamo and was the man from whom the famous "bowie knife" got its name. Less commonly known is that one of Bowie's forebears carried a coat of arms to America indicating the family could trace its ancestry back to two famous Scots, Rob Roy and his brave wife, Helen MacGregor.

The first Bowie in America settled about 1705 near the Patuxent River, in Prince George's County, Maryland. Like many early emigrants—the Boones and Crocketts among them—members of the Bowie clan were restless and lived at various times in Pennsylvania, Ken-tucky, Virginia, South Carolina, Georgia, Louisiana, and even Canada. Some of them changed the spelling of their name to Buie, more accurately reflecting its pronunciation.

James Bowie's grandfather, John, set-tled in South Carolina, married, and among his four sons were twins born about 1762. One of them, Rezin (pro-nounced "Reason"), became James's father. As a teenage boy, Rezin Bowie served in the Revolutionary War under the command of General Francis Marion, called "the Swamp Fox" by his admirers. Rezin was captured and held prisoner in Savannah, where he nearly lost his hand after a British guard struck him with a sword. As the young man recovered, he was cared for by a volunteer nurse from Savannah, Elve Jones, the daughter of

Welsh immigrants. The pair fell in love and were married in 1782.

James, the eighth of his parents' ten children, was born in Elliott Springs, Tennessee, on April 10, 1796. He had two older brothers, and two more brothers were born later. Although he's often called Jim in popular stories and movies, in his own day he answered to James.

In 1802, the family moved to the Bayou country of Louisiana, which was still under Spanish rule. (The Louisiana Purchase wasn't signed until 1803.) John, the oldest Bowie son, was seventeen, Rezin junior was nine, and James was only five. Fifty years later, John explained the family's final move, saying his father "was passionately fond of the adventures and excitements of a woodsman's life," but as the country became more settled and civilized, Rezin senior felt the need to "move on to wilder regions, where he could enjoy those sports and stirring adventures peculiar to frontier life." His eighth son would be stirred by that same desire.

In those days, the Louisiana Bayou country was full of turbulent characters, and John told a story about his parents that illustrates how naturally James came by his courage. On more than one occasion, Rezin senior had to protect his property against aggressive squatters who sought to wrest it from him. In one such encounter, a man was shot and killed. A few days later, Rezin was arrested, charged with manslaughter, and taken to the local jail.

Elve Bowie knew the sheriff was no friend to her husband and feared he would allow his prisoner to be dealt with by the squatters before a trial could be held. She fetched her horse, told a servant to bring a second horse, then headed for the jail. Elve talked the sheriff into letting her visit her husband and was allowed to enter his cell. She reappeared, "accompanied by Rezin Bowie, each with loaded pistols in their hands. While the jailer sought a place of safety, they mounted the waiting horses and rode away."

None of the Bowie children had any formal schooling, which wasn't unusual for the time and place. However, Elve had what in those days was considered a "finishing school" education and made sure her large brood learned the basics of reading and writing. She also held strong Methodist convictions and brought her children up with an understanding of Christian principles. James and Rezin also learned French and Spanish, the languages of the Bayou; the latter would be important to James when he became a Texan.

Rezin senior taught his sons what frontier boys needed to know: how to hunt and dress the game that was killed; how to plant and care for the land; how

A portrait of James Bowie in his younger years. CULVER PICTURES, INC.

to manage livestock. In Louisiana, cotton and sugarcane were important cash crops, and it was necessary to learn how and when to market them.

Rezin and James, only four years apart in age, along with their younger brother Stephen, were called "those wild Bowie boys" by neighbors, and sometimes occupied themselves by hunting alligators. When the forests of

Louisiana had been cleared, swampy areas were left behind that became "singularly infested with alligators." Among the first victims were settlers' hogs and chickens; next came landowners' hounds, and as a consequence alligator hunts became a lively sport. In one such hunt, 657 alligators were killed. (In those days, with wildlife in America so abundant, any suggestion that a species might become endangered would have seemed foolish.)

One family story tells how James rode a huge alligator that he suspected had killed his favorite hound. He leaped onto its back as it lay dozing in shallow water, wrapped his legs around its belly, then waited for a chance to plunge a knife into the beast. Even after he'd killed it, the boy kept his distance; he knew the animal would continue to exhibit muscular contractions and didn't want to be in the way of either its teeth or its tail.

Fish were often caught with a bow and arrow; gar, a fierce freshwater fish that sometimes grew to a length of twelve to fifteen feet, was a favorite prey. Equally challenging to hunt were wild cattle, said to be ancestors of the famous Texas longhorns.

James's brother John told about the "entirely original" (if cruel) way his younger brother hunted bears, which ravaged settlers' corn patches. James found a large, hollow cypress "knee" in the swamp, then drove sharp iron spikes downward through it so they resembled the teeth of a fish trap. Honey was poured into the knee, then the trap was placed near where a bear was likely to come looking for corn. As soon as it caught the scent of the honey, the bear thrust its head deep into the trap; the spikes pierced its muzzle when it attempted to withdraw, creating a death mask that prevented the animal from seeing or protecting itself. The animal then "became an easy prey to his gleeful captors."

By the time Jim was eighteen years old he'd been to New Orleans ("the Paris of the South") and to Natchez. He admired the wealth and sophistication he saw, and knew a more exciting world awaited him in such places. Although their father was a simple, hardworking man, Rezin and James were intrigued by the self-indulgent habits of the sons of rich plantation owners, for whom gambling, drinking, dueling, and womanizing were lively pastimes.

A contemporary who knew James described him as "young, proud, poor, and ambitious, without any rich family connections or influential family friends to aid him in the battle of life." He wasn't totally without assets, though; he was more than six feet tall, well built, and weighed about 180 pounds. His blue-gray eyes were deep-set, his glance penetrating, his cheekbones prominent; his brown hair was tinged with red from his father's side of the family and folks who knew him remarked, "By many of the fair ones he was called handsome."

So it probably surprised no one when, in 1814, the eighteen-year-old youth left home, settled in Bayou Boeuf, and cleared a piece of land. He supported himself mostly by cutting timber, sawing planks, then rafting them downriver for sale in New Orleans.

He barely eked out a living, yet selling lumber gave him a chance to rub elbows with those who were better off. He was said to have a winning way, with the sort of rough social grace that others—men and women alike—found attractive. He enjoyed the company of his betters, not merely because they were better, but because he knew that in the world of commerce, good business connections were important to a man's success.

Louisiana was rapidly becoming settled, meaning land values rose quickly. James observed others speculating in land on a grand scale but didn't have the kind of money it took to obtain large tracts that could later be sold piecemeal for huge profits. However, there *was* a trade at which he knew large sums could be made quickly. He broached the idea to Rezin, who also became interested, so the brothers entered the slave-trading business.

The importation of slaves into the

United States had been legal until 1808, when a no-import law was passed by Congress. The price of slaves then skyrocketed because they were soon in short supply. A slave purchased for twenty dollars in Africa or for three hundred dollars in Cuba (the headquarters of illegal traders) could be resold for up to one thousand dollars to southern plantation owners.

In 1818, the Bowie brothers were introduced to the famous French pirate, Jean Lafitte, who, for having aided General Andrew Jackson in 1815 at the Battle of New Orleans, was pardoned by President Madison for past crimes of piracy. Lafitte, a Frenchmen who had come to America by way of the West Indies, was a shrewd businessman who—as soon as the new no-import law was passed—realized a fortune could be made in black-marketing slaves, and he hired "agents" to do so. He invited the Bowie brothers to visit him at his heavily fortified home, Maison Rouge, near Galveston, Texas, where he lived in kingly splendor.

The brothers were entertained with food and wine, and agreed to join Lafitte's army of agents. John Bowie also joined his younger brothers in slave trading and left an account of their activities. (He made no mention of the ethical issue involved in selling human beings as if they were livestock.) "We . . .

purchased forty negroes from Lafitte at the rate of one dollar per pound, or an average of $140 of each . . . we continued to follow this business until we'd made $65,000, when we quit and soon spent all our earnings." They were in the slave business for about two years before another, more exciting adventure attracted James's attention.

In June 1819, James Long, a doctor who had fought against the British in the Battle of New Orleans, and now was eager to acquire cheap land, set out to free Texas from the grip of its Spanish rulers. Bowie apparently met the doctor through Lafitte and decided to join the expedition. With seventy-five men, Long marched into East Texas, captured the town of Nacogdoches, then declared Texas to be an independent republic. The invasion collapsed, Nacogdoches reverted to Spanish rule, and Long was later assassinated in Mexico City.

After the abortive Texas venture, James traveled widely, visiting Natchez, New Orleans, even New York, all the while making new friends. Then he joined his brothers in running a plantation and by 1826 had enough money to begin speculating in land. The brothers subsequently won a large lawsuit in Arkansas Superior Court over some contested claims; James was never able to hang on to money, though, and soon squandered it all.

At about this time, James was involved in a street brawl in Alexandria, Louisiana, one that would make a certain knife the most famous weapon in the history of the American West. He had gotten involved in local politics and made an enemy of Major Norris Wright, who was competing with him in land deals. One day, when the two men met by accident on the street, Wright drew a pistol and fired at Bowie; Bowie drew his own pistol but it misfired. Bowie then attacked Wright with his bare hands and might have killed him had not friends pulled him off.

A year later, at noon on September 19, 1827, Bowie joined a group of men intent upon settling a debt of honor that involved the good name of the sister of one of them. The men and their adversaries met at a sandbar along the Mississippi River a few miles west of Natchez, which had become a favorite place for conducting duels. James was a witness for Samuel Wells, who was defending his sister's honor; Wells's opponent was Dr. Thomas Maddox, who had as his witness none other than Bowie's old enemy, Norris Wright.

Wells and Maddox each fired, missed twice, then agreed to settle their squabble with a handshake. Others in the Maddox party weren't so easily satisfied and were eager to do damage to Bowie in particular. He was shot in the hip and fell to the ground. James managed to pull himself to his feet, drew a large knife from his belt (some said it looked like a butcher knife), and charged his attacker, a man named Crain. Wright, James's old enemy, saw the scuffle as a chance to get rid of Bowie for good and also shot at him.

Bowie returned the fire, striking Wright, who then attacked Bowie with a thin sword concealed in his cane. As Wright plunged the blade into Bowie's chest, James pulled the major toward him. "I twisted the knife until I heard his heart-strings sing," Bowie said later. Others from the opposition also fell upon Bowie, who—with Wright's sword still stuck in his chest—fought them all off with the knife.

A doctor who was present at the duel removed the sword from Bowie's chest and the bullets from his arm and hip. James suffered heavy blood loss and spent months in Natchez recovering from his wounds. His act was considered to be clearly one of self-defense, and no murder charge was brought against him. Newspapers carried reports of the duel, and Bowie's name became famous, in particular the fact he'd defended himself with "a big knife." From that day onward, James Bowie and his knife were inseparable in people's minds.

Exactly who invented that famous knife is still a matter of lively debate. Of course, knives weren't new to the frontier; Indians used stone knives to scrape hides and scalp enemies, and Spanish conquistadors always carried knives. British and French traders, anxious to make friends of Indians, often gave them knives as gifts. A man named Jesse Cliffe, a blacksmith who worked for Rezin Bowie, has been named as the man who made the knife James used at the battle on the sandbar; Captain Rees Fitzpatrick, a gunsmith from Natchez, also has been credited.

One story told that Jim, who remembered how his gun had misfired in the previous encounter with Wright, had the knife specially made from a fourteen-inch metal file just prior to attending the duel. Another story claimed Bowie had a blacksmith named Snowden craft the knife to resemble a hunting knife he'd always been especially fond of.

However, most historians agree that it was Rezin Bowie, *not* James, who actually invented the bowie knife. In 1838, Rezin himself took credit for the knife in a letter written to *The Planters' Advocate.* "The first Bowie knife was made by myself . . . as a hunting knife. . . . The length of the knife was nine and one-quarter inches, its width one and a half inches, single edged, blade not curved." Rezin went on to explain that he had, indeed, given the knife to James to use in self-defense but that its original purpose was only as a hunting tool.

After the battle in which Bowie defended himself against three would-be assassins, word of the knife spread quickly. Men who heard about the fight asked blacksmiths to "make one like Bowie's." "Knife schools," which instructed new owners on how best to use the knife as a defensive weapon, became popular. The knife's fame even spread to England, where copies of it were made in Sheffield and Birmingham, then exported to America.

In 1828, after Bowie had recovered from his wounds, he decided to move to Texas. He believed he'd made too many enemies to live peacefully in Louisiana; in addition, some of his land deals were beginning to sour. Opportunities to speculate in land were about worn out in Louisiana, Mississippi, and Arkansas, but were just beginning in Texas. He still was looking for a fortune and believed it was possible to make a large one if he headed west.

At that time, Texas still belonged to Mexico, which had recently gained its independence from Spain. Stephen Austin had been granted permission by the Mexican government to settle a certain number of Americans in the area and was given the respected title of *empresario*. Such emigrants (about

twenty thousand had arrived before Bowie) usually settled in eastern Texas. Bowie, however, rode deeper into the interior, to San Antonio, then a charming Spanish town of less than three thousand citizens.

Bowie, with his knack for making friends and his ability to speak Spanish, made the acquaintance of one of the most powerful men in San Antonio, Don Juan Martin de Veramendi. He soon met Veramendi's family, including the oldest of his seven children, seventeen-year-old Ursula. Bowie was thirty-two, nearly twice her age, but was not immune to the young lady's charms.

Perhaps not all of Ursula Veramendi's charms were of the romantic kind, however. In 1824, the Mexican government had passed a law declaring that Mexican citizens were to be given preference in the distribution of land in Texas, and had made Catholicism the official religion. Bowie's aim was to succeed in business, and he no doubt reasoned that it would be in his best interest to marry into a powerful local family and become a Catholic. He was baptized on June 28, 1828, and also applied for Mexican citizenship.

Prior to making a marriage proposal, Bowie made a trip home to urge Rezin to join him in Texas. While on the trip, he also met Sam Houston, who had resigned his post as governor of Tennessee and intended to settle in Texas to practice law. Houston, three years older and two inches taller than Bowie, took an instant liking to the younger man. The two had much in common: both were outdoorsmen; both were charismatic leaders whom others were eager to follow. Neither could have guessed the next time their paths crossed it would be under far more dramatic circumstances.

In 1830, after selling his Louisiana properties to his brothers, Bowie settled permanently in Texas. He became a member of the Texas Rangers and was given the honorary rank of colonel. Samuel Fisher, who would later serve in Sam Houston's cabinet, remarked that "the most valuable emigrant you have ever had is James Bowie."

Bowie resumed his friendship with Don Veramendi, who was now the tax collector and *alcalde* (mayor) of San Antonio. Lovely Ursula was now eighteen, and James requested the family's permission to court her. On April 22, 1831, he signed a dowry contract requiring him to provide his prospective bride with $15,000 or property of equal value.

Bowie didn't have much cash, but he had property that—on paper, at least—was worth about $250,000, a fabulous sum for those days. What he neglected to reveal was that ownership of much of that property was being contested in court, and that his claims might end up being worth nothing.

The marriage took place on April 25, 1831; Bowie gave his age as thirty. (He was thirty-five.) In spite of his paper fortune, the bridegroom had to borrow money from his new father-in-law for the wedding trip to Natchez and New Orleans! Nevertheless, the trip was a great success, and Ursula charmed everyone she met. Bowie was described as "supremely happy" and devoted to his bride.

The Bowies' first home was a small stone-and-adobe house on a piece of land belonging to Ursula's father. Before long they moved into the spacious Veramendi home, where James was "treated as a son and furnished with money and supplies without limit," in the words of his father-in-law. As the result of his new family connections, Bowie again became involved in land speculations, and a year after his marriage, he became the father of a daughter, Marie Elve.

However, marriage couldn't change Bowie's essential nature, which was that of a bold adventurer. He spent months searching for the lost Spanish silver mines of San Saba, two hundred miles northwest of San Antonio. He apparently obtained some old maps from his wife's family, and with Rezin's help and a crew of thirty men, he might have been very close to finding the treasure. The area had been reoccupied by the Comanches and Apaches, however, which made any real search, let alone mining, impossible. Later, with the Texas Rangers, Bowie took part in several skirmishes against various tribes and became a hero to his followers because of his daring and for his fair-minded consideration not only of his friends but of his foes.

In 1833, Mexico and parts of Texas were stricken by an outbreak of cholera. Bowie, who was about to return to Louisiana on a business trip, believed his wife would be safer in the mountain country of Coahuila than in San Antonio. Ursula was about to give birth to her second child, so the Veramendi family accompanied her. Rather than find safety in the mountains, they found the opposite: the epidemic struck in September; more than five hundred people lost their lives, including the Veramendis, Ursula, her daughter, and her newborn son, who had been named after his father.

When news of the tragedy reached Bowie, he was devastated. Acquaintances said that from that moment on he was a changed man. He spent the next year wandering restlessly between Texas, Mississippi, Louisiana, and Mexico. He sold his Texas holdings at a loss; for a time he drank heavily; he neglected his

appearance, which was very much out of character. However, it was at this time that his portrait was painted by Benjamin West in New Orleans, and a copy of it now hangs in the chapel at the Alamo.

The year 1833 was notable for something other than Ursula Bowie's death. Her godfather, General Antonio López de Santa Anna, was elected president of Mexico. Santa Anna made no secret of his hatred of Anglos and his intention to drive them out of the country. As a result, the previously cordial relations between Texas and Mexico deteriorated rapidly.

The opening salvo of cannon fire in the Texas war for independence was heard on the morning of October 2, 1835, at Gonzales, where 150 Texans held off about the same number of Mexicans. The cannon being fired was a small brass weapon that Mexico had permitted Texans to use to fight off Indian attacks; now, Santa Anna demanded its return.

The Texans refused to surrender the cannon, and a Mexican force under the command of Lieutenant Francisco Castaneda was dispatched to Gonzales to take it by force. Castaneda vowed not to return without it, but the Texans loaded the cannon with scrap iron, wrote "Come and take it" on it, then fired when Castaneda approached. Unnerved, the lieutenant beat a hasty retreat.

On October 3, the Mexican government abolished the Texas state legislature, causing Americans all across the nation to rally to the Texans' cause. On October 8, Sam Houston asked for volunteers, promising "bounties of land . . . to those who will join our ranks with a good rifle and one hundred rounds of ammunition." Volunteers from twenty-two states and five nations, including England, answered the call.

On November 3, 1835, members of thirteen municipalities of Texas met at San Felipe to form a provisional government for an independent state. Stephen Austin asked to be relieved of his duties, and Sam Houston was elected commander in chief of all military forces. In a preliminary battle in San Antonio, the Texans, with a force half the size of the Mexicans', got the best of General Cos, Santa Anna's brother-in-law, in a battle called the Grass Fight. Cos retreated to Mexico, having lost 150 men; the Texans lost 12.

When a message was delivered to Houston with news that Santa Anna's forces were about to cross the Rio Grande and were preparing to attack San Antonio, Bowie immediately offered to lead a contingent of volunteers to defend the Alamo, where rebel supplies were stored. Thirty men agreed to follow Bowie, and Houston instructed them to remove all munitions from the Alamo to keep them out of enemy hands, then to blow the place up, since "it would be impossible to hold the town" once the Mexican forces arrived. Bowie and his men headed for San Antonio, arriving on January 19, 1836.

They found Colonel James Neill already there with more than a hundred men. There were few arms or artillery left, however, because previous Texas freedom fighters had already confiscated them for other battles. When Bowie informed Neill of Houston's order to blow up the Alamo, Neill declined to do so. Bowie himself agreed but noted that it would be essential to get additional arms and supplies.

Because of Bowie's previous connections in San Antonio, he traveled freely about the city, and friends kept him informed of the movement of Santa Anna's troops. Word was passed to him on January 27 that several thousand Mexican soldiers were marching toward the city. Bowie quickly sent a message to Houston, requesting "men, money, rifles, and cannon powder." Bowie also wrote to the newly elected governor of Texas, Henry Smith, declaring, "The salvation of Texas depends . . . on keeping San Antonio out of the hands of the enemy. . . . Colonel Neill and myself have come to the solemn resolution that we will rather die in these ditches than give it up. . . ."

An unknown artist's interpretation of the fall of the Alamo. NORTH WIND PICTURE ARCHIVES.

In early February, Bowie's men were joined by Lieutenant Colonel William B. Travis, and next by Davy Crockett and twelve other Tennesseans. Enmity developed between Travis and Bowie, mostly over the issue of rank. The former was a commissioned officer in the regular army, while Bowie was a volunteer in the militia. Bowie had requested a commission from Houston, but none had been forthcoming, a matter that embittered him. Travis insisted that he ought to be in charge, but Bowie, four-teen years older, couldn't see himself taking orders from the younger man.

Sometimes, James Bowie's solution to a problem was to get roaring drunk, and he did so now. Travis complained angrily to Governor Smith about Bowie's behavior. Then the two men came to an agreement: Travis would command the regular army, Bowie would retain command of the volunteers. But Bowie had another problem: He had become seriously ill with a malady that Dr. Amos Pollard, the surgeon at the Alamo, couldn't diagnose. (Some historians believe it was tuberculosis; others say it was a combination of pneumonia and typhoid.) The issue of command was fully resolved after Bowie broke a hip in a fifteen-foot fall from a scaffold while helping mount a cannon for defense of the Alamo. The injury, combined with his worsening illness, almost totally disabled him, and Travis took command of all forces.

On February 26, Davy Crockett, who had arrived only days before, made an entry in his journal, describing the situation: "Colonel Bowie . . . is worth a dozen common men in a situation like ours . . . he manages to crawl from his bed every day that his comrades may see him. His presence alone is a tower of strength."

All the while, Santa Anna drew nearer; his force numbered about five thousand men and contained 1,800 pack mules, thirty-three wagons, and two hundred ox-drawn carts. He was enraged over General Cos's defeat and intended to settle the score. The Texans hoped the cold winter weather would slow Santa Anna's drive toward the city, but in late February a sentry posted in the tower of the Cathedral of San Fernando reported the Mexican army was in sight.

Santa Anna was surprised to discover the Texans had chosen to make their stand at the Alamo, rather than at the Mission of Concepción, two miles to the south, which was a much more formidable stronghold. By contrast, the Alamo, built by Franciscan priests in 1718, was vulnerable to attack by a strong force. Military historians believe the decision to defend the Alamo was a major reason for the debacle that soon took place.

As the Mexican army approached the city, Bowie called fifteen-year-old Gertrudis Navarro and her older sister to his bedside. The girls were Ursula's cousins, and he assured them they would be safe within the Alamo, saying, "Do not be afraid. I leave you with Colonel Travis, Colonel Crockett, and other friends." Then he signed a dispatch written by Travis, once again requesting assistance from Houston. "In this extremity, we hope you will send us all the men you can spare." The "extremity" was that Santa Anna had draped a blood-red banner from the bell tower of the cathedral, a signal to the besieged Texans that no quarter would be given.

Nevertheless, Bowie sent a message to the Mexican general requesting a conference. Santa Anna refused, saying the rebels' only recourse was to surrender unconditionally. This, of course, was exactly what Bowie had pledged never to do.

On March 1, fifty-eight delegates met in Washington-on-the-Brazos, a village of only a dozen cabins, to declare Texan independence from Mexico. Sam Houston was elected commander in chief, and Travis's appeal was read aloud to those present. Little did the delegates realize that even as the message was read, the Alamo was only days away from being overrun.

Seven men survived the final attack, which came on March 6, 1836. One of them, Davy Crockett, had been in Texas barely a month. He and his six companions were taken before Santa Anna, who ordered their execution, even though one of his own officers made a plea for their lives. The Navarro girls survived, as did Travis's black servant. Sam, James Bowie's servant, apparently died with his master. After the Mexicans stormed the Alamo, they went from room to room, executing the rebels when they were found. When informed of her son's death, which came a month before his fortieth birthday, Elve Bowie said simply, "I'll wager no wounds were found in his back."

Many stories exist about James Bowie's final moments, including one that he struggled upright in his sickbed, braced himself against the wall, and died with pistols blazing, his famous knife at his side. It seems more likely that he was far too ill to defend himself. One witness reported he was shot twice through the head as he lay helpless on his hospital cot.

The men who defended the Alamo came from twenty-two states and from five nations; eight were Mexicans. Most of the volunteers were young, between fourteen and twenty years old. Among the group was a jockey from Arkansas, a hatter from New York, a poet from North Carolina, a painter from England, and a man whose uncle, James Madison, had been president of the United States. The bodies of the dead men were stacked ignominiously in a pile in the courtyard, fuel was poured over them, and a torch was put to their funeral pyre. A year later, the remains of Bowie, Travis, and Crockett were placed in a single coffin and taken to the Cathedral of San Fernando.

It is a commonplace to say men "die as they have lived," but in Bowie's case it was certainly true. All his life, he had been a restless seeker of adventure and fortune, always quick to become involved in what his brother Rezin called "a medley," or a fight. At the very end, James Bowie was still adventuring, and his final medley became the most celebrated frontier battle of all, making him a legend in books, movies, and songs. It could be said that he'd found his fortune at last.

Jim Bridger

1804–81 Trapper, trader, scout. Discovered "the Great Salt Lake" in 1824; an early explorer of what became Yellowstone Park; founder of the Rocky Mountain Fur Company and Bridger's Fort. Principal guide for Colonel Albert Sidney Johnston's campaign during the Mormon War. Many sites in West named for him, yet he never learned to write his own name.

Jim Bridger was born on March 17, 1804, in a tavern owned by his father near Richmond, Virginia. His mother worked as a barmaid, though not for long, because the business failed and was turned over to creditors. The year of Jim's birth was memorable for something other than his entry into the world: Lewis and Clark began their expedition up the Missouri River to find an overland route to the Pacific Ocean.

Not long after the tavern was lost, the family also had to give up their farm near Fredericksburg. The Bridgers then did as many others had in those early days when beset by failure or bad luck: They turned their eyes west, to what some called "the Land of Beginning Again."

Jim was eight years old when the family resettled at Six Mile Prairie in 1812, across the Mississippi from St. Louis. In those days, St. Louis was devoted almost exclusively to the business of fur-trading. The Ojibwa Indian name *Missi Sipi* meant "great river," and it was a broad, brown highway that brought furs downriver from its upper reaches and from its major tributary, the Missouri. Along with furs came tales of even greater riches to be had by those daring enough to seize them.

For five years Jim's parents struggled to carve out a life for themselves, but they continued to be plagued by misfortune. Nothing could have seemed worse to her three children than the death of Chloe Tyler Bridger.

An equally terrible loss followed: The

A photograph of Jim Bridger by Carter. NORTH WIND PICTURE ARCHIVES.

elder Jim Bridger died. Then despair was heaped on despair when Jim's younger brother died as well. Thirteen-year-old Jim and his sister were taken in hand by an aunt who came to look after them, and within a few months the boy was apprenticed to Phil Creamer, a blacksmith, in whose shop he spent the next five years. Jim Bridger had not only been orphaned but now became indentured, compelled to work without pay while he learned the trade of blacksmithing. He was what some called "a bound boy."

Bridger might have lived and died in Creamer's blacksmith shop had it not been for an advertisement that appeared in a St. Louis newspaper on March 20, 1822. Jim had never learned to read, so someone must have told him what it said: "TO ENTERPRISING YOUNG MEN! The subscriber wishes to engage one hundred men to ascend the river Missouri to its source, there to be employed for one, two or three years."

The ad had been placed by William H. Ashley, lieutenant governor of Missouri and brigadier general in the state militia, and his business partner, Major Andrew Henry. Ashley declared that the "object of this company is to hunt and trap. . . . [the men] will direct their course to the Three Forks of the Missouri, a region . . . which contains a wealth of furs not to be surpassed by the mines of Peru." Apparently no one questioned how many furs were to be found in the mines of Peru.

The advertisement asserted the party of men chosen for the expedition would be those "who have relinquished the most respectable employment and circles of society for this arduous but truly meritorious undertaking." The reality was somewhat less glorious. With few exceptions, it was army deserters, wanted criminals, runaway slaves, and indentured servants who formed the cadre that the Ashley-Henry company crammed into a pair of keelboats headed upriver.

There was one notable standout among the motley specimens hired that spring: Jedediah Smith, soon to be greatly admired by young Bridger. The twenty-three-year-old Pennsylvanian could quote from the Bible as easily as any schoolmaster, and later was noted for his role in laying out the Oregon Trail. Also on board were bad-tempered Mike Fink and his friend, a gunsmith named Carpenter. Both were dead shots and amused themselves—and any audience that gathered around—by shooting tin cups full of whiskey from the top of each other's head.

No matter who made up that westward-bound group, for an indentured boy of eighteen the expedition was an opportunity for freedom. The first of the two keelboats owned by the Ashley-

Henry company left St. Louis on April 3, 1882; the second departed a month later. Jim Bridger wasn't taking a chance on being left behind and made sure he was on the first one. He was the youngest on board and traveled light: other than the clothes on his back, his only possessions were a single blanket, an old Kentucky rifle, a tin cup and plate, a powder horn, a shot pouch, and a heavy knife. He was a tall, quiet boy, thin but possessed of a blacksmith's muscular arms and shoulders. He had blue-gray eyes, a hooked nose, and a head of thick brown hair. When he looked back at St. Louis, did young Jim Bridger have any idea it would be seventeen years before he saw a town again?

Major Henry knew exactly where he was headed because he'd already been up the Missouri as far as the Three Forks, in present-day Montana. The aim of the Ashley-Henry company was to eventually put three hundred trappers in the wilderness, but hunting and trapping were perilous activities. The Blackfoot Indians were fiercely hostile and made relentless war on white men who dared invade their territory. There was another adversary to contend with: John Jacob Astor of New York, called "the richest man in America," was in the process of establishing the American Fur Company and had recently opened an office in St. Louis; his men would compete for the same furs the men of the Ashley-Henry party sought.

The expedition reached the Platte River in mid-May 1822. When the river became shallow, ropes were tied to the boats, which were then hauled upriver by men and horses pulling from the shore. Men had already begun to desert the company; when the boats came to Fort Recovery at the mouth of the White River, the last outpost where men could desert with any hope of getting back to St. Louis safely, nine more did exactly that.

At last they arrived at the Mandan villages near present-day Bismarck, North Dakota, where Lewis and Clark had wintered in 1804. In early August, a party of Assiniboin Indians ran off the expedition's horses, and as a result the final struggle to the mouth of the Yellowstone River was a grueling one. The 1,800-mile journey had taken four and a half months.

Major Henry immediately began construction of a trading post. Fort Henry—consisting of four log buildings connected by stockaded walls—was finished by late September; then the men scattered into the wilderness to set their traplines. Each man was supplied with several stout iron traps weighing about five pounds each, and the work was demanding even for a tough young fellow hardened in a blacksmith's shop. A mature mountain beaver weighed twenty-five to forty pounds, and Bridger soon learned that animals trapped at the higher elevations—6,500 to 10,500 feet—possessed the most luxuriant fur.

In October, Ashley himself made a visit to the post, bringing with him men to replace the deserters, plus horses to replace those stolen by the Assiniboins. He selected certain men to go into the Powder River country, but young Bridger wasn't one of them. Ashley brought an anvil, a forge, and an iron with him because he knew that traps would need to be repaired and that other ironwork—hinges, locks, gate latches—would need to be crafted. Jim had escaped his indentured status in Phil Creamer's shop only to find himself smithing in the wilderness!

The long winter settled in; time passed slowly at Fort Henry, causing tempers to fray, resulting in a famous western tale. Mike Fink complained bitterly about inadequate whiskey rations and moved out of the fort into a nearby cave, the entrance of which he blocked with brush to discourage visitors. After a time, his friend Carpenter joined him, but later they had a falling-out. When a new whiskey ration was issued, the two men were talked into mending their feud. To prove there were no hard feelings, someone suggested they perform their famous cup trick again.

Carpenter won the coin toss and got to fire first; his aim was as perfect as ever. Then it was Mike Fink's turn. He was an excellent marksman—but to bystanders' horror, this time he missed. Carpenter slumped to the ground, a bullet hole in the middle of his forehead. When Fink was accused of murdering his former friend, he started to reload his rifle, as if to shoot the next complainer. A man named Talbot was quicker and shot Fink through the heart. Even now, to call a man "a fink" is to imply he's a despicable scoundrel.

In June 1823, news came from upriver that a Blackfoot war party had killed four trappers near the Great Falls of the Missouri; seven men in another trapping party also had been killed. Two men, Jed Smith and a French Canadian trapper, staggered back to Fort Henry to report more bad news having to do with an encounter with Arikara Indians that had left thirty trappers besieged and in need of rescue. By late July word came that the government was sending in U.S. troops to humble the Indians.

Some 230 soldiers arrived from Fort Atkinson during the summer, raising the spirits of the trappers. Five keelboats moved upriver, and a party of Sioux who had joined the group in order to make war on their old enemies, the Arikara, also went along. Colonel Henry Leavenworth proved to be a rather timid leader, however, and the trappers were dismayed when they discovered he was actually negotiating a peace treaty with the Indians.

Major Ashley then gathered together what horses and weapons he could find, loaded his supplies, and decided to abandon Fort Henry and move farther up the Yellowstone. It was Jed Smith who led the expedition west across unknown territory—and this time, Jim Bridger, now nineteen years old, went with him. Each new foray into the wilderness would provide him with information that he seemed able to store in his mind in an encyclopedic fashion. He soon gained a reputation for never forgetting what he'd seen—or where he'd seen it.

Early in September 1823, Bridger was involved in an incident that has since taken on the gloss of a fable. One of the older men in the expedition, gray-bearded Hugh Glass, went out to hunt for fresh meat, with George Harris as his only companion. Glass heard what he thought was a buffalo cow along the creek, and motioned Harris to be quiet. He hoped to surprise the cow but was surprised himself: his quarry was a mother grizzly with two yearling cubs. Harris managed to kill one of the cubs, but the female attacked Glass. The screams of Harris and Glass drew the attention of the rest of the expedition,

who quickly shot the mother bear and her other cub, but by that time Glass had been severely mauled. His ribs were crushed; half his scalp was torn off and hung loosely over one ear.

Glass was alive but in so much pain he couldn't be moved, and the expedition camped for the night at the site of the disaster. It was assumed Glass wouldn't live till morning, but when dawn came the tough old man was still breathing. Major Henry wasn't willing to delay any longer and decided to leave Glass to his fate. He asked for a volunteer to remain with the dying man until he took his last breath. When no one stepped forward, Jim Bridger finally did. Henry was reluctant to leave so young a man to face such an ordeal and asked for a second volunteer; John Fitzgerald then came forward, but not before he'd wangled an extra forty dollars in pay from the major for himself and Bridger.

After four days, Glass was still breathing. Fitzgerald grew restless; on the fifth day, he stripped Glass of his most important possessions—a rifle and knife—and Bridger reluctantly agreed to accompany him in pursuit of the rest of the expedition. No one knows how many days Hugh Glass lay alone in a daze, but he finally managed to crawl to the river to drink. He survived on berries and roots, and when he finally reached Fort Kiowa, two hundred miles from where he'd been abandoned, he told trader Joseph Brazeau that he needed a rifle. He intended to hunt down and kill the two men who had deserted him.

Brazeau happened to be outfitting a party headed toward the Mandan villages along the Missouri, where Glass was sure he'd find Bridger and Fitzgerald. Toussaint Charbonneau, who with his young wife, Sacagawea, had accompanied Lewis and Clark to the Pacific, accompanied the trapper upriver. It was early December 1823 when Glass finally reached the mouth of the Yellowstone, the site of Fort Henry. However, Henry's expedition had already moved onward, to a new outpost near the Bighorn River. Glass went in pursuit and found his quarry there. Henry warned that there would be no killing, and excused Jim's conduct by saying he "was only a boy." No blood was shed—but the words "only a boy" must have humiliated Jim Bridger.

In early 1824, Major Henry sent men upriver on snowshoes to trade with the Crow Indians, who called themselves the Sparrowhawk People. Bridger no doubt was glad of the chance to escape the fort and the presence of Hugh Glass, who was still recovering from his wounds. Wintering with the Crows, who were agreeable hosts and from whom Bridger learned the Crow language, was

so pleasant that only a few of the Ashley-Henry men were ready to leave camp in midwinter to establish spring camps in the Wind River country. When Jed Smith decided to head out, Bridger was one of those who volunteered to go along.

Jim spent his twentieth birthday in the Wind River Range, which came honestly by its name. Gannett Peak, at 13,785 feet, is the highest point in the northern Rockies, and winter blasts coming off such slopes were so fierce that men had a hard time getting campfires started or keeping them going. The season ended with many furs harvested, as well as a sudden change in management: Major Henry, for reasons not documented, gave up his partnership with Ashley and vanished from the West. After his departure, it was Jedediah Smith who formed a new partnership with Ashley, and most of the trappers, young Bridger included, took contracts running through July 1827. The beaver harvest that year was estimated by a St. Louis newspaper to have been fifty thousand dollars.

The Wind River Bend of the Bighorn was the site of another unusual Bridger adventure. While his companions portaged on land, Jim piloted a raft made of driftwood down the infamous twenty-mile Bad Pass along the Montana-Wyoming border, a feat never before accomplished. The river ran through a narrow gap in the mountains; precipices rose nearly eight hundred feet on either side, blocking out the sunlight; in the stream bed, rock ledges dropped three to five feet at once, creating deadly white-water rapids.

It was something of an accident that Jim Bridger became the first white man to look upon the Great Salt Lake. The 1824–25 winter meeting, or rendezvous (a French word meaning "meeting place"), took place along Bear River in Utah. The river was a curiosity because it seemed to flow north out of the western end of the Uinta Mountains, while the neighboring Green River of similar size flowed southward from the same mountains. A debate arose as to what the river was all about, and apparently Bridger decided to solve the "riddle of the Bear" once and for all. Although historians differ as to how Bridger made the trip, some believe it was in a bullboat that he built of fresh buffalo hides stretched taut over green willow hoops.

Bridger returned from his trip and announced that the Bear emptied into a great lake, the waters of which tasted brackish. Robert Campbell, an Ashley employee, documented the event in a letter to the U.S. government geographical service: "Jim Bridger [followed] the course of the river and determined which way it flowed. This took him where the river passes through the mountain, and there he discovered the Great Salt Lake. He went to its margin and tasted the water, and on his return reported his discovery. . . ."

The fact that the water was salty caused some to believe it was an arm of the Pacific Ocean, but in the spring of 1826, four others explored it again and validated Bridger's discovery: It was indeed a landlocked salt lake. For an untutored twenty-year-old man, this discovery was equal to earning a Ph.D., and it laid a mantle of glory on young Bridger's shoulders. No one would ever think of him again as "only a boy."

Sometime during the early 1830s, Jim received his first and only serious wound. He had been trapping beaver deep in Blackfoot country and during an Indian attack was struck by an iron-tipped arrow. He carried the arrowhead buried in the flesh of his hip until a young missionary doctor—Marcus Whitman—removed it at the Green River rendezvous in August 1835. The Reverend Samuel Parker witnessed the incident: "Doct. Whitman . . . extracted an iron arrow, three inches long, from the back of Capt. Bridger . . . a difficult operation, because the arrow was hooked at the point [of] a large bone, and a cartilaginous substance had grown around it."

The surgery was performed without anesthetic; those who gathered around were more impressed than ever by thirty-one-year-old Jim Bridger's fortitude. When Bridger met Father Pierre de Smet in 1839, the priest asked him how it could be that such untreated wounds didn't become infected in the wilderness. De Smet recalled that Bridger "answered humorously: 'In the mountains meat never spoils!'"

Bridger, following Jed Smith's example, formed a new partnership with other trappers, among them Tom Fitzpatrick and Milton Sublette, to form the Rocky Mountain Fur Company. In 1833, the company was able to divide sixty thousand dollars for three years' work. Around this time, Bridger, like many mountain men, including his friend Kit Carson, made another change in his life—he took an Indian wife. He married the daughter of a Flathead Indian chief in a ceremony performed in June 1834.

Very little is known about this young woman, and her name has been lost to history. She died several years later, after giving birth to her third child, a daughter named Mary Josephine. Bridger's son, Felix, born in December 1841, was baptized by Father de Smet. Much later, an older daughter, age eleven, was among the fifty men, women, and children who were captured by Cayuse Indians from the mis-

sion home of the Reverend Marcus and Narcissa Whitman in Oregon on November 29, 1847. The Whitmans and eleven others were murdered; Bridger's daughter was reported to have died in captivity in March 1848.

Beaver had been so relentlessly trapped out of western streams by the major fur companies, not to mention the smaller independents, that, not surprisingly, it became harder and harder to make a living as a trapper. As a result, Bridger took up trading in late 1842. In partnership with French Canadian Louis Vasquez, he took over an unfinished post on the Black Fork of the Green River in present-day southwest Wyoming. Composed of what one observer described as "two or three miserable log cabins, rudely constructed," surrounded by a tall picket fence rather than a stockade, the post was located along the direct route to the Great Salt Lake, which later became known as the Mormon Trail. The fort was frequented by folk who were characterized by James Reed, a survivor of the Donner party disaster, as "[as] great a set of sharks as ever disgraced humanity. . . . Vasquez and Bridger are the only fair traders in these parts."

In a letter dictated to a clerk in 1843, Bridger described his plans for the future of his post, which was the first in the West to cater not only to trappers and Indians as had been the custom, but to the increasing number of settlers moving across the country. "I have established a small store with a Black Smith Shop, and a supply of iron in the road of the Emigrants . . . they, in coming out are generally well supplied with money, but by the time they get [here] are in want of all kinds of supplies. Horses, Provisions, Smith work, &c, brings ready cash from them. . . . I will do a considerable business . . . !"

The partnership was doomed, however, because neither Bridger nor Vasquez especially cared for the business end of their enterprise. Jim often left the post to spend months in the wilderness as he'd always done, while Vasquez was described as "drinking and frolicking." Bridger shouldn't have been surprised to discover that Vasquez's accounting methods were questionable; he ended up suing his partner.

One of Bridger's jobs as a trader was to take furs to market. As he did so in July 1842, he came upon his old friend Kit Carson, guiding a newcomer to the West. John Charles Frémont, heading a U.S. Army Corps of Topographical Engineers, was interested to hear Bridger's report that conditions in the country he intended to travel in were "exceedingly dangerous" due to roving bands of hostile Sioux. Frémont said his men became alarmed enough to consider desertion and that Kit Carson "fully supported the opinion given by Bridger." Bridger offered to guide Frémont's group himself but instead left Carson with instructions for the best route to take to avoid a confrontation with the Sioux.

Bridger met with Brigham Young and the Mormon pioneers in Wyoming on June 28, 1847, in what began as an agreeable association. Since he was well acquainted with the area of the Great Salt Basin, Bridger was able to give the Mormon leader valuable information as to its potential for settlement. The relationship which began so well had soured by 1853, however, when the Mormons became angered over the fact that Bridger's Fort sometimes sold arms and ammunition to the Indians. In addition, the Indians' high regard for Bridger—who spoke the language of several different tribes and was familiar with their customs—was perceived as a threat to Mormon domination of the area. The fort was raided, and later burned to the ground, presumably under the orders of Brigham Young, who was by then governor of Utah.

After the death of his first wife, Bridger married a woman from the Ute tribe; she died in July 1849, after giving birth to a daughter named Virginia, who would become her father's caretaker in his waning years. He needed someone to care for his three children and was

PART OF THE CAMP AT FORT BRIDGER.

A woodcut made around 1850 shows part of Bridger's Fort. NORTH WIND PICTURE ARCHIVES.

married for a third and last time, to Little Fawn, a young Shoshone woman, one of Chief Washakie's thirteen handsome daughters. Later, they were remarried in a Christian ceremony performed by Father de Smet, and Little Fawn was listed on the certificate as Mary Washakie Bridger. In 1852, Jim settled his new wife and three children on a 640-acre farm that he bought in Jackson County, in western Missouri. Then he sent Mary Josephine, six, and his son Felix, ten, to St. Louis to be educated by Father de Smet.

While visiting in St. Louis in the spring of 1854, Bridger met Sir George Gore, a visiting Irish nobleman, who was organizing a hunting party and needed a guide. Bridger set up the expedition, which eventually included "40 men, 112 horses, 12 yoke of oxen, 14 dogs, 6 wagons, and 21 carts." The sixty-year-old Irish nobleman's party wintered in 1855–56 on the Tongue River after spending a summer of unparalleled butchery on the plains. He and his companions reportedly killed 2,500 buffalo, 40 bears, and "uncounted small game" such as elk, deer, and antelope.

Bridger used part of his pay from the Gore expedition to pay for a trip to Washington, D.C., to submit his request for compensation for the Mormon burning of his fort. President Buchanan had removed Brigham Young as the governor of Utah and sent federal troops to Salt Lake. Then on September 27, 1857, Brigham Young declared war on the United States.

Ten days later, Bridger was called upon to guide eight companies under Colonel E. B. Alexander to the Green River for a showdown, and Chief Washakie offered 1,200 warriors for the coming war against the Mormons. Alexander was an ineffective leader, and Colonel Albert Sidney Johnston, who would later die at Shiloh in the Civil War, took command. It was Bridger who—five years after the burning of Bridger's Fort —led Johnston's forces into Salt Lake City.

If Jim had revenge on his mind, it could not have been very sweet, because the city was empty. At Brigham Young's orders, its thirty thousand inhabitants had temporarily abandoned it and moved en masse to Provo, Utah. Bridger didn't receive compensation for his fort and, disgusted with his failure to recoup any of his losses, left the army in July 1858.

At home in Missouri, further personal sorrow awaited Bridger. Mary Washakie died from the effects of childbirth as her predecessors had, leaving Bridger with a new son, William. Bridger stayed only a season with his children, however, because he accepted an offer in early 1859 to guide a mapmaking expedition to the Yellowstone country for the U.S. Army Corps of Topographical Engineers. He hired caretakers for his motherless children and headed west again. The expedition lasted two years. Then in 1862 he guided a military detachment escorting some federal judges into Utah Territory. He also arranged for a new home to be built in Westport, Missouri, for his children and their new caretakers, Mr. and Mrs. George London.

During the early 1860s, Colonel E. Z. C. Judson, who wrote under the pen name Ned Buntline, met Jim Bridger. Not long after, "Bridger stories" began to circulate in the eastern press, making Jim famous in a way he'd never imagined he would be. It was Buntline who also would make William F. Cody famous a few years later.

General Grenville M. Dodge called on Bridger in January 1865 to guide the Eleventh Ohio Infantry to Fort Laramie to subdue hostile Sioux and Cheyenne; he became a lifelong admirer of the mountain man. "As a Guide he is without equal," Dodge wrote. "He was a born topographer; the whole West was mapped out in his mind, and such was his instinctive sense of location and direction that it was said of him that he could smell his way when he could not see. . . . He could make a map of any country he had ever traveled over, mark out its streams, mountains and obstacles correctly"—remarkable achievements for a man who'd never had any formal schooling.

After arriving at Fort Laramie, Bridger served as guide to General Pat Connor's Powder River expedition, where the Sioux, under Chiefs Red Cloud and Crazy Horse, were terrorizing the northern edge of the frontier. Bridger protested an edict issued by Connor on a July morning as the troops left the fort, to "attack and kill every male Indian over twelve years of age." Bridger knew that such a measure could only worsen the situation, but Connor paid no heed. Bridger must have realized that he was held in contempt; at age sixty-one, he was viewed by the younger man as an aging, out-of-touch frontiersman, not up to the demands of a changing West.

Connor's expedition reached the Tongue River country in August; Connor attacked a camp of Arapahos, who had not at that time been hostile to whites, burned their village, and took eight women and thirteen small children captive. He was relieved of his command and sent back to Fort Laramie. Later, Bridger was appointed chief guide for Fort Phil Kearny at the suggestion of General Grenville Dodge.

Colonel Henry Carrington succeeded Connor but was not a great improvement to Bridger's way of thinking. It was Carrington's job to open up a wagon road around the Bighorn Mountains, straight through the Sioux hunting grounds to the gold fields of Montana, and to begin construction of military posts along the way to guard travelers headed west. Called the Bozeman Trail, this route took no account of the trail Bridger himself had laid out a year earlier, in 1864, which wisely avoided travel through the heart of Indian hunting territory. Bridger predicted that the Sioux under Red Cloud and Crazy Horse would never tolerate such an invasion of their favorite buffalo grounds.

Bridger was at Fort Phil Kearny in December 1866 when—true to his prediction—the Sioux chiefs surrounded it. Captain William Fetterman was sent out with a detail of eighty men to rescue members of a woodcutters' train that was besieged in the hills west of the fort. His instructions were explicit: Rescue the woodcutters and return, but do not become involved in any battle with the Indians. Crazy Horse and a few followers acted as decoys to tempt Fetterman into pursuing them; ignoring orders, Fetterman fell for the ruse. Bridger, who was well acquainted with Indian military strategy, could have told the captain that many more Sioux were waiting in ambush, and he probably was not surprised when every man in the Fetterman detail was slaughtered.

The famous Western painter Frederic Remington made this drawing of Jim Bridger in old age. CORBIS-BETTMANN.

In July 1868, Bridger returned home to his farm in Missouri. At age sixty-four, his health was failing. He was crippled with rheumatism and suffered from an enlarged goiter that might have been caused by decades of drinking iodine-deficient mountain water. Worst of all for a man like Bridger, his eyesight was badly impaired.

He made a home with his daughter, Virginia, who had married Captain Albert Wachsman in her father's home in Westport on February 25, 1864. His youngest son, William, lived nearby.

His older son, Felix, served with the Missouri Artillery during the Civil War, then with General Custer from 1866 to 1871. Once again, Bridger tried to get government compensation for his losses at Bridger's Fort, but it was not until eight years after his death that the family finally received a small payment of six thousand dollars.

Virginia wrote to General Dodge that Bridger's "eyes were very bad. . . . I got father a good old gentle horse so that he could ride around and have something to pass the time. . . . He named this old horse Ruff. . . We also had a dog that went everywhere with father. . . . The faithful old dog, Sultan, would come home and let us know that father was lost. . . I would go out and look for him, and lead him and the old horse home on the main road."

In old age Bridger was often called—with great respect—"the Old Scout." In 1876, Bridger's son Felix died. Five years later, on July 17, 1881, Bridger, aged seventy-seven, was laid to rest beside him in the family plot in Westport. Not long after, son William also was buried beside his father and brother.

In December 1904, the hundredth anniversary year of Bridger's birth, General Dodge had the Old Scout's body removed to a specially selected site in the Mount Washington Cemetery in Kansas City, where his final resting place is now marked by a seven-foot monument.

"I found Bridger a very companionable man," General Dodge recalled. "He familiarized himself with every mountain peak, every deep gorge, every hill, and every landmark in the country. . . . So remarkable a man should not be lost to history!"

History did not lose Jim Bridger. Countless sites in many western states are named in his honor: the town of Bridger, in Montana; Bridger Creek, in Utah; Bridger Lake, just outside Yellowstone National Park; and in Wyoming, Bridger National Forest, which was dedicated in 1941 by President Franklin Roosevelt. All are worthy memorials to the orphaned bound boy from St. Louis, who set out for the West at age eighteen and never looked back.

Martha Jane Cannary (Calamity Jane)

1852–1903 Bullwhacker, scout, adventurer. Worked on a construction gang for Union Pacific Railroad; wore men's clothing; claimed to have married Wild Bill Hickok. In her lifetime she was scorned by some, yet also was considered to be the one-of-a-kind individual who "made the west the West."

Her nickname summed up her life. The word "calamity" brings to mind disorder and ruination, something totally out of the ordinary. Martha Jane Cannary was all of that, and maybe a little bit more. Although she sometimes was described more glamorously as the "Belle of the Bull Trains," the "Wildcat's Kitten," or the "Queen of the Prairie," she preferred "Calamity Jane," and it's the name the world remembers her by.

But who *was* Calamity Jane? It has been hard for historians to separate fact from fiction, partly because the woman known by that name was an accomplished and lively storyteller who played fast and loose with the truth. However, it's important to remember that in her day telling fantastical yarns about oneself really wasn't considered to be a vice. Rather, it was a sort of entertainment, and many others besides Calamity Jane indulged in the habit.

In her autobiography, *Life and Adventures of Calamity Jane: By Herself*, Martha Jane Cannary reported that she was born on May 1, 1852, in Princeton, Missouri. Census records in Mercer County are not clear about even that most elemental fact. A family by the name of Conarray, originally from Tennessee, is listed, but with only a mother as head of the family. A certain J. T. Canary, a farmer from Ohio, is listed as the head of a family that included five girls and three boys, but only one of his children's birth dates approximates

Calamity Jane dressed and equipped as a scout. BUFFALO BILL HISTORICAL SOCIETY, VINCENT MER-
CALDO COLLECTION.

the one Calamity Jane claimed for herself—and it belonged to a boy.

One story that was circulated about Martha Jane's early life was that she had been born to the wife of an ex-soldier near Douglas, Wyoming, in 1860. Indians attacked the family ranch in 1861, the story went, killing everyone except the mother and daughter, who traveled by night to nearby Fort Laramie. The mother soon died, and the orphaned girl-child was adopted by soldiers at the fort and raised by them—surely the most fanciful of all the tales that surround Martha Jane Cannary's origins.

Since there is no concrete proof of when or where she was born, readers will just have to trust that in this case she was honest. According to Martha Jane, her parents, Robert and Charlotte Cannary, emigrated from Ohio to Missouri and began to clear land for a farm in the northern part of the nation's twenty-fourth state. Martha Jane—she says the family always called her Marthy—was her parents' oldest child, and was later joined by two brothers and three sisters.

Clearing land in those early times was backbreaking work, and the Cannary family couldn't make a go of farming. As was so common among all kinds of folk in those days, the response to failure was to turn west, hoping that fortunes would improve. Jim Bridger's family had done exactly the same thing when they traveled from Virginia to St. Louis in 1812. However, it might have been more than a failing farm that prompted the Cannary clan to move on. During the Civil War, the state of Missouri had been divided in its loyalties, half for the Union, half for the Confederacy; when the war ended, gangs of ruffians roamed the countryside, pillaging as they went, causing many people to feel unsafe. Whatever the reason, Marthy reported in *By Herself* that in 1865 "we emigrated from our home in Missouri by the overland route to Virginia City, Montana, taking five months to make the journey."

Such trips—undertaken by many families who were looking for cheap land and a fresh start—were especially hard on women, old and young alike. In spite of hardship, though, proper female behavior was considered important, and the mothers of most girls made sure their daughters wore bonnets to protect their fair complexions from the blistering prairie sun, and took care that their dresses concealed their ankles. If a girl rode horseback, as Narcissa Whitman certainly did on her wedding trip to Oregon in 1836, she rode sidesaddle.

Marthy, only thirteen when the trip West was made and apparently of a headstrong nature even then, borrowed trousers—perhaps from one of her brothers—and rode astride like a boy, a scandal in that day. "I was at all times with the men when there was excitement and adventures to be had," she proudly asserted in her memoir. "By the time we reached Virginia City I was considered a remarkable good shot and a fearless rider for a girl of my age."

Why didn't the Cannary family, who were farmers, head for the coast of Oregon as many others were doing, where crops could be raised so easily? In spite of a name that evoked an elegant way of life, Virginia City in eastern Montana was situated in rough, dry, sagebrush-choked country where it was hard to grow rocks, let alone crops. No doubt the attraction of the place was based on the discovery of gold in 1863 in a creek that ran down Alder Gulch. By the time Marthy and her family arrived, fifteen thousand gold seekers were already there to keep them company. No housing was available for newcomers, who often had to sleep under their wagons, in crude shelters, or in a motley assortment of tents.

Exactly what happened to the Cannary family after its arrival in Virginia City isn't known, but they must have moved on rather soon, because Marthy says that her mother died in 1866 at Black Foot, Montana, and was buried there. Marthy then left for Utah, where her father died a year later. No one now knows what happened to Marthy's younger brothers and sisters; only a sister, Lena, who reappeared in her life at a later date, has ever been mentioned.

In the beginning of her adventures in the West, Marthy did the sort of work that most women did who needed to support themselves: she worked as a cook and did laundry. Such occupations must have seemed mighty tame to a girl who had enjoyed riding horseback, hunting, and joshing with male companions.

Marthy's decision to continue wearing men's clothes might have come about because, dressed as a boy, she found it a lot easier to get the kinds of jobs she liked. Being slender and athletic, perhaps it was simple to pass herself off as a stripling boy, and her disguise might have lasted much longer if she hadn't been prone to flirting with her male companions.

After joining a crew of men working on the Union Pacific Railroad, she generally behaved in a sassy, outrageous manner. Suspecting that the "boy" among them was nothing of the kind, the men slyly suggested a swim in a nearby stream one evening after work. Marthy blithely peeled off her clothes and joined them without a single modest thought—and the next day was ordered by the crew leader to leave with the next wagon train headed east.

In 1872, Marthy had contact with her

sister Lena, who at age fifteen had married John Borner, a German immigrant. According to relatives, Marthy wasn't welcome in the Borner home because of her rough manners. Lena became the mother of several children but reportedly died at age twenty-nine from complications of a broken hip at her ranch near Lander, Wyoming.

Marthy claimed that she got her famous name during a military campaign in 1873, when she was twenty-one years old. "It was on Goose Creek, Wyoming, where the town of Sheridan is now located," she reported in her memoir. She boasted that she had by this time become an Indian scout at Fort Sanders and was accompanying the commander of the fort, Captain Egan, on a detail to quell an uprising of the "Nursey Pursey" Indians. (Surely she had in mind members of the Nez Percé tribe.) Captain Egan was shot, and when Marthy saw him reel in his saddle, she rushed to his side in time to save him from falling off his horse. She was able to pull him onto her own horse, then got him safely back to the fort. When the captain recovered, he laughed and said, "I name you Calamity Jane, the heroine of the plains."

Did it really happen that way? Captain Egan allowed that it didn't, and historians are more than willing to believe him. Rather, they say, in the West a girl or woman was commonly called a "jane." In fact, during the Lewis and Clark expedition, William Clark often referred to Sacagawea as "Janey" in his journals. It isn't much of a reach, then, to imagine that someone simply prefaced that ordinary name with "calamity," which very well summed up young Martha Jane Cannary. No matter how the name was acquired, the one on whom it was bestowed relished it. Whenever she arrived in a new town, it was said that she liked to swagger into the nearest saloon and announce loudly, "The name's Calamity Jane, and the drinks are on me!"

However, it apparently *is* true that Calamity became a bullwhacker, or a driver of four- to six-hitch teams of oxen that were used to carry goods all over the West. Her pay would have been much better than what she could have expected to earn as a cook or laundress—between fifty and seventy-five dollars a month, plus free meals. Unfortunately for her health in later years, Calamity also acquired a strong liking for whiskey and drank as recklessly as any man. She also learned how to curse with as much abandon as her companions.

In 1875, after Custer announced that he'd found gold in the Black Hills, the rush was on, and Calamity joined in, not because she was interested in gold but because she loved adventure. She claimed that at this time she went to work as a scout for Custer. Calamity said that if she hadn't had to swim across the Platte River with an important message, thereby catching a cold from which it took her two weeks to recover, she certainly would have accompanied the yellow-haired general on his ill-fated expedition to the Little Bighorn. It was there that he and all of his troops were slaughtered by the Sioux in June 1876. That is regarded as another of her tall tales, yet Calamity Jane was indeed in the Black Hills during this period: her name appears in several newspaper articles and in the diaries of others who were there at the time.

Calamity Jane was becoming infamous everywhere she went because of her brash conduct, and more than once she was called a "camp follower"—that is, the kind of woman who followed men from place to place doing laundry for them or being paid for sexual companionship. It's doubtful that Calamity Jane continued doing laundry, but it's quite possible that she did engage in prostitution. She was described as "always in male company, riding bucking broncs, horse racing, target shooting usually at some store sign or street lamp, and helping diminish the supply of liquor or joining in some gambling games."

At this time she lived in a dugout in Rock Springs, Wyoming, "the front having the appearance of a tumbled down shack with one narrow door and window on each side. Bright red shades were drawn over these windows. The only time she spent in this so-called house was to sleep or entertain her masculine friends." However, the writer (whose work is in the Wyoming Historical Research Department in Cheyenne) went on to say, "Even though she caused considerable excitment and worry . . . no recollections can be made of her doing any unjust [deed] or harm to anyone. She was her own worst enemy."

Calamity not only liked whiskey, she also liked to marry, and did so with regularity—at least a dozen times, according to her own count. If divorces were ever gotten between these marriages, there is no record of them. The most famous of her "husbands" (it's unlikely that formal marriage contracts ever bound her to such men) was Wild Bill Hickok. In her memoir, Calamity said they'd met at Fort Laramie when she was twenty-four years old. He was older by fifteen years and already a legend in the West, having just returned from a tour of the East with Buffalo Bill Cody's "Wild West" show.

Calamity said she and Wild Bill traveled together to Deadwood, Dakota Territory, in June of 1876 and were married there by a preacher. She often displayed a crumpled bit of paper to

Calamity Jane at the grave of Wild Bill Hickok around 1900. Three years later she was buried beside him. LIBRARY OF CONGRESS.

document her claim. The writing on it was in pencil and grew fainter with the passing of time, but no one could detect a preacher's name on it—in any case, Bill Hickok already had a wife. Calamity said she didn't know of any previous marriage and that she suspected nothing amiss when Hickok asked her to keep their wedding a secret.

Instead, Calamity reported that she started a job as a Pony Express rider between Deadwood and Custer, a distance of about fifty miles. Then fate intervened and ruined what she might have hoped would be a happy life. On August 2, 1876, after one of her return trips to Deadwood, Calamity Jane discovered that Bill Hickok had been shot to death while playing poker at the Number 10 Saloon. After a chase, Jack McCall,

Hickok's murderer, was captured, tried, and hanged in Yankton, Dakota Territory.

No one knows now exactly what the nature of the relationship between Calamity Jane and Wild Bill Hickok really was, but his death apparently affected her deeply. She began to drink even more heavily than before. Whether folks believed the two were ever truly married is debatable, but Calamity was able to tell the kind of tale about tragic love that was sure to pry another glass of whiskey out of a sympathetic listener.

She took several more husbands, adopting such names as Dorsett, Somers, Hunt, Steers, and Dalton. The *Carbon County Journal* noted in its August 30, 1886, issue that Calamity Jane swore out a warrant in Rawlins, Wyoming, for the arrest of Steers because he'd hit her with a rock and cut her lip. He was fined, but they later patched up their quarrel; a month later, both were jailed because of another drunken quarrel. When they finally left town, it was together, on foot—and she was the one who carried their baggage!

In Calamity's defense, her admirers pointed out that she always tried to befriend her "sisters in sin," that she cared for neglected and abandoned children from time to time (perhaps because she knew only too well what it was like to be abandoned), and that she often nursed the sick. Her skill even caused some on the frontier to compare her to Florence Nightingale.

As often happened with frontier characters, it was ultimately an outsider—an easterner at that—who made Calamity Jane famous. Just as Ned Buntline brought Buffalo Bill Cody to the public's attention, Edward Lytton Wheeler, also called Ned, did the same for Calamity. He was two years younger than she and had begun writing stories when he was only a schoolboy. By the time he was twenty, he was selling tales of adventure and derring-do to news magazines in Philadelphia. Some of the stories had titles such as "Hurricane Nell, the Girl Dead-Shot" and "Wild Edna, the Girl Bandit," indicating he had a pronounced interest in heroic, headstrong damsels.

Soon Wheeler began writing yarns that featured a character named Calamity Jane, who often was paired with a male companion called Deadwood Dick. In these stories, which were among the most popular he ever wrote, the heroine was always elegantly dressed in buckskin, velvet, and gold jewelry, and was "regally beautiful." Whether the real-life Calamity was beautiful or not no one could agree; some of her contemporaries said her hair was a beautiful red color; others claimed it was black as a raven's wing. One of the earliest photographs of her, taken when she was in her twenties, shows an unsmiling, steady-eyed girl who is neither beautiful nor unbeautiful.

Calamity Jane left the Northwest in 1883 and journeyed to California. By 1884 she moved on to Texas; she later reported that while she was in El Paso, "I met Mr. Clinton Burk . . . who I married in August 1885. As I thought I have traveled through life long enough alone and thought it was about time to take a partner for the rest of my days. On October 28, 1887, I became the mother of a baby girl . . . who has the temper of its mother."

In spite of marriage and motherhood, Martha Jane Cannary's life seemed destined not to be serene. As time passed she drank more or less continuously. Mr. Burk (also spelled Burke) appeared only intermittently, and no one is sure what happened to her daughter, though there was a rumor that the child was placed in the care of nuns at a convent school in South Dakota. Calamity neglected her appearance more than usual, was often clad only in rags, and frequently was thrown in jail until she sobered up from a binge.

In the mid-1890s, when Calamity was in her forties but looked much older, someone suggested that she do exactly as Bill Cody had done—join a western show and capitalize on her connections to "the Wild West." Her first appearance was in January 1896, at the Palace Museum in Minneapolis, where for a dime viewers could listen to Calamity tell about her exploits with Buffalo Bill and Wild Bill, and all of her pony-express-riding, Indian-fighting, scouting-for-General Custer adventures.

However, Martha Jane was not a born performer, as her male counterparts— Buffalo Bill Cody in particular—seemed to be. On stage, she was tongue-tied and embarrassed, and she hated having the eyes of an audience trained on her. To give herself courage, she went back on her pledge not to drink and sometimes appeared for her performances in a sadly inebriated state. It wasn't long before she was fired.

The *Daily Leader* of Cheyenne reported that "Calamity's one over-ruling passion now is her love for strong drink." She also was a cigar smoker, which did not meet with the approval of at least one reporter, who wrote that "together with the jug she kept at her side, the vile cigar which she smoked made her look anything but the beautiful woman which novelists and story writers have said so much about."

A few years later, someone helped her write her memoirs, and they were published in a small booklet under the name Marthy Cannary Burke. It was suggested that she sell them personally at the Pan-American Exposition in New York in 1901. She attempted to do so,

Calamity Jane two years before her death. CORBIS-BETTMANN.

but again the public experience was so humiliating that she quickly fled back to the West.

Because of the way she'd lived, Calamity Jane was old long before her time, and her health showed the effects of her intemperance. In Sundance, Wyoming, a storekeeper named William Fox remembered that in June 1903, "a nondescript woman who had the appearance of great age" drifted into town. Hardly anyone could believe the poor wretch was Calamity Jane, and those who had known her in earlier days could hardly believe their eyes. "All traces of her former vitality and aggressiveness were gone. She . . . looked eighty."

In July 1903, Calamity went to Deadwood, her old stamping ground, for the last time. She died a few weeks later, on August 1, 1903, at age fifty-one, in a hotel room above the saloon where she'd lifted many a glass with rowdy companions. The proper folk of Deadwood who had once looked down upon her now realized that she had brought a measure of fame to their town and ought to be respected for it.

The Old Pioneer Society of Deadwood gave Calamity Jane a funeral that would have made her exclaim grandly, "The drinks are on me!" She was buried in a white dress that someone had provided, rather than the stark black dresses she sometimes wore or the male garb in which she seemed to feel so comfortable. After the service, her flower-covered coffin was carried up to the Mount Moriah Cemetery on a hill overlooking Deadwood. She had asked to be buried beside Wild Bill Hickok, the one man she might have cared more for than any of the others, and she lies there today.

More than twenty-five years after Martha Jane Cannary's death, a woman stepped out of the shadows of history, claiming to be the daughter of Calamity Jane and Wild Bill Hickok. She said the story of her birth had come to light only after she'd found her mother's diary in an old trunk, and the tale she told was as exciting as any Calamity herself could have invented.

Not long after Wild Bill's death in the Number 10 Saloon, according to the story, Calamity had given birth to a daughter in a cave near Deadwood. Mother and child were discovered there by a Captain O'Neil, an employee of the famous Cunard steamship line. (No convincing explanation was given for what he was doing on the prairie, far from any ocean.) The captain and his English wife were happily married, though childless, and desperately wanted a baby of their own. In order to give her infant daughter a better life, Calamity agreed to give "Janey" up for adoption. A search through Cunard records revealed no Captain O'Neil, and after a flurry of attention, the woman who claimed to be Calamity's daughter faded from public view. One can imagine the yarn would have gotten a hearty laugh from Calamity herself.

Martha Jane Cannary was an eccentric, a one-of-a-kind lady who refused to be what the world expected her to be. It could be said that she was a liberated woman long before the term became fashionable. Her life and legend were colorful and dramatic, yet in personal terms one suspects she paid dearly for it all. As someone suggested, "She was her own worst enemy"; yet the West wouldn't have been what it was without her.

Kit Carson

1809–68 Hunter, trapper, scout. Called "King of the Mountain Men." Guide for Colonel John Charles Frémont's expeditions to map the Oregon Trail; fought for the Union in Civil War. Appointed as Indian agent for Pueblo, Ute, and Apache tribes by President Polk.

Christopher Houston Carson was born so late on Christmas Eve, 1809, that many biographers list his birthday as Christmas Day. His mother, Rebecca Robinson of Greenbrier County, West Virginia, was Lindsey Carson's second wife and became a stepmother to five children when she married. By the time Christopher was born, Rebecca had already given birth to five children of her own, making the three-room cabin on Tate's Creek in Madison County, Kentucky, full to the rafters when the smaller-than-average new baby came into the world on a snowy December night.

In 1811, Lindsey Carson sold his Kentucky farm and moved his large family to Missouri. Kit—a nickname settled on the boy before he learned to walk—wasn't quite two years old, and rode with his mother as the family headed west. He said later that the long trip, with his chubby baby legs wrapped around the pommel of her saddle, was the reason he grew up so bandy-legged.

The family hadn't been settled long in Howard County when the War of 1812 was declared. This war paired unresolved territorial conflicts with the British on one hand with increased resistance by the Indians to white settlers on the other. Settlers' families were forced to seek shelter from hostile Indians in small log huts built close to the walls of such defense posts as Fort Kinkead, Fort Cooper, or Fort Hempstead, and after one skirmish, Lindsey

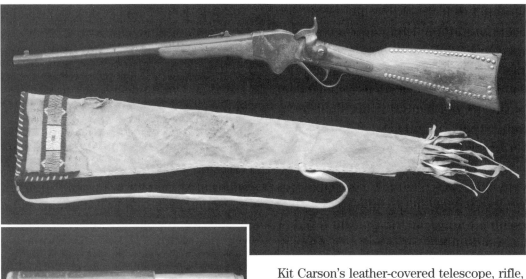

Kit Carson's leather-covered telescope, rifle, and deerskin rifle boot are displayed in the Kit Carson Museum, Taos, New Mexico. PHOTOGRAPH BY ANTHONY RICHARDSON.

Carson came home with part of his left hand shot away.

On Kit's fifth birthday, December 24, 1814, a treaty ending the war was signed, and by the time he was six the Carson family had resettled near Franklin, in the central part of Missouri. There was a new baby in the house now, a daughter named Mary Ann, who became Kit's favorite sister. Later, two more sons were born, Sarshall and Lindsey junior, making for a family of fourteen children.

Kit was nine years old when his father was killed by a falling tree as he cleared timber from his homestead. Together with Robert, fifteen, Matilda,

thirteen, and Hamilton, eleven, the boy helped keep Rebecca Carson's farm going. Four years later, when his mother married Joseph Martin, a neighboring widower with several children of his own, thirteen-year-old Kit—usually so quiet and mild-mannered—became hard to manage.

By mutual agreement, he went to live with his older half-brother William on a nearby farm. Even there, he was a problem, and not long afterward he became the ward of John Ryland, a future Missouri state supreme court judge. During this time, Kit had very little formal schooling. Many years later, he told Jessie Frémont, wife of Colonel John

Charles Frémont, "I was a young boy in school when the cry came, 'Indians!' I jumped for my rifle, threw down my spelling book, and there it still lies."

When Kit was fifteen years old—blue-eyed, lightly freckled, still small for his age—it was decided he should learn a trade, partly to deal with his troublesome behavior, mostly to give him a skill by which to earn a living. He was apprenticed to a saddlemaker in Franklin, a worthy craft in a day when men did most of their traveling by horseback. But Kit had been raised out-of-doors, and laboring day after day over a workbench with a pile of leather at his side, an awl in his fist, and a wooden saddle frame in front of him must have seemed more like a punishment than a privilege.

What made the experience tolerable was that Kit enjoyed the company of his employers, David and William Workman, who were intensely interested in stories of the continuing western migration. The saddle shop was a natural gathering place for anyone traveling by horseback, which included nearly everyone headed up the banks of the Missouri River to Dakota Territory, or down toward the Southwest along the Santa Fe Trail and thence to Mexico.

In 1821, Mexico won its independence from Spain and became a free republic. The new nation welcomed commerce with the United States, and extravagant profits—as much as six times a merchant's original investment—were being made by enterprising American traders. Of course, such stories weren't entirely new to Kit; his brothers Andrew and Robert had already joined a crew led by George Sibley and were busy surveying the Santa Fe Trail, while his half brother Moses had joined the Missouri Fur Company and had been up and down the river many times. In 1825, William Workman himself decided to join a trade caravan.

When Kit vanished from the saddle shop in August 1826, two years after having taken up his apprenticeship, David Workman posted an announcement in Franklin's newspaper, the *Missouri Intelligencer*, on Friday, October 6:

> Notice is hereby given to all persons, that CHRISTOPHER CARSON, a boy . . . small of his age, but thick set, light hair, ran away from the subscriber . . . to whom he had been bound to learn the saddler's trade, on or about the first day of September . . . one cent reward will be given to any person who will bring back the said boy.

To wait more than a month before announcing Kit's disappearance, as was required by law, and then to offer a mere penny for his return might have been

David Workman's way of helping the boy seek a life more congenial to his nature.

Late in life, Kit Carson recalled his flight: "I had the fortune to hear of a party bound for that country to which I desired to go. I made application . . . and without any difficulty, I was permitted to join them." So it was that in November 1826, Kit found himself in Santa Fe, located on a plateau nearly seven thousand feet above sea level, surrounded by pines and buoyed by the dry, sparkling air of the surrounding desert.

Kit's first job was as a "cavvy," a herder of the extra horses and mules that trade caravans took along to replace sick or stolen animals. He didn't get on well with the caravan leader and decided not to remain with it. Instead, he wintered at the home of a retired hunter and trapper, earning his keep at various make-do jobs, one of which led him to Taos, where he found work as a cook. He didn't want to be a cook any more than he wanted to be a saddle-maker, but because he was considered "too young, too small, too green," he couldn't find work with another caravan.

Kit became fluent in Spanish, and in the spring of 1828, when a party of merchants heading for Chihuahua, five hundred miles south of Santa Fe, needed an interpreter, he was hired on the spot. Afterward, Kit worked briefly in the copper mines in Chihuahua. Back in Taos in 1829, he met Ewing Young, a successful trader and trapper, who had gotten up a party of forty men with the intention of trapping and hunting along the Salt and Verde Rivers. Kit, who would always be shorter than his peers, was no longer as young nor as green as he once had been; in the four years since his escape from the saddle shop in Missouri, he'd earned the respect of other adventurers for his horsemanship, skill with a rifle, and unpretentious demeanor.

For the next ten years, Carson traveled with others whose occupation was harvesting beaver pelts to meet the fashion demands of eastern and European gentlemen who wore tall beaver hats; he became known as one of "the mountain men." The names of the hunting and trapping sites that became home to Carson and his companions were imbued with a certain rough magic: Wind River . . . Wild Horse Creek . . . the Bighorns . . . Brown's Hole . . . Prairie du Chien . . . the Rattlesnake Range . . . Powder River . . . Stinking Creek.

After receiving a large paycheck in April 1831 for the sale of a sizable stack of beaver pelts, Carson reflected on his own and his companions' opinion of their new wealth: "Trappers and sailors are similar in regard to the money that they earn so dearly, daily being in danger of losing their lives. But when the voyage has been made . . . they think not of the hardships and danger . . . [but] are ready for another trip."

Carson's new wealth consisted of something much more valuable than beaver pelts, however, and could not be measured in mere dollars. By the time he was twenty-two years old, he was intimately acquainted with vast tracts of land later to be called the Midwest: Kansas, Missouri, Minnesota, Iowa, and the Dakotas; the Mountain states of Wyoming, Colorado, Utah, Idaho, and Montana; and lastly, the Northwest states of Washington, Oregon, and California.

In the summer of 1835, Kit, now a man of nearly twenty-five, attended his first rendezvous at the mouth of Horse Creek on the Green River. He participated in a social event called a "soup dance," the purpose of which was to enable young Indian women to indicate their preferences for young men who caught their eyes. Waanibe, a young Arapaho girl (one translation of her name is "Singing Grass"), found Carson pleasing. He must have returned her interest and, like many of his companions, decided to take an Indian wife. They were married by a Protestant minister at Bent's Fort, near present-day La Junta, Colorado.

The market for pelts waned as beaver hats went out of fashion, and after Waanibe told Kit she was expecting a child, he realized he needed to stabilize his income. When he was offered a contract by the large, prosperous trading company of Bent and St. Vrain to become their professional hunter, he accepted eagerly. Charles Bent became the first governor of New Mexico in 1846; his partner, Cerin St. Vrain, a Frenchman who had become wealthy in the fur trade, remained Kit's friend till the end of their days.

Carson's job at the fort was to supply its twenty-five inhabitants with fresh meat from November through March, for which he was paid the sum of five hundred dollars. Several men were put under his command, but although the country was rich with game, Carson knew the job wouldn't be easy. He would have to contend with Cheyennes and Comanches, who considered the area to be their special hunting grounds; mountain lions and wolves competed for the same antelope and deer he would be looking for; buffalo herds, once a reliable supply of meat, were no longer as abundant as they had been. Only a man of Carson's wilderness skills could have fulfilled the fort's contract.

The following year, a daughter was born to Waanibe, whom her parents named Adaline, after one of Kit's favorite cousins. About 1840, Waanibe gave birth to a second daughter but died shortly after, leaving Kit a widower with two small children. He soon married a Cheyenne woman, but perhaps the role of stepmother didn't suit her, for she dissolved their union in the traditional Indian manner, by placing his personal belongings on the ground outside the tipi they shared.

In 1842, Carson took Adaline (no clear record exists regarding the fate of his younger daughter) back home to be raised by his sister Mary Ann in Independence, Missouri. He then boarded a steamer headed for St. Louis, where he chanced to met Colonel John Charles Frémont.

A few months earlier, this native of Georgia, a former mathematics instructor and four years younger than Carson, had been commissioned by the U.S. Army Corps of Topographical Engineers "to make a survey of the Platte or Nebraska River, up to the head of the Sweetwater," plus the first section of the Oregon Trail. When Carson learned the colonel needed a guide, he approached Frémont. "I told him I had spent some time in the mountains . . . [and] could guide him to any point he wished to go," Carson reported in his memoirs. He was promptly hired at one hundred dollars a month.

Frémont, describing his first meeting with Carson, noted that "I was pleased with him . . . a man of medium height, broad-shouldered and deep-chested, with a clear steady blue eye and frank speech and address; quiet and unassuming." Frémont's tendency to make hasty judgments made the relationship between the two men difficult in its early stages, yet Carson once remarked that he felt "under more obligation to Colonel Frémont than to any other man alive."

The two men agreed that their goal for 1842 would be to get through the Wind River Mountains of the Rockies in what would become the state of Wyoming. The group consisted of twenty-eight men, including Frémont's twelve-year-old nephew, Randolph Benton. A professional hunter named Maxwell was hired; Canadian voyageurs (rivermen) provided the muscle power for the journey; and on June 10 the trip commenced. That autumn, when the job was finished, Carson returned to Bent's Fort, hoping to take up again the job of professional hunter. St. Vrain, however, offered Carson a new position in Taos and an increase in salary.

In Taos, a town Kit had come to think of as home, he met a Mexican girl from a prominent family. He was baptized in the Catholic faith and in February 1843 married Josepha Maria Jaramillo, a month shy of her fifteenth birthday. The bride was described by observers as "a beauty . . . of the haughty, heartbreaking kind." Kit quickly hired an escort to bring his part-Arapaho daughter from Missouri to Taos to meet her new step-mother.

Josepha remained close to her family—wisely, it turned out, because throughout her marriage she was separated from her husband for long periods of time. Frémont called upon Carson again during the early months of his new marriage, this time to help him map the lands west of the Rockies, and the party left Kansas on May 29, 1843. Kit assumed that when they reached their destination, the Columbia River in Oregon, the journey would be over, but Frémont proceeded on into Nevada. A high mountain pass in the Sierra Nevada range—ever after called Carson Pass—led them into California, where they rested at Sutter's Fort in February 1844. The 5,500-mile trip had been a terrible one, the men arriving at the fort on the verge of starvation amid reports that their horses were so hungry they'd eaten each other's tails.

There was an urgency about this expedition that had little to do with furs or trade. Ever-increasing numbers of immigrants from Europe were arriving in New York, a city that could scarcely absorb another family. The U.S. government reasoned that if such people could be moved westward, pressure on east-

A drawing of Kit Carson guiding Colonel John Charles Frémont. THE NEW YORK PUBLIC LIBRARY PICTURE COLLECTION.

ern cities would be relieved. To the immigrants, most of whom couldn't afford to own property in their native countries, the prospect of acquiring land was an irresistible lure. However, it was important to construct a case for American rights to western lands by mapping and exploration, thereby combating British claims to them. Thomas Hart Benton, a powerful senator (and Colonel Frémont's father-in-law), argued successfully for a U.S. policy that would facilitate acquisition of such lands in the West.

One result of Frémont's second expedition was the publication of his official *Report of the Exploring Expedition to the Rocky Mountains, 1842, and to Oregon and North California, 1843–44*, released by the U.S. War Department in 1845. More than 250,000 copies of the report were circulated, and because of the generous praise that Frémont heaped on his guide, Kit became a celebrity almost overnight. Newspaper and magazine articles dubbed him "the King of the Mountain Men," and resolutions in both houses of Congress recommended that Frémont and Carson be honored for their accomplishments. Thirty-six-year-old Carson would enjoy few private moments again during his lifetime. America was hungry for heroes, and he instantly became one.

The U.S. Congress voted to annex Texas in 1845, a step that was certain to lead to war with Mexico. Frémont, eager to play an influential role in the conflict, was anxious to have Carson join him for yet another expedition. They met at Bent's Fort in March, ostensibly on a mission for the U.S. Corps of Topographical Engineers. The following

months saw the team cross the Rockies, proceed to the Great Salt Lake, and thence enter California once again.

Now the true nature of Frémont's third expedition became apparent: he took an active part in arousing pro-American sentiment among Californians, in anticipation of the war that was officially declared against Mexico on May 13, 1846. Frémont was sent with one hundred men to Monterey to act as a protective force after the Stars and Stripes had been raised there, but his relationship with his superior, General Stephen Watts Kearny, was troubled from the beginning. Kit Carson became embroiled in their disputes, which ended with charges of insubordination against Frémont; he was court-martialed and dismissed from the army. Since Kit didn't hold a military commission, no charges were filed against him.

In January 1847, Kit received shocking news: there had been an Indian massacre in Taos that had driven Josepha from their home. She was safe, but the disaster had taken the life of Charles Bent, Kit's longtime friend, who, after his marriage to Josepha's sister Ignacia, also had become a brother-in-law.

During one lengthy stay in Washington, after delivering a message from Frémont to President Polk in which the colonel defended himself against his court-martial, Carson became well acquainted with Frémont's wife. Jessie Frémont noted in her memoirs that he grew restive in the city, and when she asked what troubled him, Kit remarked about men of government: "They are princes here in their big houses, but on the plains *we* are the princes. What would their lives be without us [out] there?"

In 1853, Carson was appointed agent of Indian affairs for the Apache, Ute, and Pueblo tribes. Earlier than other men, he had recognized that native tribes, whose proud people once provided for their own welfare by hunting and fishing, could no longer do so as wild game in the mountains and on the plains became scarcer due to encroachment by white settlers. He concluded that "the government can have but one alternative, either to . . . clothe them or exterminate them."

Carson demonstrated his compassion by suggesting that Indians should be taught farming skills, such as the Navajo had already adopted, to replace the hunting skills that would no longer support them. Such an education, he believed, was "one mode of saving them from annihilation . . . [or] they will continue to sink deeper into degradation."

The fact that Kit Carson could neither read nor write was a serious handicap to him in his career as an Indian agent, inasmuch as he was required to fill out many government reports and keep his accounts in order. John Mostin, a clerk in Carson's employ, took care of such tasks and in 1856 also took dictation from Kit for his memoirs. The original manuscript went undiscovered for decades but came to light in 1905; after it had been authenticated, it was acquired by the Newberry Library of Chicago.

Carson established himself as a fair and honest Indian agent who, because he could speak their language, earned the trust of his native clients. But on April 15, 1861, after the Confederate firing on Fort Sumter, President Lincoln declared war. Carson immediately left his position as agent on May 24 and in August was commissioned a lieutenant colonel in the pro-Union New Mexico Volunteers, where he quickly rose to the rank of full colonel. By this time, Kit was the father not only of Adaline, but also of William, Christopher, Charles, and Teresina; several other children had been adopted into his household, including a young Navajo girl.

At the outset of the Civil War, the Confederacy was not as great a threat to New Mexico as were various Indian tribes—the Navajo, Apache, Comanche, Cheyenne, and Ute—who still were not resigned to the loss of their old way of life. As these tribes witnessed the whites fighting one another, they decided to carry out their own campaigns,

Kit Carson as an army colonel. CULVER PICTURES, INC.

hoping to retrieve the land that had been taken from them. Kit Carson's appearance in the mountains around Taos at the head of a column of seven hundred men temporarily dampened Indian hostilities. The Ute tribes returned to their homes, Apaches and Comanches scattered, and the Cheyennes sent a peace delegation to meet with Carson.

However, the Navajos, the wealthiest and most powerful of all the Southwest tribes, had only grudgingly accepted the encroachment of white settlers, and now they decided to make a final stand. Farms and ranches in what is now northwestern New Mexico and northeastern Arizona were systematically looted and destroyed. Settlers were killed, their wives and children kidnapped, livestock stolen. Soon the Navajos threatened Colorado and Utah, yet few Union troops could be spared to fend them off.

There are many chapters in the history of the American frontier that are troubling to read, and such a chapter was about to open in the career of Kit Carson. There was no doubt that Navajo depredations needed to be stopped, and Carson's superior, General James H. Carleton, developed a plan that closely resembled William Tecumseh Sherman's "scorched earth" policy following the capture of Atlanta toward the end of the Civil War.

So it was that Kit Carson found himself ordering his troops to level Navajo villages, to destroy their fields of corn, to burn their peach orchards. Sheep and cattle were slaughtered in great numbers, their carcasses left to rot in the sun. The more successful his plan was, the more depressed Carson became.

"I can take no pride in this fearful destruction," he told Josepha in a letter dictated to his clerk. "My sleep is haunted by dreams of starving Navajo women and children." In April 1864, the Navajos—their livestock gone, their villages demolished, their women and children starving—surrendered unconditionally. In one of her rare recorded statements, Josepha told General Sherman that the misery visited upon the Navajo nation was ever present in her husband's mind.

The Civil War entered its final phase, and on April 9, 1864, General Robert E. Lee surrendered at Appomattox Court House in Virginia. Kit continued to be active in subduing the Kiowa, Cheyenne, and Arapaho tribes. By this time, he'd been engaged in military battles for four and a half years; he was now a tired, war-weary man of fifty-six. No doubt he welcomed an appointment in 1866 as the commanding general of a peacekeeping force of 1,800 men at Fort Garland, Colorado, which would allow him more time to spend with his family, who moved from New Mexico to be with him. The farm in Taos was sold for forty thousand dollars, and Kit and Josepha never saw it again.

In October 1867, Carson's military career was abruptly terminated. He had headed out one morning to inspect the country around Fort Garland, an aide-de-camp his only companion. His horse spooked; Kit was thrown off and knocked unconscious. An examination by two doctors at the fort indicated that in addition to a head injury he had an aneurysm of the aorta, the major vessel of the heart; in that era, there was no treatment for such a condition.

He retired from his position as commander of Fort Garland and moved to nearby Fort Lyon. In the spring, however, it was Josepha who became gravely ill after the birth of another daughter, and she died in April. Her death, after a quarter century of marriage, deeply affected Carson, who died a month later, on May 23, 1868, at the age of fifty-eight. A year later, the bodies of Kit and Josepha were disinterred and were laid to rest in Taos, where their old home now is maintained as the Kit Carson Museum.

The notice that appeared in the *Rocky Mountain News* announcing the death of Kit Carson was subdued and appropriate. Soon, however, his life was lavishly embroidered by newspaper and magazine articles that portrayed him as a man larger than life, capable of extraordinary feats of heroism and bravery. A myth was woven around him that still, in modern times, makes it difficult to separate fact from fiction.

Some commentators, however, sought to topple Carson from his pedestal. "Kit Carson was a good type of a class of men most useful in their day, but now as antiquated as Jason of the Golden Fleece or Ulysses of Troy . . . all belonging to the dead past," General Sherman said.

Such an assessment seems unjust. After all, Kit Carson had enjoyed a life that embraced not one but four careers. He had been a trapper and a hunter; a guide for three Frémont expeditions; served many years as a respected Indian agent; and was an astute and capable military man, rising to the rank of brigadier general. He was, indeed, a good type of man, most useful in his day—and that should be more than enough.

George Catlin

1796–1872 Painter. Followed his father into the practice of law, but in his twenties discovered painting, which became a consuming passion. Was befriended by William Clark, of Lewis and Clark fame, and vowed to paint "the wild people beyond the Mississippi" while they still lived in their natural state.

Born in Wilkes-Barre, Pennsylvania, on July 26, 1796, George was the fifth of lawyer Putnam Catlin's fourteen children. Putnam himself, at age thirteen, had served as a piper during the Revolutionary War. His mother, the former Polly Sutton, was only seven years old when she was captured by Indians during a massacre; she was rescued unharmed, but her father, one of the few male survivors of the disaster, had to swim across the Susquehanna River under a hail of bullets and arrows.

While George was still an infant, the family moved to a farm forty miles from the city, and when he was ten, he suffered a wound that left him with a scar he bore the rest of his life. He and two other boys were practicing hurling a tomahawk against a tree. George stood closer to the tree than was prudent, and when the tomahawk glanced off it struck his left cheek, cutting through to the bone. The wound took months to heal and left the boy with what some called "the mark of the Indian." No one could have guessed how prophetic it would prove to be.

The Susquehanna River valley was a paradise for George and his brothers; they hunted, fished, and explored, accumulating a wealth of knowledge about the woods and its creatures. The Catlin farm was located along a much-used trail that headed west and was traveled by Indian fighters, trappers, and hunters bound for Ohio, or by those returning from travels even farther away. Such men often stopped at the Catlin home, giving George a sense of what lay beyond his own sheltered valley.

When he was in his teens, George entered Wilkes-Barre Academy. There, he studied the Greek classics, history, geography, astronomy, and math, for which his parents paid tuition of six dollars per quarter. Then, in 1817, Putnam Catlin announced he'd saved enough money to send his fifth child to the prestigious Reeve and Gould law school in Litchfield, Connecticut. During a short span of fifty years, the school had turned out U.S. vice presidents, Supreme Court judges, and presidential cabinet members.

When he enrolled at age twenty-one, George had reached his full height of five feet eight inches and weighed a wiry 135 pounds. His hair and complexion were dark and his eyes intensely blue, and the neighborhood girls had begun to pay him special attention.

In Litchfield, his father's birthplace, young George called on relatives and was welcomed warmly by his cousins Flora Catlin and Mary Peck, who taught art classes at Miss Pierce's Academy. It was under his cousins' instruction that George first learned how to use crayon and watercolor. During this era, miniature portraits, painted on ivory, were fashionable items in many upper-class households, and when George exam-

ined some excellent ones created by Anson Dickinson of Litchfield, he assumed the painter had studied in Europe. Not at all, his cousins informed him; rather, Dickinson was entirely self-taught.

Young Catlin began to paint in any spare time that he had after tending to his law studies. When he graduated in October 1818, he set up a law practice in Lucerne County, Pennsylvania. He was successful, but painting and sketching dominated more of his time and thoughts than the law. Later, he wrote about the years from 1819 to 1823: ". . . another and stronger passion was getting the advantage of me, that of painting, to which all my pleading soon gave way. . . .[So] I very deliberately resolved to convert my law library into paint pots and brushes, and to pursue painting as my future."

He wasted no time following through; the law library was sold, and he set up a small studio on Walnut Street in Philadelphia. George looked forward to entering his work in the spring exhibit of the Pennsylvania Academy of Art, and he often visited the Philadelphia Museum, where he had a chance to see the collection of artifacts from the Lewis and Clark expedition. He was delighted when he discovered that four—not one but *four!*—of his miniature portraits were selected for the exhibit in

May 1821. As a result, he was invited by Rembrandt Peale, a noted painter, to drop by his studio to meet other artists, Thomas Sully and John Naegle among them. The following year, George's luck was even better: six of his portraits were selected by the academy.

George's brother Julius, eight years younger and now a cadet at West Point, forecast great success for George. The prophecy was fulfilled on February 18, 1824, when the twenty-seven-year-old painter was elected to the Pennsylvania Academy of Art. In three short years, George had achieved greater success than he'd ever believed possible.

Yet something gnawed at his soul. He was making a good living as a painter— but did he want to spend his life in the city, painting portraits of people who could afford them? He thought often of the Lewis and Clark exhibit he'd seen. "My mind was continually reaching for some branch of enterprise of the arts, on which to devote a whole lifetime of enthusiasm," he later wrote.

During the winter of his election to the academy, a delegation of Indians on their way home from Washington, D.C., visited in Philadelphia. The Indians' stoic, noble bearing and their exotic clothing of leather, fur, and feather ignited Catlin's imagination. Much later, he wrote that the "history and customs of such people, preserved by pictorial illustrations . . . [are] themes worthy of the lifetime of one man." He believed in his heart *he* was that man.

George concentrated on developing a style of painting that would be suitable for his new mission. He knew the meticulously detailed style suitable for miniatures on ivory was useless for what he had in mind. Rather, he needed to approach his new models with swift, brisk brushstrokes; in addition, the portraits had to be life-size.

As a means of practicing this new style, Catlin used a model to whom he had regular access: himself. His self-portrait does more than tell us what Catlin looked like in 1824; its quick, sure brushwork demonstrates how far he'd come in his quest for a new method of portraiture.

He still did some work on commission, however, and in December 1824, he painted the first of three portraits of De Witt Clinton. In addition to being the power behind the construction of the Erie Canal, Clinton was governor of New York, leader of the Republican Party, and an influential member of the American Academy of Fine Arts.

In May 1826, Catlin was elected to the Academy of Fine Arts (known today as the National Academy of Design), and was thereby assured of a career as a painter of famous, wealthy white Americans. He remained committed to his desire to paint the natives of the West, however, and began making frequent trips to nearby Indian reservations in western New York State. His first known Indian portrait was of the famous Seneca statesman and orator, Red Jacket, signed and dated at Buffalo, New York, in 1826.

Catlin had someone who shared his dreams: his brother Julius. After graduating from West Point, Julius was stationed on the western frontier in present-day Arkansas. He so thoroughly shared George's plan for the future that he resigned from the army in September 1826 in order to promote his brother's artistic career.

Catlin became a frequent guest at Governor Clinton's mansion, and at a party there met Clara Bartlett Gregory, the daughter of a wealthy family. They fell in love and were married in an evening ceremony on May 10, 1828, at St. Peter's Episcopal Church in Albany. The painter was thirty-two; his bride was twenty.

George now had a wife whom he loved—but he was about to suffer a loss that would affect him deeply. The Franklin Institute in Rochester, New York, had ordered a copy of one of his De Witt Clinton portraits; when it was finished, George asked Julius to deliver it. While in Rochester, Julius joined a group of friends for a swim in a nearby river and was drowned. George was determined not to forsake the dream he and Julius had shared, and he continued to paint portraits of Indians from the nearby reservations: Oneidas, Tuscaroras, Ottawas, and Mohegans. Nevertheless, the loss of Julius wore him down; he lost weight and developed a cough that caused some to wonder if he had consumption. (Today, we call it by its right name, tuberculosis.) Worried about her husband's health, Clara took him to Richmond, hoping he'd recover in a warmer climate.

The Virginia Constitutional Convention of 1829–30 was then in session, and Catlin was commissioned to paint a picture of the assembled body. The composition is witty—the face of each man, all 101 of them, including the likes of James Madison, James Monroe, and John Marshall, was carefully painted as if it were a miniature portrait! Witty or not, George had made up his mind to abandon the career of a society painter; Clara supported his decision, as she did to the end of her life. Her family was scandalized and couldn't understand why a young man with a brilliant career would throw it all away to paint "savage red men in the wilderness."

In 1830, Catlin went to St. Louis, at that time a bustling city of fifteen thousand; his mission was to meet a man who knew more about the West than

An etching of the young George Catlin, reproduced by photogravure. NORTH WIND PICTURE ARCHIVES.

anyone else alive, General William Clark. After the completion of the Lewis and Clark expedition, Clark served as superintendent of Indian affairs, until his death twenty-five years later. It was his responsibility to grant government trading and hunting licenses, and no man could trade, hunt, or travel in the West without his approval.

Catlin knew the meeting with Clark could make or break his plans, and he armed himself with the most impressive letters of introduction he could obtain and a collection of his best Indian portraits. Clark recognized the value of the project that Catlin outlined to him and was impressed that the painter didn't ask for government funding or for any special assistance.

As if to test Catlin, Clark invited him to paint in his office, where Indian delegations came almost daily, and was impressed not only by Catlin's ability to paint a picture swiftly but also by the rapport he established with those who sat for him. The chance to paint Indians in Clark's office whetted Catlin's appetite to paint them in their own settings and on the hunt, so in July 1830, he accompanied Clark on a treaty-making expedition to Prairie du Chien along the upper Mississippi in present-day Wisconsin. There, he met members of Iowa, Sioux, Omaha, Sauk, and Fox tribes and began his mission—that of painting "the wild men" in their native element.

Later, Catlin made two more trips, the first up the Missouri as far as Fort Leavenworth in the northeastern corner of Kansas, a gathering place for Delaware, Potawatomi, Shawnee, and Kickapoo tribes. He painted the portraits of notable chiefs, among them Notch-ee-ming-a, No Heart, the principal chief of the Iowas, and Ten-squat-a-way, a brother of the famous Shawnee chief, Tecumseh. The second trip with Clark was to the villages of the Konza (Kansas) tribe, along the Kansas River.

Catlin rejoined his wife, but in the spring of 1831 was off again, this time on a trip up the Platte River with Major John Dougherty. Their travels took them to what in 1834 became Fort Laramie in Wyoming; the route they followed later was named the Oregon Trail. Catlin painted portraits as he traveled, but by now he had conceived of an even grander project: the recording and documentation in writing, as well as in painting, of primitive Indian ceremonies and customs then unknown to most white men.

One of the many acquaintances Catlin made in St. Louis was Pierre Chouteau, the manager of John Jacob Astor's American Fur Company. Chouteau was planning a two-thousand-mile boat trip upriver to Fort Union, the company's westernmost outpost, deep in the heart of Sioux country. The boat, built to Chouteau's specifications and named the *Yellowstone*, left St. Louis on March 26, 1832, with Catlin on board. Many colorful characters also made the trip, among them Wi-jun-jon, the son of an Assiniboin chief, who was returning from a visit to Washington. He had been sent east to represent his people wearing traditional Indian garb but returned wearing his idea of a white man's military outfit: blue broadcloth suit trimmed with gold, high-heeled black boots, a tall beaver hat, and red kid gloves. The "uniform" was completed by a large blue umbrella.

The Missouri River, which some wags said was "so thick it cracked going around the bend," or so muddy "you have to drink it with a fork," foiled the travelers. In May, the *Yellowstone* went aground near what is now the capital of South Dakota, and Catlin set off with others on the overland trip to the trading post of Fort Tecumseh (soon to be named Fort Pierre in honor of Chouteau). Catlin was greeted by William Laidlaw and Kenneth MacKenzie, employees of the American Fur Company.

Laidlaw was married to a Sioux woman, and he arranged to find good subjects for Catlin to paint. The first to sit for a portrait was One Horn, a Sioux chief, but it was difficult to find other Indians willing to be painted. They became alarmed when they saw the life-size likeness of One Horn and regarded the whole process as "bad medicine." The Indians noted that in the painting, One Horn's eyes were open, and asked, "How can he sleep at night?" It was One Horn himself who reassured them. "Look at me. Am I harmed? No. And you will not be harmed."

Catlin won the Indians' respect because he had a deep regard for their customs; in return, the Sioux performed the rarely seen Dance of the Chieftains for him, which Catlin immortalized in a painting. He also painted the bear dance, the scalp dance, the sun dance, and a special ceremony called "smoking the shield," to which a young man invited friends and well-wishers for a dance and feast while the skin of a new rawhide shield was shrunk and hardened over a special fire built in a shallow pit.

When Catlin suggested painting one or more of the women of the tribe, the Sioux objected vigorously. They pointed out that women did nothing important, such as hunt or take scalps. They only built fires, cooked food, tanned skins, made clothing, and raised children!

One portrait session ended in tragedy. As Catlin was painting Mah-to-tchee-ga, Little Bear, a chief of the Hunkpapa

In this self-portrait George Catlin recorded the interest of a group of Mandans as he painted their chief. RARE BOOKS DIVISION, THE NEW YORK PUBLIC LIBRARY. ASTOR, LENOX, AND TILDEN FOUNDATIONS.

tribe (the band into which Sitting Bull would be born in 1834), Shon-ka, Dog, of the Bad Arrow Points band, came to view the proceedings. He was a sullen man, disliked by other Indians, but when he exclaimed that Little Bear was "only half a man," the onlookers fell silent. Dog pointed to the painting, which showed Little Bear in profile, and declared that Catlin had painted him thus because the other half of Little

Bear wasn't worth anything. Later, in a confrontation, Dog shot away the half of Little Bear's face that hadn't appeared in the portrait. A few months after Catlin's departure, Little Bear's followers tracked down Dog, killing him and his brother, Steep Wind.

When the *Yellowstone* was able to navigate again, the travelers pushed hard for Fort Union, eight hundred miles up the Missouri, making as few stops as possible. At one stop, not far from Fort Union, Wi-jun-jon—still outfitted in white man's finery, carrying his blue umbrella and a keg of whiskey under his arm—went ashore to rejoin his Assiniboin kinfolk. Catlin observed that they greeted him coolly, and only after their curiosity became unbearable did they consent to listen to his tales of Washington. The *Yellowstone* set off before Catlin could witness the final chapter of Wi-jun-jon's homecoming: the Assiniboin decided that their former protégé, whom they had chosen themselves to go east, was a liar and a fool. He was ridiculed and shunned, and after several months he was murdered by his own people.

The *Yellowstone* arrived at Fort Union on June 16, 1832. The fort was at the mouth of the Yellowstone River, close to the present Montana-North Dakota border. Here, Catlin met members of the Cree, Blackfoot, Piegan, and Crow tribes. "I am traveling in this country not to advance or prove theories, but to see all I am able to see and tell it in the simplest and most intelligent manner," wrote Catlin in his *Letters and Notes on the Manners, Customs, and Conditions of the North American Indians*, published in 1841. He added, ". . . for these uncontaminated people . . . I would be willing to devote the energies of my life."

Catlin observed something that caused him distress: it was plain that the buffalo would eventually become extinct and that liquor would defeat the Indians more surely than anything else. He discovered that his acquaintance Chouteau had a clever plan to defeat a new law forbidding shipment of liquor into Indian territory: rather than smuggle liquor into the country, he decided the simplest thing would be to build a distillery at Fort Union.

The trip downstream gave Catlin a chance to paint the Mandans, who called themselves the People of the Pheasants. It was with the Mandans that Lewis and Clark had wintered in 1805–06, just before setting out to find the Northwest Passage to the Pacific. Mandan ancestry remains something of a mystery; they were a light-skinned people who had blue or gray eyes and hair that varied from dark to light and often grayed prematurely. The Mandans were perhaps the most civilized and peaceful of all the Plains Indians, their homes well tended, their clothing the most carefully decorated, their personal cleanliness remarkable. Catlin wondered if this tribe was descended from Welsh seamen under Prince Madoc, who legend hinted might have come to the New World during the Middle Ages.

In spite of their love of fine things, however, the Mandans weren't sure they wanted their portraits painted, even though James Kipp, agent for the American Fur Company, praised Catlin's work. In particular, Mah-to-he-ha, Old Bear, an influential medicine man, was opposed to the project. Catlin handled the matter diplomatically. Early one morning, he asked Old Bear to come to his studio and remarked that since coming to the village he had admired the medicine man's fine appearance. His previous paintings, Catlin explained, had been made only to perfect his skills so that he'd be able to do justice to a man as handsome as Old Bear. Such words worked their magic on the medicine man, and he hurried away to dress for the occasion. When Old Bear saw the full-length likeness of himself, he became Catlin's staunchest supporter.

When James Kipp visited Catlin in New York City in 1838, however, he had a melancholy story to tell about the Mandans. The year before, fur traders had unwittingly infected the Indians with smallpox; within two months, nearly the entire village was dead, and the thirty or forty survivors were taken captive by the Arikaras. Later, when the Arikaras were attacked by the Sioux, the Mandans ran forward, calling out to the Sioux to kill them, for they no longer wanted to live. They were obligingly hacked to death.

Catlin was reunited with his wife in Pittsburgh after 86 days of nonstop painting. He returned with a wealth of material: the likenesses of people from 27 different tribes in more than 135 pictures, including 66 portraits, 36 scenes of Indian life, 25 landscapes, and 8 hunting scenes. Catlin could have rested his career on what he'd accomplished, but he soon returned to St. Louis to get ready for another painting trip. Pierre Chouteau objected because Catlin had been outspoken in his criticism of the fur company's practice of supplying whiskey to the Indians as well as the white man's depredations of the buffalo herds. Catlin remained in St. Louis, hoping Chouteau would change his mind; when he didn't, the painter went home to Pittsburgh and in April 1833 exhibited more than a hundred of his Indian paintings. They were hailed as "most extraordinary . . . [they] constitute a most valuable addition to the history of our continent."

Catlin's work had exhausted him, and he spent the winter in Mexico, where his brother James was a banker. Next, he obtained permission from the secretary of war to join a group traveling into Comanche territory. In the spring of 1834, Catlin joined the First Regiment of Mounted Dragoons at Fort Gibson, who were about to commence a trip across the southern plains to the Rocky Mountains. The expedition was the first effort by the U.S. government to acquire Mexican-controlled lands in the Southwest. Among the officers on the expedition was a young West Point graduate, Lieutenant Jefferson Davis, who would one day become the president of the Confederacy in the Civil War. This trip gave Catlin the chance to paint the Cherokees, Choctaws, Creeks, Seminoles, Chickasaws, Senecas, Osages, and Delawares.

The southern expedition was handicapped by illness among both men and horses, due in part to the extreme heat, recorded as high as 108 degrees. Many men died, and Catlin himself—delirious and clinging to life—had to be carried in the baggage wagon back to Fort Gibson, where he was cared for by a Dr. Wright. Later, on a journey up the Mississippi, this time to Fort Snelling in what would become the state of Minnesota, Catlin sketched members of the Ojibwa, Fox, and Sauk tribes.

The winter of 1835–36 was devoted to making plans for organizing a new exhibit. It wasn't until July 1836, in

Buffalo, New York, when he was nearly forty years old, that Catlin displayed for the first time all of his paintings and the thousands of Indian costumes, weapons, and artifacts he'd collected in what he called "an Indian Gallery." Tickets were sold to his lectures, for this was how he intended to earn a living now that he was the father of his first child, Elizabeth.

In December 1837, an incident occurred that caused Catlin to shut down his exhibit and travel to Fort Moultrie in South Carolina. Chief Osceola, the "Tiger of the Everglades," who for six years had outwitted the military might of the U.S. Army, had been captured; he was imprisoned and died of malaria in spite of Catlin's efforts to rescue him. The surgeon at Fort Moultrie cut off the chief's head and took it home; when he wanted to punish his young sons, he hung Osceola's head on their bedstead. Catlin was outraged and decided to move his entire exhibit to Washington, where he intended to lobby the federal government for more humane treatment of the Indians.

Catlin was warned that crusading on the Indians' behalf would wreck his finances and further undermine his health. Nevertheless, he opened his exhibit in Washington, D.C., in 1838 and campaigned for "a national park" for the Indians, making him the first American to call for what later became the national park system. He won some converts, Daniel Webster and Henry Clay among them.

Later, Catlin took his exhibit to Baltimore, Philadelphia, and Boston, continuing to lobby Congress to purchase his entire Indian Gallery and establish a United States National Museum. A friend suggested that he take his paintings to London. Hoping to shame Congress into taking a more active interest in his projects, Catlin announced plans to do exactly that. Congress continued to dawdle, and the artist discovered he'd laid a trap for himself: he didn't really want to leave America but was obliged to carry out his threat. The decision came at an awkward time: Clara was expecting a second child, and his elderly widowed father was ill and might not live until his son's return.

On November 25, 1839, forty-three-year-old George Catlin sailed for England with eight tons of freight, six hundred paintings, and thousands of Indian costumes and artifacts. In London, he rented three huge gallery rooms in Piccadilly for the sum of three thousand dollars a year. The public response was greater than anything he had hoped for, but the strain of constant lecturing and socializing was physically exhausting.

Back in America, Clara gave birth to a second daughter, while in England, Catlin pursued the possibility of publishing an expanded version of the letters he'd written home from the frontier. London publishers hesitated to undertake the printing of two thick volumes plus 312 steel engravings, so Catlin decided to publish it himself. Too hastily published and containing many flaws, the book came out in October 1841, cost twelve dollars, and was an instant success, enabling Catlin to arrange for Clara and his children to join him.

The following year, 1842, brought birth and death: a third daughter was born, named Victoria in honor of the British queen, and back home Putnam Catlin died. Plans were made to return to America, but not before the exhibit toured Manchester, Liverpool, Edinburgh, Dublin, and many other cities. The trip home was further delayed by the arrival in London of promoter Arthur Rankin, who showed up with nine Ojibwa Indians from Canada to add to the exhibit. Catlin objected to this cheap display, but Londoners were crazed with a desire to see Indians, and soon Catlin and Rankin were making four hundred dollars a day from their exhibit.

When one of the Indians, Cadotte, fell in love with a young English girl, proper Victorians were scandalized, and attendance at the Indian Gallery dropped to almost nothing. During these turbulent times, there was one happy note: Catlin's first son, George junior, was born.

By April 1845, Catlin had moved his family—and the remaining Indians—to Paris, where he opened exhibits and lectures on June 3, 1845. But the Indians grew homesick, and when Little Wolf's wife died, they decided they wanted to return to America. Clara, too, wanted to return as soon as possible, but she was ill with pneumonia and Catlin spent many days nursing her. She was far sicker than anyone realized and died on July 28, just short of her thirty-eighth birthday.

Catlin needed money desperately and got a commission from King Louis Philippe to make fifteen copies of his Indian paintings, a project that he commenced in January 1846. He was fifty years old now, father of four motherless children, and beset by debts. He launched a new campaign to get the U.S. government to buy the Indian Gallery collection for a sum of sixty-five thousand dollars. American painters who lived in Paris rallied to his cause, and a bill was passed in Congress, resulting in the establishment of the Smithsonian Institution.

Before the museum could get under way, however, the Mexican War broke out. To support himself and his children, Catlin accepted another commission from King Louis Philippe, this time for twenty-seven paintings representing La Salle's four-year journey from the Great Lakes to the Mississippi. When typhoid fever broke out in Paris, Catlin's daughters fell ill, then his son. The girls recovered, but after a brief illness, little George died. Although Catlin forced himself to continue to paint, observers noted that his work was second-rate.

As Catlin struggled, awash in personal problems, a political storm brewing in Europe erupted in the revolution of 1848. Louis Philippe fled the country; soldiers of the Second Republic broke into Catlin's apartment and, while he watched, shredded his paintings with bayonets. Having lost his benefactor, and needing money to support his family, Catlin wrote a hasty tract, *Eight Years' Travel and Residence in Europe;* the book was published in 1848, to scornful reviews.

Efforts to revive interest in Congress for purchase of Catlin's collection were attempted; finally, the House of Representatives voted to buy them, but the Senate refused to go along. One of the negative votes was cast by Jefferson Davis, who as a young lieutenant had been on the expedition with Catlin to Comanche territory in 1834. He cast a nay vote because the southern slave

George Catlin's 1832 oil portrait of the chief of the Blackfoot nation. NATIONAL MUSEUM OF AMERICAN ART, SMITHSONIAN INSTITUTION. GIFT OF MRS. JOSEPH HARRISON, JR.

owners whom he represented were hungry for Indian lands and wanted no public sympathy aroused on behalf of Indians.

Catlin's world caved in. Creditors stripped his apartment of its furnishings while his daughters looked on; Clara's wealthy brother, Dudley Gregory, arrived in Paris and angrily took custody of his sister's children. An American benefactor, Joseph Harrison, head of the world's largest railroad locomotive–building firm in Philadelphia, paid off the principal debts against the Indian Gallery, then crated up the paintings and returned with them to America. Catlin, aged fifty-six, penniless and deaf, could offer no resistance.

Catlin suffered through the cold Paris winter of 1852–53; unable to heat his small room, he spent hours at the Bibliothèque Imperial. There, he met a man who told him grand tales about ancient Indian gold mines in the Crystal Mountains of northwest Brazil. Catlin obtained a British passport "incognito . . . as kings and emperors do," he later wrote, and sailed to South America. There, he traveled to Venezuela, up the Orinoco River, then crossed the Crystal (Tumucache) Mountains. The search for gold was in vain, and he turned to painting the Indians of South America as he'd once painted those in the North. His sole companion was Caesar Bolla, a half-black escaped slave from Havana. Between 1853 and 1858, the two men made three extensive trips: up the Amazon to its source, across Argentina, all the way to Tierra del Fuego at the southern tip of the continent; up the west coast of the continent to the Aleutian Islands, crossing the Bering Sea to Siberia; finally, a return trip across the Rockies, descending at last into Mexico. There, at Yucatán, Bolla and Catlin said good-bye to each other after more than five years together. Catlin's next years were spent in Antwerp, Belgium, making reproductions of his own works. At age sixty-two, his hearing so impaired that it was difficult for anyone to converse with him, he lived a frugal and friendless life. In 1870, at age seventy-four, he finally returned to America, after an absence of thirty-one years. His daughters, who had lived in affluent comfort with their mother's relatives, welcomed him warmly. He was honored with an exhibit at the Smithsonian, and at last, in 1871, his paintings were hung in the National Museum, his life's most cherished dream. When he became ill in 1872, Catlin moved to Jersey City to be closer to his daughters, and died there two days before Christmas.

It isn't known why he wasn't immediately buried next to his wife and son in the Gregory family plot in Brooklyn; a year passed before he was laid to rest there on a beautiful wooded knoll. No stone marks the spot, perhaps reflecting family animosity toward the man they believed was responsible for the death of Clara and young George. But George Catlin didn't need a monument. He left one in paint and in prose—not to himself, but to the "the wild people beyond the Mississippi," to whom he'd devoted his life's energies.

John Chapman (Johnny Appleseed)

1774–1845 Orchardist, eccentric. In his youth, became a disciple of the Church of the New Jerusalem; combined his new faith with skills as an orchardist, then devoted a lifetime to planting apple trees throughout Pennsylvania, Ohio, and Indiana, where settlers headed west would eventually make their homes. Was also called "the apple man" or "the seed man," but the nickname "Johnny Appleseed" is the one we remember him by.

Sometimes a figure from history becomes so enshrouded in myth and fable that he or she seems not quite real. Often, there is scant firm documentation about such a person, and what little is known comes down to us in the form of legend or anecdote, as have famous tales about England's King Arthur and Robin Hood. That's somewhat the case with John Chapman, making it natural for us to ask, "Was there really a Johnny Appleseed, or did someone just make him up?"

No doubt the baby boy born on a Monday during apple-picking time, September 26, 1774, seemed real enough to his parents, Nathaniel and Elizabeth Chapman. The new baby, who seemed puny at first, joined a four-year-old sister, also named Elizabeth. One of the infant's Yorkshire ancestors, Edward Chapman, had emigrated to Boston in 1639, and when he died in 1678 was able to leave his wife "ten good fruit-bearing trees." It was by no means a trivial legacy in those early times, and perhaps it foreshadowed John's own interest in orchards.

The baby's mother, twenty-six-year-old Elizabeth Symonds (sometimes spelled Simonds), was the fifth child of James Symonds, one of the earliest settlers in Leominster, Massachusetts. He had built one of the first frame houses in the area, so solid it was still standing 150 years later.

At John's birth, the village of Leominster numbered about nine hundred per-

A contemporary artist's representation of Johnny Appleseed. OHIO HISTORICAL SOCIETY.

sons, and Nathaniel Chapman scratched a living for his family from a small rented farm and by doing carpentry for his neighbors. He also was one of the original Minutemen, who had dedicated themselves to protecting the community from the British. The villagers knew a break with England was just around the corner, and Nathaniel was eager to participate in the coming fight for independence. He'd already served eight months' duty with the Continental Regiment, and he later fought at Bunker Hill.

The winter of 1775 in the colonies was a harsh one, and Elizabeth Chapman struggled with the demands of keeping up a husbandless household. She was a frail young woman and grew even more so during the time Nathaniel served with General Washington in New York in 1776. Finally, on June 3, she set down her thoughts in a letter to her husband. He kept it the rest of his life, then passed it on to his daughter Elizabeth. It read, in part:

"Loving Husband—I am no better than when you left me. . . . My cough is something abated, but I think I grow weaker. . . . I must bid you farewell and if it should be so ordered that I should not see you again, I hope we shall both be as happy as to spend an eternity . . . in the coming world which is my desire and prayer." The cough she referred to was very likely caused by tuberculosis,

a common and almost-always fatal illness in colonial America.

On June 26, 1776, three weeks after writing to her husband, Elizabeth gave birth to her third child, a boy she named after his father. She never recovered from the birth and died a month later; in August, Nathaniel junior also died. Exactly how little Elizabeth and two-year-old John were cared for after their mother's death isn't known; most likely it was Elizabeth's younger sisters, Ruth and Rebekah Symonds, who took charge of the motherless pair.

In 1777, Nathaniel enlisted in the militia for three more years and was made captain of a company of wheelwrights. In July 1780, shortly before his discharge, he married seventeen-year-old Lucy Cooley from the village of Longmeadow, a few miles west of Leominster. Johnny (we'll assume he might have been called by this familiar nickname) was six, and his father's new home was quickly filled with half sisters and half brothers—eventually, there were ten in all. It has been hinted that Nathaniel wasn't the ablest of providers, that he was a man who, as summed up in a saying of the time, had "more stock than fodder."

The small house in Longmeadow, described as "a tiny structure . . . one of the oldest in town," was close to a river on one side and to woods on the other.

Perhaps Johnny learned at a very early age that he could exchange a noisy, crowded household for the solace and calm of the wilderness. Family stories paint a picture of a little boy who soon came to regard the woods as the place where he felt most truly at home, and where he developed an unusual fondness for green growing things as well as for all animals and birds.

Johnny attended an elementary school in Longmeadow, where he learned his numbers and fine cursive handwriting. He was eight when the Revolutionary War ended, the result of which was that Britain ceded all territory south of the Great Lakes and east of the Mississippi River to the colonies. In 1789, when he was fifteen, the Constitution was drawn up, and the new nation began to expand at an even faster pace than before. Johnny's half-siblings were growing too, which must have made the small house in Longmeadow more cramped than ever. It was time for the family's oldest boy—whose continuing fondness for the woods now might have been considered a bit odd—to begin earning his own way in the world.

However, exactly *what* Johnny did or *where* he did it can only be surmised by historians, for no records of the next several years have been left by family, friends, or Johnny himself. Those years can be speculated about, however, and various Chapman family legends give some hints.

One story tells that in 1792, eighteen-year-old Johnny and his half-brother Nathaniel, only eleven, set out for an uncle's house in Olean, a small settlement in western New York. When they arrived and found the place empty, they moved in and lived on their own before traveling on. (The boys musthave felt as if they were on a real holiday!) Pennsylvania had been made safer after General "Mad Anthony" Wayne's defeat of the Indians at the Battle of Fallen Timbers in 1794, and the next hint of Johnny's whereabouts is that by the mid-1790s he had apprenticed himself to an orchardist in the Susquehanna region.

Apples were an important staple in the diet of colonial Americans. They were relatively easy to grow, could be stored for long periods, and were used in a variety of ways—eaten fresh, preserved by drying, cooked into apple butter, or made into vinegar and cider. Vinegar was essential for making pickles and other preserves, while apple cider was always a pleasure to drink—and many pioneer men were especially fond of it after it "hardened," or fermented into alcohol.

As a child, Johnny had been baptized; like most young folk of his day he probably attended Sunday school regularly and found no reason to question his faith. Then, in the 1790s, a new religious movement gained converts among the American colonists, and Johnny was swept up by it too. At age twenty-three, he became a dedicated Swedenborgian disciple, or a follower of the teachings of Emanuel Swedenborg, a Swedish scientist and inventor. Swedenborg believed he'd been given a divine appointment to interpret the Scripture in a new way, and founded the Church of the New Jerusalem, often referred to by its followers simply as "the New Church."

The core of the new creed was a mystical sort of love of God for man, of man for God, and of both for all creation. It was a warmer, more emotional brand of religion than the cold, stern Calvinist faith John Chapman had been raised in. Swedenborg had written, "Man is so created as to be in the spiritual world and in the natural world at the same time"; such words must have had great appeal to someone who already was very much in tune with the woods and its creatures. Was Johnny already a practicing orchardist at the time of his conversion? Probably; in any case, his new, benevolent vision of man's duty on earth became wedded to a love of his fellow man that expressed itself in what came to be a lifelong apple-planting mission.

By 1795, America's westward expansion was proceeding quickly, and the Pennsylvania legislature had established three new towns: Erie (old Fort Le Boeuf), Franklin (old Fort Venango), and Warren, near the Allegheny River. The Holland Land Company began selling real estate in the area, and in the winter of 1797 John Chapman's name appeared in the trading-post records of Edward Hale at Franklin, a village of only ten families. One historian surmised that Johnny probably had "selected a spot for his nursery—for [that] seemed to be his primary object . . . on the big Brokenstraw."

The "big Brokenstraw" was a creek that flowed into the Allegheny River six miles below the village of Warren. Indians called this region Cushanadauga, because the rich bottomland was covered in summer with tall grass that in autumn fell over of its own weight, causing it to look like broken straw. Thus began what became one of Chapman's orcharding methods: He picked a two- or three-acre site near a river, where the land was rich and the soil moist enough to support the trees once they'd been planted. Next, he enclosed the tree nursery with rude fences made of brush, coming back only periodically to tend to it. However, none of this property actually belonged to him; rather, he did what others of the time often did—he "squatted" on the land. Sometime during the 1790s, Johnny also may have traveled as far north as the edge of Lake Erie.

Where did Chapman obtain apple seeds? In those days, it was a fairly common practice to collect them from someone who ran a cider press, which in the older settlements usually was a commercial cider-making operation. Such seeds could be obtained for next to nothing, then were washed, dried, and sorted by the purchaser. They could be planted directly into the soil and nursed as seedlings or could be carried long distances in leather saddlebags, as Chapman often did.

Between 1797 and 1804, Chapman apparently stayed in the Franklin region, helping "others more than he helped himself," noted one historian. He "took up land several times, but would soon find himself without any, by reason of some other person 'jumping' his claim." Some folk suggested that Johnny was a lazy drifter, but the truth was the land laws of that era often didn't favor small owners. As with many other notable early-day frontiersmen—Daniel Boone being the most famous example—Johnny might have found himself clearing land, getting it ready for planting, then being ousted from it by a savvier claim-seeker. As a result, it seemed that he often worked for nothing. Perhaps that didn't concern him, for one anecdote quoted him as saying, "The bees work without wages. Why should I not do the same?"

In a federal census report in Pennsylvania in April 1801, Johnny was listed as a "head of family"; it didn't mean he had married—he never did—but it was the way census takers of the time identified young men more than eighteen years of age who were living on their own. Relatively few men on the very edge of the raw frontier were married because only the hardiest women were willing to tolerate such a life; most women came only after the settlements became more stable. Yet it was the sort of life John Chapman found comfortable and from which he never really departed. Indians still populated the region, Senecas in particular, and Chapman came to know them well and to speak the language of several other tribes.

John's older sister Elizabeth had married Nathaniel Rudd in December 1799, and a promissory note signed by the future Johnny Appleseed at Franklin on February 4, 1804, gives a hint that his career had begun in earnest: ". . . for value received I promise to pay Nathaniel Chapman . . . the sum of one hundred dollars in land or apple trees with interest till paid as witness my hand." Was the Nathaniel mentioned his sister's new husband, his father back in Longmeadow, or his half-brother Nathaniel? No one now can be sure.

R. L. Curtis recalled that he knew

Chapman quite well at this turn-of-the-century time, when he himself was only a child of eight or nine. "He was a singular character," Curtis remembered. "He was very fond of children and would talk to me a great deal, telling me of the hardships that he had endured." Although Chapman never had children of his own, it delighted him to bring colorful ribbons to settlers' little daughters or to share tall tales with their young sons. And always—at great length and in a clear, sharp voice—Chapman shared the beliefs of the New Church.

During these early days Johnny also earned a little money chopping wood for neighbors, and fanciful yarns grew up around his wood-chopping feats—such as that he could do as much in one day as most men could do in two. Other stories were soon passed around—how he'd walked several miles barefoot on the surface of an icy river to demonstrate his unusual endurance. Tales also were told about how he slept in hollow logs when no other shelter was available, lining them with leaves for extra warmth and comfort.

Early in his career Johnny also adopted a peculiar way of dressing—peculiar even for the frontier. He believed clothing should be worn for utility, not adornment, and was oblivious of any sort of fashion awareness. If someone wanted to buy a tree from him but had no money, Johnny gladly accepted old worn-out clothing as payment. He never wore stockings, and his shoes were other men's castoffs; if by chance he could find only one shoe or boot, he left the other foot bare. One early pioneer told of seeing Chapman wear a tin pot as a head covering, one that he later used for cooking a frugal meal of cornmeal mush or stew. None of this was the result of foolishness; rather, it reflected Johnny's belief that personal deprivation in this life would guarantee him a better one in heaven.

Physically, Chapman was a small, slender fellow, said to stand about five feet nine, weighing only 125 pounds. His hair was fine and dark, worn shoulder-length and tucked behind his ears; his eyes were deep-set (some anecdotes say those eyes were blue, some say brown). His skin was weathered to a nutlike color due to living constantly out-of-doors. His appearance and behavior were so odd that it was once remarked that "our hero may be considered insane by those who never knew him."

Of course, Chapman was by no means the first man to introduce apples to the country he traveled through. Before Johnny was born, the French had carried the fruit into the Great Lakes region and then into the Mississippi Valley. Many other frontiersmen had established small orchards: Ebenezer Zane on the Pennsylvania side of the Ohio River, Jacob Nessley on the Virginia side of it, and Rufus Putnam at Marietta, Ohio. What made Johnny unique was that he was able to move so easily with the westward migration because he had no wife, no children, nor any permanent dwelling to tie him down.

Experienced orchardists knew, even in those long-ago times, that starting apple trees from seeds wouldn't produce an ideal apple. Much was already known about the importance of grafting buds or limbs onto seedlings to produce larger, tastier fruit. But that would have been too expensive and time-consuming. Therefore, apple trees often were started from seeds, and nursed along to seedlings, which then could be transported easily. Later, when a seedling had become a thriving tree, the pioneer who'd purchased it could "topwork" the tree by grafting onto it buds taken from better stock.

The lands through which Johnny traveled were not yet heavily settled, and he often crossed paths with wolves, bears, snakes, and wild pigs; yet there are no legends that he was ever injured. Nor was he ever harmed by Indians, who came to regard him as a medicine man and to respect his peace-loving nature. Johnny had developed a keen interest in herbal medicine and used pennyroyal, catnip, horehound, dandelion, winter-green, mullein, and rattleroot to treat his own or others' ailments. He often used dog fennel, a rather foul-smelling plant reputed to be good for treatment of ague—now we call it malaria—and he carried its seeds wherever he went. Unfortunately, dog fennel was a pest weed and soon infested the entire region, much to settlers' disgust.

By the early 1800s, Johnny had penetrated the Licking Valley of Ohio. A historian in 1862 interviewed persons who could still remember the apple man and said that his "name is found recorded among those voting at the first election ever held in this district." Among the few residents of the area were a half-wild fellow named Andy Craig, and John Stilley, his wife, and their twelve children. It has been assumed that Johnny established his first Ohio tree nursery along the west bank of a creek near Craig's place sometime between 1801 and 1804, because he had seedlings ready for sale by 1806.

The year 1804 was a special one in Johnny's life not only because he was living part of the time in Ohio, but because his family was too. His father, stepmother, and many siblings had moved to a settlement called Duck Creek, fifteen miles from Marietta, Ohio. Nathaniel died there in 1807, and Lucy was still there when the census of 1810 was taken. She died about 1830.

In September 1809, thirty-five-year-old John Chapman paid fifty dollars for two town lots in the village of Mount Vernon, Ohio, named after President Washington's home in Virginia. It was his first real estate purchase; however, owning land didn't mean he actually settled down on it. He was on the move constantly, tending to his many nurseries, even traveling back to Pennsylvania to take care of the ones he'd established there.

Johnny was living near Mansfield, Ohio, when the War of 1812 broke out. When the British incited the Indians against the colonists, Johnny volunteered to hurry through the night to Mount Vernon to get help from the captain of the local militia. Along the way, he took time to warn many settlers of the coming danger.

Soon, Johnny's property interests began to take on long-range significance, and on May 31, 1814, he and a Mrs. Jane Cunningham signed a ninety-nine-year lease in Ohio for a quarter section of land—160 acres—a few miles from the village of Mansfield. There are no documents or letters that reveal what sort of personal relationship these two may have had, but they apparently saw eye to eye about business. The lease cost ten dollars, a small sum by modern standards, but substantial in those times. Not long after, Chapman signed another lease in Madison Township; the following winter he purchased more land in Wayne County.

Did John Chapman ever seriously seek a wife? No one knows that he did, yet one anecdote describes his experience with a certain young lady and gives an indication of his romantic expectations. According to a tale told by a family named Rice, John once befriended the young daughter of another family and took pains to watch over her as she grew up. However, when she was fifteen he happened to call at the family's cabin and discovered her holding hands with a young fellow. A witness reported, "He thought the girl was basely ungrateful. After that time she was no protegee of his."

However, at midlife Chapman did indeed acquire a family—that of his half-sister, Persis, nineteen years younger than he, who was only twelve when Nathaniel and Lucy moved their large brood to Ohio. Persis later married William Broom, and sometimes Johnny lived with them, often giving William employment in his orchards as payment for room and board. He was devoted to Persis's children, and when Chapman moved to Indiana, the Brooms followed him there.

One of the few records that document Chapman's association with the New Church was a letter written from

Manchester, England, by a society that published the writings of Emanuel Swedenborg. Dated January 14, 1817, it gives one of the earliest written accounts of what Chapman was doing in the wilderness. "He procures what books he can [from] the New Church; travels into the remote settlements, and lends them wherever he can find readers, and sometimes divides a book into two or three parts for more extensive distribution and usefulness. This man for years past has been in the employment of . . . sowing apple seeds."

Wiliam Schlatter, a wealthy Philadelphian and also a Swedenborgian, indicated in a letter written in November 1822 to the Reverend N. Halley of Virginia that it was he who had supplied Chapman with the books that were being distributed. He referred to Chapman's work in Ohio, noting, "They call him John Appleseed out there. . . . I corresponded with [him] for seven years." This is the first written reference to the name by which everyone now remembers him.

Johnny's life might have seemed that of a vagabond, but he kept records of his business much like any other tradesman. His usual price for an apple tree was a "fip-penny-bit" (did that mean one-fifth of a penny?). Often, he had more money than he wished to be bothered with and used the surplus to provide care for old horses. All his life, his regard for the world included animals as well as humans.

Johnny established a one-acre apple plantation in Coshocton County, Ohio, the year his father died. A valuable document now owned by the Boy Scouts of Mansfield, Ohio, is proof that it was still operating in 1812: "October 1812, for value received I promise to pay or cause to be paid to Benjamin Burrell one hundred and fifty trees at my nursery near John Butlers in the month of March such as they are when called for. John Chapman."

Chapman's nursery stock must have been hardy, for a tree planted by K. B. Cummings was still standing in 1881. It was twelve feet in circumference, and although it bore no fruit, it still set out blossoms each spring. Another Chapman tree that was cut down showed seventy rings, indicating its advanced age.

Through the years, Chapman often stopped for rest and a meal at the cabin of a Mr. and Mrs. Worth along the St. Joseph River a few miles from Fort Wayne, Indiana, and he went there for a final time in March 1845. He'd gotten word that some cattle had broken through the brush fence surrounding one of his nurseries, and he hurried there to repair it. The Worths noted that he was exhausted and seemed to be suffering from "the winter plague," which today we would call pneumonia.

Johnny ate a meal with the family (one account says that it was a simple one of bread and milk); then, as usual, he slept on the floor by the hearth (he always refused a bed). His condition had worsened by morning, and although a doctor was called, it was too late. The precise date of Chapman's death is uncertain but it is generally accepted as occurring on March 18; he was seventy years old.

A notice in the *Fort Wayne Sentinel* observed that "the deceased was well known throught this region. . . . He submitted to every privation with cheerfulness and content. . . . His death was quite sudden. We saw him in our streets only a day or two previous."

Samuel Fletter, who built Chapman's coffin, described the unusual garments the deceased man was wearing at the time of his death: "a coarse coffee-sack, with a hole cut in the centre though which he passed his head," served as Chapman's shirt. "He had on the waists of four pairs of pants . . . ripped up at the sides . . . buttoned around him, lapping like shingles so as to cover the whole lower part of his body, and over all these were drawn a pair of what once were pantaloons."

Richard Worth, son of the family with whom Chapman had so often stayed, reported that "we buried him respectably in the Archer family burial plot." The

Harper's Monthly magazine published this drawing of Johnny Appleseed in the midst of a discussion with a preacher. OHIO HISTORICAL SOCIETY.

plot was located on an elevated patch of ground overlooking the St. Joseph River. The precise site probably wasn't marked, but in 1916, the Indiana Horticultural Society selected a spot to memorialize Chapman at the top of the knoll. In 1935, an imposing granite boulder bearing the inscription "He Lived for Others" was set in place.

John Chapman was regarded by some as a wastrel; a history of Venango

County, Pennsylvania, published in 1890, forty-five years after his death, curtly dismissed Johnny's activities. "John Chapman's . . . sojourn [here], owing to his thriftless disposition, was only temporary. . . . As soon as the settlements began to increase he . . . drifted further westward."

The writer could not have realized that Johnny's habit of drifting amounted to much more than mere restlessness. It was part of a plan that had taken shape in his head when he was a very young man, a vision to which he remained faithful until the day of his death fifty years later. He left a legacy of goodness and godliness that could serve as a model for any of us, and the names of those early apples have the resonance of a sturdy colonial hymn: Early Chandler, Roxbury Russet, Seek-No-Further.

Long before Chapman died, at the Fifth General Convention of the New Churchmen in Philadelphia in June 1822, a committee reported on the work being done by one of the church's most active disciples. It concluded: "Having no family, and inured to hardships of every kind, his operations are unceasing. . . . As we are told in holy writ, [he] that 'turn many to righteousness shall shine as the stars forever.'" It is a pleasing way to remember John Chapman, now known around the world as Johnny Appleseed.

William Clark

1770–1838 Explorer, mapmaker, Indian official. The Clarks believed that whichever of their children inherited red hair would become a person of great accomplishment. The man known to the Indians as "the Redheaded Chief" lived up to his family's myth and became a legend as the result of the seven-thousand-mile journey he made with Meriwether Lewis to explore the West. Ironically, Clark's life *after* the expedition tells just as much about the kind of man he was.

More than one biographer has noted that William Clark is so well known for his association with Meriwether Lewis that the men's names are thought of as a single one spelled "Lewisandclark"— with Clark always taking second place in people's minds.

Many men would have resented standing in the long shadow cast by the man whom President Thomas Jefferson picked to lead what he called the "Corps of Discovery," a fact-finding mission to explore the land west of the Mississippi River. The reason it didn't bother Clark might be due to the fact that, having had a very famous older brother, he'd gotten quite used to standing in someone's shadow. General George Rogers Clark had been the conqueror of the Old North-west Territory (Kentucky, Ohio, Illinois) during the War of Independence, was a confidant of General Washington, and became a national hero.

George Rogers was already eighteen years old when his little brother William was born in Caroline County, Virginia, to John Clark and the former Ann Rogers on August 1, 1770. "Billy" (later called Will by the family) was his parents' ninth child, and like the man with whom his name would later be so closely linked, he also was descended from ancestors who'd come from the British Isles. (His were Scotch; Meriwether Lewis's were Welsh and English.) The first Clarks reached Jamestown in the late 1600s and are identified only as "Clark & wife" in surviving records. Although Lewis also was born in Virginia four years after

Captain William Clark of the Lewis and Clark expedition. CULVER PICTURES, INC.

Clark, and although both families were friends of Jefferson's, the paths of the two men never crossed while they were growing up.

All six of the Clark sons (there also were four daughters) became soldiers; the oldest five took part in the Revolutionary War. All survived except the oldest, John, who died while he was a prisoner of the British. William was only six when the war started, and his own military service would come during the Indian wars along the new nation's western borders, in the territories of Kentucky and Ohio.

While his five oldest sons fought in the War of Independence, father John made his own contribution by giving George Rogers large sums to help outfit his army unit, money he assumed the state of Virginia would reimburse when the war was over. After the state declined to do so, the family decided to mend their fortunes by heading for the Kentucky frontier in 1784, when William was fourteen. The trip was a long one, and they didn't arrive until the following year.

William grew up along Bear Grass Creek, not far from Louisville, in a new home called Mulberry Hill. (His future friend Lewis's boyhood home in Virginia was called Locust Hill.) There were no schools on the frontier at that time, but William had his older brothers' help, es-

pecially that of George Rogers, who had been educated in private schools where he'd studied Latin, Greek, history, and science. The one thing the boy didn't learn was grammar, and he went through life fracturing the English language in a lively fashion.

After the British were vanquished in the Revolution, the U.S. Congress decided the new nation no longer needed a large standing army, and by 1784 military forces had declined to a mere seven hundred troops. It was true the British had lost the war, but they remained in the New World as agitators, while the Spanish and French also had land claims they intended to pursue. Each of the three European powers encouraged the Indians to hold back the rising tide of American settlers, and they supplied arms and advice. It soon became clear that some sort of an army was needed to protect families who were moving west, and in 1788 settlers took matters into their own hands by organizing groups of militia to protect themselves.

In 1789, at age nineteen, William joined the local militia. When Congress decided to increase the size of the regular army, he enlisted in 1791 and became a lieutenant a few months later. In September 1792 he was assigned to General "Mad Anthony" Wayne's western command, and for the next four years he lived as a field officer in the

Indiana-Ohio territory. Such service taught him how to survive in the wilderness, gave him a chance to learn practical skills such as mapmaking, and provided him with a keen knowledge of Indian character and respect for the Indian's view of the encroachment by whites on ancestral lands.

While serving under General Wayne, Clark and his troops were escorting a supply pack train of seven hundred horses and seventy men through the wilderness when they were set upon by Indians. Even though they were badly outnumbered, Clark was able to drive the attackers off, and he won the general's commendation. In August 1794, Clark served with Wayne in the Battle of Fallen Timbers, which destroyed the Indians' power and put an end to the border wars for several years to come.

General Wayne was impressed by the abilities of his tall, red-haired officer and selected him for special intelligence-gathering missions down the Ohio River. Clark traveled to Indian villages near Spanish outposts in the Cumberland and Tennessee Valleys and went down the Mississippi as far as New Madrid, in present-day Missouri, where the Spanish officials who met him described him as an "enterprising youth of extraordinary activity."

In 1795, General Wayne transferred a twenty-one-year-old fellow into Clark's company of Chosen Rifle sharpshooters. The chap had just been acquitted of court-martial charges brought by his superior officer, a Lieutenant Eliott, who accused him of breaking into his quarters, insulting him, and challenging him to a duel. Clark discovered the newcomer was only four years younger than he was, had also been born in Virginia, and that his family were friends of Thomas Jefferson's. The fellow's name was Meriwether Lewis. In the six months they spent together, the two men became good friends, in spite of the charges that had been leveled against Lewis. They parted in 1796 and apparently had no contact with each other during the next several years.

Clark enjoyed the rigors of military life, but because of persistent bouts of ill health—very likely he suffered from recurrences of malaria, which was a common ailment on the frontier—he resigned his lieutenant's commission on July 1, 1796, and returned to Mulberry Hill. In addition to recovering his health, there was plenty for William to do at home. George Rogers had remained a bachelor, and although he'd once been a famous war hero, Congress had declined to reward him with any financial compensation. He'd fallen into debt, had grown depressed, and had let his business affairs become a mess, all of which was made worse by the fact that he drank more whiskey than was good for him.

Clark spent months dealing with creditors as he tried to put his brother's affairs in order. Then in 1799, when John Clark died, Mulberry Hill was left to him, rather than to any of the older sons, giving William even greater responsibilities. The estate was sizable: 7,040 acres of Kentucky land, a grain mill, a distillery, and twenty-four slaves. It was about this time that Clark met a young lady named Julia Hancock. (He misheard her name, though, and believed it was Judith.) She was a cousin, and he began to think of marriage. But that would have to wait because he was about to receive an invitation to make history.

Seven years after he and Lewis parted, Clark received a letter from his former acquaintance. It was dated June 19, 1803, but had taken a month to arrive at Mulberry Hill. It contained an intriguing suggestion. Lewis introduced it by first noting that because of the "friendship and confidence which has subsisted between us, I feel no hesitation in making to you the following communication." Clark read further and must have taken a deep breath as he discovered what Lewis intended to do.

"My plan is to descend the Ohio in a keeled boat thence up the Mississippi to the mouth of the Missourie, and up that river as far as it's [sic] navigation is practicable . . . [and then] reach the Western Ocean." Lewis went on to ask if they could meet on August 10 to discuss the trip in greater detail, and he described the type of men he hoped could be recruited for such an undertaking: "good hunters, stout, healthy, unmarried men, accustomed to the woods, and capable of bearing bodily fatigue." If Clark knew of any such men in his neighborhood, Lewis advised him to keep them in mind. Lewis added that President Jefferson "has authorized me to grant you a captain's commission. . . . Your situation . . . will, in all respects, be precisely such as my own." In other words, they would be co-commanders of the expedition. The promise of a captaincy to a man who'd previously been a lieutenant must have been a powerful enticement.

Lewis concluded by offering Clark a way to gracefully refuse the offer; if the press of family or business prevented him from accepting the invitation, Lewis requested that his old army acquaintance simply accompany him "as a friend part of the way up the Missouri. I should be happy in your company."

After discussing the offer with George Rogers, Clark penned an answer the following day. Lewis received it ten days later, on July 29, 1803, and its directness gives the reader a clue as to

why Lewis thought so highly of his former commander, though perhaps not of
his spelling. Clark conceded that the
project was "an amence [immense] undertaking fraited [freighted] with numerous difficulties," but "my freind I
can assure you that no man lives with
whome I would prefur to undertake &
share . . . Such a trip than yourself."

Lewis had chosen well. In addition to
both men being six feet tall and physically fit, he and Clark had much in common: each was young, intelligent, and
enjoyed adventure; each was a capable
woodsman; each had military experience; each knew how to command men.
Yet their differences were equally important and would serve the best interests of the expedition: Lewis could be a
hot-tempered, broody man, while Clark
was outgoing, friendly, and rarely given
to wrath. Lewis was better educated and
more comfortable with abstract ideas,
while Clark was a down-to-earth, practical man of action. Throughout their long
journey together, under circumstances
that would have tried the patience of
saints, there is no record of any serious
discord between them.

In preparation for the trip, which was
expected to last about two years, Clark
deeded Mulberry Hill to his oldest
brother, Jonathan, and built a small log
house for George Rogers in Clarksville,
which was on the north bank of the

Ohio River, while Louisville was on the
south bank. Clark decided to take with
him a servant, York, a black man who
had served the Clark family since his
birth and whose own father, Old York,
had also served the family. He was
about the same age as William and was a
man of exceptional size and strength;
later, he would make a deep impression
on the Indians, who had never before
seen a black man. Unlike the two captains, York was married and left behind
his wife, Rose.

After Lewis arrived at Clarksville on
October 15, 1803, the men spent two
weeks getting ready to set out for Fort
Massac, on the north bank of the Ohio
about thirty-five miles from its junction
with the Mississippi. The group consisted of handpicked hunters, woods-
men, and frontiersmen. Some had
special skills such as blacksmithing;
others knew how to communicate with
Indians in sign language; some were experienced boatmen, carpenters, or gun-
smiths. Clark made it clear that Lewis
could veto any of the selections of the
men he'd made, and in return Lewis offered Clark the same privilege. From the
beginning, the two men cooperated fully
with each other.

A newspaper in Louisville declared
that the captains planned to make up a
party of about sixty men, although
Jefferson's original suggestion had been

only a dozen. A small party was deemed to be safer because it would seem much less alarming to the Indians—or, for that matter, to the British, French, or Spanish—who would naturally view the American venture into the West as the first step in a process of territorial expansion. (Indeed it was, but Jefferson took great pains to downplay that aspect of the trip.) The group that left Clarksville on October 26, 1803, also included Seaman, a large black Newfoundland dog that Lewis had purchased for twenty dollars. (Some biographers have recorded the dog's name as Scannon, but experts attribute that to a mistaken deciphering of Lewis's handwriting.)

Although Lewis had hoped to get much farther upriver before winter set in and the rivers froze, when the fledgling expedition reached the Wood River in December, it was plain a winter camp would have to be made. Tents were pitched; then permanent cabins were built at the juncture of the Missouri and Mississippi Rivers. It was at Camp Wood in April 1804 that a devastating piece of news arrived that could easily have sabotaged the relationship of lesser men than William Clark and Meriwether Lewis.

Clark's commission did indeed arrive from Washington, but to the dismay of both men it was one for a second lieu-tenant, not a captain! The letter from the secretary of war, Henry Dearborn, stated that the "organization of the Corps of Engineers is such as would render the appointment of Mr. Clark a Captain in that Corps improper." The lower rank had been approved and signed by both Jefferson and the Congress; there was nothing to be done.

No one knows why Jefferson reneged on his promise. Did he fear it would be natural on such a long journey that the best of men would be bound to disagree, and that if Lewis had a superior rank it would automatically prevent a paralysis of leadership? In any case, Lewis was as embittered as Clark, but he had committed himself to the principle of co-commanders and told Clark that "it will be best to let none of our party or any other persons know any thing about the [commission]." In Washington, Clark may have been viewed as a second-in-command; in the West, as Lewis had promised, they shared the leadership of the expedition equally, and none of their men was ever the wiser.

At Camp Wood, Lewis and Clark made their final selection of men to accompany them up the Missouri. When the final cut was made the group numbered twenty-three, including York. The youngest, George Shannon, was eighteen; the oldest, John Shields, was thirty-eight. Among the group were two brothers, Reuben and Joseph Field, and Charles Floyd, whose father had served with George Rogers Clark in the Revolution. John Colter, a twenty-eight-year-old Virginian, had been one of the first enlistees and would later become famous as the first white man to pass through what is now Yellowstone National Park. Six other men were hired to go only as far as the next winter camp; they would return in the spring with all of the scientific data and artifacts that had been collected to that point.

Lewis spent much of the winter buying supplies, and Clark spent his time drilling the members of the crew as he had once drilled his soldiers. When the men had too much time on their hands they quarreled with each other, stole meat from the local farmers, and drank too much. By spring, however, they had been turned into professionals, and discipline problems were less common.

On May 14, 1804, Clark led the expedition members and three boats away from Camp Wood and upstream to St. Charles, a village twenty miles up the Missouri River; Lewis, still off buying supplies, would join them later. The group stayed five days at St. Charles, gathering more food, and the local townsfolk gave a party in their honor. On May 20, Lewis rode into camp with additional last-minute supplies, and the

following day the boats were loaded, were shoved off from shore, and their bows turned west. Clark's entry in his journal was as practical as he was: "May 21st 1804 Monday—Set out at half passed three oClock under three Cheers from the gentlemen on the bank." The greatest exploration in American history had begun.

The job of getting upriver was immensely hard. Sometimes the boats were rowed; if the wind came from astern, sails could be raised; mostly, though, the vessels were pushed upstream with iron-tipped poles by teams of men standing on deck. In shallow or rough spots, the boats had to be dragged along by men (sometimes with horses) who pulled with ropes from the shore. Not everyone had water-related chores; the hunters spent most of their time moving ahead along the riverbanks looking for game. When they made a kill, the animal was dressed out, then hung from a tree limb for the boatmen to pick up.

Lewis spent most of his time on shore not merely because he enjoyed getting off by himself, but because he wished to catalog and collect as many new forms of plant and animal life as possible. Clark, who was an experienced boatman from his days serving General Wayne, took charge of the vessels and also took responsibility for mapping the

Charles M. Russell's painting of York with Indians and members of the expedition. MONTANA HISTORICAL SOCIETY. GIFT OF THE ARTIST.

course of the Missouri, about which not much was known at that time.

Near present-day Kansas City, the Missouri made a great arc, and whereas at the outset the expedition had been headed into the sun, now it faced almost due north; it would not turn west again until it reached Dakota Territory. On the Fourth of July, 1804, the captains gave each man an extra measure of whiskey to celebrate the nation's birthday, and by July 21, after two months of travel, the expedition reached the mouth of the Platte River. Clark estimated they had traveled six hundred miles—and to everyone's amazement, no Indians had yet been sighted.

Now the men began to see a country that only a few traders and trappers knew much about. A strange new animal was killed by one of the soldiers; it was a badger, which none of the men had ever seen before, and was the first scientific discovery of the expedition. On August 1, Clark celebrated his thirty-fourth birthday and noted in his journal that he ordered (from York, who acted as a cook for him and Lewis) "a Saddle of fat Vennison . . . [and] a Desert of Cheries, Plumbs." He noted further that the countryside was a wonderful place "for a Botents [botanist] and a natirless [naturalist]"—which gives a reader not only a sense of the moment but another example of Clark's creative spelling.

Toward the end of August, Sergeant Charles Floyd fell ill. In spite of attempts by Lewis to save his life, the young man died, becoming the only person to perish on the arduous two-year trip. It is now believed he died of a ruptured appendix, which was nearly always fatal in those times; a stream near where he was buried was named Floyd's River on Clark's map.

When the expedition stopped at a village of Arikara Indians in early October 1804, the captains invited the chiefs to a drink of whiskey, as was a customary gesture, then were taken aback when the offer was indignantly refused. The Indians said they were surprised the captains would offer them such a thing, because it "made them act like fools." York, however, was a sensation among the Arikara, who had never before seen a man with black skin. He let them try to rub the color off, then played with the children, roaring as he chased them around the village, telling them he was a wild beast that Captain Clark had tamed. Finally, Clark ordered him to quit, because he "made himself more turibal [terrible] than I wished him to doe [do]."

By late September, Clark noted in his journal that the weather was getting cold; the skies were streaked with geese heading for warmer climates; the first snow fell on October 24. The following day, the three boats tied up in front of five Mandan villages along the riverbank in what is now western North Dakota. Traders and trappers rarely went farther than this point, and it was judged to be a good place to build a winter camp.

Downstream from the Indian villages, the captains located a spot on the north side of the Missouri, seven miles below the mouth of the Knife River, which was well supplied with wood for building cabins. Trees were felled immediately because the weather grew steadily colder; sometimes it snowed the whole day, but soon a camp consisting of eight small cabins and two storage rooms, with stockade walls enclosing the compound in a triangular shape, was ready to be occupied. The captains named it Fort Mandan, and soon Indians from the nearby tribes came to visit, as did several French Canadian trappers and traders.

On November 4, Clark recorded that

"a french man by Name Chabonah . . . visit[ed] us." Toussaint Charbonneau brought along his two young Indian wives, Sacagawea and Otter Woman; he had lived among the Indians for several years and knew some of the local languages. Charbonneau informed Clark that his wives were from the Shoshone (also called the Snake) tribe, who lived near the mountains. Lewis and Clark knew they would be needing horses when they got close to the Rockies and hired Charbonneau as an interpreter—but since it was his wives who spoke Shoshone, they stipulated that the younger girl accompany him on the trip. No doubt they picked her because Otter Woman had a small child. Apparently neither captain noticed that Sacagawea was six months pregnant, because it wasn't mentioned in their journals.

In the deep of winter, temperatures on the plains dropped well below zero, yet on January 10, 1805, Clark noted in his journal that Indians could spend a night out on the prairie without a fire, with merely a buffalo robe to sleep beneath, and survive handily. They could "beare more Cold than I thought it possible for a man to indure," he wrote.

In spite of the cold, Clark realized that the members of the expedition must be kept busy, and he continued to hold regular drills, kept sentries posted, and conducted a daily weapons inspec-tion. He knew that an idle soldier was a bored soldier, which in turn inspired bad behavior, just as it had back at Camp Wood. During the holidays, the explorers and Indians attended each other's parties, giving everyone a break in the monotony, and once again York was the man of the hour.

Lewis spent considerable time ministering to the Indians' medical needs; one time he amputated the toes of a boy who was suffering from frostbite and who might otherwise have died of gangrene. In February, his most unusual doctoring experience was to act as a midwife for Charbonneau's seventeen-year-old wife, who was having a difficult labor. At the suggestion of another French Canadian trader, René Jussome (also spelled Jessaume), Lewis mixed pieces of a rattlesnake's tail with water and gave it to the young woman, who delivered a healthy son ten minutes later. The baby was named Jean Baptiste by his father, but his mother always called him Pomp, which meant "leader" or "firstborn" in Shoshone. Lewis may have delivered her child, but it was Clark with whom the young woman formed a deep friendship. He called her "Janey" and often referred to her son fondly as "my little Pomp."

By the end of March 1805, ice began to melt in the Missouri; snow gave way to rain; ducks and geese returned from the south. On April 7, the boats—including six new canoes that had been made from cottonwood trees during the winter—were put in the water, and the expedition (which now included a young Indian mother and her two-month-old baby) headed upstream again. Two days later, the six men who had been hired to go only as far as the Mandan village packed their boats and headed back to St. Louis. On board were the samples and specimens that had been collected thus far: plants, minerals, insects, mice, the skeletons of two pronghorn antelope, even some live creatures—four magpies, a prairie dog, and a grouse. Only one of the magpies and the prairie dog made it to Washington alive. Clark's map of the country west of the Mississippi also was sent, which one historian called "a masterpiece of the cartographer's art."

In its first four days, the expedition covered more than ninety miles, reaching the mouth of the Little Missouri River, which meant that now they headed straight into the western sun again. When they passed a stream entering the Missouri from the south, Clark named it after the girl he hoped to marry when the journey was over, Julia Hancock—but since he'd misheard her name, he called it the Judith River, by which it is still known today.

On June 3, 1805, they passed the junction of two large rivers. Jefferson's order had been to follow the Missouri to its source, and the expedition leaders were bound by honor to do exactly that. But which was the true Missouri that would lead them to the Rockies and to the Shoshones? Was it the northwest fork of brown, muddy water that looked very much like the river they'd been traveling on? (All of the recruits believed it was.) Or was it the clear stream that came from the southwest? Clark took some of the men and explored thirteen miles of the clear river for almost two days; Lewis took the rest of the men and did the same with the muddy river. It was true that the clear water didn't seem "right," inasmuch as the Missouri was usually brown and muddy, but they agreed its clearness indicated it came straight out of the mountains, that the pebbles covering its bottom had been washed downstream aeons before. Lewis named the northwest branch Maria's River in honor of his cousin, whose "celestial virtues and amiable qualifications" he admired. The apostrophe has been removed, and now the river is called simply the Marias.

During Lewis's exploration of the Marias, Sacagawea and some of the men became ill. The young mother was so sick that the expedition halted for a time while Lewis treated her with quinine, then with water from a nearby sulfur spring. Within a few days she was well enough to travel, and when the expedition came within sight of the Great Falls of the Missouri, the captains knew they'd made the right decision in following the southwestern branch because the Indians had said they would come to such a place if they followed the correct river.

The long portage around the falls was commenced and was nearly completed when a fierce thunderstorm came up. Clark, Charbonneau, and Sacagawea and her baby sought refuge in a deep ravine with walls of rock ledges. No one expected the gully to fill so rapidly with water, but, as Clark later wrote, before they could escape "a roling torrent with irrisistable force driving rocks mud and everything before it" was upon them. Clark was able to get Sacagawea and her baby to safety (Charbonneau seems to have looked out for his own skin), but lost his compass in the process. Happily, it was later rescued from the mud.

When the expedition reached the Three Forks of the Missouri, the captains were once again faced with deciding which fork was the "true" Missouri. Each of the forks was given a name in honor of the men in Washington who had made the journey possible in the first place: the Jefferson River (for the president), the Madison (for the secretary of state), and the Gallatin (for the

secretary of the treasury). Lewis decided the point at which the three rivers merged was actually the headwaters of the Missouri, 2,500 miles from the point at which it emptied into the Mississippi near St. Charles, Missouri.

Toward the end of July 1805, Sacagawea told the captains she recognized the country they were traveling through, that it was the area where she'd been kidnapped many years before as a child of about twelve. It was good news because both Lewis and Clark were anxious to obtain the horses they'd need to get over the mountains before winter settled in. They looked forward to meeting some of Sacagawea's people, and when they finally did it was to discover that the chief of the tribe was none other than Cameahwait, Sacagawea's brother. His meeting with his long-lost sister was an emotional one during which both shed tears, and he promised to provide horses for the rest of the journey.

The expedition headed north along the Bitterroot River, near what is now the Montana-Idaho border. For ten miserable days they climbed up the Lolo Trail. Since it began to snow early high in the mountains, the route was already snow-covered, making travel difficult, and was strewn with fallen timber. Food was in short supply for both men and animals, and finally three of the mares' colts were killed for meat.

At last, on November 7, 1805, Clark wrote in his journal, "Great joy in camp we are in view of the Ocian, this great Pacific Octean which we been so long anxious to See. And the roreing or noise made by the waves brakeing on the rockey Shores . . . may be heard distinctly."

After exploring the countryside for the best place to build a winter camp, Lewis found a place three miles up a stream that flowed into the Columbia; today it's called the Lewis and Clark River. The selection of the site was put to a vote so that each recruit could have his say; surely such democratic practices were one of the reasons the entire journey had been such a success. Construction of cabins was begun in early December, and on Christmas Day, 1805, the members of the expedition were able to celebrate the holiday within the shelter they named Fort Clatsop, in honor of the local Indian tribe that had been so helpful. "Celebrate" might be too grand a word because, as Clark noted, "our Diner concisted of pore Elk, so much Spoiled that we eate it thro' mear necessity. Some Spoiled pounded fish and a fiew roots."

The winter was a long, rainy, dreary one, during which the captains tended to their journals, sent men down the coast to make salt for the return journey, and kept their eyes peeled for any sign of trading ships on the horizon. They had hoped to be able to board such a vessel for an easier trip home, but because of the season, no ships appeared. On March 23, 1806, on a day when there was a rare bit of sunshine, the captains turned the fort over to Comowool, the most helpful of the Clatsop chiefs, and the expedition turned toward the east for the return journey.

It was still early enough in the spring that travel was difficult due to snow and rain, but crossing the Continental Divide wasn't quite as hard, since this time they knew the way. Although food was hard to find, no horses needed to be killed for meat, and by the end of June 1806, they were over the mountains. At this juncture, the two captains decided to split their command, with Lewis taking nine men and reexploring the Marias River area, while Clark took the rest of the men, plus Sacagawea and her child, back to the area of the Three Forks of the Missouri.

Clark and his men fared well on their journey, and on July 25 stopped to examine a two-hundred-foot rock tower that was visible for miles in all directions. The monolith was already decorated with many Indian drawings, so Clark carved "Wm. Clark July 25 1806" into its surface and named the place Pompey's Pillar, in honor of Sacagawea's son. (For some reason, an *e* was added to the boy's name and thus it appears on historical place maps.) Lewis had a far livelier time, encountering a band of hostile Blackfoot Indians, and worse, being shot in the buttocks by one of his own men as they hunted for elk. When the two parties met again on August 12, Clark was alarmed not to see his friend Lewis among the recruits; he was lying in the bottom of a boat, still recovering from his wounds.

The journey downstream was swift, and on August 14, the explorers arrived back at Fort Mandan. John Colter asked to be released from duty, for he intended to stay in the West a good while longer, and three days later everyone else proceeded downriver toward St. Louis. Before parting from Sacagawea, Clark offered to take Pomp home with him, to raise and educate as his own child. He had grown very fond of the boy whom he described as "a butifull promising child," but Sacagawea said she could not let him go until he had been weaned; however, she and Charbonneau promised to bring him to St. Louis in a year's time.

The expedition tied up at Camp Wood, its point of origin, on the morning of September 23, 1806, two years and five months after its beginning. The journey to the Pacific had covered 4,134 miles; the journey home was a bit shorter, or 3,555 miles, for a total of more than 7,500 miles. At the end of the trip, each man was paid his salary—which was double what had been promised—plus 320 acres of land. Lewis was given 1,600 acres, and Clark 1,000; Lewis refused his allotment, saying that Clark must receive an equal amount. Then the captains proceeded together as far as Louisville, Kentucky. Clark stopped there to stay with his family, and Lewis continued on to Washington, where he arrived just before Christmas.

On January 10, 1807, Lewis attended a gala reception in the capital, while Clark, who could have shared such honors if he'd been present, was in Virginia to ask for Julia's hand in marriage. Later that year, Lewis was appointed governor of the Louisiana Territory, with headquarters in St. Louis, while Clark was recommissioned as a brigadier general in the Louisiana militia (making him the fifth of the Clark brothers to become a general), and also was stationed in St. Louis.

Clark married Julia Hancock on January 10, 1808, a year after his homecoming, and they moved into a house in St. Louis that Lewis had selected for them. They had five children, three of whom survived to adulthood; Clark named his firstborn son Meriwether Lewis. The marriage lasted twelve years, until Julia's death in 1820; a year later,

Clark married her cousin, Harriet Radford, and they had two children. When she died ten years later, Clark remained a widower.

In 1813, after the Louisiana Territory was renamed the Missouri Territory, President James Madison appointed Clark its governor. He governed ably for seven years. When James Monroe became the nation's fifth president, Clark was named the superintendent of Indian affairs in the West, a post he held for almost seventeen years. It was an appointment the Indians welcomed, for they knew "the Redheaded Chief" had a deep sympathy for their concerns, that he attempted to treat them as fairly as possible.

Among Clark's early visitors in St. Louis were Sacagawea, her husband, and Pomp. Clark lived up to his promise to raise the boy as his own, and at age nineteen Jean Baptiste was befriended by a German nobleman and taken to Europe to finish his education in grand style.

From the moment the expedition was over, Clark's life proceeded smoothly, but it troubled him that the life of his good friend Lewis became so tormented. Lewis had been a brilliant explorer, but dealing with the intrigues of appointive office was very difficult for him, and although Jefferson desired that the expedition's journals be published as quickly as possible, Lewis seemed unable to get them edited. In July 1809, Lewis was informed that the government would not pay certain expenses he had incurred during the expedition. He sold some of his land grants to clear up the debts, then headed for Washington to explain his side of the matter.

Before Lewis left, Clark spent several days with his friend, helping to put his accounts in order, and agreed to meet him in Washington at a later date to give further moral support. Lewis left St. Louis on September 3, 1809, and the following day Clark wrote a worried letter to his brother Jonathan, noting that "if his mind had been at ease I Should have parted [from him] Cherefuly."

But Lewis's mind was not at ease. Rather, he was deeply troubled and drank heavily, which further disordered his thinking. He was in such a state of emotional exhaustion that when he stopped at Fort Pickering in mid-September, the post commander, Captain Gilbert Russell, detained him, fearing the explorer might take his own life. A week later, when Lewis seemed recovered, Russell allowed him to go on. Later, someone reported that he overheard a still-anxious Lewis mutter to himself that he was sure his old friend Clark would soon be coming, that Clark could put things aright.

Late on the afternoon of October 10,

Lewis arrived at Grinder's Stand, a small, rustic establishment along the Natchez Trace that took in travelers. Mrs. Grinder prepared him a meal but he had no appetite. He paced about restlessly; then she saw him cast his eyes "wishfully towards the west" and comment on what "a sweet evening" it was. Sometime during the early morning hours of October 11, Lewis shot himself in the head; the ball only grazed his skull. He took up another pistol and shot himself in the chest. The ball passed downward and emerged near his backbone. Mrs. Grinder, whose husband was absent on business, heard the commotion but was afraid to venture out into the darkness. At the first light of morning she called her servants and went to Lewis's room, where she found him barely alive. He asked for water, then died shortly after sunrise.

Clark received word of the death as he was preparing to go to Washington himself. "I fear this report has too much truth," he wrote to Jonathan. "O' I fear the weight of his mind has overcome him." Jefferson was notified and observed that Lewis "had from early life been subject" to depressions and a troubled mental constitution.

Clark was distressed that the journals of the expedition had still not been published—journals that would make clear to the world the kind of man Lewis had

A page of William Clark's notebook includes a sketch of a trout. NORTH WIND PICTURE ARCHIVES.

been—and he met Jefferson at Monticello to discuss the matter. Jefferson, whose brainchild the expedition had been in the first place, seemed to be the ideal man to put the journals in order and see to their publication. However, the ex-president had come to a time in life when he wanted nothing more than to tend his gardens. Clark finally persuaded young Nicholas Biddle to take the job.

Biddle was something of a boy wonder: he had been admitted to the University of Pennsylvania at age ten, completed the work needed to graduate three years later, then went on to Princeton, where he graduated at age fifteen. He had married a wealthy woman and now had the time, the intellect, and the inclination to take on the job. The book appeared in 1814; 1,417 copies were printed, and sold for $6.50; for the next ninety years they were the only printed account of Clark's amazing journey with his good friend Lewis.

William Clark died in St. Louis on September 1, 1838, at age sixty-eight, at the home of his son, Meriwether Lewis Clark, and his funeral was said to be the largest the city had ever seen. He had lived almost thirty years after Lewis's death and left the world just as the West was changing faster than either of the great explorers could have imagined: John Jacob Astor's fur traders had gone into every nook and cranny of the wilderness where a beaver could be trapped; Marcus and Narcissa Whitman were the first white couple to cross the Rockies. In 1835, Texas declared its right to independence from Mexico, and Samuel Colt patented a single-barrel rifle; in 1836, Davy Crockett and Jim Bowie died at the Alamo; Samuel Morse exhibited his telegraph in New York in 1837; in the last quarter of the century the Indians Clark had endeavored to treat fairly saw their lands shrink and were driven onto reservations.

The thirteen red morocco-bound journals that Lewis and Clark brought back (seven were Lewis's, six were Clark's) have preserved an adventure and an era that readers still enjoy reading about nearly two hundred years after the expedition ended. It was the habit of the two men to work on their journals at the same time, the better for each to corroborate the other's account of events, and a sense of eager anticipation can still be felt in one of William Clark's final entries:

"Friday 25th Septr. 1806—a fine morning we commenced wrighting."

William Cody (Buffalo Bill)

1846–1917 Guide, hunter, showman. At age eleven carried messages for a freight company; served in the Civil War, hunted buffalo to feed Kansas Pacific Railroad workers, acted as guide for General Custer. His adventures attracted attention of dime novelists; by degrees, he went into show business, where he "out-Barnumed Barnum."

Isaac Cody, of English and Irish descent, was a widower with a five-year-old daughter when he married schoolteacher Mary Ann Leacock (also spelled Laycock) in 1840, and together they had seven children. Their second son, William Frederick, was born on February 16, 1846, in Le Claire, Iowa.

Called Will by his family, the boy was seven when his brother Samuel, older by five years, was killed after Bettie, the family mare, reared back and fell on him as he was bringing cows in from pasture. The loss so distressed Mrs. Cody that a short time later Isaac moved the family west to the Salt Creek valley of Kansas, a few miles west of Fort Leavenworth.

Isaac got a government contract putting up hay for the nearby fort, and in spite of Samuel's fate, Will soon got his first horse, a little sorrel named Prince. Perhaps the boy's interest in showmanship was sparked as he watched an older cousin break the pony and teach it such tricks as how to kneel on command.

The year after the Codys' arrival at Fort Leavenworth, Congress passed the Kansas-Nebraska Act, which allowed citizens of western territories to decide for themselves whether or not to permit slavery. After Isaac Cody joined the Salt Creek Squatters Association, he found himself embroiled in fierce local debates about the issue. Many emigrants to Kansas were Missourians who intended to expand slavery; the Codys came from a state where it wasn't practiced.

Isaac opposed the expansion of slavery and wasn't shy about saying so. At a meeting on September 18, 1854, he got into a bitter argument with Charles Dunn, who stabbed him in the chest, puncturing a lung. The newspaper account of the incident observed that "the settlers on Salt Creek . . . sustain Mr. Dunn in the course he took," labeled Isaac "a noisy abolitionist," and noted—with regret—the injury hadn't been serious enough to cause his death.

Colorful stories were woven around this incident, among them that Will, aged eight, threatened to kill Dunn and actually carried out his mission several years later. The truth seems to be that Dunn only lost his job. Revenge *was* taken upon the Codys, however. Isaac's horses were run off, and three thousand tons of hay he'd put up for Fort Leavenworth mysteriously burned.

In the summer of 1856, when Isaac Cody was on business in Grasshopper Falls, thirty-five miles away, a roving gang of proslavery advocates called Border Ruffians decided to teach the Codys another lesson. They lay in wait for Isaac, hoping to catch him on his return, but a neighbor discovered the plot and urged Mrs. Cody to warn her husband. Will was sick with the flu but insisted on being the one to get word to his father. His sister Julia, three years older, saddled Prince, and the feverish boy took off at a hard gallop. Eight miles from home, he was

spotted by the Border Ruffians, who called out, "That is the damned abolitionist boy; let's go for him!"

Will whipped his pony into a lather, becoming sicker as he tried to outrun his pursuers. Then he remembered that a Mr. Hewette lived not far away; if he could get to Hewette's house, he was sure he'd be safe. He made it—just barely—having nearly run Prince into the ground and gotten so ill he'd vomited all over the poor beast. While Mr. Hewette took care of the pony, Mrs. Hewette bathed the young hero and put him to bed. Will felt better in the morning and continued his journey.

Isaac Cody died in the spring of 1857, due partly to the stab wound he'd received earlier. With both father and older brother gone, Will became the man of the house and went to work for a neighbor, driving an ox team for fifty cents a day. When the job was finished, he told his mother he'd like to work for the firm of Russell, Majors, and Waddell at nearby Fort Leavenworth, which hauled freight in fleets of wagons to army outposts.

Will, age eleven, was hired as an express rider to deliver messages from the firm's headquarters to its outlying offices. The boy was given a mule to ride and a place to sleep, and was ordered to report for work at eight the next morning. On his first day, he was given a message, but when Russell saw the boy in the store not long after, he scolded him for not tending to business. Will explained he'd already delivered the message and was waiting for another assignment.

Of all the figures in western history, William Cody is the one about whom it's most difficult to separate fact from fiction, mostly because of Cody himself. He loved telling yarns and told them with gusto, embroidering them as he went along, but paying little attention to truth or the chronology of events. For example, the story that he'd killed an Indian at age eleven was a fabrication, causing one historian to remark that it was "unfortunate that Cody so clouded the truth," because the reality of his life was compelling enough.

Will worked next as an ox herder on a trip to Utah. Trooper Robert Peck of the U.S. Cavalry recalled in his memoirs that Cody was a "boy of eleven or twelve years. . . . He gave no visible signs then of future fame, and only impressed me as a rather fresh, 'smart-ellick' sort of a kid." But one of the bull-whackers informed Peck that the boy "was already developing wonderful skill at riding wild horses or mules, shooting and throwing a rope."

On April 3, 1860, the Pony Express was inaugurated, backed by Will's earlier employers, Russell, Majors, and Waddell, who invested $100,000 in the project, which included 190 stations, five hundred horses, and eighty riders. The boy reportedly became one of the first couriers; however, several scholars dispute whether Cody actually rode for the Express. Just the same, the advertisements posted to hire such boys fit him to a fare-thee-well:

WANTED

YOUNG SKINNY WIRY FELLOWS not over eighteen. Must be expert riders willing to risk death daily. *Orphans preferred.*

Cody claimed in his autobiography that he kept the job for only two months, and the heyday of the Pony Express itself likewise was short: less than two years after its beginning it was replaced by the wireless telegraph. Nevertheless, there are dozens of fantastic stories about Cody's experiences as a plucky boy rider, most of them creations of press agents, dime novelists, and Cody himself.

The Civil War commenced in April 1861, and for a time Will, age fifteen, made excursions into Missouri with other young men to steal horses from the Confederates. When his mother discovered what he was up to, she insisted that he quit—perhaps in the nick of time, for shortly afterward the leader of the group was ambushed and killed.

For the next two years, Will did odd jobs around Fort Leavenworth, then joined a freight outfit headed for Denver. When he got a letter from his sister Julia reporting that their mother was near death, he hurried home and was at her side when she died on November 22, 1863. Cody later wrote, "I loved her above all other persons," and young though he was, he sought to drown his sorrow in alcohol. (The habit would cause problems the rest of his life.) He claimed he couldn't remember enlisting in the Seventh Kansas Cavalry, only that "after having been under the influence of bad whiskey, I awoke to find myself a soldier." He reported for duty on February 19, 1864, three days after his eighteenth birthday; he was described in official records as having brown hair and eyes and standing five feet ten inches in height.

The most important Civil War battle Will took part in was at Tupelo, Mississippi, on July 14, 1864, when the Seventh Kansas Cavalry defeated the famous Confederate general Nathan Bedford Forrest. According to one fanciful tale, Will also acted as a spy, but records show that he was on regimental duty as a private until his discharge in September 1865, after one year and seven months of active duty.

He may not have been a spy, but during a brief tour as an orderly in St. Louis, Will met the young lady who would soon become his wife. Louisa Maude Frederici was a handsome girl with exceptionally large, dark eyes, and the pair joshed between themselves about being engaged. Many years later, Cody recalled wryly, "Boylike, I thought it very smart to be engaged. . . . I asked if she would marry me . . . [and] jokingly she said 'yes.'" After he returned to Kansas, Louisa pursued him with letters, insisting that he keep his word, and Cody said, "I concluded to do it"—not exactly the comment of an eager bridegroom!

The couple were married in St. Louis on March 6, 1866; Louisa was twenty-three years old; Will was twenty. Following the ceremony they boarded the steamer *Morning Star* and headed upriver to Fort Leavenworth. The marriage was troubled from the outset, inasmuch as the pair had very different expectations of their life together: Louisa didn't care for the rawness of the West, while Will didn't care for anything else. A contemporary of Cody's observed that he was a "primitive natural man . . . who could never be domesticated"; others said, less charitably, that all his life he was "an innocent boy" who loved a fine time.

The couple moved into Cody's mother's old home, where Will tried his hand at hotel keeping. The venture wasn't successful, and within six months he headed west to Salina to seek other work. Louisa returned to her family in St. Louis; it would be the first of many separations.

Scouts and guides were in demand by the U.S. Army, and Cody quickly found a job. One of the first was with young General George Custer, who needed a guide to take him cross-country from Fort Hays to Fort Larned. Shortly before Christmas, 1866, Cody became the father of a baby girl and returned to St. Louis long enough to agree that she be named Arta.

Back in Kansas, Will joined one William Rose in a partnership to take advantage of the coming of the Kansas Pacific Railroad. Cody left his scouting job to help lay out a town to be called Rome, through which it was believed the railroad would pass; a hotel, three or four stores, several saloons, and two hundred houses were built. On paper, Cody considered he was worth $250,000, and he moved his wife and baby daughter to Rome. Alas, the town was abandoned when it was decided Hays City would be a better site. Rather than becoming the prosperous founder of a city, Cody was reduced to grading a roadbed on which the rails were to be laid.

When the road-grading job was finished, Cody went to work as a buffalo hunter for Goddard Brothers, suppliers of meat to the Kansas Pacific. He was contracted to bring in twelve buffalo per day and was paid a whopping five hundred dollars a month because the work was so hazardous. The name "Buffalo Bill" first appeared in print in an article in the *Leavenworth Daily Conservative* on November 26, 1867. It stuck like a burr, and a popular jingle celebrated Cody's growing fame as a hunter:

> Buffalo Bill, Buffalo Bill
> Never missed and never will;
> Always aims and shoots to kill
> And the company pays his buffalo bill.

There were many Bills in the West, and a lot of them hunted buffalo, so Cody wasn't the only Buffalo Bill beyond the Mississippi. There was a Buffalo Bill Mathewson in Kansas, Buffalo Bill Cramer in Montana Territory, Buffalo Bill Wilson in New Mexico, Buffalo Bill Brooks in Dodge City, and Buffalo Bill Tomlins in the Black Hills. As Cody's fame blossomed, it often was necessary to refer to him as "the *true* Buffalo Bill."

In 1868, Cody and a certain Billy Comstock agreed to a buffalo shoot-out; the affair was arranged by officers from Fort Hays and Fort Wallace, and attracted spectators from as far away as St. Louis, including Louisa and baby Arta. The event was to commence at eight in the morning and conclude at four in the afternoon; each hunter went into the same herd at the same time, killing as many buffalo as possible. The score at the end of the day was Cody 69, Comstock 46, and the festivities reportedly were made lively by large quantities of champagne.

Not everyone was an uncritical admirer of Buffalo Bill; Theodore Davis, a reporter for *Harper's Weekly*, observed that Cody "was by nature a dandy. . . . When we ordinary mortals were hustling for a clean pair of socks . . . I [saw] Buffalo Bill appear in an immaculate boiled shirt . . . a jacket of startling scarlet . . . the long wavey hair that fell in masses . . . was glossy from a recent anointment of some heavily perfumed mixture." It seems Buffalo Bill was a showman even before he became one.

When the train tracks reached Sheridan, Wyoming, the job of hunting buffalo was over. From 1868 until 1872, Cody fought Indians, carried military messages, and acted as a guide for the U.S. Army. His services were greatly admired, and in June 1869 he received a one-hundred-dollar bonus for "extraordinarily good services as a trailer and fighter." In July 1869, he participated in the attempted rescue of Mrs. Alderdice and Mrs. Weichel, who had been captured by Chief Tall Bull's Cheyennes. The ladies lost their lives, but Tall Bull

was killed and Cody was given credit for his death.

Whether or not Cody killed Tall Bull (many doubt it), the story was the stuff of legend, and Ned Buntline, a part-time temperance lecturer and writer of dime novels, was enthralled. On December 23, 1869, Buntline's first installment of a serial titled *Buffalo Bill, the King of the Border Men*, advertised as "the wildest and truest story ever wrote," appeared in the *New York Weekly*.

Buffalo Bill's only son, Kit Carson Cody, was born November 26, 1870, a year that marked another important event in Cody's life. General Henry Davies, member of a group of wealthy would-be buffalo hunters from New York City, hired Cody to guide them on a hunt. Davies described his first sight of the slender, six-foot-tall scout: "mounted on a snowy white horse . . . dressed in a suit of light buckskin, trimmed with fringes . . . he realized to perfection the bold hunter and gallant sportsman of the plains." The trip was considered a huge success by the New Yorkers, who hunted for 194 miles along the mountains bordering Medicine Creek, killing more than six hundred buffalo and two hundred elk. (No one explained why a party of sixteen men needed so much meat.)

When the young Grand Duke Alexis of Russia arrived on the western prairie in January 1872, Cody was recruited again. A previous acquaintance of Cody's—General Custer, who, four years later, would fatally encounter Sioux warriors along the banks of the Little Bighorn in Montana—also participated in the royal hunt. For his services, the duke presented Cody with a gold purse, a diamond stickpin, a coat of Russian fur, and jeweled cuff links. More valuable, however, was the notoriety gained as the result of being the duke's escort.

As a consequence of his contacts with the likes of the grand duke, Buffalo Bill was invited to visit New York, where he was hosted at a dinner and reception at the Union Club. At about this time, Buntline's story, *Buffalo Bill, the King of the Border Men*, was being dramatized on stage—heady stuff for a young man only twenty-six years old. Buntline quickly wrote additional episodes, including *Buffalo Bill's Best Shot* and *Buffalo Bill's Last Victory*. After a six-week visit, Buffalo Bill returned to the plains, but a plan was hatching in the fertile imagination of Ned Buntline.

Buntline knew a performer when he saw one and urged Buffalo Bill to represent himself on stage. He said four magic words that persuaded Cody to try it: "There's money in it." Buffalo Bill might not have been a polished actor, but from his first appearance in Chicago

he dominated the show, which also featured Texas Jack, a sometime scout and Indian fighter, and Buntline himself. Louisa attended the opening on December 23, 1872. Then Buntline moved the show to Cincinnati, Rochester, and Buffalo; the Boston opening in March 1873 grossed an astonishing $16,200.

The *Boston Journal* was enthusiastic: "The play is an extraordinary production of more wild Indians, scalping knives and gun powder to the square inch than any drama ever before heard of." Not all reviewers were impressed; a critic at the *New York World* noted, "As drama it is very poor slop," but admitted that "Cody enters into the spectacle with a curious grace . . . [and] is remarkably handsome."

When Buntline departed from the show, publicity was handled by John M. Burke, an ex-actor, who devoted the next thirty-four years of his life to making Buffalo Bill the legend the world remembers. Under Burke's stewardship, Cody began a new way of life in earnest. He toured theaters from fall to spring and moved his family to Rochester, where, perhaps for the first time in their marriage, Louisa was happy. *The Scouts of the Plains* became a hit, and for a time Wild Bill Hickok also starred in the production. During the summer, Bill went back to the plains, where he con-

"Buffalo Bill" photographed with Chief Sitting Bull in 1885. NOTMAN PHOTOGRAPHIC ARCHIVES, MUSEUM OF CANADIAN HISTORY, MONTREAL. PHOTOGRAPH BY WILLIAM NOTMAN.

tinued to work as a scout and hunter; however, he was astute enough to realize that the Indian wars were mostly over, that there was no future in guiding a few rich men around the prairie.

On April 20, 1876, while Cody was starring in a two-day run in Springfield, Massachusetts, he received news that Kit, not yet six years old, was ill with scarlet fever. He hurried home, but his only son died shortly after. It was a loss from which some said Cody never recovered.

Against the advice of friends, Buffalo Bill took his show to the West Coast in 1877; he was warned the show wouldn't play well in California, which, ironically, would be the birthplace of the most popular type of movie of all time, "the western." His opening night in San Francisco was impressive at a time when tickets could be bought for as little as twenty-five cents, and although the run was planned for only two weeks, it lasted five. Soon, Bill was making enough money to buy the ranch of his dreams in Nebraska, which he named Scout's Rest.

Cody took part in one final Indian battle shortly after the Custer debacle along the Little Bighorn, during which he supposedly killed the Cheyenne chief, Yellow Hand (again, scholars differ on whether he did or didn't). The publicity that surrounded the encounter made John Burke realize that this was the kind of fame that could be turned into cash, and Cody himself became obsessed with the idea of turning his life on the plains into drama. To do so, he needed money, and one way to get it was to write more dime novels with himself as the hero. He wasn't a writer, but with the help of Burke, Buntline, and even his sister Helen, tales such as *Boy Chief of the Plains*, *Buffalo Bill at Bay*, and *Pearl of the Prairie* were cobbled together, to the public's delight.

Cody first met Nate Salsbury, an actor and stage manager, in New York in 1882, and listened carefully as he proposed a new venture called "a wild west show," conducted out-of-doors, and embodying "the whole subject of horsemanship." The idea was instantly appealing, but when plans didn't come to immediate fruition, Cody organized a Fourth of July "Old Glory Blow Out" celebration in Nebraska later that year, featuring a stagecoach holdup, horse races, reenactments of Indian skirmishes, and a sharpshooting contest. The event attracted people from 150 miles around and was in a sense a rehearsal for the kind of show that later became so hugely successful.

When Salsbury and Cody still couldn't come to an agreement about their venture, Cody formed an association with William "Doc" Carver, an internationally known marksman who had show business aspirations of his own. They named their company Cody & Carver's Wild West, and staged their first show in Omaha on May 17, 1883, before an audience of eight thousand. Although the show was a success, Carver decided to leave it, and Cody finally cast his lot with Salsbury. About this time, Cody was called home again by family tragedy: his eleven-year-old daughter, Orra, died on October 24, 1883. Only two children now survived: Arta, the firstborn, and a new baby, Irma, only a few months old.

By April 1884, at an opening in St. Louis, the Wild West company included six-foot five-inch Buck Taylor, the King of the Cowboys, and a superstar had been added—a twenty-four- year-old Ohio farm girl named Phoebe Anne Moses, better known as Annie Oakley, or "Little Sure Shot." Neither Cody nor Salsbury was eager to hire her, but they gave her a chance at a three-day engagement. "I went right in and did my best before seventeen thousand people," Annie said. She became the show's opening act and stayed on for seventeen years.

Cody copyrighted "Buffalo Bill's Wild West Show," and by 1885 it had played in more than forty cities in the United States and Canada, including New York, at Madison Square Garden. For a time, Chief Sitting Bull was a special added attraction, and one season ended with a profit of $100,000, an enormous sum for the day.

Queen Victoria's fiftieth year on the British throne was celebrated in 1887 with a Golden Jubilee, and one of the events scheduled in London was called an "American Exhibition." Cody's Wild West show was invited to appear for six months, turning Buffalo Bill into an international sensation. From that time on, although he'd never had a military rank higher than private, Cody became known as "Colonel Cody." When the show sailed for England on March 31, 1887, it carried the specially built Deadwood stagecoach, 97 Indian performers, 180 horses, 18 buffalo, 10 elk, 10 mules, 5 wild Texas steers, 4 donkeys, and 2 deer. Amazingly, only one animal—a horse—died during the stormy Atlantic crossing.

The show was set up on twenty-three acres in London's East End, with a grand opening on May 9. The weather had been rainy, and Cody worried about how things would go; luckily, the skies cleared just in time. The first performance was hugely successful, and Queen Victoria, who had been in seclusion for twenty-five years after the death of her husband, Prince Albert, attended on May 11. Her enthusiastic approval guaranteed huge audiences for the remainder of the tour.

Arta Cody, now twenty-one, came to

London and was received in London society. After the final performance in London on October 31, 1887, Cody took the show to other major English cities. The final performance was in Yorkshire on May 5, 1888. Three weeks later the Wild West show was welcomed back in New York by cheering crowds. The *New York Evening Telegram* called Cody a "hero of two continents," and as the result of Salsbury's shrewd management, Cody earned half a million dollars.

After a rest at his Nebraska ranch, Cody opened the show in Paris in May 1889. During his stay, he was painted by Rosa Bonheur, one of the most fashionable artists of the day. Her portrait of him mounted on a dapple gray steed now hangs in the Buffalo Bill Historical Center in Cody, Wyoming. At age forty-three, Cody was beginning to feel the strain of being a star. Yet when the Paris show closed he moved on to Spain and then to Italy, where he appeared in Rome, Florence, Bologna, Milan, Venice, and Verona.

The Wild West show played to European audiences for two more years. The next big target was the Chicago World's Fair in 1893, where Cody performed before an estimated six million people. The show now included an act of Cossack horsemen, as well as Arabian and Mexican acts. When Chicago mayor Carter Harrison's re-

quest that fair officials allow poor children free admission was refused, Cody himself offered it to them, as well as free ice cream and candy; fifteen thousand boys and girls enjoyed the afternoon of their lives.

The Chicago performances resulted in other engagements, including a 126-day run in Brooklyn. There were 321 performances in 1895, and in spite of his reputed drinking problems, Cody never missed one; 1899 was an even bigger year, with 11,111 miles traveled and 341 shows performed. "Side shows" grew up around the Wild West show, featuring giants, midgets, glassblowers, snake handlers, and fortune-tellers. Yet James Burke, Cody's publicist, insisted that vulgar circus terms never be used in connection with the Wild West company, and that the "show grounds" must always be called the "exhibition grounds."

It is likely that Cody never appreciated how much money flowed through his hands. He enjoyed showering family, friends, and employees with gifts. He built a sixteen-room mansion at Scout's Rest, where he ran 3,000 head of cattle and 1,500 horses. He bought a second ranch in Wyoming, established a town nearby, named Cody in his honor, and started its first newspaper, the *Shoshone Valley News*. When his sister Helen married, he gave her a thirty-thousand-

Rosa Bonheur's oil painting of Bill Cody in 1889. BUFFALO BILL HISTORICAL CENTER, CODY, WYOMING. GIVEN IN MEMORY OF WILLIAM R. COE AND MAI ROGERS COE.

dollar home; when he became enamored of a young English actress, Kate Clemmons, he spent eighty thousand dollars to establish her career. A mining venture in Arizona drained an estimated half million dollars from his pockets.

When Nate Salsbury died on Christmas Eve, 1902, he left behind a troupe numbering five hundred, and Cody took the show to Europe for a four-year tour. James Bailey took over Salsbury's job as financial manager. Then he too died, leaving the show somewhat in debt. Misfortune struck in France in 1905, when two hundred horses came down with a serious glandular disease and had to be shot. Rumors began to circulate about how the Indians in the show were treated, but it seems their greatest difficulty might have been simple homesickness.

Moving pictures soon brought images of the Wild West to even the smallest city, cutting down demand for live performances. Although Cody's show continued to earn profits, they were not sufficient to keep ahead of creditors. In 1905, Arta Cody died during proceedings in which Bill, after thirty-nine years of marriage, pressed for a divorce from Louisa. The judge found in favor of Mrs. Cody, refused to grant the divorce, and ordered Cody to pay all court costs. The unfavorable publicity damaged Buffalo Bill's reputation and added to his financial woes.

By early 1912, Buffalo Bill was a weary sixty-six-year-old, his long white hair now so thin he needed to wear a toupee, and the Wild West show was deeper in debt. Cody made a deal with Harry Tammen, unscrupulous owner of the *Denver Post*; in exchange for a loan of twenty thousand dollars, Cody allowed his show to be merged with the Sells-Floto Circus, owned by Tammen, and gave up his copyright to the name "Buffalo Bill's Wild West Show." Due to complicated financial machinations, Cody soon found himself unable to pay his workers or feed his animals, and by 1913 the show was put on the auction block. In order to repay his loan, Cody became, in a sense, Tammen's slave, performing when and where he was told.

Nevertheless, the Cody Club of Wyoming hosted a grand party for Bill's sixty-ninth birthday in 1915. The following year the idea of Wild West shows of any kind seemed out of place in an America about to enter its first world war. Desperate for money, Cody performed with the "101 Ranch Show." His health steadily deteriorated, and behind the scenes he often had to be helped onto and off his horse. In November 1916, he appeared in public for the last time in Portsmouth, Virginia.

Ill with a cold and bothered with kidney trouble, Cody retreated to his sister May's home in Denver, where a doctor suggested that the mineral waters at Glenwood Springs might help. Cody and his older sister Julia set off, but he barely withstood the journey and returned to Denver. Just past noon on January 10, 1917, William Cody died, a few weeks shy of his seventy-first birthday. Six weeks later, his longtime friend and promoter, John Burke, died, some said of a broken heart.

Messages of adulation came from around the world, but death didn't solve Buffalo Bill's troubles. Immediately, disagreements arose about where he ought to be buried. His will clearly stated his wish to be laid to rest on Cedar Mountain in Wyoming; it was rumored that Cody's old partner, Tammen, wanted Cody buried in Colorado for publicity reasons and paid Louisa ten thousand dollars to make sure that he was. He rests there now, in a bronze casket encased in a granite vault atop Lookout Mountain, overlooking Denver. He had been a grand performer who made "the Wild West" real for Americans of all ages and circumstances, yet as one biographer noted, "Cody lived with the world at his feet—and died with it on his shoulders."

Crazy Horse

1841–77 Sioux chief. When gold was discovered in the Black Hills, the already troubled relations between the Sioux and whites worsened. Crazy Horse refused government order to give up tribal ways, joined Sitting Bull on the Little Bighorn River in 1876. Government sent General George Armstrong Custer in pursuit; the result was a tragedy that still compels the imagination of military historians and admirers of Indian lore.

It was a Sioux custom to camp each summer in the Pa Sapa, or Black Hills, the highest mountain range between the Atlantic Ocean and the Rockies. The Indians believed these mountains were the home of Wakan Tanka, the Great Spirit, and Bear Butte in particular was considered to be a sacred place. There, in 1841, on an evening in August, the Moon of Ripe Plums (some historians give the year as 1840 or 1842), the wife of a Sioux holy man, delivered her second child, a boy.

From the beginning, the infant looked unlike other Sioux babies: he had a fair complexion and wavy, light brown hair. Settlers and soldiers who saw him often whispered "captive" among themselves, implying that he might be a stolen white child. As the boy grew older, he was smaller than his peers, and unusually quiet, which further set him apart. Since a Sioux boy wasn't given a formal name until he was old enough to make a vision quest, little boys were known only by their nicknames. Everyone called this one Curly.

The Sioux nation into which the light-haired boy was born was composed of the Seven Council Fires, connected to one another by a root language and the twin traditions of buffalo hunting and making war on other Plains tribes. Curly belonged to the Oglalas, meaning "to scatter one's own"; other tribes in the council were the Brulés, Miniconjous, Two Kettles, Sans Arcs, Blackfeet, and Hunkpapas. Sitting Bull, perhaps the

An undated portrait of Crazy Horse. CORBIS-BETTMANN.

most famous Sioux chief of all, belonged to the Hunkpapas.

As he grew up, Curly played the games that his companions played; their aim was to prepare a boy to be brave in battle and swift on the hunt. There was time for simple fun too: in winter, children sledded on buffalo ribs; boys played a game on the ice similar to hockey; plum pits were used like dice, because Sioux of all ages were fond of gambling games.

One of the most important events in a boy's life was the formation of a special partnership with another boy his own age. Such a friendship was called a *kola*. High Back Bone, nicknamed Hump, became Curly's best friend. Other close companions were Lone Bear and He Dog.

When Curly was eleven, he joined Hump and other boys on a horse-catching expedition in the sand hills of what is now northwestern Nebraska. He caught himself a fine buckskin pony and was the first of the boys to break his mount for riding. Later, he gave the horse to his younger brother, Little Hawk. Perhaps because of his small size, Curly seemed especially eager to prove himself worthy, and he soon gained a reputation for exceptional daring and fearlessness.

In August 1851, U.S. government agents called for a gathering of Plains Indians at Fort Laramie. In order to guarantee the safety of white settlers traveling along the Oregon Trail, called the "Holy Road" by the Sioux, the government decided it would have to pay for their safe passage. In return for granting trouble-free travel through Indian country, tribes that signed a treaty were promised annuities. Such annuities, to be paid once a year, would be in the form of blankets, clothing, coffee, tea, tobacco, salt, sugar, and beads. At this conference, Conquering Bear was chosen as the spokesman for the Sioux.

It wasn't easy for Conquering Bear to maintain order among his young men, however, and two years after the treaty was signed, a young warrior named High Forehead stole an old cow from a Mormon wagon train. It was the sort of petty crime that often had been committed before, but this time the owner of the cow hurried to Fort Laramie and demanded that something be done.

The fort was commanded by twenty-eight-year-old Lieutenant Hugh B. Fleming, only two years out of West Point. His associate was an even younger West Pointer, Lieutenant John B. Grattan, who had little respect for Indians, once boasting that he could whip the whole Sioux nation with twenty good soldiers! When Lieutenant Fleming decided that High Forehead must answer for his crime, Grattan requested permission to bring the wrong-doer to justice.

The following morning, August 17, 1854, leading a volunteer force of thirty-one men, Grattan headed for the Sioux camp a few miles away. Conquering Bear was ordered to surrender High Forehead, and when he didn't comply quickly enough, Grattan lost his temper. (It was rumored that he had been drinking.) Thirteen-year-old Curly watched Grattan order his men to fire directly into the camp. Conquering Bear, whose job it had been to maintain peace, was shot nine times. There was no chance for Lieutenant Grattan to savor his victory because he and his entire command were slaughtered by outraged Oglalas and their Brulé cousins.

The death of Conquering Bear left Curly deeply troubled. In his short life, he had seen many things change for the Sioux: every year, more *wasichus*, or white men, arrived on the plains; the great buffalo herds were vanishing; ancestral lands were being settled by people who built log cabins and sod huts, and put up fences.

Curly decided it was time to seek a vision, to find out what *his* place in Sioux life should be. Much is known about the light-haired boy's dream, for the Sioux talked openly about such matters. In 1868, Curly even recounted his dream to a white man, William Garnett, a fur trader and part-time interpreter.

The boy retreated alone to the nearby sand hills. To induce a trance, he went without food or water and tortured himself by cutting and scratching his flesh with sharp stones. He was scalded by the sun during the day; he shivered through the cold prairie night. After three days, no vision had appeared, and he assumed he was not yet worthy of one.

As he was about to give up the quest, Curly suddenly saw a man mounted on a spotted horse riding toward him. The stranger wore a smooth round stone tied behind his ear; a lightning bolt was painted across his cheek; hailstones decorated his chest. He wore a single hawk feather in his hair, and the bullets and arrows flying past him apparently had no power to do him harm.

In the final phase of the vision, Curly saw the rider surrounded by his own people, who tried to pull him off his horse and pin his arms to his sides. The dream faded, then the boy fell into a deep sleep. When he wakened, his father and Hump were standing over him, angry that he'd been gone from camp so long without telling anyone of his whereabouts. Humiliated, Curly decided to keep his vision to himself.

In the wake of the Grattan disaster, the U.S. War Department ordered six hundred troops under Brigadier General William S. Harney, hero of the Mexican

War, into Sioux country to instill fear in the hearts of the Indians. Early on the morning of September 3, 1855, Harney attacked Chief Little Thunder's encampment of Brulés, relatives of Curly's mother, killing eighty-six members; seventy women and children were captured.

The Sioux called for a gathering at Bear Butte to discuss the increasing problems faced by the Seven Council Fires. More than seven thousand gathered, and the group included many who were familiar to Curly: his uncle, Spotted Tail; his cousin, Black Elk; seven-foot-tall Touch-the-Clouds; famous Red Cloud; the great orator, Sitting Bull. Perhaps it was here that fifteen-year-old Curly also met Red Cloud's beautiful niece, Black Buffalo Woman, who would play such an important role in his life.

Toward the end of the council, Curly decided to tell his father about the vision he'd had two years earlier. His father, a holy man, recognized the importance of the dream and announced to all who had gathered that henceforth his son would be called Tashunka Witko (*tashunka* meaning horse, *witko* meaning strange or awe-inspiring). "I give him a new name. . . . I call him Crazy Horse," the boy's father declared.

In adulthood, a Sioux male joined an *akicita*, a secret society. Such societies,

in which membership was by invitation only, had names such as Brave Hearts, Kit Foxes, or Lance Owners. One of the functions of such organizations was to act as tribal policemen within the camp; Crazy Horse became a member of the Crow Owners.

When he was twenty-one, Crazy Horse commenced his courtship of Black Buffalo Woman. Sioux girls were strictly chaperoned, however, and the couple could meet only briefly. In addition, this beautiful young woman was admired by many, and Crazy Horse had to wait his turn. In the summer of 1862, while he was gone on a hunt, Black Buffalo Woman abruptly married a brave named No Water. Stricken, Crazy Horse exiled himself from the tribe for two years and went to live with relatives in the Powder River country.

In 1863, Crazy Horse became friends with a white soldier, Caspar Collins, whose father was the new commander at Fort Laramie. Collins was an affable young man, and Crazy Horse taught him the Sioux language, explained Sioux customs, and took him on hunts. The two men seemed to genuinely enjoy each other's company, but when their paths crossed two years later it would be under tragic circumstances.

During the years 1861–65, most U.S. military forces were needed for duty in the Civil War, and as a result, the government maintained a fairly low profile on the western plains. An incident at Sand Creek, Colorado, on November 29, 1864, signaled a dramatic change and remains a dark chapter in U.S. military history. Chief Black Kettle of the Cheyennes was camped peacefully with several hundred followers when he was attacked without provocation by troops from nearby Fort Lyon under the command of Colonel J. M. Chivington. One hundred and fifty people, mostly women and children, were killed and mutilated in what an official congressional report later called "barbarity of the most revolting character."

The Cheyennes immediately sent word to their allies, and the Oglalas, Brulés, and Arapahos agreed to join in making war on the whites. A war party of a thousand men, including Crazy Horse, set out to avenge the massacre at Sand Creek. As always, Crazy Horse painted himself as the man in his vision was painted, wore a small smooth stone on a rawhide thong behind his ear, and put a single hawk feather in his hair. The Indians attacked Julesburg in Colorado Territory, killing fourteen soldiers and stealing as many goods as could be carried off. For six days they terrorized the countryside, stealing horses and cattle. When the raids were finished, Crazy Horse returned to his tribe, who, noting

the plunder that had been collected, decided to follow the warpath themselves. It was a decision that made permanent peace between Indians and whites impossible.

When the Civil War ended, greater numbers of U.S. troops were quickly sent west to quell the unrest on the plains. The Sioux and Cheyennes did not wait quietly for fate to overtake them but gathered in the Moon of Chokecherries Ripening, July 1865, to discuss their future. Crazy Horse was twenty-four years old, still somewhat shorter than his companions, about five feet eight inches tall, weighing about 140 pounds. His skin and hair had darkened slightly over the years but were still unusually light-colored. Red Feather, an Oglala, described him as "a nice looking man, with brown, not black hair, a sharp nose, and a narrow face. His hair was very long, straight, and fine in texture."

On July 26, a skirmish between the Sioux, Cheyennes, and federal troops occurred at the Platte River Bridge, during which Crazy Horse recognized a man riding a big, hard-to-handle gray horse. It was his old friend, Caspar Collins. Crazy Horse shouted to his allies not to harm the young man, but the Cheyennes ignored his warning. When the unmanageable horse bolted into their midst, young Collins was killed instantly.

That same year, Crazy Horse was chosen to be a shirt wearer. The job of shirt wearers was to enforce decisions made by tribal elders. Others chosen were Young Man Afraid, American Horse, and Crazy Horse's close friend, He Dog. These young men pledged that the welfare of their people would always come before personal goals or desires. They were given beautifully decorated shirts made from the tanned white hides of bighorn sheep.

In early 1866, U.S. peace commissioners arrived at Fort Laramie with promises of more gifts if the Indians would stop harassing travelers on the Bozeman Trail, which had been blazed by John Bozeman in 1862 to allow travelers to head for the gold fields in Montana. Yet even as government agents parleyed for peace with the Indians, forts were being built along the Bozeman Trail—among them, Fort Phil Kearny in the Bighorn Mountains and Fort C. F. Smith in Montana. The Sioux regarded this as an act of treachery. They retaliated on December 21, 1866, by attacking Fort Phil Kearny, killing Captain William Fetterman and eighty troops. There were Indian losses too: Lone Bear, the friend from days when he'd still been called Curly, died in Crazy Horse's arms.

In the spring of 1868, peacemakers from Washington came to Fort Laramie with yet another proposal. The army agreed to abandon the forts along what was now called "Bloody Bozeman" and promised that all of present-day South Dakota, including the Black Hills, would become a Sioux reservation. No whites would be allowed on this reserve, and in return the Sioux had to promise not to oppose completion of the Union Pacific Railroad.

Red Cloud signed the treaty and journeyed to Washington to meet the U.S. president, where he warned the government that he might be unable to control younger men such as Crazy Horse. The light-haired warrior had the confidence of his people, however, and was honored by being appointed a lance bearer in 1869. These lances, nine feet in length, had been in the Oglala tribe for more than three hundred years. As Crazy Horse's friend He Dog explained, they "were given to the younger generation who had best lived the life of a warrior."

Crazy Horse had never forgotten the love of his youth, Black Buffalo Woman, and often visited the camp where she lived with her three young children. It was a custom among the Sioux that if a wife wanted her freedom, a husband was expected to accept a gift of horses and let her go. No Water was a possessive man, however, and refused to give up his wife.

Nevertheless, Crazy Horse and Black

Buffalo Woman decided to live their lives together and rode away from camp, making no effort to disguise their intentions. No Water pursued them and shot Crazy Horse in the face, smashing his upper jaw. Crazy Horse recovered from his wound, but elders of the tribe advised Black Buffalo Woman to return to her husband. Crazy Horse, who had taken a vow to put the welfare of the tribe above personal concerns, was ordered to give up his position as a shirt wearer. It seemed that his reputation among his people had been ruined.

Another loss awaited Crazy Horse. His brother Little Hawk was killed in a fight with gold miners near the Yellowstone River. Not long after, Crazy Horse decided to marry Red Feather's sister, Black Shawl, and it was she who rode with him to recover his brother's bones, to wrap them in a red blanket and return them for proper burial. Then, in a battle with the Shoshones, hereditary enemies of the Sioux, Crazy Horse suffered yet another blow: High Back Bone, the *kola* of his boyhood, was killed. Crazy Horse, only thirty years old, had in a short time suffered the loss of four important loved ones: Lone Bear, Black Buffalo Woman, Little Hawk, and now High Back Bone.

Within a year, Crazy Horse became the father of a baby girl and devoted himself to activities that would earn back the respect he'd lost over the incident with Black Buffalo Woman. For example, rather than keep Little Hawk's pony herd to himself—which was his right, according to custom—he gave the horses away to others in the tribe. His many efforts were noted by tribal elders, and when Sitting Bull, ten years older than Crazy Horse, was chosen chief over the Sioux, Crazy Horse was named second-in-command.

The Sioux had long known there was gold in the Black Hills, but they hoped the fact would remain a secret. The Indians knew too well what the discovery of gold would mean. It had been responsible for the destruction of the Platte River hunting grounds as emigrants traveled through on their way to California; it was the reason the Bozeman Trail cut through the Powder River country as white men traveled to gold fields in Montana. Therefore, when rumors began to circulate about the presence of gold in the Black Hills, it was clear to the Sioux what would happen next.

If they had any false hopes, they were dispelled on July 25, 1874, when a thousand troops descended on the Pa Sapa to document rumors of the precious metal. The force was commanded by a man whose name would be forever linked to Crazy Horse's—General George Armstrong Custer. (Ironically,

Custer's boyhood nickname also had been Curly.) After Custer emerged from the Black Hills to give newspapermen a glowing account of what had been discovered, white men began arriving in large numbers to stake out mining claims.

During these tense times, yet another personal loss awaited Crazy Horse. His daughter, as light-skinned and light-haired as he was himself, died of cholera. After her death, friends said that he grew even quieter and more reserved than before.

The discovery of gold in the Black Hills presented a problem to the U.S. government, which in the treaty of 1868 had declared these sacred mountains "set apart for the absolute and undisturbed use and occupation of the Indians." The treaty continued, "The United States now solemnly agrees that no persons . . . shall ever be permitted to pass over, settle upon, or reside in the territory."

When gold fever reached epidemic proportions, however, agents from Washington pressed the Sioux to sell the Black Hills to the government. In September 1875, commissioners from the East arrived to discuss the matter. The Sioux were divided among themselves as to what to do; many believed the *wasichus* were too powerful to be held back and that it would be wise to

agree to a good deal if one were offered. In previous treaty negotiations, such Indians had been dubbed "friendlies" by the government, but "hostiles" such as Crazy Horse and Sitting Bull were determined never to concede to white demands. "One does not sell the land upon which the people walk," Crazy Horse said.

The Sioux turned down an offer of $400,000 a year for mineral rights in the Black Hills, or $6 million for an outright sale. The government was stymied; an excuse to seize the lands was needed, and one was soon concocted: the Sioux were accused of making war on the Crows, which meant the Crows needed government protection. A declaration of war against the Sioux was made on December 6, 1875, by President Ulysses S. Grant, and a deadline was given to all Sioux to abandon their old ways and report to government agencies within six weeks. If they refused, U.S. troops would be sent to hunt them down.

Crazy Horse responded by moving his people north to join Sitting Bull, who also declined to obey the government order. However, most of the Sioux—about ten thousand of them—now lived near the various Indian agencies as friendlies. Only three thousand remained hostile; Crazy Horse and Sitting Bull knew they needed more men to fight a war, and they sent runners to the agencies, inviting young men to join them. By February, the Moon When Grain Comes Up, Sioux warriors began to leave the agencies by the hundreds. Crazy Horse's old friend, He Dog, was among them.

Word soon came that a thousand men under the command of General George Crook, in addition to many Crow, Shoshone, and Pawnee scouts, were in pursuit of the hostiles. On June 17, 1876, Crazy Horse led his men, including Bad Heart Bull, Black Deer, and Good Weasel, in a standoff battle against Crook's men at Rosebud Creek, then re- treated to join Sitting Bull along the banks of the Little Bighorn River in east- ern Montana.

The morning of June 25 dawned hot and windless. A week had passed since the battle along the Rosebud; Crazy Horse's scouts kept track of General Crook and confirmed his retreat. However, the scouts reported a new threat: a 600-man cavalary regiment was approaching the Little Bighorn. About three o'clock, when everyone in the Sioux camp was resting, a tower of dust was seen rising in the air toward the south.

The Sioux immediately gathered up their weapons and ponies. Women and children scrambled for cover. The Sioux were not aware that the large force had been divided into three parts. The first,

under Major Marcus Reno, commanding 131 men, and the second, under Captain F. W. Benteen, commanding 113, had traveled all night; exhausted, they were not prepared for what awaited them. In the battle that ensued, 40 of Reno's men were killed and 13 wounded. The war- riors wanted to finish them off, but Crazy Horse's scouts informed him that a third and larger contingent of troops under the command of General Custer was approaching just below the eastern bluffs.

Crazy Horse, riding at the head of a thousand warriors, forded the Little Bighorn, circled around behind the sol- diers, and attacked them from the crest of a hill. Chief Gall came up at them from below. For the Seventh Cavalry, there was no escape. In the battle that followed—which has been estimated to have lasted barely an hour—Custer and approximately 225 troops were killed. An Arapaho warrior later said, "Crazy Horse . . . rode closest to the soldiers . . . [who] were shooting at him, but he was never hit," a manifestation of the vision Crazy Horse had had as a boy of thir- teen.

The government was outraged by the death of Custer and his troops. In August 1876, Congress declared that no food or provisions could be given to any Indians, even those living peaceably at the agencies, until all Sioux agreed to give up the Black Hills, the Powder River country, and the Bighorn territory. In September, Chiefs Red Cloud and Spotted Tail finally signed an agreement.

Crazy Horse, still committed to the old ways, retreated deep into his old haunt, the Powder River country. Winter came early that year; hunting was poor, grass for the horses was scant, the weakest animals were slaughtered for food. Crazy Horse realized that although the Sioux had been victorious at the Little Bighorn, the war itself had been lost.

In January 1877, Sitting Bull fled with his followers to Canada, the "Land of the Grandmother," so named in honor of Queen Victoria. He urged Crazy Horse to accompany him, but the younger chief declined. On May 6, 1877, with nearly a thousand followers, including his headmen—Little Big Man, He Dog, and Bad Road—Crazy Horse surrendered at Camp Robinson in Nebraska.

The light-haired warrior must have been surprised to discover how famous he was among the white soldiers. They were fascinated by the man who had defeated General Custer, and they often visited him at his camp on Little Cottonwood Creek near Camp Robinson, bringing money and gifts. "Other Indians got very jealous," Red Feather remembered. Crazy Horse's for-mer allies, including his uncle, Spotted Tail, became anxious about Crazy Horse's growing notoriety among the whites and whispered to the soldiers that he would never remain peaceful for long.

To make certain Crazy Horse behaved himself, it was decided he should be arrested and put in jail. During a scuffle in front of the guardhouse where he was to be confined, the second part of Crazy Horse's boyhood vision was fulfilled: while his old friend Little Big Man seized his arms to prevent him from defending himself, a soldier plunged a bayonet deep into his back, then thrust it a second time through his kidneys.

Crazy Horse's aged father was summoned; He Dog and Touch-the-Clouds joined him. The wounded chief whispered, "Tell the people it is no use to depend on me anymore," and an hour later, a few minutes past midnight on September 5, 1877, Crazy Horse died. He was thirty-six years old.

"His parents placed his body on a travois and took it away," Jennie Fast Thunder reported later. "[They] never told anyone where they put the body of their son and no living Sioux knows where it is." Crazy Horse's cousin Black Elk summed it up best: "It does not matter where his body lies, for it is grass; but where his spirit is, it will be good to be."

A drawing depicting the funeral procession of Crazy Horse. STOCK MONTAGE.

After Crazy Horse's death, the fate of the Indians was one of continued loss. The Nez Percé surrendered in Montana after a 1,200-mile flight from General Howard's troops. Sitting Bull returned from Canada and was murdered, along with his seventeen-year-old son Crow Foot, at the Standing Rock reservation in 1890. One result of Sitting Bull's death was the Wounded Knee massacre, in which three hundred unarmed Sioux men, women, and children were slaughtered by the U.S. Army and buried in a mass grave on New Year's Day, 1891. The Seven Council Fires would burn no more.

Davy Crockett

1786–1836 Backwoods hunter, soldier, politician. Called "the gentleman from the cane"; served in Tennessee legislature, later three terms in U.S. Congress. Primary interest was assisting pioneers acquire homesteads in the new western territories at a fair price. His death at the Alamo made him a legend.

A biographer of this famous American quickly discovers there are two Crocketts. The first was known to friends and family as David; he grew up, married, was elected to office, wrote books, and died under that name. At his death, a man named Davy was born—a larger-than-life hero, slayer of hundreds of bears, a man who faced down General Santa Anna at a Texas mission, his rifle spitting fire, the cry "Remember the Alamo!" on his lips. For better or worse, we have all come to think of that man as Davy, and that's how he'll be referred to here.

Davy Crockett's exact birth date was not recorded, but Crockett himself gave it as August 17, 1786, and pinpointed the location as near the Big Limestone River, Greene County, in eastern Tennessee. A stone slab now marks the spot where his parents had settled three years earlier.

John Crockett, of Scotch-Irish descent, and his wife, the former Rebecca Hawkins, had emigrated from North Carolina. John, whose parents had been massacred by the Creeks in 1777, had fought against the British at King's Mountain during the Revolutionary War. Davy was the fifth child among nine that included three girls and six boys, and the first of the brood to be born in Tennessee.

It is impossible to understand Davy Crockett without knowing something about his time. At his birth, the Constitution had not yet been drafted; George

Washington had not yet been elected the first president of the new nation; the country was almost exclusively agricultural. Only five cities in the United States had a population of more than 10,000: New York, 33,000; Philadelphia, 28,000; Boston, 18,000; Charleston, 16,000; and Baltimore, 13,000. Only one-tenth of America's citizens lived west of the Allegheny Mountains.

By 1827, the balance had shifted dramatically: now, one-third of the population lived west of the mountains. Davy Crockett strode onto the scene just as interest in the West was ignited among Americans; there, land could be had for free or for as little as twenty-five cents an acre. It was an era of increasing trust in the rule of the people rather than rule by an elite class. Davy Crockett was made for such times, and the times were made for Davy Crockett.

Davy was a small boy when his father, who had recently lost his homestead due to indebtedness, opened a tavern along the road from Abingdon to Knoxville, where travelers could rest themselves and their stock. There, Davy was in constant contact with travelers, adventurers, and explorers of all kinds. Davy didn't attend school, nor did any of his brothers or sisters. Until he was seventeen, he couldn't read, write, spell, or do sums; instead, he grew up admiring the willingness of men to be responsible for themselves, to endure hardships, and to use rifles to make their way in the wilderness.

In 1798, when Davy was twelve, his father hired him out to Jacob Siler, a Dutchman who had stopped at the tavern while driving a herd of cattle to Rockbridge County, Virginia, and who needed help continuing his journey. Davy went willingly, eager even then for adventure. Siler, who owned a fine Prussian rifle, has been credited with teaching the boy how to handle a firearm. But when the Dutchman attempted to force Davy to work beyond the terms of their agreement, Davy left in the dead of a snowy might, determined to return home. Luckily, he soon met travelers who remembered stopping at his father's tavern themselves and who helped him return.

In Davy's absence, something new had come to the area: a school had opened. John Crockett was determined that his sons would have the education that he'd never had himself, and Davy and his brothers were dispatched to a small log building with an earthen floor, presided over by schoolmaster Benjamin Kitchen. Davy's school experience lasted one week. He got into a fight with a bigger boy and clobbered him with a rock. He realized that his father would thrash him soundly for such behavior and wasted no time hiring out to a neighbor, Jesse Cheek, who was driving a herd of cattle to Virginia. This time, the boy was gone for two and a half years, returning in 1802.

Davy discovered his family's fortunes hadn't improved during his absence, a problem that was to haunt his own life as well. John Crockett owed two debts: thirty-six dollars to an Abraham Wilson, forty to a Quaker named John Kennedy—large sums in those times. Within six months, at his father's request, Davy worked off the first debt. He began to work off the second one to Mr. Kennedy in the summer of 1803. During that time, John Kennedy's lovely niece came from North Carolina to visit her uncle, and seventeen-year-old Davy promptly fell in love.

The young lady's refusal to consider him as a suitor in spite of his eager attentions caused Davy to take stock of himself. *Ah*—it must be his lack of education that was the problem! He enrolled in a nearby Quaker school, attending four days a week while continuing to work for Kennedy two days a week. The arrangement continued for six months; Davy learned how to read and write a bit and to do simple sums. His formal education amounted to about one hundred days.

Having once fallen in love, Davy found it even easier the next time. He proposed soon after being introduced to sixteen-year-old Mary Finley—called Polly by her family—the red-haired daughter of an Irish family that was nearly as poor as the Crocketts. Polly's father was able to provide a dowry of only two cows and their calves; then the couple were married on August 14, 1806, three days before Davy's twentieth birthday.

Davy settled down to the kind of life led by most young men of his time: farming, clearing land, raising crops and livestock, hunting the surrounding forests and meadows for extra meat. For Davy, the latter was always a pleasure, never a chore, and he became expert with a rifle, winning so many local shooting contests that others quit competing.

"We worked on for some years, renting ground and paying high rent [but] it wasn't what it was cracked up to be," Davy wrote in *A Narrative of the Life of David Crockett of the State of Tennessee*, published in 1834. "In this time we had two sons . . . as I knowed I would have to move sometime, I thought it was better to do it before my family got too large." In addition to a wife and two small sons, Davy now had an old horse and a couple of halter-broken two-year-old colts. With his father-in-law's help, he packed up and moved over the mountains to the fork of Mulberry Creek on the Elk River in Lincoln County, Tennessee.

Davy Crockett, based on a painting by J. G. Chapman. CORBIS-BETTMANN.

Crockett was sure he'd made a good decision and wrote in his *Narrative* that he "found this a very rich country. . . . It was here that I began to distinguish myself as a hunter. . . . Of deer and smaller game I killed abundance, but the bear had been hunted in those parts . . . and were not so plenty as I could have wished." No sooner was the family settled than Davy's urge to move on in search of an even better place became irresistible; in 1811, the Crockett family moved again, this time to Franklin County, where they settled on Bean Creek, near what is now the Alabama border.

It was here that circumstance began to mold Davy Crockett into the man remembered in history. By 1813, the Indians onto whose lands white settlers had steadily encroached were growing ever more resentful. In particular, the Creeks, who had sided with the British during the Revolutionary War, resisted what was happening to their tribal lands—lands rich in lumber resources as well as game. Inevitably, the eagerness of white settlers to appropriate such lands caused wrath among the native people.

The massacre at Fort Mimms was the beginning of a bloody struggle between Indians and whites, but the truth seems to be that the war was started not by the Indians, but by the whites. In the summer of 1813, 180 militiamen surprised a party of 60 to 90 Indian warriors at Burnt Corn Creek and killed many of them. In retaliation, the Creeks attacked Fort Mimms—not a military fort as such, but the stockaded residence of Samuel Mimms—located a mile from the Alabama River.

Fearing that the British or Spanish would supply the Indians with arms, Major Daniel Beasley of the Mississippi Volunteers led 265 soldiers to defend the fort, where nearly 250 other citizens had gathered for safety's sake. At noon on August 30, the Indians descended on the fort and poured through the gates, which unaccountably had been left standing wide open. Within a few hours, more than 500 people were dead, 100 children among them.

A volunteer militia was formed immediately, and Davy, along with many of his neighbors, enlisted for ninety days. When volunteers were called for to scout the movements of Indians on the other side of the Tennessee River, Davy Crockett was among those who responded. Bloody revenge was taken on the Creeks, and 186 warriors, plus women and children, were slain at Tallussahatchee in November 1813. It was during these hostilities that Davy met and learned to fiercely dislike the commander of the volunteers, Andrew Jackson, a man ten years his senior who would one day be elected the seventh president of the United States.

In early 1815, shortly after his return from the war, Polly Crockett gave birth to a daughter, and died that summer. Davy now had three motherless children to care for, one a mere infant. He asked one of his married brothers to come to live with him, but the arrangement didn't work out.

As was the custom of the day, the best way for a widower to provide care for his children was to marry again. Elizabeth Patton had lost her husband in the Creek War; she had a son and daughter of her own, plus a tidy farm. She came from a prominent family, was a large, capable woman with fine managerial skills, and within a year of their marriage in 1816, Davy's fortunes seemed to take an upward turn. His new life was followed by plans for another move, this time to a tract of territory in south Tennessee that had been opened after Andrew Jackson negotiated a treaty with the Chickasaw Indians. Here, in 1817, Crockett was appointed to his first public office as a justice of the peace.

Davy also was elected to the local militia regiment and was given the rank of colonel in 1818, a title that he kept throughout his lifetime. In 1820, he ran for the Tennessee legislature and was elected, confirming the emergence of

what came to be called "squatter democracy," as backwoodsmen rose to positions of regional influence.

The Jeffersonian ideal was that "all men are created equal," but prior to the 1820s, men such as Crockett, with their rough manners and homely speech, offended the sensibilities of better-educated men. By the 1830s, however, Crockett and those like him had captured the imagination of the public. Davy was determined to ride the crest of that wave. He was a natural speaker, had a variety of comical tall tales to tell, and possessed a rough common sense that appealed to many citizens.

During his first term in the state legislature, Crockett interested himself in matters of taxation; he voted to release landholders in western Tennessee from paying double assessments for delinquent taxes. He submitted a resolution to prevent the issuance of more than one grant for a piece of land; in 1821 a man could homestead a piece of land, clear it, improve it—only to find himself moved off by the discovery that an earlier grant had been issued to someone else. Davy also resisted efforts by land speculators to buy up tracts of land to be sold later at enormous profit.

One of Crockett's political experiences at this time harked back to the reasons for his distrust of men like Andrew Jackson—men who, he suspected, thought they were better than backwoodsmen like himself. One day after he'd risen to speak in the legislature, he heard himself referred to by a fellow member as "the gentleman from the cane"—a hick, in other words—and the expression stung. Later, he happened to come across a cambric shirt ruffle similar to the kind worn by the man who'd insulted him; he pinned it to his own coarse, homespun linsey-woolsey shirt, rousing hoots of laughter among his fellow legislators and causing his red-faced adversary to depart from the chambers.

In November 1821, Crockett, with his oldest son, John Wesley, now a boy of fourteen years, proceeded to the newly opened counties west of the Tennessee River and selected yet another homesite near the Obion River. It was the type of site that most appealed to Davy: game was plentiful (on his first day there he shot six buck deer), and it was far enough away from neighbors to suit his nature.

On the advice of friends, Crockett was urged not to run again for reelection to the state legislature but to run instead against Colonel Adam Alexander, a high-tariff advocate, for a seat in the U.S. Congress. Davy resisted, saying Congress "was a step above my knowledge," then finally agreed to run on an antitariff platform.

He was defeated by two votes and explained why in a typically whimsical way: "It was a year that cotton brought twenty-five dollars a hundred. . . . I might as well have sung salms [sic] over a dead horse, as to try to make the people believe otherwise."

That autumn, Davy busied himself providing meat for his family for the coming winter and reported that he and his companions killed fifty-eight bears close to his new homesite. He also became involved in a venture to produce barrel staves from local cypress trees. He hired several employees and built two boats that were intended to transport the staves downriver. By January 1826, the boats were completed, and thirty thousand barrel staves had been manufactured. In early February, all hands joined Davy in boarding the boats and they set out down the Obion River, headed for New Orleans.

Once they reached the Mississippi, however, things went badly awry. The men discovered they were unable to steer their homemade craft properly, but neither could they get to shore to tie them up. Finally, the boats were lashed together so as to protect the investment of barrel staves, but when they reached a treacherous part of the river called "the Devil's Elbow," the boats struck some sawyers (uprooted trees sunk below the water's surface) and the boat

Davy was on capsized. He was rescued by his companions—stark naked and nearly skinned alive because he'd been hauled so forcefully through a hole in the side of the boat that it peeled his clothes right off, along with a few layers of skin.

The barrel-stave misfortune caused Davy problems with his creditors. As was his custom in times of such stress, he took to the woods again, and in the spring of 1826 he reported that he'd taken another forty-seven bears. Other matters also kept him busy: he was placed on a committee charged with trailblazing a road from "the town of Trenton to [the] Weakley County line in a direction to Dresden," served on a jury, and soon was urged to run again for Congress.

His opponents were strong ones: Alexander, who'd won the election two years earlier; Colonel Arnold, an officer in the militia and also a lawyer; and a man named Dyer. With a loan of $250 from M. B. Winchester, in whose home he recovered after the barrel-stave accident, Davy decided to run for office again. This time he won by a substantial margin. On December 17, 1827, the gentleman from the cane arrived in Washington, D.C.; he was about to step onto the national stage.

He arrived in the city a sick man; he'd had a recurrence of what probably was malaria and had undergone a common treatment of the day, bloodletting, which left him very weak. One of Crockett's first endeavors as a national congressman was his work on the Tennessee Vacant Land Bill. It proposed to relinquish all vacant federal lands in Tennessee, with the provision that they be sold and the money used for schools. Davy's interest was not so much in education as it was in the stipulation that such lands ought to be sold at reasonable prices to the poor settlers of Tennessee. It became obvious, however, that the state of Tennessee was interested in selling such lands for *as much* as possible, rather than for as little as possible.

The rich of the nation require little legislation to help them increase *their* worth, Davy noted, but "we should, at least occasionally, legislate for the poor." Crockett believed himself to be one of those for whom he fought: "hardy sons of the soil; men who had entered the country when it lay in cane, and opened in the wilderness a home for their wives and children."

Crockett's efforts, however, went against the wishes of the party machine, best personified by James K. Polk, destined to become the eleventh U.S. president, who accused Crockett of betrayal and declared that "our man Crockett . . . [has] associated himself with our political enemies." As he battled for his constituency, Crockett (with the aid of an assistant to help him with his grammar) explained what he was attempting to do:

> I shall yet have the . . . pleasure of seeing you by firesides which you can safely call your own. You know that I am a poor man; and that I am a plain man. I have served you long enough in peace. . . . I have fought with you and for you in war. . . . I hope that you will not forsake me to gratify those who are my enemies and yours.

The wrangling over the land-use bill was intense and left Crockett on one side of the fence, and Polk and Andrew Jackson—now the seventh president of the United States—on the other. The bill itself was talked to death, tabled indefinitely, and never passed during Crockett's lifetime. It was his oldest son, John Wesley, who saw it passed in 1841, when he followed in his father's footsteps and was elected to Congress himself.

Crockett also opposed such things as the establishment of a military college at West Point (he believed it was elitist) and of pensions for Revolutionary War veterans. Again, his opposition made him unpopular with many of his colleagues. His stand on the Indian rights issue was a curious one: he seems to

have been in favor of Indians' rights, yet his backwoods attitude toward them was one of hostility, no doubt due to the fact that his grandparents had been victims of a massacre. The Indian removal bill was aimed at forcing the Indians to live west of the Mississippi—that is, to vacate their lands so that whites could take possession of them. Crockett's opposition to this bill seems to have been designed both to enhance his image in the eyes of an eastern audience and to reinforce his reputation as an anti-Jackson man.

In spite of his growing political reputation, Davy's financial situation did not improve. His one great asset—his famous sense of humor—became frayed. After the failure of his land bill, Davy seems to have become bitter, a condition not improved when he was defeated for reelection in 1831.

In December 1833, a play titled *The Lion of the West*, written by James Kirke Paulding, was produced in Washington, D.C. Whether the main character, Nimrod Wildfire, was based on Crockett is a matter of debate, but the similarities between the two were compelling: both had the title of colonel, both were westerners, and both were running for reelection.

Davy's final campaign was preceded by the publication of *A Narrative of the Life of David Crockett of the State of*

Tennessee, published in Philadelphia by E. L. Carey and A. Hart in 1834, and written with the help of Thomas Chilton, congressman from Kentucky. A book tour took Davy to the the East, where he met such notables as Daniel Webster. His appetite for reentry into politics was whetted, and he looked forward to returning to Congress, but was defeated by 230 votes.

In July 1835, Crockett told his publishers that "if I don't beat my competitor I will go to texes [Texas]." Four months later, he wrote to his brother that he was "on the eve of Starting to Texes—on to morrow morning mySelf Abner Burgin and Lindsy K Tinkle and our nephew William Patton . . . will go through Arkinsaw and I want to explore the Texes well before I return."

Although he has often been portrayed as a passionate advocate of Texan independence, it seems clear that Davy Crockett did not go there to fight for that cause. Rather, he went to explore the country, to scout the possibility of one final move to yet another new frontier. Throughout his life his eyes had been turned to the west, and so they were at the end.

Crockett left Tennessee on November 1, 1835, with three relatives and a neighbor. The group traveled down the Mississippi to the mouth of the Arkansas River, then on to Little Rock. They set out overland, following a route that conforms more or less to present-day Highway 67. Before long, Abner Burgin and Lindsey Tinkle turned back for home.

Davy's last surviving letter testifies to his intentions: "I expect in all probability to settle on the Border . . . that I have no doubt is the richest country in the world. Good land and plenty of timber and the best springs . . . good range, clear water . . . and game aplenty . . . .I would be glad to see every friend I have settled thare."

The sting of the election defeat a few months earlier no doubt had faded, and Crockett must have been buoyed up to be in such a country, to be hunting and adventuring as he had done most of his life. In addition, his name was well known, and as he wrote to his daughter Margaret and her husband, Wiley Flowers, "I have been received by everyone with open cerimony of friendship."

Almost as an aside, he also mentioned that he had volunteered for the Texas militia and would soon set out for San Antonio. Davy was shrewd enough to realize that if he intended to make this country his new home—already home to more than twenty thousand Americans—service in the militia would be essential if he wanted to run for political office again. As always, his eco-

The Alamo, San Antonio, Texas. THE DAUGHTERS OF THE REPUBLIC OF TEXAS LIBRARY. PHOTOGRAPH BY HARVEY PATTESON.

nomic situation was on his mind, for he added, "I am in hopes of making a fortune yet for myself and my family, bad as my prospect has been."

The push for statehood in Texas had been accelerating for some time, which deepened tensions between the American settlers and the Mexican rulers of the area. The U.S. government made efforts to purchase the territory from Mexico, but all offers had been rebuffed.

Davy Crockett arrived in San Antonio in February 1836, and proceeded to the Alamo, an abandoned mission within the city, founded by Franciscan priests in 1718. There, Lieutenant Colonel William Barrett Travis, along with 187 Americans, was determined to hold off the forces of the Mexican army under the command of General Antonio López de Santa Anna. Sam Houston, commander in chief of the Texas Military Forces, sent Jim Bowie to the fort with instructions to the rebels to destroy it, then to rejoin him. Travis refused to acknowledge the order and resolved to remain where he was. Bowie supported that decision.

When a message finally was delivered to Houston requesting reinforcements for those besieged at the Alamo—Davy Crockett and Jim Bowie now among them—he went to their aid, only to discover that after a thirteen-day standoff, Santa Anna's army of five thousand troops had destroyed the fort on March 6, 1836, killing all military personnel within its walls. Bowie, ill with typhoid fever, had been shot where he lay on his sickbed.

Generations of Americans have believed that Davy Crockett was the last of the defenders of the Alamo to die, that he went down with his favorite rifle, Sweet Betsy, blazing away. According to the diary of Lieutenant José Enrique de la Peña, however, Crockett was one of a half dozen survivors at 6 A.M. on the morning the Alamo was overrun. The men were delivered to Santa Anna by General Castrillon, who made a plea that their lives be spared. Santa Anna was in no mood to be forgiving; the survivors—fifty-year-old David Crockett among them—were executed immediately.

There were many times during his life when David Crockett felt that fame and fortune had eluded him. So they had. It was in death that both were showered upon him in measure that would have astonished him. No early American has had more books written about him, more songs sung about him, more movies made about him. A long-running TV series made his name known to schoolchildren not only in America, but all over the world. The fact that his name had been changed to Davy might have made David Crockett smile.

George Armstrong Custer

1839–76 Military man and Indian fighter. Graduate of West Point; served with distinction in the Civil War. Flamboyance and daring caused his downfall on the western plains, making his name one of the most controversial in American history.

His family called him Armstrong, a name that was a mouthful for the tad with bright blue eyes and reddish gold curls, so he called himself "Autie." Soon everyone else did too.

He was born on December 5, 1839, in the small town of New Rumley, Ohio. Each of his parents had been widowed; his father, Emmanuel, a blacksmith of German ancestry, brought three children to his new marriage to Scotch-Irish Maria Kirkpatrick, the mother of two. Together, they added seven more, but their first two babies died; Autie, their third child, survived, which made him special in his parents' eyes. Eventually, Nevin, Tom, Boston, and Margaret joined the cheerful, boisterous Custer household.

At age four, Autie attended militia meetings with his father. He learned to present arms perfectly, causing his papa to laugh and call him "a born soldier." It would be the first of many times the expression was used to describe Autie. When he was ten, the boy went to live with his older half sister, Lydia Ann, who had married and moved to Monroe, Michigan, twenty-five miles north of Toledo. Each summer he went home to help on the farm, however, where hard work shaped him into a strong, energetic, well-built youth who never seemed to tire.

Autie attended McNeely Normal School at Hopedale, Ohio, and in 1856, at age seventeen, began teaching school himself. Noting his blue eyes and curly, red-gold hair, one of his students, Sarah

McFarland, observed "what a pretty girl he would have made."

During the late 1850s, rumors of war between those who believed in slavery and those who did not rumbled across the United States. Young schoolmaster Custer came from a proslavery family, and he believed it was Northern fanatics who were the cause of such agitation. Mostly, however, his interests were in his own immediate welfare: he wished to further his education but had no money to do so. When a friend informed him that an appointment to the U.S. Military Academy at West Point would not only give him an education but also pay him twenty-eight dollars a month, Autie's interest was piqued. He petitioned his local congressman for an appointment to the Academy, and he got one in June 1857.

From the start, the young cadet was remarkable—but, alas, not at academics. He accumulated demerits with unseemly speed and often was within ten points of being dismissed. Nevertheless, his fine physique, strength, and boundless energy made him outstanding in horsemanship and swordsmanship, and since he was good-natured and fun-loving, he was popular with fellow cadets. One of them noted, however, that Custer was "too clever for his own good . . . [He is] always connected with all the mischief that is going on, and never studies anymore than he can possibly help."

Once, when he realized he was about to fail an exam, Custer broke into an instructor's office and stole the questions to be asked, an incident that seems to indicate the lengths to which he'd go to get himself out of a scrape—and his good fortune at not getting caught. Perhaps that was the beginning of what came to be called "Custer's luck."

When the Civil War commenced in April 1861, Custer didn't cling to his family's proslavery views. He wrote to Lydia Ann that "in case of war, I shall serve my country according to the oath I took" on admission to the Academy. Therefore, on June 24, 1861, graduating at the very bottom of his class—thirty-fourth in a class of thirty-four—twenty-one-year-old Cadet Custer became a second lieutenant in the U.S. Cavalry.

Custer's first appointment was as aide-de-camp to General George B. McClellan. Custer was the eyes and ears for McClellan in the victory at Antietam, Maryland, in September 1862. McClellan later described Custer as "a reckless, gallant boy, undeterred by fatigue, unconscious of fear. . . . He always brought me clear reports of what he saw. I became much attached to him."

After Lincoln removed McClellan from his command, however, Custer went home to Monroe, Michigan, to

Mathew Brady's photograph of General George A. Custer. CORBIS-BETTMANN.

await his next assignment. He was still a lover of good times and pretty girls, and he cut a dashing figure wherever he went. At one party he was formally introduced to Elizabeth Bacon—Libbie to her friends—whom he'd known slightly when they both were schoolchildren. The only daughter of Judge Daniel S. Bacon, one of the town's leading citizens, Libbie was two years younger than Custer, well educated, beautiful, and sought after by others. She remembered that his nickname was Autie, and was immediately smitten.

In April 1863, Custer was assigned to Brigadier General Alfred Pleasonton's staff, where he earned the rank of captain. Pleasonton was impressed by Custer's fearlessness in battle and his ability to inspire others to follow him. Pleasonton requested that Custer be promoted—and to everyone's astonishment, he was advanced four grades. At age twenty-three, he was the youngest brigadier general in the Union army and found himself in charge of the Michigan Cavalry.

At Cemetery Ridge in the Battle of Gettysburg on July 3, 1863, Custer faced the Confederate legend Jeb Stuart, who for two years had bested all Yankee cavalry sent against him. Under Custer's command, federal cavalry repulsed Stuart for the first time; the rebels were driven back by the dashing young man who rallied his Michigan company forward with the exuberant cry, "Come on, you Wolverines!"

By this time, Custer was already known for his flamboyant style of dress. He wore a black velveteen jacket decorated with double rows of brass buttons and gold braid from cuff to elbow. His trousers likewise were decorated with rows of gold braid; a red scarf was looped around his neck. Someone remarked that he looked "like a circus rider gone mad." His red-gold hair, still wavy, fell to his shoulders, and a full mustache covered a chin that a few unkind observers described as weak. He was prone to sunburn easily, which often gave his cheeks a flushed, fevered look. He even devised a personal flag: crossed white swords on a blue-and-red background. Eastern newspapers gladly took note of him and dubbed him "the Boy General."

In September 1863, Custer was wounded slightly in the leg and was sent home to Michigan for fifteen days, where his attraction to Libbie Bacon was rekindled. On February 9, 1864, although Libbie expressed concerns about his gambling habits and lack of religious devotion, they were married at the First Presbyterian Church in Monroe. After their honeymoon, Libbie began a practice that lasted most of their lives: she went with her husband on his military assignments whenever possible. When they were separated, letters became their lifeline; the ones that have survived indicate their intense devotion to each other.

In the spring of 1864, General Philip H. Sheridan took command of the Union cavalry. Custer had been stunned by the sudden departure of his second mentor, Pleasonton, in the spring of 1864, but recognized in his replacement a man he could admire. General Philip H. Sheridan was a scrappy thirty-three-year-old Irishman as bold and energetic as he was himself.

Jeb Stuart, the Confederates' idol, was killed when Custer's Wolverines won the Battle of the Yellow Tavern in Richmond, Virginia. Then, in a daring attack against Lieutenant General Jubal A. Early, Custer and five hundred Wolverines rolled over an entire Confederate infantry brigade, capturing seven hundred rebels and fifty-two officers, a feat that earned Custer the command of the Third Division. Following the battle at Cedar Creek, Custer got a second star. Not long after, Custer's brother, Thomas, nineteen years old, became his aide-de-camp.

Custer was victorious in the Shenandoah campaign in the spring of 1865, then in the battles of Didwiddie Court House and Five Forks, and yet again at Sayler's Creek on April 6. When Custer learned that a train loaded with ammunition and rations awaited General Robert E. Lee at Appomattox, he seized it before it could do Lee any good. Then, at daybreak on April 9, 1865, a lone horseman approached twenty-five-year-old Custer, presented a linen towel tied to a pole, and informed him that General Robert E. Lee wished to surrender to General Ulysses S. Grant. After four bloody years, the Civil War had come to an end.

Men who fought in the Civil War with Custer described him as "brave as a lion, fought as few men fought . . . was brave, alert, and untiring . . . [he] commanded in person . . . a born soldier." He led those men—who now wore red scarves around their necks just like their commander—down Pennsylvania Avenue past the White House on May 23, 1865, to the cheers of enthusiastic crowds.

But peace didn't nourish Custer's spirit as war had. Fortunately, Sheridan called on him to round up ragtag Confederate forces in Texas. The problem was that the Union troops under Custer's command wanted to be going home, not to Texas. They were unruly, deserting in large numbers, and to keep his men in line, Custer resorted to punishment. He threatened to put a sergeant who had fought bravely for the Union in front of a firing squad, a decision that nearly started a riot.

Such behavior on Custer's part did not create high morale, and the Boy General found himself hated rather than admired by his subordinates.

Yet Custer wasn't totally unhappy in Texas. Libbie was at his side, brother Tom still served on his staff, and he even got his father appointed as the forage agent for his division. When the Texas appointment was finished, Custer explored career opportunities in New York, intending to turn his Civil War fame into riches in either mining or railroading. He confided to Libbie, "I long to become wealthy, not for the wealth alone but for the power it brings."

When Libbie's father died suddenly, the couple returned to Michigan, where Custer considered running for political office. He learned that politics could be as fierce as warfare but concluded it was not congenial to his nature. When the U.S. War Department, at Sheridan's recommendation, offered Custer an appointment to head a new regiment, the Seventh Cavalry, he accepted with great relief.

At the end of the war, Congress had decreed that henceforth the U.S. Army would have three missions: to reconstruct the South, to protect the western frontier, and to defend the seacoasts. Westward expansion was proceeding apace, and one of the tasks of the army would be to deal with Plains Indians such as the Sioux, Cheyennes, Arapahos, Kiowas, and Comanches, who threatened the safety of white settlers. Custer and the Seventh Cavalry were ordered to Fort Riley, Kansas, and charged with protecting farming settlements in the area, as well as travelers headed down the Santa Fe Trail or out the Smoky Hill Trail to Denver. All the Indians in this area were superb warriors who had resisted invasions by the whites before. They were to prove themselves more frustrating adversaries than any Custer had yet encountered.

In October 1866, Custer, Libbie at his side, took up life at Fort Riley. Tom Custer was there too. The Seventh Cavalry itself was made up of regulars and volunteers, varying widely in age and experience, but most with little experience as Indian fighters. It was not a crack regiment by any means. Many men drank heavily and, as in Texas, deserted regularly, some drawn away by tales of gold in the Rocky Mountains.

Again, Custer—who had been admired by men in his Civil War commands—found himself as disliked on the plains as he'd been in Texas. Captain Frederick Benteen, a capable but sullen officer, detested young Custer more than most. Custer, always an optimist, told Libbie things would get better as soon as the men "had all faced death together, where the truest affection was formed among soldiers." However, the antagonism among the men in the Seventh Calvalry only deepened.

Custer's introduction to plains warfare was swift. In December 1866, the Sioux under Red Cloud and Crazy Horse attacked Fort Phil Kearny, killing Captain William J. Fetterman and his entire command of eighty men. Hunting down the culprits was no easy task, and although Custer wasn't accustomed to failure, he was given the slip time after time by the Sioux and Cheyenne warriors.

For the first time in his life, Custer's usually buoyant spirits deserted him. His depression expressed itself in cruel, thoughtless acts against his own men. Desertion became an even more serious problem; after Custer ordered a forced march, thirty or forty deserted. Enraged when he saw one group of men ride off in full view, Custer ordered, "Stop those men. Shoot them where you find them. Don't bring in any alive." Fortunately for all, the order wasn't carried out.

Custer was at Fort Wallace when cholera broke out at Fort Riley, and when he received a letter from Libbie expressing fears about her welfare, he felt compelled to rush to her side. But Fort Wallace was three hundred miles to the east; he would have to travel through dangerous Indian country—and that's precisely what he did. Shortly after

his arrival, he was arrested and charged with abandoning his post without permission, of ordering deserters shot, and of taking his troops on forced marches. On November 18, General Sheridan announced that Custer was suspended from duty and would forfeit full pay for a year. So ended the Boy General's first Indian campaign.

It is difficult to explain how the brilliant soldier of the Civil War so quickly became a troubled leader on the western plains. Part of the reason was the war itself; plains warfare was not at all like the war between the states. The Indians were not the Confederates: Indians vanished like ghosts across the treeless wastes or appeared unexpectedly out of nowhere. Added to that was the interminable boredom of plains life in dry, dusty outposts. There were no cheering crowds, no adoring troops. The weather itself was an enemy—bitterly cold in winter, blisteringly hot in summer. The effect of the whole experience was to plunge Custer into what in modern times would be called an identity crisis.

During the enforced idleness of his court-martial, Custer began to write his memoirs. Meanwhile, General Sherman, who had been appointed the commander of all western cavalry divisions and was notorious for his "scorched earth" policy against the Confederacy during the Civil War, had come to some harsh conclusions about the Indian problem on the western plains. "The more I see of these Indians the more I am convinced that they will all have to be killed," he said, and he became determined to apply his opinion to the Indian problem and bring it to its final conclusion.

Sherman realized that someone with mettle was needed to help him do so, and he telegraphed a terse request to Custer: "Can you come at once?" Custer wired back that he would be on the next train—and so he was, accompanied by his two Scotch deerhounds, Blucher and Maida. As flamboyant as ever, he also ordered Libbie to follow him as quickly as possible.

At dawn on November 27, 1868, Custer and his troops fell upon the Cheyenne camp of peaceful Chief Black Kettle along the Washita River in present-day Oklahoma; in the massacre that followed, both Black Kettle and his wife were killed, along with more than a hundred others, including many children. Custer believed the victory at Washita would help him regain his image, but in the long run the reverse occurred. He had abandoned one of his officers on the field, and Captain Benteen, who had disliked Custer from their first meeting, now despised him even more. In addition to abandoning Major Elliott to his fate, Custer did

something else at Washita that went against conventional military wisdom: he attacked an enemy of unknown strength in a terrain with which he was not familiar. At Washita, Custer's luck held; when he repeated the error eight years later, the outcome would be quite different. For the moment, however, Custer's ego was soothed, and he traded his blue-and-gold Civil War costume for the fringed buckskin outfit of a true plainsman.

Early in his career, Custer had focused his attentions on money, and that interest hadn't been forgotten. He was anxious to enjoy the lifestyle of men he'd met on his trips to New York, and in 1871, he became involved in a mining scheme near Georgetown, Colorado, regarding it as a "steppingstone to larger and more profitable undertakings." The scheme collapsed, and no fortune was ever made.

To supplement his income, Custer then began to write articles for fashionable magazines, and the first of a series appeared in 1872 in *Galaxy*. In 1874, the articles were published as a book, *My Life on the Plains*, which served to enhance his fame with the general public.

In the summer of 1872, the task of the Seventh Cavalry was the protection of railroad survey crews headed west into Montana. The expedition was something of a lark for Custer, who each day led a detail of twenty-five men out to obtain antelope, deer, or elk to provide fresh meat for the surveyors. When they neared the Yellowstone country, a favorite hunting site of Sitting Bull's band of Sioux, Custer was warned by his Indian scouts to be on the lookout for trouble. Trouble came, but although Custer was outnumbered, he won the skirmish handily. Afterward, Custer discovered that the *New York Tribune* had published his official military report, calling him "a Glorious Boy." It was exactly the sort of praise he craved.

Military life allowed for fun even beyond hunting expeditions. In 1872, Custer played host, along with Buffalo Bill Cody, to the grand duke Alexis of Russia, who was touring America. The young duke, only twenty-two years old, was an avid hunter, and Custer showed him the time of his life.

There is no doubt that Custer came to sincerely love the western plains. As he proceeded toward the Yellowstone, he wrote to Libbie, "No artist could fairly represent the wonderful country we passed over." One of Custer's fellow officers, however, Major General David Stanley, wasn't watching the countryside: he was watching Custer. "I have seen enough of him to convince me that he is a cold-blooded, untruthful and unprincipled man," he wrote. Stanley also complained that the mission was held

up each morning due to the time it took to pack up all Custer's relatives, his servants, and the cages of canaries and mockingbirds he'd brought with him.

On July 2, 1874, Custer led an expedition of a thousand men accompanied by two thousand horses and mules out of Fort Lincoln and headed for the Pa Sapa, the Black Hills, to document the presence of gold there. To guarantee the right sort of publicity, Custer included a young naturalist, George Bird Grinnell, in his party, along with four newspapermen. The first glint of gold was found on July 30, and Custer wrote enthusiastically about the Black Hills: "There are unlimited supplies of timber. . . . I know of no portion of our country where nature has done so much to prepare homes for husbandmen [farmers]."

There was a thorny problem with this wonderful discovery, however. Custer and his troops had trespassed on land that had been set aside as the Great Sioux Reservation in the Fort Laramie treaty of 1868. Custer himself admitted "the Indians have a new name for me"— *thief*—and the Sioux named the road he'd taken into the Black Hills "the Thieves' Road." Custer was undaunted, and ignoring the deep spiritual regard the Indians had for the Pa Sapa, he informed the U.S. War Department in September that "Indians . . . neither occupy nor make use of the Black Hills," and therefore the area ought to be thrown open to settlement by whites. "I shall recommend extinguishment of Indian title at the earliest moment practicable for military reasons," he wrote.

In 1875, pressure was put on the Sioux to sell the Black Hills to the government. When they refused, President Grant declared war against them and ordered all hostile Indians to report to government agencies no later than January 31, 1876, in order to make the country safe for incoming white miners and settlers. Some Indians complied, but not the famous Sitting Bull or the mysterious, never-photographed Crazy Horse.

Not all of Custer's concerns at this time were on the plains. He had accused the secretary of war, William Belknap, of profiting from trade deals with the Indian agencies. Such accusations caused President Grant great embarrassment; Custer was placed under arrest and was informed he would not be able to participate in the planned military maneuvers against the Sioux. Knowing that he was the darling of newspapermen, Custer took his cause directly to them. Ultimately, Grant relented, and the thirty-seven-year-old Custer commenced what turned out to be his last military campaign.

The Seventh Cavalry left Fort Lincoln in May 1876 with the aim of bringing in any Indians who remained hostile,

mainly the followers of Sitting Bull and Crazy Horse. In mid-June, General Crook's forces were surprised by the Sioux and Cheyennes along Rosebud Creek. Caught off guard, Crook was forced to retreat and was unable to get a message through Indian country to Custer regarding the surprising force of the Indian encampment.

Custer estimated the Indian strength at about eight hundred warriors; in fact, more than three thousand warriors had gathered along the Little Bighorn River in eastern Montana. Based on his own estimates, however, Custer was confident his Seventh Cavalry, over six hundred strong, was more than a match for whatever lay ahead. On June 22, Custer marched up the Rosebud and two days later the cavalry came across an Indian trail that was a mile wide, the ground so scarred by travois poles that it looked as if it had been turned with a plow. Custer ordered a night march, and in the morning scouts brought back an amazing report: the valley ahead was white with the lodges of more Indians than the cavalry's Crow scout, Bloody Knife, had ever seen before. Bloody Knife was alarmed, and he warned Custer to be very careful.

When a report came soon afterward that the Indians appeared to be getting ready to move on, Custer decided he had only one choice: he would have to

In 1899 Edgar S. Paxson painted this version of Custer's Last Stand. BUFFALO BILL HISTORICAL CENTER, CODY, WYOMING.

attack a day earlier than he'd planned. He ordered each cavalryman to pack one hundred pounds of ammunition and prepare for battle, then split his command into three units: Captain Benteen took three cavalry companies, Major Reno took two, and Custer himself kept five, or approximately 225 men.

The Little Bighorn varied from ten to forty feet wide and was seldom more than five feet deep at any point. On the hot, windless afternoon of June 25, 1876, Indian children were swimming and playing on its banks while their mothers worked nearby. The scene seemed peaceful, but the Indian chiefs—Sitting Bull and Crazy Horse of the Sioux, and Gall of the Cheyennes— were fully aware of Custer's approach.

Custer circled around the camp with the idea of coming upon the Indians from the north, intending to prevent any escape; Benteen and Reno went to the south. From the bluffs, Custer caught sight of what he thought was the far end of the camp. He confidently called out to his men, "We've caught them napping," and prepared to attack. But Custer's men were tired; their horses were weary after their long night march. By comparison, the Sioux and Cheyennes were rested and their horses were fresh.

Custer started down Medicine Trail Coulee but found his path blocked by Chief Gall of the Cheyennes, who had allied himself with the Sioux. Too late, Custer realized he had come upon the center of the camp, not its farthest end. He retreated to the high ground, believing that Reno and Benteen would soon come along to help him. Unknown to him, both Reno and Benteen had been caught in an Indian trap and were unable to come to his aid. Then, as Custer and his men proceeded up the slope toward the top of the bluff, Crazy Horse and a thousand Sioux warriors appeared at its crest. The expression "The rest is history" is trite, yet it painfully describes what followed.

Custer's men were sandwiched between Gall's warriors below and Crazy Horse's above. The battle lasted less than an hour—some military scholars have estimated perhaps only twenty minutes. Custer and all his men were killed, including Custer's brother Tom, his brother-in-law, and a nephew. Young Mark Kellogg, the newspaperman who was to have reported Custer's greatest victory, also perished. Custer's luck had finally run out on a sun-baked hillside in eastern Montana, in the same year that America celebrated its hundredth birthday.

Members of the Seventh Cavalry were buried more or less where they'd fallen, but Custer was later reburied at West Point on October 10, 1877, with full military honors. Custer's beloved Libbie never remarried; she lived for fifty-seven years after the death of the young man she had always called Autie, tirelessly defending his name and honor against any and all critics.

John Deere

1804–86 Blacksmith, inventor, manufacturer. When he observed that the iron-and-wood plows farmers brought to the West were not suited to tough prairie soil, he crafted a steel share out of an old sawmill blade. Twenty years later, he was making ten thousand plows a year and had changed American agriculture.

When anyone in the farm industry refers to a "John Deere," it is a machine, not a man, that is brought to mind—a grass-green machine that bears on it the logo of a leaping deer beside the inventor's name emblazoned in sun yellow. The machine and the name have traveled to every corner of the globe; yet, unlike biographers of famous American inventors such as Thomas Edison, those writing of John Deere have to dig deep to uncover the origins of the man who played a major role in revolutionizing world agriculture.

Early members of the Deere family preserved few records, but according to a privately printed family history, William Deere was born in England, where the name can be traced as far back as 1617. There had been a William de Deer in Somersetshire as early as 1327, and before that the names Robert and Dalph le Dere were recorded at Oxfordshire in 1273.

William Deere, a tailor, arrived in the New World about 1790, most likely going first to Canada, then traveling south into Vermont. It isn't known when or where he met and married Sarah "Sally" Yates, the daughter of British captain James Yates, who, when England lost the Revolution, pledged his allegiance to the new country.

The first documented evidence of William's presence in the United States was in 1800, when his name appeared on the census records of Vermont. Also listed were a wife, two sons, and a daughter, the children being under ten years of age. The Deere family Bible records that a fourth child, John, was born on February 7, 1804, in Rutland, Vermont, close to the eastern edge of New York State. The year was auspicious for something else: Thomas Jefferson had been elected the third president of the United States and would be responsible for sending Lewis and Clark on their momentous expedition the following year, the success of which would mark the opening of the West for a flood of land-hungry settlers. The energies of the Deeres' new son and of those settlers would one day converge.

Early Americans moved often, and William must have cast about for a place where his prospects would be better than they were in Rutland. Nearby Middlebury, a village of about 1,200 souls, had become an important stagecoach center and also boasted of sawmills, grist (flour) mills, cider presses, a carriage factory, and manufacturers of machines to card wool. A local craftsman named Calvin Elmer advertised his "fashionable mahogany and cherry sideboards," as well as desks, tables, and bedsteads. Epaphras Miller ran a tannery and sold his goods "for cash or exchanged for rawhides." Eben Judd had a marble-cutting factory, and blacksmith shops had sprung up to build or repair all types of iron goods.

What better place for a man to settle if he wanted to improve his tailoring business? The Deeres moved to Middlebury, where William opened a shop, as documented by an advertisement in the *Middlebury Mercury* on April 14, 1806: "The subscriber respectfully informs the inhabitants of . . . the vicinity that he has commenced in the tailoring Business . . . over M. Henshaw's Store, at the west end of the Bridge."

Citizens of Middlebury had been dissatisfied with "common schools" and had established a grammar school in 1797, then pressed the state legislature to establish a college as well. In 1800, Middlebury College was born. Nor was women's education neglected: a Miss Ida Strong started a ladies' academy at the courthouse. All of this was a boon for a tailor because the presence of professional people meant there would be a need for "fine" garments, rather than common work clothes. Indeed, William became so busy that he advertised for an assistant; such an employee was not easy to come by, however, and he continued to work alone.

Mr. Deere was so deluged with orders that he had no time to teach the trade to his oldest son, twelve-year-old William junior. As a result, the boy was apprenticed to a cabinetmaker, Hastings Warren, and went to live in the gentleman's home. In spite of the fact that the

An 1855 model of John Deere's steel plow. JOHN DEERE COMPANY.

tailoring business was good, it was often hard to collect payment from customers, and in two years William senior had acquired debts that he was unable to pay. When he got word that a cousin back home had died and left him a small inheritance, William decided to return to England. In a letter dated June 26, 1808, the elder Deere explained to his namesake that he intended to "obtain means of paying my Debts & making our family Comfortable." He also advised young William to "be Dutifull to your mother [and] Kind to your Sister & Brothers. . . . May God bless you & all the family . . . your father and friend, W R Deere."

John was only four years old when his father left, and it was the last anyone ever saw of William Deere, Sr. The family believed he had arrived safely in England but was lost at sea on the return voyage. Atlantic crossings were indeed hazardous in those days, and ships went down regularly, but records kept by the Bostom customs house of persons who perished at sea have since been destroyed. It is possible—inasmuch as he was burdened with debt and might have been unable to acquire the money he'd gone to England to collect—that a disheartened William Deere chose simply to lose himself in the teeming population of a city like London or Liverpool.

In any case, his absence from Middlebury was confirmed in the census of 1810, when Sally Deere was listed as the head of the household, with three children: John, George, and Elizabeth. Francis, about eleven, wasn't mentioned; perhaps he had been apprenticed like his older brother. Sally Deere's name also turned up on a list of new members of the Congregational church in Middlebury. Mrs. Deere continued the tailoring business that her husband had started, advertising in May 1816 that she was "happy to serve her old customers and the public on short notice."

William didn't remain as Mr. Warren's apprentice but returned home to help his mother. It isn't clear how he acquired enough education to become a schoolteacher, but in 1821 he advertised a new school for "Young Ladies and Gentlemen." Competition in that field was fierce, however, and the school apparently failed; little else is known about William except that he left the United States and went to Ireland to live.

Becoming an apprentice was a way for any boy or young man to learn how to earn his way in the world, so when John was about eleven, he went to work for Epaphras Miller, the local tanner. One of his jobs was to grind oak leaves and bark into a powder that contained a substance called tannin, which was used to preserve animal skins and gave leather its rich, distinctive color.

By the time Sally moved her tailoring business to a new location, John was old enough to take up the trade that had always interested him much more than tanning hides. In 1821, Captain Benjamin Lawrence, one of the most successful of the seven blacksmiths plying their trade in Middlebury, accepted him as an apprentice. The young man went to live in the captain's home, where he also received lessons in reading, writing, and arithmetic, plus a wage of thirty dollars—per year!

Smithing was an important part of any preindustrial community, and shoeing horses was only one among many jobs that were performed. Pots and pans, as well as door latches and gate hinges, were crafted from scratch by blacksmiths; ironwork on stagecoaches was in constant need of repair; all sorts of farm equipment needed to be made— hay rakes, scythes, and plows as well as smaller items such as shovels, hoes, and pitchforks.

When John finished his apprenticeship in 1825, he hired out to two blacksmiths in separate shops, David Wells and Ira Allen. Having two masters no doubt meant that he kept his nose close to the grindstone. In 1826 his mother died, leaving behind the family's three youngest children. Exactly how much John contributed to his siblings' upbringing isn't known because no records from that time have been preserved.

In spite of his youth, John must have been a diligent employee with a good reputation because within a year, Colonel Ozias Buel asked him to come to Colchester Falls. Buel had purchased thirty acres of land on which he was building a sawmill and a linseed-oil mill; he needed a blacksmith for the whole enterprise. For twenty-three-year-old John, it meant he could establish his own shop, which in turn meant he could propose to the young lady he'd fallen in love with.

Demarius Lamb was the third daughter in a family of six girls; her parents, William and Mary Lamb, had settled in Hancock, Vermont, at about the same time John's parents had come to Rutland. She was a year younger than he, and well educated; family legend says that she had attended Mrs. Emma Willard's School for Young Ladies in Middlebury. Mrs. Willard became the author of the famous hymn "Rocked in the Cradle of the Deep" and also taught another early American girl, Narcissa Prentiss, who became the wife of the Oregon missionary Marcus Whitman.

After their wedding on January 28, 1827, John and Demarius set up housekeeping in the village of Vergennes, north of Middlebury, and a year later their first son, Francis Albert, was born. He was named for John's second oldest brother, who had died a couple of years earlier. The Vermont census of 1830 shows that Deere had moved his family to Leicester, a village of about six hundred. Two other adults, a young man and woman, were listed in the household; were they George and Elizabeth Deere, John's younger brother and sister?

Deere bought a piece of land and built his first shop at a place called the "Four Corners," the crossroads of a stagecoach line that served Middlebury and Leicester, then extended east into New Hampshire. Within three months, he had to sell the land, probably because he needed capital in order to equip the shop. Fate was not kind, however; six months after the shop was completed a fire burned it to the ground. It was rebuilt as quickly as possible, then it burned a second time, putting John deeply in debt.

It was a bad time to be in debt, for his family had just increased by the birth of a second child and first daughter,

Jeannette (sometimes spelled Jennette). It was necessary to make another move, this time to work for someone else, where he'd be guaranteed a regular wage. Deere picked Royalton, Vermont, as his next destination, and again became an "iron monger" engaged mostly in the repair of stagecoaches. In Royalton he made the acquaintance of Amos Bosworth, part-owner of the largest hotel in town, who also was involved in the stagecoach business. Again, the Deeres settled down, and another daughter, Ellen Sarah, was born in 1832.

Royalton was a thriving community, yet migration out of it became steady as more and more folk headed west. However, it was another move within Vermont that took the Deeres out of Royalton; in 1833, they went to Hancock, Demarius's hometown. There, a local resident recalled that Deere made a log chain from discarded scythes that was "a joy to its owners, for after more than fifty years' use it had never broken."

Deere's craftsmanship became well known throughout the area. In fact, he was such a painstaking smith that he spent an unseemly amount of time on some items, thereby reducing his profit. It was said he polished the tines of his hayforks "until they slipped in and out of the hay like needles," and his shovels

and hoes were "like no others that could be bought by reason of their smooth, satiny surface." Although his meticulousness was admirable, John was regarded as "no business man."

In October 1836, Deere was still deeply in debt and a warrant was issued for his arrest; he was ordered to pay what was owed or have his belongings taken in lieu of cash. It was a time in American history when many besides John Deere were having trouble making ends meet. The country's economic climate was stormy, and such troubles weren't confined to Vermont; the worsening national economy was called the "Panic of 1837," and part of Vermont's unique difficulty was a mania that had swept the state: "the sheep craze." There were six sheep for every person in the state, making for 1.5 million animals. The fortunes of all Vermonters soon were tied to sheep, while other forms of agriculture were neglected, which in turn meant that a wide variety of farm tools were no longer as much in demand as they once had been.

The population of Hancock steadily declined, turning from a "steady stream to a freshet, not to say a flood." Words such as the ones penned by a Vermont resident to a friend in far-off Wisconsin illustrated the temper of the time: "I am fully determined to leave. . . . Write me for the best [time] you know of, for I think that I shall go West in the course of this season."

Illinois, in particular, was the subject of much publicity. One emigrant wrote back to declare it was "the Nile of America. I saw corn . . . on the stalks higher than I could reach . . . fifteen and a half feet."

Emigration was roundly criticized by Vermonters who dreaded to see friends and neighbors pull up stakes. One newspaper editor lambasted what he called "Westernism," saying that he hoped President Van Buren would soon take "efficient measures to suppress it." Often, Vermonters emigrated as entire communities. In 1832, the whole town of Benson moved lock, stock, and barrel to Page County, Illinois, and another large group settled a town in Michigan, naming it Vermontville. One of the things that made the emigrating New Englanders different from emigrants to other parts of the West was that they were usually mature folk at the midpoint of their lives—men and women with well-developed farming skills. As one historian noted, "The boy settler and his child bride were rarities."

Given his continuing financial problems, the prospect of moving west must have seemed especially attractive to John Deere. A Vermont emigrant from Illinois wrote home in 1836, "All kinds of trades do well . . . Especially carpenters

[and] blacksmiths." It might have been Amos Bosworth, Deere's old friend from Royalton, who had already made a trip there himself, who gave Deere a final push. In any case, in November 1836, thirty-two-year-old John Deere sold his smithing business to Demarius's father for two hundred dollars and pointed himself west. He left behind his son Francis, eight, the boy's younger sisters, and their mother, who was about to have a fifth child. He took only the tools of his trade and a small amount of cash. He headed for the village Bosworth had told him about, Grand Detour, along the Rock River, a hundred miles west of present-day Chicago.

Americans enjoy celebrating "the olden days," but it's unwise to glamorize such times. A man traveling through Grand Detour in 1839 described what he found: "fifteen or twenty houses, widely scattered over a low & swampy prairie . . . the scene around so gloomy & dull." The meal he sat down to in a tavern was no gourmet delight: "A broken plate of rather dingy bread—about 2 in. square of Molasses Cake—a plate of questionable butter—a few peeled onions—ye Gods, save me from the likes again!"

Another Vermonter, Leonard Andrus, already settled in Grand Detour, had built a sawmill and a grist mill, and had put up a collection of several small cabins for himself and his workers. No doubt Deere was a welcome addition to the budding community, for until he arrived the nearest blacksmith was forty miles away. And there was a job waiting for him the moment he stepped into town: Andrus's sawmill was standing idle because a drive shaft had broken. Within two days Deere had it fixed, and the mill was running again.

Deere's next task was to set up some kind of a shop for himself. One family story tells that his only cash amounted to $73.73—yet he managed to build a small smithy on a piece of rented land. More than a century later, when officers of Deere & Company decided to locate the exact site of that original shop, archaeologists from the University of Illinois used a magnetometer to pick up the general location. Then, with careful excavation, they located scrap iron, burned bricks, and finally the post holes of the original building, thirty by twenty-six feet.

All of Deere's smithing expertise was quickly put to work, and his old habit of polishing the tines of pitchforks established his reputation, just as it had in Vermont. Any time not spent at his forge Deere used to build a small home for his family. It was a story-and-a-half structure, eighteen by twenty-four feet, that was intended to be added on to later. There were two large rooms below, with a steep stairway to a large sleeping loft

above. It was only the second frame home in the village; everyone else lived in crude log cabins. Only two years after Deere's arrival, however, Grand Detour experienced a boom: in addition to Deere's blacksmith shop and the nearby grist mill, it boasted a total of eight frame houses, a tavern, and a country store.

When Demarius arrived, she was accompanied by her sister and her husband, who also intended to emigrate, and there was a new son in the family. A favorite family story tells that just before their entry by wagon into the village, Demarius alighted and walked into Grand Detour with one-year-old Charles in her arms. Her greeting to her husband was, "Here, John, I have carried him all the way from Vermont." No one guessed it at the time, but Charles would prove to be a very special son.

When New Englanders arrived on the plains, they naturally gravitated to places where they could see small patches of woods. They did so for two reasons: they needed wood for building and for fuel, and they believed that stands of oak and maple indicated richer soil. The first was true, the second was not. Soon, settlers would come to understand that for aeons the dense, fibrous roots of the shoulder-high wild grass that covered the prairie had been producing humus of great fertility beneath that flat, seemingly infertile surface. Before tapping into that richness, however, settlers needed to "break" the soil. Critical to that process was plowing under the tall grass which—when it was caressed by the wind—had reminded Indians of a maiden's long, flowing hair.

Midwestern newspapers carried advice on how the task of turning the thick prairie mat into farmland was to be accomplished—the type of equipment that should be used, the best time of year to do the job, how deeply the prairie ought to be plowed. If the area in question contained growths of redroot or willowroot, the task was doubly hard. A writer in the *Prairie Farmer* advised settlers, "Cutting off a plant at the neck is nearly always the most fatal to it," and suggested that shallow plowing was adequate because when the sod was turned over and allowed to dry, the roots would decompose. Instead, it was discovered that the roots did not rot but remained "nearly as strong as when first turned over." Other observers suggested a large plow that would go deep, which required four- to six-hitch ox teams.

Just as important as breaking the prairie in the first place was its cultivation the following season. "Some men expect their lands to work and some men expect *to work their land*—and that is the difference between a good and a bad farmer," one writer remarked,

and he warned that bad beginnings would not bring good endings. Settlers soon discovered the rich, black gumbo soil provided a special challenge: yes, it was so fertile that someone quipped that a farmer "could stick a crowbar down into it at night and it would sprout ten-penny nails by morning"; but it also was so adhesive that it stuck like tar to everything, especially to rough iron plowshares. A farmer learned to carry a special paddle-shaped device so that every few yards he could stop to scrape off the sticky black soil.

Since he was a blacksmith whose business it was to make or repair farm equipment, John Deere probably heard many stories about the problems farmers were having. Then he remembered that when he'd first came to Grand Detour and had repaired the shaft for Andrus's sawmill, he'd chanced to see a broken saw lying nearby. It was made of Sheffield steel, and he had asked if he could have it.

Now, Deere had an idea for how that blade (not a modern circle saw, as some have suggested, but a broad strip of steel with large teeth on one edge that was driven up and down by water power to cut logs into boards) might be converted into a plow that would "scour"—that is, a plow that would not attract the sticky Illinois soil to its surface. The solution would be, John believed, to polish the metal in such a way that it would be inclined to shed the gooey black gumbo in a self-cleaning fashion. Many years later, Deere himself described what he did next:

> I cut the teeth off [the saw] with a hand chisel . . . and heated what little I could at a time, shaped [it] as best I could with the hand hammer . . . finally succeeding in constructing a very rough plow. I set it on a dry-goods box by the side of the shop door. A few days after, a farmer from across the river drove up. Seeing the plow, he asked, "Who made that plow?"
>
> "I did, such as it is, wood work and all."
>
> "Well," said the farmer, "that looks as though it would work. Let me take it home and try it, and if it works all right, I'll keep it and pay you for it. If not I will return it."
>
> "Take it," said I, "and give it a thorough trial."
>
> About two weeks later, the farmer drove up to the shop without the plow, paid for it, and said, "Now get a move on you, and make me two more plows just like the other one."

On the hundredth anniversary of that first plow, one of John Deere's original three plows, owned by the Frierton family near Grand Detour—a plow which had been in continuous service until 1901!—was presented to the Smithsonian Institution. The relic shows how

Deere bent the saw blade into its unique concave configuration.

Deere's plow became so popular that he soon ran out of old saw blades; by 1844, he was ordering steel directly from Pittsburgh, America's steel capital. Previously, fine steel had to be imported from England, but by the mid-1840s technology in the United States had been improved. According to historical documents, "The first slab of cast plow steel ever rolled in the United States was . . . at the steel works of Jones & Quigg [in Pittsburgh] in 1846, and shipped to John Deere."

It was the smoothness of Deere's plows that made them special, and extensive grinding was needed to bring them to a "self-polishing" condition. The type of craftsmanship John Deere had practiced in his early days in Vermont had earned him the reputation of being a "poor business man"; now, ironically, the same craftsmanship would make him hugely successful. His polished steel plows did indeed cut through the tough prairie soil with ease, and so swiftly that the metal made a high-pitched hum, earning John's invention the nickname "the singing plow."

Although Deere is credited with giving agriculture its first steel plow, that's a misconception that should be corrected. Even before John made his first plow from a saw, plow technology had been proceeding right along both in England and in the colonies. In Scotland, wood plows had been replaced by iron as early as 1763, and an American patent on such a device was taken out by Charles Newbold in 1797. American farmers were skeptical, however, believing that metal poisoned the earth and promoted the growth of weeds. When opposition to metal faded, Jethro Wood patented an improved cast-iron plow, and by 1819 was selling four thousand of them each year.

Although Wood's cast-iron plow worked well in the sandy soil along the East Coast, it could not maintain its smooth surface in heavy western soils. John Lane, a blacksmith from Lockport, Illinois, began incorporating steel into his plows in 1831, five years before Deere's invention—and like Deere, he used the steel of a saw blade.

It was Deere, however, who clearly foresaw the commercial value of his invention. By 1839, he'd made 10 plows; then—by his own accounting—he made 40 of them in 1840, 75 in 1841, and 100 in 1842, which did not make him a major manufacturer by any means. A plow-making firm in Pittsburgh was crafting 100 plows daily by that time; when that production was combined with other Pittsburgh manufacturers, 34,000 plows were being made in that city alone. In truth, John Deere was part of a wave of improvement in farming technology.

In early 1840, the best-known plow maker in Illinois was the firm of Jewett-Hitchcock, and John Deere sold Jewett-Hitchcock plows himself. (They might have been among the hundred he claimed to have sold in 1842.) Arguments have existed as to whether Deere was any sort of a genius, and one of his former shop foremen put it succinctly: "I should not call him a man of general inventive ability. The improvements he would make [were] by practice or experimenting, more than creative or inventive." The secret was that Deere never stopped practicing or experimenting.

For tradesmen or other service providers, it wasn't an easy matter to collect payment for what was owed from folk who were struggling to make ends meet themselves, and once again Deere found himself in debt. A sign posted on the Rock River ferry boat summed up the problem all businessmen faced at that time:

> Since man to man is so unjust,
> I do not know what man to trust.
> I've trusted many to my sorrow;
> Pay today, I'll trust tomorrow.

On November 11, 1842, Deere placed a notice in the *Rock River Register:* "All persons indebted to the undersigned will save costs by making immediate payment." Deere needed the money because he was being sued for nonpayment of a debt himself. It isn't known how the case was resolved, for all the records of the U.S. courts from that era were destroyed in the Chicago fire of 1871. In terms of dollars and cents, the debt probably wasn't huge; a sample of one of Deere's bills to a customer gives a reader an idea of what costs were in those days, as well as the kind of work that was done:

PITCH FORK $ 0.92
ONE PLOW 24.00
REPAIRING BRASS KETTLE 1.00
CASING MILL BUCKET 1.75
ONE NEW [HORSE] SHOE 1.13
REPAIRING TWO [HORSE] SHOES 0.62
REPAIRING OF YOKE AND STAPLE 0.50
PIN TO WHEEL TO PLOW 0.25

In March 1843, Deere and Andrus, whose sawmill John had repaired on his arrival in Grand Detour, became partners in the business of blacksmithing and plow making, operating under Andrus's name. By combining their capital, the two men were able to build a two-story factory that was located close enough to the Rock River to harness its power. A large grinding wheel was purchased, about eight or ten men were employed, four hundred plows were produced in their first year of business, and in 1844 a third partner was added to the firm.

John also acquired a salesman: one of Demarius's nephews who had arrived from Vermont. Young Samuel Peek quickly discovered that his uncle expected everyone to hustle as he did himself, and a story from those days illustrated that Deere wasn't the easiest man in the world to work for. One of his employees was carrying plows down the stairs of the factory but wasn't moving quickly enough to suit John, who gave him a shove. The man tumbled down the stairs, could have been badly hurt, and turned on his boss in a fit of temper. Deere ran and hid from him but told his nephew, "Go find him and smooth it over. He is a damned good man, I don't want to lose him."

The year 1848 began in a tragic fashion: Deere's oldest son, Francis Albert, almost twenty, died suddenly of an unexplained illness. Then, almost before he could adjust to his loss, Deere was faced with an important decision. A railroad was being planned for the area but would bypass Grand Detour because the many bends in the Rock River would require too many bridges. John Buford was interested in attracting Deere to nearby Moline, and in May 1848 John dissolved his partnership with Andrus and moved to Moline, where the company is still located today.

Deere went into partnership again, this time with Englishman Robert Tate,

An engraving of John Deere in his later years. CULVER PICTURES, INC.

and a new, larger blacksmith shop was built. Tate noted that on a single day in September 1848, ten plows were made. John Gould, an acquaintance from Grand Detour, was taken in as a third partner to assume the bookkeeping duties that Francis Deere had done until his death.

As early as 1731, an English agriculturist had promoted the idea that seed shouldn't be broadcast by hand but should be planted with some kind of grain drill that would align the plants in straight rows to make later cultivation easier. Deere's first grain drill—nine tubes that would plant a six-foot width—was sold on March 22, 1851, and was an indication that John was already looking far beyond merely making plows.

Two years after the Deere-Tate-Gould partnership fell apart in 1852, Deere took in a new partner. Sixteen-year-old Charles, the son who'd been carried into Grand Detour in his mother's arms, came into the business and remained in it for fifty-four years. Schooling hadn't been much to Charles's taste, and he admitted that he often got into trouble with his stern, demanding father on that score. Yet he'd always enjoyed accompanying his father on trips to test out a new plow, and when he graduated from Bell's Commercial College in Chicago, his father put him to work. Finances had

always been the elder Deere's downfall, and it was Charles who put the company on a sound financial footing for the first time in its history.

By 1856, not quite twenty years after making a single plowshare from an old saw, the Deere company was turning out ten thousand plows a year. In addition to that original "breaking plow," Deere now produced a "stirring" plow, double plows, and shovel plows, not to mention cultivators, seed machines, and harrows. And a new invention was about to come on the scene: a coal-powered steam plow. British inventors had been experimenting with such a device, and in 1858, Joseph Fawkes of Pennsylvania demonstrated his own version, a strange-looking contraption called the "Lancaster." Fawkes and Deere combined their energies and won a gold medal at the Illinois State Fair in 1859.

Deere didn't dominate the farm-implement field by any means, and competition kept the company on its toes. In 1867, when the plow-making firm of Candee-Swan imitated the Deere logo, in addition to referring to their plows as "the Moline plow," a phrase the Deere company had used for many years, young Charles Deere filed a lawsuit. He won on the circuit court level, but when the case was appealed to the Illinois Supreme Court, the Deere company lost and was reprimanded on the ground that the phrase was "only a generic term," to which the Deeres had no exclusive right.

From his early days in Illinois, Deere took an active part in community life and became interested in politics. Even though his state was divided in its loyalties, John was so fiercely pro-Union that he was described in a newspaper article as "that raging abolitionist." Throughout the Civil War, the company did well, but the end of the conflict saw loss of a personal sort for John Deere. Demarius, his wife of nearly forty years and mother of his nine children, died in 1865. On a visit to his home state of Vermont, Deere reacquainted himself with Demarius's spinster sister, Lucenia, and they were married in May 1866.

Following the war, the Order of Patrons of Husbandry was formed to address the problem of declining prices for farm products. Members of the organization called it "the Grange," and referred to themselves as "Grangers." They noted that although prices for their products dropped, cost of farm equipment rose steadily; they came to believe that bankers, railroads, and implement manufacturers were conspiring against them. One particular object of farmers' wrath was the implement salesman, and the solution seemed to be to buy directly from the manufacturer, as had been done earlier in the century. But times had changed; the middleman or salesman (later called a dealer) had become an integral part of all plow makers' market strategy.

In the last half of the century, Deere equipment could be grouped into five categories: walking and wheeled plows; cultivators; harrows; drills and planters; and wagons and buggies. Deere plows won honors at a Paris exhibition in 1867 and took a first prize at the Vienna Exposition in 1873. The trademark insignia of a leaping deer was first used in 1875, and at about that time all Deere equipment was painted a bright green. Steam plowing was tried again in 1889; a Deere steam plow was advertised that could travel 2.5 miles per hour and plow 1.75 acres. The following year, when the bicycle craze hit the United States, even the John Deere Company manufactured three models: the Deere Leader, the Deere Roadster, and the Moline Special.

After his son and son-in-law assumed full control of the company, John Deere had time to enjoy other pursuits—and finally became a farmer himself! He raised registered Jersey cattle and Berkshire hogs and also became the mayor of Moline, often lending money to young businessmen trying to get a start in life, worrying as much about their future as he had about his own many years before.

Despite a trip to California to remedy some health problems, John Deere died on May 17, 1886, at age eighty-two. His funeral was said to have been the largest the city of Moline ever saw, the altar at the church fittingly decorated with a sheaf of grain and a plow made out of flowers. John Deere didn't live long enough to fully appreciate the impact he'd made on the world, but his farm equipment carried his name and the symbol of a leaping deer to all major European industrial nations, as well as to smaller countries throughout Asia, South America, and the Middle East. Not bad for a man Vermonters said made wonderful hayforks but had no head for business.

George Bird Grinnell

1849–1938 Naturalist, ethnologist, author. Graduate of Yale University; at twenty, joined a paleontology expedition to collect fossils from the central plains, Wyoming, and Utah. Naturalist for General Custer's 1874 exploration in the Black Hills; became editor and owner of *Forest and Stream* magazine. Founder of the Audubon Society; responsible for creation of Glacier National Park.

George Bird Grinnell (since his full name is such a mouthful, many biographers refer to him simply as GBG) was born in Brooklyn, New York, on September 20, 1849, the oldest of six children of George Blake Grinnell and the former Helen Lansing. The first Grinnell to arrive in the New World was Matthew, in 1630, a Huguenot from Burgundy, who spelled his name Grennell (sometimes Grenel) and settled in what is now Rhode Island. Both sides of the family were illustrious and had five colonial governors to their credit, as well as Elizabeth Alden, one of the first white children born in New England. Education was a high priority for the Grinnells and Lansings; Grandfather Lansing graduated from Yale in 1804,

the same year Grandfather Grennell entered Dartmouth.

When George was four years old, the family moved from Brooklyn to Manhattan. One of the boy's clearest memories of this period was going for early morning carriage rides with his father. As he recalled in his unpublished memoirs, "as soon as 23rd Street was passed, we were on a dirt road on which the horse could be driven at speed. . . . It must have been just about this time that Central Park was established. . . . It was then a wilderness of rocks and pasture land."

After a year, the family moved again. GBG believed the move was made because "of the children's health," that his father wanted to be farther out in the country, where the communicable diseases of the city were less apt to be a threat. Mr. Grinnell rented a house in Weehawken, New Jersey, from a Mr. Cossett, a wealthy New York merchant. The family stayed only six months, but it was long enough for GBG to have his first riding lesson, including falling from a horse for the first time (which didn't prevent him from later becoming an excellent rider).

In the grassy backyard of the estate, he remembered, "Selim, my father's gentle trotter, used to be turned for exercise. I succeeded one day in persuading the coachman, Amos Hovey, to put me on the animal's back where I sat for a little while. . . . Amos, meantime, had gone off somewhere. . . . After I had become accustomed to my perch, riding seemed so easy that I wanted the horse to move. I managed to reach a twig of a tree, and breaking it off, struck the horse with it. He jumped and I rolled off, and was found . . . between his forelegs, while he investigated me with his nose."

One of the boy's favorite retreats was Grandfather Grinnell's home in Greenfield, Massachusetts. His father's younger brother, Thomas, about twenty, still lived there, and he had a large collection of stuffed birds and animals in a room that was called "the bird room." Among Tom's many specimens was reportedly the last wild turkey killed in Massachusetts in

1849, and the hours young GBG spent with his uncle helped to foster a lifetime of interest in natural history.

When Grinnell was seven, the family moved again, this time to Audubon Park, the thirty-acre estate of the famous painter-naturalist, located in Manhattan between what today are 155th and 158th Streets, and bordered on its western edge by the Hudson River. Again, the family rented a house, this one belonging to another wealthy merchant. (The Audubon estate was home to several other large families.) Then, in 1860, his father bought the old Audubon home itself, where GBG would live for more than fifty years. The acreage was heavily wooded with chestnuts, oaks, and hemlocks; deer and elk roamed at will; there was nothing to be seen of paved streets or other "improvements." Rather, it was a wilderness, where GBG slept out under the stars for the first time; yet it was only a few miles from the hub of the busiest, wealthiest city in America.

One of the most important people in GBG's life during these years was Lucy Audubon, the widow of John James Audubon, familiarly known as "Grandma." When GBG met her, she was snowy haired, kindly, and patient when instructing children, but also "a strict disciplinarian," as he recalled. After her husband's death, she continued to live on the estate in the home of one of her sons, Victor. Victor and his brother John continued their father's work (John was a painter himself), but neither had a head for financial matters, which meant their mother needed to be partly responsible for her own support. With that end in mind, she started a school on the second floor of Victor's house, and it was she who taught GBG the basics of arithmetic.

She taught him something else just as important. Mrs. Audubon was a great believer in self-control, and since the boy had been prepared for such a philosophy by his father's similar attitude, he was equally receptive to Mrs. Audubon's. Much later, when GBG spearheaded conservation efforts in the West—such as hunters voluntarily imposing bag limits on themselves when going out after ducks and geese—they were based on principles he'd learned at Lucy Audubon's knee.

One morning, as the boy approached the Audubon house, he came upon several small birds he'd never seen before. He was determined to catch one and got a crab net from the porch. After he'd captured one of the birds, he hurried upstairs to show Grandma Audubon his prize. She explained to him exactly what it was—a red crossbill—then told him about the bird's origins and life habits, and when they went back downstairs helped him set it free again.

The homes of both Victor and John were treasure troves of interest for a curious lad. Each was filled with all sorts of specimens of animals and birds, books, and many paintings. The picture GBG liked best was one of an eagle and a lamb; he told Grandma Audubon how much he enjoyed it. She promised that it would be his one day. Perhaps he forgot about it, but she never did. After her death in 1874, GBG discovered she had specified in her will that he should have the painting, and ever after it was displayed prominently in his home.

One of young GBG's favorite places at Audubon Park was the loft in a barn behind John Audubon's home. Here too were books stacked in rows, not to mention a variety of bird and animal skins. When he was older, GBG began to read the senior Audubon's descriptions of his travels. The famous painter made his final trip to the West in 1843. He had ascended the Missouri and Yellowstone Rivers and deplored the senseless slaughter of the buffalo by white men, who often took only the tongues of the beasts, then left the carcasses to rot in the sun or to be eaten by wolves and coyotes. The artist noted that "before many years the Buffalo, like the Great Auk, will have disappeared; surely this should not be permitted."

Like other boys in similar circumstances (Francis Parkman and Frederic

A portrait of George Grinnell in early life. STERLING MEMORIAL LIBRARY, YALE UNIVERSITY.

Remington, whose biographies appear in this volume, come to mind), GBG enjoyed the outdoors so much that he treated regular schoolwork casually. When GBG was twelve, his parents enrolled him at the French Institute, housed in a country estate near what is now 170th Street in New York City. They hoped his study habits would improve in this setting. There were about fifty students, many of whom were French, Spanish, or South American and also came from privileged backgrounds. The boys played hard, and for GBG, studying still came second.

After two years, the Grinnells decided a more structured environment was needed. They sent GBG to the Churchill Military School along the Hudson River, near present-day Ossining. GBG didn't record what he might have felt at being away from home for the first time, only that he began school "as a small boy as a private in the rear rank, and finally got to be an officer in command of the company." Before he left home, Grandfather Grennell (who had preserved the original spelling of the family name) gave some advice to his grandson:

"Exercise yourself in contentment. . . . Keep your books & room in good order: file & fold all your papers, letters & compositions. Cultivate strength & clearness of voice & fluency of speech." The old man died at age ninety-one, having lived long enough to be pleased at how well his advice had been heeded.

Fifteen-year-old Grinnell was a student at Churchill when President Lincoln was shot, and his father took him downtown to City Hall, where Lincoln lay in state. Many years later, GBG wrote that he could still "remember the air of gloom that pervaded the whole city . . . the tears which rolled down the faces of women, even of some men. . . . No one old enough to observe can forget that day."

GBG was proficient in all physical activities at school but, as usual, didn't do well in academics. The family made it clear that he must go to Yale, although Grinnell admitted that "I did not in the least want to go, and tried to escape it, but my parents had made up their minds, and I was not in the habit of questioning my father's decisions." First, however, there was a problem to overcome: the boy had done so poorly that he needed extensive tutoring to make up for what he hadn't paid attention to in class, Latin and Greek in particular. GBG spent his sixteenth summer in daily cram sessions, then went with his father to New Haven in the fall, where he took the entrance exams. To everyone's satisfaction, he passed, but was put on provisional status in Greek and geometry.

His freshman year passed quietly, but

the following year he admitted to being "perpetually in trouble." One night he climbed a lightning rod on one of the buildings and painted the class numerals on the face of the campus clock with bright red paint; he was pleased that his prank required the school janitor to spend two days trying to figure a way to climb up and clean it off. GBG went too far, however, when he hazed a freshman student; he was suspended for a year, whereupon his parents sent him to Connecticut and hired yet another tutor.

The Reverend L. R. Payne was easy on GBG, and the two spent happy hours tramping about the Connecticut woods, canoeing, fishing, and exploring, the result of which was that he failed to pass his examinations again. More tutoring was required, and this time GBG was forced to tend to business. His grades improved, and as a reward his parents took him to Europe for a three-month holiday. The family must have breathed a sigh of relief when he finally graduated in 1870. Privately, GBG worried that his diploma might be held up at the last minute; he would have been as surprised as anyone else if he'd been able to see the future: ten years later, he received a Ph.D. from Yale, then an honorary doctor of letters in 1921.

During GBG's senior year, Professor Othniel Marsh, head of Yale's paleontology department (the first such department in any American university), announced that he intended to lead a summer expedition to the West to collect fossils. Marsh had already won fame for having discovered the bones of an extinct species of horse at Antelope Station, Nebraska. As a boy, Grinnell had been fond of stories of travel on the plains, and he later said that as soon as he heard of the proposed expedition he "at last summoned up courage to call Professor Marsh . . . [who] discouraged me at our first interview but said that he would inquire about me. . . . A little later he accepted me as a volunteer." Marsh and eleven young volunteers—most of whom probably hoped for nothing more than a grand summer adventure—left New Haven on June 30, 1870.

The outcome for GBG was dramatic: it changed his life and was the first of more than forty trips to the West that he would make. The plan for the Marsh expedition was to travel via the new transcontinental railroad, taking side trips along the way. In eastern Nebraska, the train was stopped because buffalo blocked the tracks. Grinnell assumed they would be able to travel again within moments, but three hours passed before the great herd passed on its way across the plains. (Perhaps he reflected that Audubon was wrong about such animals becoming endangered.) The group's destination was

Fort McPherson, near the present-day town of Maxwell. The scout at the fort was Buffalo Bill Cody, who made a deep impression on the eastern students.

"He was . . . a handsome man who wore his blonde hair long and was a striking figure," GBG wrote later. "Like many outdoor men on the plains in those early days, he wore buckskin clothing . . . he performed a most re-markable feat, when in riding after buf-falo, he killed sixteen in sixteen shots."

Marsh's party stayed at the fort for several weeks while preparations were made to go by horseback into the field to search for fossils. Grinnell recalled how mounts were selected: "We were taken out to the corral to choose our horses from a bunch of Indian ponies captured . . . at the battle of Summit Springs. . . . There were some amusing scenes as these young men, many of whom had never mounted a horse, at-tempted to ride, but most of the horses were quite gentle and did not try to get rid of their riders."

Part of Grinnell's later fame would be built upon the great empathy he devel-oped for Indians and the efforts he made on their behalf. At this time in his life, however, he was only another cal-lous easterner, as revealed by his own words in a letter to his parents, in which he regarded an Indian as not much more than a creature to be used for target

practice: "Only one Indian was seen . . . and no one was able to get a shot at him."

The purpose of the trip wasn't to shoot Indians but to collect fossils, and many examples from the Miocene and Pliocene eras were gathered along the Loup River while the soldiers stood guard on the bluffs above. For the first time, Grinnell endured the kind of physical hardships that he'd only read about: during a five-day ride across the Nebraska sand hills beneath a scalding sun when temperatures reached 110 de-grees, the students spent fourteen-hour days in the saddle. "I never realized what thirst was before," GBG remarked. Later, he and a companion became lost and found themselves trapped by a near-fatal prairie fire that singed their hair and the hides of their horses.

While he was at Bridger's Fort in Wyoming, Grinnell was completely charmed by the lives of old-time trap-pers. "They possessed that indepen-dence which all men seek," he noted. "They were masters of their own lives. When they felt like it, they pulled down their lodges, packed their possessions on their animals, and moved away to an-other place which pleased them. The pursuit of food, the attention to their traps, and the care of their livestock lent to their lives an interest which never failed. . . . While I was with them I could not imagine, nor can I imagine now, a more attractive—a happier life—than theirs."

After leaving the fort, the professor took his volunteers to Salt Lake City, where they made a courtesy call on Brigham Young, the Mormon leader, then pressed on for California. By Thanksgiving, after a trip lasting five months, Grinnell was back in New York City. Professor Marsh had returned with a collection of one hundred specimens of vertebrates, toothed birds, and a pterodactyl, all of which gave support to Charles Darwin's new theory set forth in *On the Origin of Species*, which had been hotly debated since its publication in 1859. The Yale expedition became famous for another reason: first, the West had been discovered by men with rifles and traps; next, it was mapped by military experts like John Charles Frémont; now, it would be rediscovered by men of science such as Marsh. (John Wesley Powell, whose biography appears in this volume, also was such a man, and his career parallels GBG's in several respects.)

At home, Grinnell found himself facing more personal concerns. He had begun to think of studying medicine, only to discover that his father wanted him to go into business. As a result, the young man's plans to study medicine were exchanged for a job as a clerk—

without pay—in his father's Wall Street brokerage firm. It was a prestigious office, for the elder Grinnell was the principal agent for Cornelius Vanderbilt's vast railroad enterprises. Nevertheless, it was birds rather than business that continued to preoccupy GBG. With Professor Marsh's encouragement, in his spare time Grinnell learned how to mount birds for display and began the study of osteology (bone formation).

Two years after entering his father's office, GBG—still dreaming of the West—wrote to Major Frank North, who'd been one of the military escorts on Marsh's expedition, to arrange to go on a buffalo hunt. The hunt taught him something about buffalo that he might not have been expecting to learn: that Audubon had been right. It would soon be an endangered species, and some sort of action needed to be taken by "not only the States and Territories, but by the National Government [or] these shaggy brown beasts . . . will ere long be among . . . the things of the past."

Grinnell's vacation lasted three weeks but was an inexpensive one, since he'd obtained railroad passes from some of his father's clients. The trip also cemented a lifelong friendship between Major North and Grinnell. The younger man considered North to be a "guide, philosopher, and friend," and the two planned another hunting trip, this time for elk, to take place the following year.

At home, major changes awaited GBG. In 1873, the elder Grinnell's business partner, Horace Clark, who also was Vanderbilt's son-in-law, died unexpectedly. The company was carrying a large volume of shares "on the margin," which wasn't a problem "so long as Mr. Clark was living [because] any additional margin required was always forthcoming." It was under such an economic cloud that on September 1, 1873, the senior Grinnell turned his business over to his son. What young Grinnell then faced was a baptism by fire. As he recalled later, "The [economic] panic of 1873 came on out of a clear sky, about September 20th. Trusted officers of banks and corporations disappeared with the money of institutions; the stock market promptly fell to pieces; prices dropped almost to nothing; and the Stock Exchange . . . closed its doors."

The winter was one of great financial and emotional turmoil for the Grinnell family, as well as for countless others across the country. It was then that GBG began to write for publication. As a means "to divert my mind," he recalled, "I began to write short hunting stories for . . . *Forest and Stream*, a newspaper which had been established the previous August. . . . These little stories, the first of which was published in October 1873, and dealt with my recent Nebraska elk hunt, I took to the office of

Forest and Stream." From that small beginning grew a relationship that would last forty years.

Legal action was taken against the Grinnell brokerage firm by those to whom money was owed, but after an investigation charges were dismissed. GBG's father retired permanently, and as the younger Grinnell recalled, "After he had gone, there was nothing to hold me to Wall Street." Since his 1870 trip, GBG had stayed in contact with Professor Marsh, who encouraged his scientific interests and suggested he ought to pursue a Ph.D. at Yale. Grinnell—now twenty-four years old—mustered enough courage to go against his father's wishes for the first time. He dissolved the firm of Grinnell & Company in March 1874 and went to work at the Peabody Museum as one of Marsh's assistants. There was yet no funding for salaries for such assistants, so "for three years I worked without pay, living as economically as I could. The first year I spent $535, the second year $637.50."

Later that spring, General Phil Sheridan informed Professor Marsh that a summer expedition under the leadership of George Armstrong Custer was being planned for the Black Hills of South Dakota. The general suggested that Marsh might wish to send a man along with the expedition for the purpose of documenting the flora, fauna, and fossils of the area, and Grinnell was delighted to be the man Marsh selected.

Grinnell not only met Custer, but "Lonesome" Charley Reynolds as well, whom Custer had hired as his chief of scouts. Reynolds, a thirty-one-year-old native of Kentucky, had come from a well-to-do family and got his nickname because he preferred to hunt and trap by himself. As a boy of fourteen, he'd been sent to boarding school in Indianapolis, where he believed he was treated unfairly by the headmaster. He ran away, but was afraid to return home, so he started west on foot. He became one of the most successful white hunters on the plains, and many Indians believed that he possessed "good medicine" that enabled him to entice animals to come to him.

During his stay at Fort Lincoln, where Custer was headquartered, Grinnell collected a variety of bird specimens and also spent time at Custer's house, listening to the general's tales about his exploits (Two short years later, Custer would lie dead on a battlefield in eastern Montana, a victim of his own enthusiasms.) Also present at such get-togethers was Colonel Fred Grant, the son of Ulysses S. Grant.

Finally, the expedition—made up of twelve hundred men, a thousand horses, many wagons, three Gatling guns, a herd of beef to slaughter when meat was needed, a sixteen-piece brass band, and the notorious Calamity Jane—was ready to enter the Black Hills, known to the Sioux as the Pa Sapa, or the home of the sacred spirits. It was an expedition that should never have been undertaken, because according to the Fort Laramie treaty of 1868, the land had been set aside as the Great Sioux Reservation, and whites were forbidden to trespass. Nevertheless, it was Custer's mission to find out if rumors of gold in the hills were true, and to make a report.

On July 20, the expedition entered the Black Hills. The terrain changed from level prairie to rough "bad lands," and the type of animals that were seen changed as well. Here, deer were more common than antelope or buffalo. It was midsummer, but Grinnell remembered that in the mornings "it was very cold and most of us stood shivering about the fire with our plates in our hands and our tin cups of coffee on the ground beside us while we ate our breakfast."

Traces of gold were indeed discovered on July 30, 1874. Custer, a man who was always eager for good publicity, made no attempt to keep the news quiet and sent Charley Reynolds out with the word that gold had been found. But it was not gold that Grinnell came to find, and when the expedition reached the south edge of the Black Hills in August, he continued to look for fossils along the rivers. Then on August 30, 1874, the expedition arrived back at Fort Lincoln, having taken sixty days to make the 883-mile round trip. The monograph that Grinnell wrote of his observations was for many years the definitive scientific work on the Black Hills and surrounding area. Among his observations, Grinnell noted "the gray wolf [is] one of the most common animals in the Black Hills, and hardly a day passed without my seeing several individuals of this species. . . . On one occasion I heard [their doleful] howling at midday— a bad omen, if we may trust the Indians." It was indeed a bad omen, for the discovery of gold and consequent gold rush into the sacred spirit country of the Sioux eventually led to Custer's death.

Grinnell returned to the West the following year, this time to Montana. On this trip, he gained an even deeper awareness of the unnecessary slaughter of wildlife. He'd never forgotten the reverence for such life that he'd learned from Audubon's widow, and he made his opinion clear in June 1876, when he called public attention "to the terrible destruction of large game, for the hides alone. . . . Buffalo, elk, mule deer and antelope are being slaughtered by the thousands. . . . Of the vast majority of animals killed, the hide only is taken." Grinnell also noted that the females of such species were often slaughtered at a time when they were about to deliver their young, thereby reducing the numbers of animals that would mature the following year. Grinnell was an enthusiastic hunter himself but despised such wanton slaughter and warned that "unless the destruction of these animals can be checked, the large game still so abundant in some localities will . . . be exterminated."

On his Montana trip, Grinnell discovered dinosaur fossils in the Judith Basin country, then resumed his duties at the Peabody Museum. By now he was well known to western military personnel as well as to hunters and trappers, and in May 1876, while visiting his father (who now spent part of the year in California for health reasons), Grinnell received a telegram from General Custer, inviting him to participate in another summer expedition into Sioux country. Grinnell was eager to join his old friends, yet he was preoccupied not only by his father's illness, but by a large amount of work waiting to be done at the Peabody. Reluctantly, he declined the invitation. Seven weeks later, he heard about Custer's fate in the Battle of the Little Bighorn on June 25, 1876. One of his first concerns was for Charley

Reynolds, who'd become a good friend. Soon he learned that Lonesome Charley had been killed along with Custer and his troops.

In spite of his many activities, Grinnell still contributed to *Forest and Stream* in a column called "Natural History." In the autumn of 1876, editor Charles Hallock fired the man in charge of the column. He believed the column was perhaps the most important feature of the magazine because subscribers were "among the leading men of this country and Europe." He wanted someone in charge who would be more widely respected. He asked Grinnell to take over the job, with the assurance that GBG could continue his work at the Peabody. Four years later—as Hallock himself had predicted—Grinnell became the magazine's owner, editor, and publisher, replacing Hallock himself.

After a trip west in 1878, Grinnell returned from a visit to "Buffalo Bill" Cody's ranch along the Dismal River in Nebraska, feeling poorly. He didn't realize it, but he'd gotten a case of Rocky Mountain spotted tick fever, and he nearly died. He barely managed to get home, was delirious much of the time, and remained bedridden for seven weeks. Afterward, Grinnell suffered from headaches and an inability to sleep, and when he finally went to a doctor, he was advised to change his line of

work or "be prepared to move into a lunatic asylum or the grave."

There was a less drastic solution: during the winter of 1880, he was invited to become president of the Forest and Stream Publishing Company, whose offices were in the old Times Building in New York City, and he accepted. In that same year he also received his doctorate in vertebrate paleontology from Yale. He immediately became a hands-on publisher, noting with pride, "We printed a good paper, had a large circulation, and began almost at once to make plenty of money."

His new post at the magazine kept him away from his western travels for a time, but in 1881 he made a trip to British Columbia, where he collected more fossils, hunted mountain goat and black bear, fished for salmon, and canoed for six hundred miles along the islets and inlets of the Canadian coast, which were "the most marvelous I have seen." On his return trip through Oregon, he witnessed an incident at Pend Oreille that shocked him. As Northern Pacific Railroad workers laid track through the western forests, they felled timber in a strip fifty feet wide, and the quickest way to get rid of the debris was to set it on fire. Frequently, the blaze got out of control and burned the countryside for miles around. "The woods were on fire everywhere," he wrote as he passed through the area, and later, in the pages of *Forest and Stream*, he vigorously attacked the railroad's practice, calling for "steps taken toward putting a stop to such . . . destruction of valuable timber."

In the spring of 1883, having spent more than a decade becoming familiar with the West, Grinnell decided to make a commercial livestock investment, as many other easterners had done. He bought a 1,100-acre ranch in southeastern Wyoming, three thousand head of sheep, and many horses. The altitude in that part of the country was more than seven thousand feet, and the weather was far too severe for sheep; during his first winter of ranching, Grinnell lost one-third of his stock. He sold the surviving animals in the spring and invested in cattle; they also did poorly. The venture was a financial failure, partly because he really didn't put his heart into it, preferring instead to leave ranch management in the hands of others.

In 1885, he hiked into the St. Mary's area of southwestern Montana, site of present-day Glacier National Park, which at that time hadn't been explored by any white man. It was the last surviving wilderness area in the United States, and many of the names GBG gave to various sites are still used, Grinnell Peak among them. In that same year, he somewhat unenthusiastically reviewed

Grinnell Glacier and Mount Gould. GLACIER NATIONAL PARK.

a future president's book, *Hunting Trips of a Ranchman*, by Theodore Roosevelt, in the pages of his magazine. Roosevelt was miffed and called upon GBG to discuss the matter. Rather than parting enemies, the pair began a lifelong friendship.

Grinnell had made his first trip to the West in 1870 at the age of twenty; now, a mere fifteen years later, it had changed more than he cared to admit. The proud Indians, many of whom he'd come to know personally, were now confined to desolate reservations; buffalo herds once numbering in the tens of thousands now were limited to hundreds; roads and railroads connected both coasts. "The old charm is gone," he told a friend, "for the old independence is gone." The truth was, Grinnell had arrived on the scene just as the Old West was fading, and he had been a witness to its passing.

Grinnell spent the rest of his life trying to protect and conserve the best of the West. In 1886, he founded the first Audubon Society with the support of such men as minister Henry Ward Beecher, poet John Greenleaf Whittier, and jurist Oliver Wendell Holmes. Within two years the organization had a membership of fifty thousand. In 1887, Grinnell began a two-year campaign to save the Blackfoot Indians of Montana from starvation, their dire predicament caused by the actions of a dishonest Indian agent named Young. For his efforts, the tribe named GBG Pinut-u-ye-is-tsim-o-kan, or "Fisher Cap," and made him an honorary chief. Chief Curly Bear said that had Grinnell not "come to our aid, in our time of dreadful need, our tribe, to the last man, woman, and child, would have perished."

In 1889, when he was forty years old, Grinnell published his first book of Indian tales, *Pawnee Hero Stories and Folk Tales*. It was followed by several more—*Blackfoot Lodge Tales*, *The Fighting Cheyennes*, and *By Cheyenne Campfires*—which were regarded by anthropologists such as Margaret Mead as his finest work.

Grinnell's father died in 1891, his mother in 1894, and in 1896 he concluded a $1.5 million treaty with the Blackfoot Indians for the purchase of land that in 1910 became Glacier National Park, the sum being paid out over a period of ten years. When he was fifty—still a bachelor who'd never had a family of his own—Grinnell commenced a series of books for children, featuring a boy named Jack (perhaps modeled on himself and his boyhood playmate, Jack Audubon), including *Jack among the Indians (1900)*, *Jack in the Rockies* (1904), and *Jack, the Young Cowboy* (1913). In 1902, at age fifty-three, he met and married Elizabeth Kirby Curtis, a widow from Boston, who assisted him in the publication of his major work, *The Indians of Today*.

After he gave up his editorial post at *Forest and Stream* in 1912 following a tenure of thirty years, GBG traveled widely through the West he loved so well (curiously, he chose never to live there permanently), became president of the National Parks Association, and received a doctor of letters degree from Yale honoring him "for what you have done to publish in the world of letters a fast vanishing world of American life."

George Grinnell and his wife standing on a glacier. GLACIER NATIONAL PARK.

In 1925, President Calvin Coolidge awarded him the Theodore Roosevelt Medal, which cited him for preserving "vast areas of picturesque wilderness for the eyes of posterity. . . . Glacier National Park is your monument."

In 1929, Grinnell suffered his first heart attack; he died nine years later in New York City on April 12, 1938, at age eighty-eight, having been confined to a wheelchair for several years. The world that he'd seen change so much during his life-

time was about to change even more radically than he ever could have imagined: eight years after his death, the atomic bomb was dropped on Hiroshima; the world he'd known was no more.

Toward the end of his life, Grinnell—who became known to the Pawnees as White Wolf, to the Cheyennes as Wandering Bird, and to the Gros Ventres as Gray Clothes—wrote to a friend, "I have had barrels of fun. In fact, I suspect that there is no one living who ever had so good a time. . . . " *Field and Stream* magazine called him "the grandfather of conservation," but as Grinnell knew better than anyone, the work of conservation is never finished. As he wrote after the founding of the Boone and Crockett Club in collaboration with Theodore Roosevelt, the objectives of the club were more "in the field of protection than in that of destruction . . . [because] it became apparent that on all hands the selfishness of individuals was rapidly doing away with the natural things of this country."

Therefore, Grinnell made himself responsible for protecting Yellowstone National Park from private development; placing over a hundred million acres of land into a forest preserve system; operating the Bronx Zoo; restricting the hunting of deer with lights and dogs; founding the American Game Association; and helping pass the Lacey Act, which prohibited the killing of birds merely for their decorative feathers.

George Bird Grinnell's most eloquent testimonial is in his own words. In an article about Glacier Park, published in 1886 in *Forest and Stream*, he imagined his own end: "I see pass before me, as in a vision, the forces and faces of grave, silent, gentle men, whom once I had called my friends. . . . They have kindled their last camp-fire, they have . . . crossed the Great Divide. . . . None have risen, nor can arise, to fill the places left vacant. The conditions which made these men what they were . . . no longer exist."

James J. Hill

1838–1916 Railroad magnate. Emigrated to Minnesota from Canada at age eighteen, worked as a freight clerk. Ten years later became agent for St. Paul and Pacific Railroad and later organized a syndicate to purchase it. Renamed the Great Northern, Hill's railroad was responsible for settling more emigrants in the West than any means before its time. Hailed as the "Empire Builder," he also was despised as the "Red River Pirate."

James Jerome Hill, born on September 16, 1838, in Ontario, Canada, was the first living son of James Hill and the former Ann Dunbar. Their first child, who died not long after birth, also was named James. Since it was a Hill family tradition that the oldest son be called James, the name was given to the new baby as well. The young couple, both emigrants from Ireland, met and married in Ontario, then settled on a fifty-acre farm in 1833. Athough they'd come from Ireland, neither was Catholic; James was Baptist, Ann was Methodist, and their children were educated in a Quaker school.

Only a year separated Jim and his younger brother Alexander, and the two were chums throughout their boyhood, hunting, fishing, and playing together after their chores were done. When Jim was nine years old, they experimented making bows and arrows; somehow, an arrow Jim fitted into his bow flew backward, hitting him in the right eye. The eye was dislocated from its socket, but a local doctor was able to replace it so that muscular control was maintained. However, Jim lost the sight in that eye, something many people never knew.

The Hill household was exceptional in its day because it was well stocked with books. In spite of having the sight of only one eye, Jim's favorite hobby was reading, and *Ivanhoe* and *Don Quixote* were among his favorites. After reading a biography of Napoleon, young Jim—who had always been known simply as "James Hill" like his father, grand-father, and great-grandfather before him—fancifully bestowed upon himself the middle name Jerome, in honor of the emperor's brother.

Jim attended Ackworth Academy, a Quaker school, in the village of Rockwood, fifty miles west of Toronto. Subjects offered included grammar, algebra and geometry, bookkeeping, history, and geography. He also studied surveying, which would one day become one of his most valuable skills. The boy boarded by the week at the school and paid part of the fee from money he'd saved himself.

In 1848 Hill's father gave up farming and moved the family to the village of Rockwood, where he opened an inn and tavern. Life became easier than it had been on the farm, and the family had more time to spend together. On Christmas Day, 1852, however, when young Jim was fourteen years old, the family's comfortable life came to an abrupt end when the elder James died unexpectedly after a short illness.

Jim spent the next four years clerking in general stores in Rockwood. His first job, for a Scotsman named Passmore, paid a dollar per week. Stores and shops in the village catered to the needs of farmers and stockmen, and the boy learned how to keep books, how to order goods from the cheapest suppliers,

and how and when to extend credit to customers. Then Ann Hill gave up trying to run the tavern by herself and moved to the nearby village of Guelph. There, Jim worked as a grocery clerk, but after eight months he found himself unemployed. It would be the first—and only—time he would ever be without work.

In 1856, when Jim Hill was eighteen years old, expansion in Canada was hampered by the huge wilderness that lay between its eastern cities and the province of British Columbia to the west. The government in Quebec, rather than see its young people drift away to the congested cities along the United States' eastern seaboard, actually encouraged emigration to the American Midwest.

As a result, there soon were more than six thousand French Canadian residents in Kankakee, Illinois, eight thousand in Iowa, and nine hundred in Kansas. A former neighbor from Rockwood who had traveled to Minnesota promised Jim that jobs there were easy to find. Later, school chums went to look over the Red River country along the Minnesota–Dakota Territory border and came back with other exciting tales. It was enough to interest Jim, and he set out in July 1856, with six hundred dollars he'd saved. He got as far as Syracuse, New York, where he went to work for a farmer, earning enough to

A trestle on the Northern Pacific line. NORTH WIND PICTURE ARCHIVES.

move on to New York City, then to Philadelphia, and finally to Minnesota.

The city life of St. Paul, then a crude, bustling frontier town perched on the edge of the Mississippi River, was concentrated along a few muddy blocks near the levee. Five hotels faced the river; five newspapers were kept busy reporting the comings and goings of steamboats from New Orleans, St. Louis, and Dubuque. The young adventurer from Canada actually intended to move on; he fancied he would like to go to the Orient, but he remained in Minnesota for the next sixty years.

Young Jim had promised to write to his grandmother as soon as he arrived, and he sat down to do so. "I am in . . . the shipping business," he reported proudly. "My salary is twice as much as

I could get in Canada and work is easy, all done in an office." St. Paul was an inspired choice for a young man like Hill; as one commentator of the time remarked, "Every man here is determined to make his mark." The boy who'd given himself a middle name definitely aimed to do so.

When young Hill arrived, steamboats were still the primary means of transporting cargo in the Midwest, and the shipping firm that hired Hill felt lucky to get him. His skills were out of the ordinary for the time: he was good at adding columns of figures; he wrote a clear hand, important in a day before typewriters or word processors; and he was willing to work long hours. There was plenty for a shipping clerk to do because everything needed by emigrants or newcomers to set up households or farms had to come up the river and be unloaded on the docks: cookstoves, wagons, harnesses, even livestock. The fur trade still accounted for much cargo, but before long the export of lumber and flour became even more important. A grist mill had been built near St. Paul—a city still often called by its nickname, "Pig's Eye"—and by 1861 it was milling 250,000 barrels of flour a year.

Contrary to what he'd told his grandmother, Jim didn't spend all of his time in the office. He soon became a wharfmaster for the firm of Borup and Champlin, where he had a chance to learn all about shipping rates, routes, and schedules. Nor was all of his life devoted to business: he helped rescue an eleven-year-old boy about to drown in the Mississippi, organized a bear hunt across the river in Wisconsin, and chased down a runaway cart horse on the main street of St. Paul. There were occasional fistfights too. Hill described how, while walking home late one evening, he and a friend were accosted by two men who had stepped out of "one of those low rum holes. . . . I hauled off and planted one-two in Paddy's grub grinder and knocked him off the sidewalk."

Hill joined the Pioneer Guard, whose job it was to defend the city from attack, and won a first prize for marksmanship in spite of having only one good eye. Considering the mood of the Sioux Indians, who could not have been pleased at the rapid encroachment of settlers into the area, there was always the possibility of conflict. Also, rumors of a civil war between the North and South were rolling across the nation, and no one knew yet what it might mean for the Midwest.

On September 9, 1861, an event took place on the banks of the Mississippi that changed forever the development of the western United States: in a drizzling rain, the steamship *Alhambra* pushed a barge toward the St. Paul docks that bore a huge brass-and-iron monster—a railroad locomotive. It was stored over the winter, until tracks could be built to connect the "twin cities" of Minneapolis and St. Paul. In the spring, James Hill helped load three wooden freight cars—little realizing, perhaps, that what he'd just done would someday make him one of the richest men in America.

By the time the Civil War (a war Hill volunteered for but never fought in because of his sightless eye) turned in the favor of the Union, the young man from Canada had gained valuable experience in transportation and the merchandising of staples such as wood, grain, coal, and salt. He also had earned the reputation for being a fellow who made things happen. The commodore of the Northwest Packet Company offered young James Hill a job. Hill's employers knew how valuable he was and wouldn't let him go, but Hill kept his contacts open with the competing firm. Then, in March 1865, the twenty-six-year-old Hill was appointed freight and passenger agent for *both* the Northwest Packet Company and its ally, the Milwaukee and Mississippi Railroad.

An immediate challenge faced Hill: how to resolve the problem of transferring freight between steamships at the docks and rail cars a few hundred feet away on the riverbank. Draymen (wagon drivers) could do the task, but Hill calculated that it would add one dollar to each ton of freight. He decided that an all-weather warehouse, its floor level with the dock, with railroad sidings nearby, was the answer. Freight could be protected from rain or snow during a shortened transfer process, and the warehouse would cost less than employing crews of draymen.

In February 1866, Hill invested $2,500 of his own savings in the warehouse venture. More importantly, he struck a deal with his new business partners: he would draw $1,500 a year in salary (other clerk-solicitors of the time were earning $1,000), with the promise of a bonus if he made the business profitable. The firm was called the James J. Hill Company, and a warehouse 100 by 330 feet was built, which in his words was "splendid."

Success didn't come without struggle. Competition with the Milwaukee & St. Paul Railroad caused Hill sleepless nights. As he wrote, he'd had "a terrible long siege of it figuring and figuring." But figuring was Hill's most remarkable skill; by 1867, profits were soaring, and his reputation as a shrewd businessman increased. He also was known as a decent fellow, often buying a train ticket for someone who'd run out of luck or lending a few dollars to those who needed it. However, he always considered such help a loan and expected to be paid back in full. When a man didn't repay a twenty-dollar loan, Hill sternly reminded him in a letter, "Now, John, I have no such amount to lose." It was just one example of Hill's genius: he was scrupulously attentive to even the smallest detail of his business.

The year 1867 was notable for something else: Hill arranged to have a piano shipped from the East and suggested that the agent for the Red Line in Chicago, for whom he'd done many favors, ought to be willing to "carry my music box 'Phree' without any loss." He also ordered two hundred calling cards for "Mr. and Mrs. James J. Hill."

The bride-to-be, Mary Theresa Mehegan, was the daughter of Irish immigrants who had settled first in New York, where she was born in 1846. When Timothy Mehegan's tailoring business failed, the family journeyed west to Minnesota. In 1854, when Mary was eight, her father died on Christmas Eve (ironically, both Mary and James lost their fathers at Christmastime), leaving the family penniless. When she was older, Mary worked as a waitress at the Merchants' Hotel, where James and his friends often dined. Mary was a reserved and dignified girl whose staunchest friend was Father Caillet, the French priest at her parish church.

After the couple's engagement was an-nounced in June 1864, Father Caillet realized that if Mary married James Jerome Hill, already one of the best known men in St. Paul, she would need the kind of education that would befit the wife of a rising young tycoon. With his encouragement—and financial help from James and some of his friends—she went off to St. Mary's Institute, a convent school in Milwaukee. There, she learned the arts that would be required in her new life: French, music, and polished manners. The couple were married in a simple ceremony on August 19, 1867; the bride was twenty-one, the groom was twenty-nine, and home became a modest dwelling in St. Paul. A year later a daughter, Mary Frances, was born, and two years later, a son, James Norman. Eventually there would be seven daughters and three sons in the family.

Rail trade in the Midwest didn't proceed only on an east-west axis; travel north into Canada was also important. The Hudson's Bay Company was still an economic powerhouse, and even though the fur trade was waning, a half million dollars in furs harvested by American trappers passed north through St. Paul in 1870. That winter, Hill left St. Paul and headed north himself along the Red River, his destination Pembina, where he hoped to negotiate a peaceful settlement of the Riel Rebellion. Louis Riel, a *metis*, or half-French, half-Indian leader,

James J. Hill (center) at the height of his power, photographed with financiers Charles Steele of the House of Morgan (left) and George F. Baker of the First National Bank. BROWN BROTHERS.

aspired to set up an independent nation in Canada or, failing that, to request annexation by the United States of what is now the province of Manitoba.

Part of the trip was made by dogsled, but Hill was dissatisfied with the guide he'd been given and sent him back to Fort Garry. Alone in Indian country, Hill realized that his life might be in danger and decided to cross over to the west side of the river where he might be safer. He built a raft of branches, stripped to his underwear, then splashed through the icy water to the other side. On shore, he and his team huddled under blankets and buffalo robes, their combined body heat keeping them warm. He became so fond of the team's lead dog that he took it back to St. Paul as a pet.

One important result of the trip to Pembina and back was that it fully acquainted Hill with the entire Red River valley. He could see its potential for settlement by emigrants, so in the summer he began to build flatboats to carry freight to the Canadian provinces. The extension of the main line of the St. Paul and Pacific Railroad to within a hundred miles of the Red River achieved Hill's goal of making railroads and waterways work together. He formed a partnership in August 1870 with the Griggs brothers; the firm built its own steamship, the *Selkirk*, and soon Hill and the Griggses held a monopoly on river transportation—a fact warmly resented by Canadians.

Until the Civil War, most farms and small towns throughout the Midwest were heated with wood. Even railway locomotives were powered by wood. In the East, the age of coal had already arrived, and Hill realized it would soon come to the Midwest. He resolved "to get as many people using coal as possible. In a country as thinly wooded as this and settling up so fast a large coal business must build itself up in a very short time."

Hill began to read everything he could about coal and made it a priority to gain a monopoly on importation into St. Paul of the finest anthracite from the East. He pressed the railroad to use coal in its shops, and in 1875, with new business partners, Hill became the principal supplier of coal northwest of Chicago. The Northwestern Fuel Company was founded in 1877, with Hill as its first president; from that date until the 1940s, the St. Paul–Minneapolis area was among the most important fuel-distribution centers in the United States.

By this time Hill was the father of five children, and a new baby was on the way. He was thirty-nine years old, his dark hair had receded, and he had put on weight, all of which made his appearance more impressive than ever. At the time of his marriage, Hill calculated that if a man could acquire a fortune of $100,000 he ought to be able to retire and live a gentleman's life. He now was worth about $150,000 and could have done as he'd once planned, but it wasn't really money that interested Jim Hill. Rather, it was the irresistible fascination of work itself, of making bigger deals, of taking greater risks and seeing them pay off.

He began to buy small, failing companies—iron foundries or saloons, for example—and turned them into profitable businesses. He leased soft-coal fields in Iowa; he ran for the post of alderman in St. Paul and was defeated, ending his interest in holding public office. He realized that his method of dealing with people was often considered brash and that he could do more behind the scenes than by being a politician himself.

All of Hill's various activities created in him a keen appreciation of what a railroad in the West could mean. Improvements in railcars—such as the invention of a sleeping car by George Pullman in 1864 and of the air brake by George Westinghouse in 1868—as well as improvements in construction of rail beds that allowed use of more powerful locomotives meant that rail travel was the wave of the future. Hill realized that since there was no boat travel up the Mississippi during winter months, settlers could save a year of travel time if they were able to go by train.

First, however, he needed to gain control of rail use in the region. Using his customary fact-finding talents, Hill set out to gather information on the legal and financial tangle in which the failing St. Paul and Pacific Railroad was foundering. The effort required voluminous correspondence, trips to stockholders' meetings in New York, and

fending off other buyers. Many other railroad owners from the East were interested in the region, but Hill played them "judiciously against each other," and was able to reach a tentative agreement in March 1878 to gain local control.

The agreement stipulated that a certain amount of rail line had to be completed by December 1878, requiring Hill to work swiftly to gather together grading crews and rails for the task. Hill and his partners, who included an old St. Paul friend, Norman Kittson, as well as George Stephen and Donald Smith of Canada, completed the work that was required, and the governor of Minnesota issued a certificate for the new railroad on January 9, 1879. Capital stock was fixed at $20 million and common stock at $15 million; mortgage bonds were authorized in the amount of $8 million—yet at the very moment he was dealing with such huge sums, Hill was writing a sharp note to a delinquent customer of the Northwestern Fuel Company for payment of a $27.50 debt!

One of Hill's first acts in 1880, after he was appointed the general manager of the St. Paul, Minneapolis & Manitoba Railroad—thereafter referred to simply as "the Manitoba"—was something he had postponed since his arrival in St. Paul twenty-four years earlier: he decided it was a good time to became an American citizen.

As he traveled about to check on his rail line, Hill observed even the minutest details of his enterprise in a small notebook: a "platform of depot wants one eighteen-foot plank for repairs"; a train engineer "dumped his fire on the ties and burned them in two or three places"; or "flatcar No. 1269 has two broken truss rods and should be repaired." In 1881 a newfangled contraption—a typewriter—was added to Hill's office. It was a device that should have made correspondence easier, but it would be many years before he gave up writing all correspondence in longhand—nearly every scrap of which has been saved for scholars and historians to examine.

In addition to managing his "rolling stock," as engines and railcars were called, Hill also learned that the business of running a railroad depended on *employees*. Like any owner of a large business, either then or now, Hill hoped men would always be willing to work for what he was willing to pay them. However, in August 1880, two hundred men walked off their jobs in St. Paul to protest the layoff of other employees. The following day, five hundred workers gathered in the railyard. Hill treated them all to a stern lecture: "The time will never come when you can dictate who shall be hired and who discharged. I work for a living, as you do, and

always expect to. . . . [And] when we are all dead and gone, the sun will still shine, the rain will fall, and this railroad will run as usual." The following day, everyone was back on the job; Hill later discovered that not all labor-management disputes could be resolved so easily.

Hill's efforts to extend his line to the Pacific Coast developed slowly in the form of "stub" lines connecting various small Minnesota villages and towns, because he had no land grants west of the Minnesota border. By 1883, 937 miles of new line had been laid on the Manitoba road. Thousands of emigrants were moving into the Red River valley, but there still was constant competition from the likes of the Northern Pacific and the Milwaukee, which Hill referred to as "wolves" or "foreigners."

Hill watched the westward progress of the Northern Pacific Railroad with an anxious eye. Under the inspired direction of Henry Villard, the NP line from Duluth to Tacoma was completed in 1883 and became the second so-called transcontinental railroad in the United States (the Union Pacific was the first). Meanwhile, Hill had to patch his line together piecemeal. True, his line had helped populate Canada, but what about the vast American Northwest? Hill made up his mind to lay claim to it.

In order to get across Montana, Hill

arranged to have a bill introduced in Congress that would waive restrictions included in the Indian Reservation Act. It failed to pass, partly due to the efforts of an equally powerful railroad man, Jay Gould, a major stockholder in the Union Pacific, who naturally did not welcome competition.

Hill decided to confront Gould in person. Of course, someone of Gould's standing was not an easy man to see, and when Hill appeared in Gould's office a receptionist crisply informed him that Mr. Gould was not available. Hill paid no attention and barged into Gould's private office. The startled New York financier looked up to see before him "a gorilla of a man, with an abnormally long torso and abnormally short legs, with a prodigiously heavy chest and neck . . . thick, sinewy arms, and limbs like granite columns. . . . One good eye blazed like a living coal . . . and from between the huge teeth there came a succession of hoarse, growling barks." No one knows exactly what the two men said to each other. What *is* known is that Hill's next request to pass through Indian lands was approved by Congress.

Even before the bill was passed, Hill had organized the Montana Central Railroad Company in 1886, stockholders being a few of his personal friends. At that time, the westernmost end of the rail line was at Minot, North Dakota, and Hill intended to lay track to Great Falls, Montana, in as short a time as possible. To do so required grading crews of 8,000 men and 3,300 teams of horses working day and night; laying the track and building bridges required an additional 650 men. Chief contractor for the project, which commenced on April 1, 1887, was D. C. Shepard, who later said that it was "very doubtful . . . track will ever be laid again in seven and one-half months at the average of 3 1/4 miles per day," a record that is still astonishing.

One of the plums to be plucked in Montana was the freight traffic out of Butte. The city had started out as a gold-mining camp; when the gold boom ended, a commoner but an equally important metal was discovered: copper. Mile-high Butte, situated on "the richest hill on earth," soon made Hill even richer than he was. Until the arrival of Hill's railroad, the Union Pacific handled all freight in the region, but Hill promised Marcus Daly, one of the men known as "the copper kings," "When our lines are continued through to your place, we hope to be able to furnish you all the transportation you want . . . at such rates as will enable you to largely increase your business."

Of course, Butte was not the end of Hill's dreams. It was plain that the

Northwest was a region of great wealth in terms not only of mining, but also of livestock, wheat, lumber, and coal. Back home, Hill had already established grain elevators in Duluth, Minnesota, that held as much as 1.8 million bushels of grain and had coordinated his rail lines with Great Lakes barge traffic.

In September 1889, Hill reorganized and combined his enterprises, creating the Great Northern Railway Company. At midnight on January 31, 1890, the company officially took over 2,700 miles of rail line and at its board meeting laid plans to push the line all the way "to some suitable point in Puget Sound." Hill hired a surveyor, John F. Stevens, to find "the Lost Pass of the Marias" through the Rocky Mountains. As a result of his survey training as a schoolboy in Canada, Hill had always been careful to lay track in a way that avoided excessive grades; if the pass lived up to its legend, it would offer a passage to the coast along the lowest possible elevation.

The Flathead and Blackfoot Indians had supposedly used such a pass, and a map made in 1840 indicated its presence. Some men claimed to have traveled through it, but Lewis and Clark were not among them, having crossed the Rockies farther to the south at Lemhi Pass in the Bitterroot Mountains. With a Flathead guide, Stevens stumbled

"by mere chance" on the fabled pass almost without realizing he'd found it. It would make Hill's line to the Pacific Coast even more cost-efficient.

When Hill visited Spokane in 1892, he was welcomed with open arms because the city believed it had been victimized by the Northern Pacific, the only line that served it, which set freight rates at whichever level pleased management. Now, with competition from the Great Northern, it was believed the economic climate of the city would improve.

However, Hill pointed out that Spokane, because of its geographic location, was a hard city to get into, and even harder to get out of. Elevation again was the problem; Hill informed a reporter from the *Spokane Review* that the grade was "one-quarter of a per cent higher than we want to go," and then drew a vivid illustration of what such a seemingly small sum meant. "The extra quarter of one per cent is equivalent to having to lift one thousand tons thirteen feet in the air for each mile of road traversed." He warned that the cost of such a project might be prohibitive.

There was a solution, of course—and Hill made it plain that it was up to Spokane itself to provide it. Hill demanded a free right-of-way—and got it. The line was then extended to Seattle, over bitter objections by the Northern Pacific. The last rail of the Great

Northern's line to Puget Sound was laid on January 5, 1893, thereby connecting St. Paul to Seattle, 1,816 miles away.

That year was better known for something else: an economic crisis hit the United States, and many railroads failed. The Santa Fe went into receivership, as did the Union Pacific. Only one major line was left unscathed: the Great Northern—a remarkable fact, considering that Hill's railroad had been built entirely *without* government subsidies.

When Hill's archrival, the Northern Pacific, went bankrupt in August 1893, it slashed rates to compete with the Great Northern. Hill promptly lowered his own rates. It was a costly move, but he held to it. The economic woes of the country led to a fresh problem: the American Railway Union called a strike against the Great Northern, demanding higher wages. At first, an outraged Jim Hill was inclined to break the strike by force, but he settled for arbitration, and after eighteen days his trains were running again.

Bankruptcy meant that the Northern Pacific was ripe for plucking, and in collaboration with J. P. Morgan of New York, Hill proceeded with plans to gain control of it. An antimonopoly suit forbidding such a merger was filed, and the U.S. Supreme Court ruled against Hill's group. Hill was not a man to be defeated, however. If the railroad could not be purchased, then he and his associates would gain control by becoming major stockholders; they proceeded to do so, and the new organization was called the Hill Lines.

Hill was now fifty-eight years old; forty years had passed since he'd arrived in St. Paul. His mind and health were as vigorous as ever, but it could be said that his appearance and personality had changed a great deal. His thinning hair was snow white, his physique more bearlike than ever, his temper shorter. One day he tore a telephone off the wall of his office, smashed its wooden box to smithereens, and pitched everything out the window. When one of his office clerks vexed him, he demanded to know the man's name. When the trembling fellow told him it was Spittle, Hill fired him on the spot, roaring, "I don't like your name and I don't like your face!" When the village of Wayzata, Minnesota, sued the Great Northern over some inappropriately placed outdoor toilets and won its case, Hill was so furious that he moved the depot two miles out of town, declaring that the ungrateful villagers could now walk.

When the century turned, James Hill met his match in the person of Edward Harriman, another prominent railroad wizard. Harriman, ten years younger, was the opposite of Hill in physique and manner. He was a frail, nearsighted man, shy and soft-spoken, and could easily have been mistaken for one of his own bookkeepers. He was a stockholder in the Illinois Central, went on to join the syndicate that purchased the Union Pacific, then bought into the Central Pacific and Southern Pacific roads. His aim was precisely the same as Hill's: to dominate rail travel from the Great Lakes to the Pacific.

Their test of wills, dubbed "the Battle of the Giants" by newspapers, came to a head in the struggle over who would gain control of the Chicago, Burlington & Quincy Railroad. Hill and his associates quietly bought stock in the Burlington line, gaining control of it by 1901, and they believed they had achieved their goal. Harriman was not to be outwitted; he, in turn, began to secretly buy stock *in one of Hill's own lines*, the Northern Pacific. Hill was oblivious of what was going on until, while on a trip to the Northwest, he noted a sudden rise in the stock price of Northern Pacific shares.

Hill realized that someone was trying to undermine his operation, and he dealt with the challenge in a characteristic manner. In Seattle, he hitched his private luxury railcar to a locomotive, ordered the tracks cleared, and headed for New York City at full throttle. Once there, he discovered the plot that was afoot: if Harriman couldn't have the Burlington, he planned to seize the Northern Pacific.

It was Friday; 150,000 shares of Northern Pacific stock were hastily purchased by Hill and his associates. On Saturday, Harriman decided to buy another 40,000 shares himself, to ensure his position, but because his broker was attending religious services that day, the order was not carried out. By Monday, the stock market was in a panic as the titans battled it out. Prices climbed; prices tumbled. The matter was ultimately resolved when Harriman was given representation on the NP board, but all control remained in Hill's hands.

The battle damaged other companies; U.S. Steel stock prices fell, and many people across the country lost money. Social commentators observed that the battle among three rich men—Hill, Harriman, and J. Pierpont Morgan—had wiped out the life savings of ordinary citizens, but when Morgan was asked if he wished to make a statement about the crisis, he replied, "I owe the public nothing."

Something else happened that year that would change the attitude of many citizens toward corporate giants. In September 1901, President McKinley was assassinated, and Theodore Roosevelt became president. Roosevelt was severely critical of what was called "the Northern Pacific panic," and early in his administration the new president instituted Sherman Anti-Trust proceedings against Hill, Harriman, and Morgan. The railroad men went to court, but in 1904 the U.S. Supreme Court upheld Roosevelt's decision.

In spite of that setback, Hill's fortunes continued to multiply. At the urging of his sons, Hill purchased land in the Mesaba, Minnesota, area, which turned out to have huge iron ore deposits; he leased mineral rights to U.S. Steel, who in turn used his railroad for shipping. To settle a bitter dispute over sixty-five thousand acres of land in the Red River valley that Hill claimed belonged to him, Congress agreed to let him select other comparable lands, and—shrewd man that he was—he chose the finest timber acreages in Montana, Idaho, and Washington. He then formed an alliance with an old acquaintance, Frederic Weyerhauser, who became the greatest lumber baron of the twentieth century.

The state of Minnesota infuriated Hill by fixing rates for freight and levying penalties against those who did not abide by them. Hill refused to observe such rate schedules and refused to pay penalties when they were imposed. He fought the cases through the Minnesota courts, lost them all, and then went before the U.S. Supreme Court, where he lost again. Embittered at his treatment in the state where he'd made his fortune and lived for fifty years, Hill bought a home in New York City in 1906 and con-

sidered leaving Minnesota permanently. His ties in the Midwest were too strong, however, and he returned to his palatial home on Summit Avenue in St. Paul. The truth was that he'd lived long enough to be both admired and despised, as a popular jingle indicated:

> Twixt Hill and Hell, there's just one letter;
> Were Hill in Hell, we'd feel much better.

For fourteen years, Hill had groomed his second son, Louis (whom he deemed more fit for top management than his namesake, James Norman), to take over the leadership of the Great Northern, and in June 1907 he resigned to become chairman of the board. Not that Hill ever actually retired; he pursued railroad interests in Oregon, which brought him once again into conflict with Edward Harriman. This time, it was more than simply a paper war; this one involved hand-to-hand combat with axes, picks, and shovels in Deschutes, Oregon, with loss of life for both Hill and Harriman employees.

At seventy-three years of age, Hill drove the last spike in the new rail line at Bend, Oregon, on October 1, 1911, before a cheering crowd. Rail connections always brought growth: the population of Bend was 536 when Hill's line arrived; ten years later, it was 5,415, a growth of 910 percent. Hill then cast his eye on San

Francisco but died before he could see that dream materialize; Louis, however, saw it come true.

In his later years, Hill enjoyed his collection of European paintings—Corot and Millet were his favorites—and took a keen interest in all types of agricultural affairs, giving many speeches at state and county fairs. He had, after all, been a Canadian farm boy once upon a time, and he proudly pointed out that he'd made seven thousand head of the best cattle available to Minnesota settlers, and almost as many hogs.

Hill died on the morning of May 29, 1916, after nine days of what he had referred to as "an indisposition," an infected hemorrhoid, which could have been treated successfully had he tended to it properly. By the time doctors from the Mayo Clinic in Rochester, Minnesota, were called to Hill's home, gangrene had set in and there was no hope. Many of the glowing obituaries following his death pointed out the same amazing fact: that Hill had built a railroad from the Great Lakes to Puget Sound without a nickel's worth of federal aid. It was perhaps his most remarkable monument.

Throughout his long career, Hill kept two things uppermost in mind. He knew that if he could build railroads, immigrants would settle nearby. He knew, too, that the interdependent relationship between people and railroads would benefit both. By 1910, newcomers had homesteaded more than four million acres in Montana alone; by 1922, 42 percent of that state was settled by homesteaders who had been induced to come west by Hill's enthusiasm. Montana was not the Red River valley, however, and there was an unforeseen consequence: at least 80 percent of the land that had been so hastily settled was not really fit for agriculture, and the type of deep plowing that was recommended helped bring drought to the high plateaus. The figures speak for themselves: in 1900 the grasslands of Montana yielded 25 bushels of wheat to the acre; by 1919, the yield was 2.4 bushels, forcing many emigrants to give up their land. If James J. Hill had lived long enough to see the empty farmsteads along his rail line, he might have had second thoughts.

Hill's prediction of 1893, that the sun would always shine on railroads, also turned out differently than he could have foreseen. Today, in most parts of the United States freight is carried by eighteen-wheel tractor-trailer rigs, and rails have been replaced by four-lane highways; passenger travel is now done mostly by air. As a result, many miles of railroad have been abandoned and torn up. Hill's empire has been dismantled—a fact that surely would astonish him.

Sam Houston

1793–1863 Statesman, soldier, politician. At age sixteen, spent three years living with the Cherokees, which gave him "a deep sympathy for the Indian character." Served in U.S. House of Representatives, later became governor of Tennessee. Made his first trip to Texas in 1832, fought for its independence, became its first senator and later its governor.

"My life and history are public property," Sam Houston declared when he was sixty-eight years old, "and it is the historian's privilege to record the good as well as the evil I have done." In Houston's life there was much of the former and a little of the latter.

Houston's Protestant Scotch-Irish ancestors emigrated to Pennsylvania in the 1730s, then moved down the Shenandoah Valley to Virginia. They established themselves on the western side of the Blue Ridge Mountains at Timber Ridge in Rockbridge County. Major Samuel Houston, a career military officer, married Elizabeth Paxton, the daughter of other Scotch-Irish immigrants, and they became parents of six sons. The fifth boy, born on March 2, 1793, was named after his father; he was always called Sam, rather than Samuel, to distinguish him from the elder Houston. Later, three daughters were born, making for a family of nine children.

Sam was said to be his mother's favorite, and she apparently didn't complain when he roamed the woods and fields around their Timber Ridge home rather than doing chores with his brothers. He started school late, at age eight, but most of his education took place at home, where his father kept a small library that became one of young Sam's favorite hideaways. Geography and literature appealed to the boy, but he despaired of ever being good at math.

The major's military duties kept him away much of the time, but Elizabeth Houston ran the plantation efficiently.

Like many estates of the time, the Houstons' was self-sufficient: grains and meat were raised for family consumption; cloth was woven on the premises so clothing could be made; shoes were stitched by hand. Tobacco was the main cash crop, but no whiskey was distilled because the Houstons' conservative religious beliefs forbade it. As a grown man, however, Sam's relationship with liquor would be the topic of considerable scandal.

Major Houston died suddenly in September 1806, while he was on an inspection of a Virginia militia unit. Prior to his death, he had made plans to move his family west to Tennessee, where other Houstons and Paxtons had already established themselves. In 1807, after she'd settled the family's business affairs, Elizabeth undertook the journey herself. A pair of Conestoga wagons were loaded, she gathered together her brood of nine children, and they set off on the hard, three-week trip to Blount County, near Maryville, just across the North Carolina border. Her fifth son, then fourteen, would remember her during that trip as "a heroine. . . . She was nerved with a stern fortitude."

Along with establishing a new home, Elizabeth acquired an interest in a general store in Maryville. Because Sam showed no interest whatever in farm management, he was often sent to the store to help his older brothers, John and James. Being a merchant didn't appeal to the boy any more than farm management did, and his marks at the Porter Academy also were indifferent. Yet he maintained a deep interest in literature and memorized a translation of *The Iliad* by the time he was fifteen. The heroic adventures of Achilles, Hector, and Odysseus left an indelible mark on him and armed him with a sense of language that later made him a dramatic orator and a gifted writer.

In his early teens, Sam often was mysteriously absent from the farm or the store for a few days at a time, and when he returned, offered no explanation of his whereabouts. He was reprimanded by his mother, and although he had been her favorite, a distance grew between them. In a sense, Sam became a silent, stubborn stranger to his family—a very tall stranger at that, fully six feet two inches in height, his hair tinged slightly with red like his Scots ancestors, his eyes a cool blue.

Sam never explained why he decided to exile himself permanently from his birth family when he was sixteen years old. He simply packed his favorite books and walked away to become the member of a new family among the Cherokee Indians, the type of family that apparently better fulfilled his needs.

The Cherokees, more than other

Indian tribes, had adjusted themselves to the white man's ways; they had become farmers, adopted some of the white man's dress, and intermarried with whites. When Chief Ooleteka (his name is spelled several ways), whom whites called John Jolly, learned that Sam's father had died, he offered to adopt him as a son. Sam accepted the invitation and was given a new name—Kalanu, or Raven. The raven was a sacred bird to the Cherokees, and the name indicated that the newcomer was held in high esteem.

Sam's mother sent his older brothers to fetch him home from where he was living with the three-hundred-member Cherokee band on Hiwassee Island, where the Tennessee and Hiwassee Rivers converge, near present-day Dayton, Tennessee. Sam declared that he was happy where he was, but when the brothers left they were quite sure he'd soon follow. They misjudged him; he stayed where he was for three years. He read, hunted, fished—and would remain spiritually bound to Indians till the end of his days.

The reasons that drew nineteen-year-old Sam back to his own people are as mysterious as the ones that drove him away. One of the first things he needed when he got home was a job, and though he didn't have much formal education, he became a schoolteacher. He must have surprised his students, for he appeared wearing moccasins and his hair was braided in a plait that hung down his back, Indian fashion. He charged eight dollars per pupil—a hefty sum for the time—to be paid in thirds: cash, corn, and cotton cloth. He had as many as eighteen students, some of whom were middle-aged men, and he said that it was one of the most satisfying times of his life.

The experience was brief, however, lasting only six months. Once again Sam needed a job. The War of 1812 (which pitted Americans against the Indian tribes that gathered under the leadership of Tecumseh to take a stand against endless encroachment by whites into their lands) had commenced, and army recruiters, accompanied by a piper and a drummer, soon appeared in Maryville. The recruitment process was simple: silver dollars were placed on the drum, and whoever picked one up thereby indicated his intention to enlist. On March 1, 1813, one day short of his twentieth birthday, Sam Houston plucked a dollar from the recruiters' drum. His family was indignant that he'd signed up as a common soldier when, considering the family's position in the community, he could easily have gotten a commission. "I would rather honor the ranks," he retorted.

Houston didn't stay in the ranks long;

he was a sergeant by the end of April and was transferred to the Thirty-ninth Infantry. Even more significant than the military experience he got was his meeting with General Andrew Jackson, who would become the seventh president of the United States. Although Jackson, in his mid-forties, was more than twice Houston's age, the two men had much in common: each had lost a father early, each had an influential mother, each was headstrong.

In the Battle of Horseshoe Bend against an uprising of Creek Indians who had killed several hundred white settlers at Fort Mimms, Houston was wounded both by arrows and by rifle fire as he leaped a barricade. He nearly died from loss of blood, and Jackson was so impressed that he gave Houston a battlefield promotion to second lieutenant. Houston was wounded too badly to remain on duty, and was carried home to his mother's house. A thousand Creek warriors lost their lives at Horseshoe Bend, and Sam told her, "The carnage was dreadful." He didn't mention that he himself had played a part in the savagery by ordering his men to cut off Indians' noses as a way of counting the dead. Considering his feelings about his Cherokee friends, what he'd done must have caused him deep regret.

It took Houston several months to recover, and finally he headed for Washington to seek better medical attention. When Jackson defeated the British in New Orleans, the end of the war meant a reduction in the size of the army. Houston didn't want to be discharged and took pains to make sure that he wasn't by writing letters to influential men in Washington, among them the representatives and senators from Tennessee, plus the secretary of war, James Monroe. He was admitted to the regular army in 1815, and his actions were a preview of how shrewdly he could play the game of politics.

At the conclusion of the war, the U.S. Army was divided into two parts, the Northern Division and the Southern Division. Command of the latter naturally went to Andrew Jackson, who was given permission to set up his headquarters at his plantation near Nashville (known as the Hermitage), where Houston reported for duty with his old chief. He was promoted to first lieutenant, and with it came the handsome salary of thirty dollars a month.

In 1817 Houston was appointed to the better-paying job of agent for his old friends, the Cherokees, who were protesting what they said was a fraudulent treaty foisted upon them to cede 1.3 million acres of land to the United States in exchange for cash and other, less desirable land. Sam needed to convince his old father-friend John Jolly that it would be wise to accept the government's offer of land in Arkansas, but he soon found himself entangled in a web of political intrigue. The secretary of war, John C. Calhoun of South Carolina, and Senator John Williams had no love for Houston's mentor, Andrew Jackson; they accused Houston—whom they knew to be Jackson's protégé—of corrupting the Indians by supplying whiskey to them and trafficking in slaves. Sam was eventually cleared of the charges but was understandably embittered by the experience. To Jackson's dismay, Sam resigned from the army on March 1, 1818, precisely five years to the day after he'd enlisted.

Houston began the study of law in Nashville under Judge James Trimble, a distant kinsman. He studied hard but found time to visit Jackson often at the Hermitage, only nine miles away, where he was treated like a son by the general and his wife, Rachel, who had no children of their own. Because of his fine reading skills and excellent memory, the study of law came easily to Houston; he compressed the eighteen-month course into six, passed his bar examination in December 1818, and won the first case he tried.

He settled in Lebanon, Tennessee, thirty miles east of Nashville, and set up a law practice that quickly became successful. Within two years, Houston was appointed a colonel in the state militia, then became the attorney general for Davidson County, Tennessee, a post that would give him the kind of political experience he wanted. He was active in social events such as amateur theater and also began to spend more time than was seemly in a popular local pub, the Nashville Inn.

As Houston groomed himself for greater things in Tennessee, like many other Americans he also began to hear more and more about Texas. Spain had ceded Florida to the United States, but contained in that agreement was a clause forbidding the U.S. to intervene in Texan affairs. Influential Americans, however—among them Andrew Jackson—had expansionist dreams, which made Texas a constant topic of conversation. In 1819, Dr. James Long had built a fort on Galveston Island and gathered a militia around him (James Bowie was among the group), with the hope of establishing an American influence in the area. The effort was a failure: Long was captured and executed in Mexico City in 1821 (but his wife, Jane, gave birth to the first American child born in Texas and came to be called "the mother of Texas").

Although Houston purchased shares in the Texas Association of Tennessee, a land-speculation company inspired by Moses Austin's efforts in 1822 to gain approval for a colonizing contract with Spain, his primary political and business interests remained in Tennessee. His next step up the political ladder was his election as a representative to the U.S. Congress in 1823. In the same election, his good friend Jackson was elected to the U.S. Senate, and they set off for Washington together—a Washington which at that time included such American legends as Daniel Webster and Henry Clay.

One of Houston's and Jackson's aims was to get Jackson elected to the presidency, but it was John Quincy Adams who was elected in 1824. The Jacksonians were dismayed and formed an anti-Adams coalition that eventually would be the foundation of the Democratic Party. As a first-year congressman, one of Houston's interests was the promotion of funding for public works in the western states—roads, bridges, canals. He also kept up a lively social schedule and at age thirty-two was one of the most popular bachelors in Washington.

Getting Jackson elected to the presidency was still high on his agenda, and both men knew it would be an advantage to have a "friend" in Tennessee. Consequently, Sam decided to run for the governor's office in his home state. Those who opposed Houston accused him not merely of being a stalking horse for Jackson but of being "excessively vain." The

vanity was intentional; in Congress, Houston had modeled himself after staid gentlemen such as Webster and Clay; in Tennessee he discarded such drab dress in order to increase interest wherever he appeared. An observer described one of Sam's costumes:

". . . a standing collar, ruffled shirt, black satin vest, shining black silk pants gathered to the waistband with the legs full . . . a gorgeous red-ground, many-colored Indian hunting shirt fastened at the waist with a huge red sash . . . an immense silver buckle, embroidered silk stockings, and [shoes] with large silver buckles."

Sartorial splendor must have had an effect because the thirty-four-year-old Houston became governor of Tennessee in 1827. Staunch opposition made the election harder to win than he'd anticipated, however, and it saw a young anti-Jackson Tennessean named Davy Crockett rise to national prominence. An observer, Julia Connor of South Carolina, happened to meet the new governor the year he was elected and noted in her journal that she was somewhat disappointed because Houston did "not possess talents of the highest order." She was willing to concede that he was handsome but regarded him as a manipulative charmer.

A year later, Andrew Jackson was successful in his bid to become president, further enhancing Houston's position on the national scene. Sam had also became a frequent guest at Allenwood, John Allen's home on the Cumberland River bluffs, twenty miles east of Nashville. Allen—an acquaintance from Houston's army days—had become a wealthy planter, married, and was the father of several children. His fifteen-year-old daughter, blond Eliza, was a fine horsewoman, and in spite of their age difference, the governor eventually began a proper courtship of the young lady with her family's blessing. They were pleased by the prospect of having a daughter married to such a powerful, influential man, and the new governor—in addition to admiring the young lady—realized that a handsome young wife would make running for reelection easier.

The pair were married in a candlelight service on January 22, 1829. Houston was resplendent in a black velvet suit and a Spanish cape lined with scarlet satin. (Few descriptions remain of the bride's gown!) From the beginning, however, the marriage seems to have been an unfortunate mismatch; among the reasons for Eliza's disenchantment might have been her husband's drinking habits. She also stated that he was "insanely jealous and suspicious" and sometimes locked her in her room. It was also said that Eliza had married to please her family rather than

herself. After three months of matrimony, Eliza packed her bags and returned to her astonished family, which lost no time circulating the scandalous news that their daughter had been mistreated.

The Tennessee public was intolerant of such behavior on the part of a gentleman; Houston was burned in effigy in several towns and admitted, "I am a ruined man." He resigned from office on April 16 and destroyed all his private papers, which explains why no one knows much about what really happened between the couple. On April 23, Houston rode out of Nashville in disgrace and headed west. One of his Tennessee enemies gleefully remarked, "He rose like a rocket and fell like a stick."

Houston knew there was one place he could go to ease his pain and disappointment: back to the Cherokees. On May 20, 1829, he returned to John Jolly's band, now living on the banks of the Arkansas River, near the well-traveled "Texas Road." Once again Sam melted into Indian life, officially becoming a tribal member in October 1829. He married a woman named Tiana Rogers, the beautiful part-Indian daughter of Jack Rogers, a Scots trader. (Among her descendants was the famous American humorist Will Rogers.)

Unfortunately, Sam Houston carried his real enemy with him: his passion for whiskey. His consumption became legendary, earning him the nickname Ootse-tee-ar-dee-tah-skee, or Big Drunk. His behavior shamed him in the eyes of his Cherokee friends, and when, in a drunken rage, he struck his adopted father, he had to make a public apology before the Cherokee Council.

Problems with his Cherokee friends were overshadowed in 1831 by news from home that his mother was dying. Sam was able to be at her bedside at the end, and the loss seemed to temporarily bring him to his senses. He had never really given up dreams of a political life, and when he returned to Arkansas, he told his Cherokee wife he intended to go to Washington. He made a bigger splash in the capital than he could have foreseen: on April 3, three days after his arrival, Houston picked up a newspaper and read that Congressman William Stanbery of Ohio had just made slanderous statements about him in a speech.

He immediately demanded an accounting from Stanbery, who ignored the request. When Houston met his accuser on a Washington street shortly thereafter, he attacked the congressman with a cane, called him a "damned rascal," and thrashed him soundly. Houston was arrested and hired Francis Scott Key (a well-known defense attorney in addition to being the author of "The Star--Spangled Banner") to defend him.

After a long trial, during which Jackson, his old mentor, gave him money to buy a coat "of the finest material . . . with a white satin vest" to replace his Indian garb, Sam was merely reprimanded and fined. What the trial did was to make him a national celebrity. As Houston said himself, "I was dying out . . . but they gave me a national tribunal for theatre and set me up again."

Better even than having gotten off lightly for his attack on Stanbery, Houston had time while in Washington to pursue his interest in Texas, which now was constantly on his mind. President Jackson and many of his influential friends likewise were still interested in the fate of Texas and believed a revolution was brewing there. Once again Sam headed west; this time he carried a government passport dated December 6, 1832, permitting him to make treaties with frontier Indian tribes.

One of the stops along the way was to visit Tiana. Divorce among the Cherokees was a simple matter: Houston declared that he intended to part from her and deeded her the house they had shared, some land, and two slaves. Then he crossed the Red River into Texas; he didn't look back.

The Texas that thirty-nine-year-old Sam Houston entered in December 1832 was "a remote and dangerous frontier, huge in area, vague in definition . . . meagre in development." Its native inhabitants included the Comanche, Apache, and Yaqui Indian tribes; it had been explored in the 1500s by the conquistadors, then in the 1700s Spanish officials who were headquartered in Mexico City began to build presidios, or forts, northward to colonize the area. Spain finally granted Mexico its independence in 1821, and unauthorized American settlers, lured by the prospect of cheap land, began to drift across the Sabine and Red Rivers, or up from the Gulf of Mexico. By 1830, Americans outnumbered Mexicans in the area by three to one, and it was said that "G.T.T." (Gone to Texas) was being scratched into ever more homesteaders' doors north of the border.

The type of men who settled the area were described by Houston himself as "a class of noisy, second-rate men, who are always in favor of . . . extreme measures." The country was ready for the leadership of a man like Houston, and he was ready for the country. He established a law practice in Nacogdoches, sent President Jackson glowing reports about what could be accomplished in Texas, fell in love again (and again, the young lady did not return his sentiments), and converted to Catholicism, so as to make Mexican citizenship easier to obtain.

Americans were not the only ones interested in Texas, however. General Antonio López de Santa Anna became president of Mexico in 1833 and was determined to make it part of Mexico. He was as aware as the Americans were of the potential wealth of the country, and he made it clear that *norteamericanos* were no longer welcome.

On September 14, 1835, as the push by white settlers for Texan independence became more intense, Houston was appointed commander of Nacogdoches's small militia, and he declared, "The work of Liberty has begun." A month later he was put in charge of all Texas military forces and in November took part in a meeting to draft a "Declaration on the Causes of Texas Taking Up Arms." Next, a provisional state government was established, with Henry Smith as president.

The Alamo, which would play such a symbolic role in the struggle for independence, had been built in 1718 by Franciscan priests and was originally called the Mission of San Antonio de Valero. When the Franciscans left it in the 1790s, it was renamed the Alamo, a Spanish word meaning "cottonwood tree." It had been a place of peace for 120 years, but that was about to change.

A volunteer force headed by Colonel James Bowie headed toward San Antonio, with the intention of securing

William Huddle's 1886 painting depicts the surrender of Santa Anna following the battle of San Jacinto. Sam Houston, wounded in the battle, gestures to Santa Anna, inviting him to sit on an ammunition box to his left. ARCHIVES DIVISION, TEXAS STATE LIBRARY.

the city—including the Alamo—for Texas. Houston considered that to be a mistake, inasmuch as Santa Anna had a far larger force, and his orders to Bowie were explicit: ". . . blow up the Alamo and abandon the place, as it will be impossible to keep up the Station with volunteers." Bowie saw the matter otherwise, and so did Colonel Neill, who was already at the Alamo; the two men decided that the Alamo must be held at all costs. To the end of his life, Houston refrained from outright criticism of

Bowie, but he believed that his former friend had deliberately betrayed him.

Santa Anna himself led the Mexican troops in the Battle of the Alamo. Besieged inside were 183 Americans, including not only James Bowie but Davy Crockett as well. Santa Anna draped a scarlet banner from the tower of the Church of San Fernando, a signal that no quarter would be given to the Americans, and refused Bowie's request that negotiations be held. The Alamo was overrun by Mexican troops on

Sunday, March 6, 1836; all inside were killed and their bodies burned.

Santa Anna had only a few weeks to savor his victory; on April 21, 1836, Houston, with a small force, defeated the Mexican general at San Jacinto in a battle that was said to have lasted less than twenty minutes. Mounted on his white stallion, Saracen, Houston himself was probably the first man ever to utter the famous war cry "Remember the Alamo!" He was severely wounded in the ankle, but when the battle was over, six hundred Mexican troops lay dead and Texas belonged to the Americans.

Santa Anna was captured as he tried to escape in the uniform of a private, and Texans wanted to execute him on the spot. Houston was shrewd enough to realize that the Mexican general was worth far more alive than dead, and spared his life, but it was an act that his enemies would throw in his face to the end of his career.

On September 5, 1836, less than four years after his first arrival in the state, Sam Houston was elected the first president of the Republic of Texas with 79 percent of the vote—surely one of the most astonishing resurrections of any American political career. Mirabeau Lamar was elected vice president, a fact that later would cause Houston considerable grief. At his acceptance speech, Sam drew the sword he'd worn at the Battle of San Jacinto from its scabbard and held it dramatically in front of him, declaring, "I have worn it . . . in defense of my country; and should the danger to my country again call for my services, I expect to resume it, and respond to that call . . . with my blood and life"—words that earned him loud applause.

The republic that Houston inherited owed debts of half a million dollars, yet was nearly bankrupt; the total population was only about thirty-five thousand, many of whom were women, children, and slaves. Lamar continued to press for Santa Anna's execution, but Houston stoutly opposed it and had the support of President Jackson, who advised that nothing would "tarnish the character of Texas more than such an act at this late period." The Mexican general was finally returned to Mexico in February 1837.

Now began the long struggle toward recognition in the U.S. Congress of the independence of Texas and its eventual annexation as a state. Houston's previous experience as a legislator from Tennessee now proved invaluable. In April 1837, the seat of government moved to the new town of Houston, a few miles from the San Jacinto battlefield. The place was no more than a tacky collection of tents and shanties, but by the end of the year the population was twelve hundred souls.

Because of his close relationship with the Cherokees, Houston never was comfortable with Andrew Jackson's policy of Indian "removal" and made serious efforts to set aside suitable lands for the fourteen thousand Indians within the Republic of Texas. Southern emigrants, however, wanted to be rid of Indians altogether. The Indian question was further complicated by the fact that problems developed with Mexican dissidents who sought to ally themselves with the Indians. Houston urged the Cherokees "not to take up the Tomahawk, nor will I allow other men to raise it against you."

In 1839, on a visit to Spring Hill, the home of William Bledsoe, an Alabama businessman, forty-six-year-old Houston met Margaret Lea, only twenty. He was impressed, and this time so was the lady. Houston prolonged his visit, and when he left, he asked her to continue to think of him. The rest of his summer was spent with Andrew Jackson in Nashville, where conversation was directed toward the annexation of Texas. Opposition in Congress was strong because abolitionists had strengthened their position throughout the United States and opposed bringing any state into the union whose population was one-quarter slaves.

Then the scandal over the fate of Indians in Texas further galvanized the antiannexation forces. Lamar, the second president of Texas, had called for the removal or annihilation of all Indians in the new republic. In July 1839, the Cherokees were defeated and fled to the north. One of Houston's old friends, Chief Bowl, was killed, wearing a sword and sash that Kalanu had given to him long before.

On his way back to Texas, Houston stopped to see Margaret Lea again. The young lady's mother was dubious about the match, but Margaret was not and accepted his offer of marriage. On May 9, 1840, the couple were wed. Sam's friends believed he'd been a bachelor too long and doubted that he could reform his wild ways. But the marriage apparently was a happy one, producing eight children and lasting until Houston's death twenty-three years later.

The moment he left office in 1838, Houston and his friends began to lay plans for his return as the president of the Republic of Texas. They dreaded what Lamar had in mind; he opposed annexation to the United States and dreamed of enlarging Texas deep into Mexico. His monetary policies were a disaster (Lamar simply printed money when he needed it; the currency became worthless and was derisively nicknamed "red backs"), and the republic was in danger of economic collapse.

Houston's campaign for a second term was launched, whereupon the opposition labeled him a coward, a poor lawyer, a bad general, and a drunk.

Nevertheless, Houston was reelected in September 1841. A thousand people—nearly the whole city—attended his inauguration in Austin, Texas. He appeared dressed in common linsey-woolsey clothing, an old hat, and Indian moccasins. This time his costume was intended to impress upon the citizenry that the republic was in serious financial trouble. His message illustrated his understanding of what lay ahead for Texas: "We have arrived at a crisis in our national progress. . . . The facts must be submitted in their simplest dress." Among other things, Houston advised Texans to cease involving themselves in the internal affairs of Mexico, which was costly and produced no results.

Throughout Houston's second term, the question of annexation hung over his head. The population of Texas was still under 100,000, one-quarter of whom were slaves. New settlers were desperately needed. This concern, coupled with his efforts to grant Indians their proper rights, kept Houston busy— and he even managed to remain popular. In 1843, Houston and Margaret became parents for the first time, having a son who was said to be the image of his father.

Andrew Jackson, though no longer president, continued to do what he could to promote annexation. A treaty finally was gotten through Congress, but ratification was not to be—not yet.

Houston left office and returned to the new home that he had built along the Trinity River near the small town of Liberty. He opened a law practice and seemed settled for perhaps the first time in his life. But he was soon to lose the most important man in his life, the one to whom he had turned in times of crisis since their first meeting. Andrew Jackson died in June 1845; if he had lived a few months longer he would have seen one of his fondest dreams come true: on December 29, 1845, the state of Texas was recognized by the U.S. Congress.

Houston's name was put forth when the first Texas legislature met in 1846 to select two senators. He was elected in February, and on March 2 celebrated his fifty-third birthday and the tenth anniversary of the birth of Texas. He went to Washington, while Margaret, who was expecting another child, remained in Texas. He no sooner arrived in Washington than some observers detected the gleam of further ambition in Sam's eye: could he perhaps become president not merely of the Republic of Texas but of the whole United States? "Were I the nation's ruler," he wrote to his wife, "I could rule it well." However, when the presidential election of 1852 rolled around, even though "Houston for President" clubs had sprung up around the country, Sam didn't enter the race but supported Franklin Pierce, who went on to win.

One of the greatest challenges that arose during the period Houston served in the senate was the question of slavery—that is, whether it should be permitted in the new states that entered the union. In 1850, Henry Clay introduced a compromise bill to the U.S. Senate that was intended to resolve the issue. The bill provided that the North could have its way on some matters and the South could have its way on others, thereby avoiding any more talk of secession.

In 1854, however, the issue came up again, this time in regard to the territories of Kansas and Nebraska. A new congressional bill made it possible for Kansas and Nebraska to decide for themselves about slavery. Houston argued vigorously against it, declaring, "If this bill passes, it will convulse the country from Maine to the Rio Grande." Houston was bitterly criticized in his home state, but he held firm to his position. "Because the entire South is wrong," he replied, "should I be wrong too?" It is a question that does him everlasting honor.

Houston served in the Senate for nearly fourteen years, continued to be a staunch supporter of the Union, and denounced the "reckless and mischievous agitators" who promoted secession, because he clearly foresaw that it would be disastrous for Texas. He called upon "friends of the Union . . . to sacrifice their differences upon the common altar of their country's good." Houston was nothing if not a realist: he knew that the North had more money, more men, and more industry, and would eventually defeat the South in the event of a war.

Although Houston was far from home, living alone in a city known for its many temptations, he finally was able to control his drinking habits. In fact, he began addressing temperance societies and attended church regularly. Back in Texas, his family now included not only Sam junior but three daughters as well. In 1855, C. E. Lester published the *Life of Sam Houston: The Only Authentic Memoir of Him Ever Published*, with the input of the book's subject. It immediately aroused a storm of criticism among Houston's Texas enemies, who called him a "demagogue" and an "egoist." His sojourn among the Cherokees was labeled "mystical nonsense," and his decision at San Jacinto to spare Santa Anna's life once more became a topic of debate. It was plain that Houston could no longer count on the type of support he'd once enjoyed.

Newcomers were settling Texas in large numbers and now the slave population accounted for fully one-third of citizens. Houston chose not to run for reelection and gave his final Senate speech in March 1859, the day after his sixty-sixth birthday.

He talked of retirement, but if his friends and family took him seriously, they didn't know him as well as they should have. By summer he was talking of running for governor of Texas, and when the "Black Republicans" (those favoring slavery) nominated a strong slavery candidate, Houston threw his hat in the ring. The issue of secession still consumed his interest, and the words of one of his speeches, very Lincolnesque in their grandeur, galvanized voters, who elected him with 60 percent of the vote— making him the only American to have been governor of two different states.

"Mark me, the day that produces a dissolution of this [Union] will be written in history in the blood of humanity," Houston declared. "All that is horrible in war will characterize the future of this people. Preserve the Union and you preserve Liberty."

Houston hadn't yet arrived in Austin to take office when the radical abolitionist John Brown stormed the military arsenal at Harpers Ferry, Virginia, on October 16, 1859. He was hanged two months later, becoming a hero to the an-

tislavery movement and a hated symbol to slaveholders. When Lincoln won the presidential election in 1860, a committee of secessionists demanded that Governor Houston follow the example of Georgia and South Carolina in preparing to leave the Union.

Throughout 1860, rumors of rebellion spread throughout Texas, but Houston governed according to his own understanding of morality: He provoked Texans by pardoning a slave named George who had been sentenced to hang for hitting a white man; as Houston saw it, there had been "peculiar and aggravated circumstances" that justified the black man's act. Earlier, he had intervened in the punishment of a black boy who had been sentenced to 750 lashes for burglary. Neither act endeared him to Texans.

The Texas secessionist movement was successful; in March 1861 secession was approved by a three-to-one vote. Houston then gave what might have been his noblest speech in a lifetime of noble speeches. Calling it an address "To the People of Texas," Sam reaffirmed his love for Texas but refused to take an oath of allegiance to the Confederacy. "I am ready to lay down the office rather than yield to usurpation and degradation," he said. "I love Texas too well to bring civil strife and bloodshed upon her. . . . I shall make no

An engraving after a photograph of Sam Houston taken by Mathew Brady.

endeavor to maintain my authority as Chief Executive of this State. . . . I will not yield those principles, which I have fought for and struggled to maintain."

A week later, Houston was asked to vacate the governor's mansion; within thirty-six hours, he and Margaret and their seven children were gone.

Lincoln himself had conferred with Houston, offering the embattled governor fifty thousand troops to maintain order. Houston declined, pointing out that it would mean civil war in the state. But a national civil war was very near at hand, and it commenced on April 12, when Confederate forces fired on Fort Sumter in Charleston Harbor. This time it wasn't Houston who went off to war; it was his son, Sam junior, who enlisted in the Confederate army. He was wounded at the Battle of Shiloh in April 1862 and was listed on the rolls of "Dead and Missing." Weeks later word came that he had been wounded and was very much alive, and he came home to recover in September 1862.

After abdicating the governor's office, the Houstons moved to Huntsville. Rumors persisted that "Old Sam" might attempt to run for office again. It was true that he hadn't lost interest in politics, but his health caused his family concern. He had developed a cough, and the old wound he'd gotten at Horseshoe Bend almost fifty years earlier still sometimes oozed and caused him pain. Houston made out a will in April 1863, but contrary to a popular story, didn't free his slaves in it.

Houston followed the war news carefully and toyed with the idea of urging Texas to take itself out of the Confederacy and call itself a republic again. On July 4, 1863, two decisive battles were lost by the South: Robert E. Lee was defeated at Gettysburg, while a thousand miles away, Vicksburg fell to Ulysses S. Grant. Sam was certain the worst was only beginning. Later that month, he caught a cold, then developed pneumonia. On Sunday evening, July 26, 1863, as Margaret read his favorite passages from the Bible aloud, his breathing became labored. When she reached out to take his hand, he murmured, "Texas . . . Texas . . . ," then was gone.

Gone was one of the most colorful men in American history. He was buried on a rainy day in Huntsville; a plain pine board was erected bearing his name and the date. A decade passed before a twenty-five-foot slab of gray Texas granite took its place, with Andrew Jackson's words etched into it: "The world will take care of Houston's fame."

Houston left behind more than four thousand letters and documents comprising more than two million words. He had led a life easy to criticize: he drank too much, had a disastrous first marriage, and could be manipulative; yet many of his speeches are as fresh today as when they were written and reveal a man of deep integrity. He was nearly always on the right side of the important issues of his time.

Meriwether Lewis

1774–1809 Explorer. At age twenty, he answered Washington's call for volunteers to put down the Whiskey Rebellion; later fought at the Battle of Fallen Timbers. When Jefferson asked him to lead an expedition to the Northwest, Lewis selected an old friend, William Clark, as his partner. Their journey has been called the "most excellent exploration . . . in the history of America."

The boy born on August 18, 1774, in the shadow of the Blue Ridge Mountains of Albemarle County, Virginia, was christened Meriwether, his mother's maiden name. The thousand-acre Lewis estate, only nine miles from Thomas Jefferson's Monticello, was surrounded by lush fields of bluegrass and woods of locust trees, which gave the family home its name, Locust Hill.

On his father's side of the family, the new baby (a sister, Jane, was born first; a brother, Reuben, came later) claimed a Welsh heritage; on his mother's side, there was a combination of English and Welsh ancestors. The legend on the family crest read, *Omne solum forti patria est*—To the brave man, everything is done for his country.

Lieutenant William Lewis died when Meriwether was five years old. He was returning to active duty in the Continental army after a brief visit with his wife and children on a cold November day; when he tried to ford the flood-swollen Rivanna River his horse was swept from under him and drowned. The swim to shore severely chilled the lieutenant, and he died of pneumonia a few days later at age forty-six. His oldest son blamed his father's death on the redcoats, and more than twenty years later his anti-British sentiment was still strong.

A family acquaintance believed Meriwether inherited his courage and determination from his mother. Lucy Lewis, only twenty-seven when she was widowed, was a self-reliant woman, handy with a rifle, and looked after her children with resourcefulness. One day, a buck deer leaped into her yard; she cornered it against the house, shot it, butchered it, then fed the meat to her family.

Her son learned such lessons well; once, he stood his ground when charged by a bull, then shot the animal dead in its tracks. Not that the boy needed to shoot domestic livestock for food; the country where he lived was rich with game, as the names of locations such as Elk Run, Buffalo Meadow, and Red Bear Hollow testified. Wild turkeys, ducks, and geese populated the ponds, and fish filled the creeks—a paradise for any boy who loved the outdoors.

Lucy remarried in 1780, and the family moved to Georgia. Compared to Virginia, Georgia was a rough frontier, and the boy's stepfather, Captain John Marks, built a cabin at the very edge of the forest. Meriwether, who was intensely curious about the world around him, closely observed the new animals and plants he encountered; the knowledge he acquired would serve him well many years later.

When he was thirteen, Meriwether returned to Locust Hill. After his father's death, the estate had been left in the care of his uncles, but as the oldest son he now was expected to take part in its management. He also attended Albe-marle Classical School, where geography was one of his favorite subjects. A classmate described the boy's character as one of "great steadiness of purpose, self-possession, and undaunted courage." His physical person was somewhat less remarkable; he was considered "stiff and without grace; bowlegged, awkward, formal and almost without flexibility."

Meriwether wanted to continue his education at the College of William and Mary, but at the insistence of his uncles he became the full-time overseer of Locust Hill. It was his brother Reuben, three years younger, who went on to college and became a doctor.

In 1790, Lucy was widowed again. Meriwether fetched his mother back to Locust Hill, along with Reuben and Jane, plus John and Mary, his half siblings. Now that he was the head of a family, Meriwether tended to his duties more energetically than ever, causing Thomas Jefferson to note approvingly that the young man was "an assiduous and attentive farmer."

Did eighteen-year-old Lewis chafe at the sedentary life of a gentleman farmer? Perhaps. In any case, it was whiskey that changed his life—not the drinking of it, but the chance to participate in a battle over the liquor tax that had been imposed on it by Alexander Hamilton, the U.S. secretary of the treasury. The "whiskey counties" of Penn-

The young Meriwether Lewis in a portrait by Charles-Balthazar-Julien-Févret de Saint-Mémin. CULVER PICTURES, INC.

sylvania—Fayette, Allegheny, and Washington—angrily objected to such a tax because whiskey, not money, was a medium of exchange among tradesmen in those days. However, the tax had to be paid in cash, which was always in short supply. Opposition was organized under the leadership of a lawyer named David Bradford.

Tax protesters attacked revenue officers, robbed the U.S. mail, and defied judges' orders. President Washington hoped the matter could be settled peacefully, but in August 1794 it became necessary to call up thirteen thousand militiamen from nearby states to put down the revolt. One of the first volunteers from Virginia was twenty-year-old Meriwether Lewis. Washington himself marched with his inexperienced troops as far as Bedford, Pennsylvania, but no real battle ever took place. As the army neared Pittsburgh, Bradford and the resisters fled to Louisiana, which was still controlled by Spain.

No doubt there was some disappointment among the recruits that enemy opposition collapsed so easily, yet young Lewis believed he'd found his true calling. He remained in Pittsburgh with a contingent of troops whose job it was to maintain order, and in November 1794 he wrote cheerfully to his mother that he was "quite delighted with a soldier's life." He was eligible for discharge from the militia in early 1795 but enlisted in the regular army instead. His next assignment was with General "Mad Anthony" Wayne in the Battle of Fallen Timbers, which subdued a confederation of Wyandot, Delaware, Shawnee, Ottawa, and Chippewa Indians, ending the Indian wars in the Ohio country.

In November 1795, Lewis was involved in a scandal that one might not have expected of him, but one which, ironically, also involved whiskey. Black moods sometimes settled over Meriwether, and it's possible that liquor had, indeed, become a problem for him. He was hauled before a court-martial hearing on a charge of being drunk, breaking into the quarters of a superior officer, threatening him, and challenging him to a duel. Lewis entered a plea of not guilty and was acquitted. He returned to duty but was transferred to the Chosen Rifle Company at Fort Greenville, Ohio. His commander there was a red-haired chap named William Clark, four years his senior. The two quickly became friends, but they didn't serve together long because in July 1796 Clark resigned his commission and went home to settle some tangled family affairs.

Lewis remained in the army, undertaking a variety of duties. It was he whom General Wayne usually chose to carry urgent express dispatches; he commanded an infantry company that took over Fort Pickering, a new post on the Mississippi. He became a recruiting officer in Charlottesville, Virginia, was promoted to full lieutenant in 1798, then made captain in 1800. He was appointed paymaster for his regiment and showed a talent with numbers. He seemed headed for a traditional military life and apparently welcomed it.

Destiny tapped him for a different fate. On February 23, 1801, twenty-six-year-old Lewis received a letter from his old neighbor, Thomas Jefferson, who had just been elected the nation's third president. The election was a close one, and Jefferson wanted a man by his side whom he could trust without question. Who better than the son of old family friends, a young man he'd always thought well of?

Jefferson invited Lewis to become his private secretary and made it clear that acceptance wouldn't mean he'd have to give up his military career. Rather, Lewis could retain his rank and would even be eligible for promotion while serving in Washington. Jefferson added that Meriwether was his first and only choice, and he would be treated "as one . . . of my family." The president also hinted that he had other, even more exciting jobs in mind. Four days later, Lewis sent his reply: "Not a moment has been lost in making the necessary arrangements in order to get forward to the City of Washington with all possible dispatch."

Jefferson, a fifty-eight-year-old widower whose two married daughters were settled in lives of their own, wanted not merely a secretary but an aide-de-camp. Lewis soon became the president's shadow; he answered all correspondence, arranged state dinners, and became privy to state secrets, all the while making use of Jefferson's fine library. The likes of philosopher Thomas Paine were frequent guests at the White House, dinner conversations were never ordinary, and Lewis got the sort of education he'd always dreamed about. For example, in December 1801, when Jefferson couldn't deliver the State of the Union message to Congress himself, he sent Meriwether Lewis in his place.

Sometime early in 1802, Jefferson invited Lewis to help him plan an expedition to search for an all-water, western passage to the Pacific Ocean. At that time, little was known about the country beyond the Mississippi, but many believed a series of connecting rivers—principally the Missouri and the Columbia—might enable travelers to get all the way to the Pacific by boat. Jefferson called his expedition the "Corps of Discovery," then asked Meriwether Lewis to be its leader. It was, in fact, the real reason he'd asked Lewis to come to Washington in the first place.

The United States at that time had been independent of Britain for only nineteen years and consisted of sixteen states (the original thirteen, plus Vermont, Kentucky, and Tennessee). European nations still pressed their claims in the New World: Spain had stretched its Mexican interests into California; France owned vast tracts west of the Mississippi; Russia had colonized Alaska and was casting greedy glances down the western coast. Most competititve of all, of course, was England. Even though the colonists had won the War of Independence, there were English outposts throughout eastern Canada, and it was rumored more forts would be constructed all the way west to British Columbia.

Jefferson was determined to protect American interests. For more than twenty years, he had pondered the nature of the country west of the Mississippi, and in Meriwether Lewis he was sure he had a man who could help him find out more about it. As one biographer put it, "If George Washington is the father of our country, then surely Jefferson is the father of the American West."

Jefferson told Lewis the exploration must be a peaceful one. His mission would be to map the country, find out about its animals and plants, and especially to establish good relations with the Indians, to learn as much as possible about their customs and languages while taking care to "treat [them] in the most friendly and conciliatory manner." (Sixty years later, the government's Indian policy would be far less benign.)

Jefferson realized his young protégé needed a crash course in scientific investigation and sent Meriwether to Philadelphia to be tutored by respected experts. Benjamin Smith Barton instructed him in botany; Caspar Wistar taught him the basics of astronomy; Dr. Benjamin Rush tutored him in the practice of medicine.

Outfitting the expedition, however, was left up to Lewis. It was the sort of organizational project that ideally suited his temperament. He divided his purchases into ten categories: mathematical instruments, arms, ammunition, clothing, camp equipment, food and provisions, gifts for Indians, means of transportation, medicine, and material for making packs for all of the aforementioned items. Included in the arms category were a pair of pocket pistols for himself, each with secret triggers.

He didn't skimp on the "gifts for Indians" category: there were beads of blue, white, red, yellow, and orange; bright calico shirts; handkerchiefs of muslin or silk; eyeglasses and mirrors; bells, scissors, needles, sewing awls, and thimbles; fish spears and fishhooks;

rings, earrings, and brooches; and a dozen peace medals with the profile of Jefferson on one side, a pair of hands clasped in friendship on the other.

The medicines he assembled were the best available for the time: Epsom salts; calomel; powdered bark (probably quinine); drugs such as opium and laudanum; borax; camphor; and spices such as cinnamon, clove, and nutmeg, which often were used to treat common ailments. He also gathered together almanacs and scientific tables for use in determining longitude and latitude; books on minerology, botany, and nautical astronomy; books on medicine and health; maps; and thirteen journals bound in red leather in which to document the expedition's findings.

Timing was critical because Lewis hoped to travel at least three hundred miles up the Missouri before winter froze the river and made travel impossible. In Pittsburgh, he arranged for the building of a pirogue, a small, flat-bottomed boat (a second was purchased later), and a fifty-five-foot keelboat with a thirty-two-foot mast, capable of carrying ten tons of cargo. He also designed a collapsible canoe that weighed only 99 pounds and named it *The Experiment*; when tested, the craft proved able to carry a load of 1,770 pounds. As a companion/mascot, he bought himself a black Newfoundland dog for twenty dollars and named it Seaman (some references give the dog's name as Scannon).

Most importantly, on June 19, 1803, Lewis found time to write to an old acquaintance—red-haired William Clark—inviting him to join the expedition. He asked Clark to keep the project "inviolably secret" because the Louisiana Purchase, whereby France agreed to cede fifteen million acres of western land to the United States at a cost of four cents an acre, had not yet been signed. (News of the signing in Paris on April 30, 1803, didn't reach America until July; it was finalized March 10, 1804.)

On July 29, Clark's reply was received. He was "much pleased" and would be happy to share the "dangers, difficulties and fatigue" of such a venture. So continued the relationship of two men whose names became so intertwined in American history that someone said it was if they were a single person named "Lewisandclark."

Clark assisted in recruiting men for the venture, but Lewis warned him not to accept those with "soft palms"—men who hoped for a grand adventure but weren't up to hard work. On August 31, 1803, the party left Pittsburgh and headed down the Ohio River. Drought had made the water level low, and teams of horses on the riverbank had to drag the boats along. The expedition turned into the Mississippi at Fort Massac, went upriver, then stopped at the mouth of the Wood River, seventeen miles from St. Louis. There, Camp Wood was established, and the expedition wintered until mid-May 1804.

Lewis had promised Clark that he would be given a captain's rank if he joined the expedition, but while at Camp Wood news came that Congress had refused to approve the commission. Both men were embittered, though not at each other. Lewis pledged that as far as he was concerned, the crew would never be informed of Congress's refusal, and he would address Clark as "Captain" and respect him as such.

As a result, expedition members were never aware of the difference in rank between the two men; but the difference in their personalities was clearly evident from the beginning. Lewis was by nature a taciturn man who held people at arm's length and who probably wasn't amused by nicknames the crew gave him: "Captain Merry," "Merry Lewis," and "Merry Weather." By contrast, Clark had a steady disposition, seldom became angry, and was always approachable. Lewis's name would come first in history books, but expedition members usually preferred to deal with Clark.

On May 14, 1804, the Corps of Discovery left Camp Wood. The group consisted of its two leaders, nine Kentuckians, fourteen soldiers, two French voyageurs, an interpreter, Clark's black slave, York, and Lewis's Newfoundland dog. The youngest man in the party was eighteen-year-old George Shannon of Pennsylvania; the oldest was John Shields, thirty-eight, a blacksmith. John Colter, twenty-eight, would become famous for a discovery he made after the expedition was over. Together, the crew turned westward, toward what the French called *le pays inconnu*, the unknown land.

The expedition soon came upon many species of plants and animals that white men had never seen before. All were carefully recorded and described in the captains' journals, and whenever possible, Lewis preserved specimens for shipment back to Jefferson. When the crew came upon a village of prairie dogs, which they called "barking squirrels," they managed to capture one of the animals by flooding its burrow with buckets of water. Badgers, jackrabbits, antelope, and coyotes (Clark called the latter "prairie wolves") also were new to the travelers.

In August, Sergeant Charles Floyd became ill, and when Lewis noted that his condition was worsening he tried to ease the young man's pain with medication. On August 20, 1804, Floyd asked Clark to write a letter for him, but he died before he could dictate a word. It's now believed that he died of a ruptured appendix, and to him belongs the dubious honor of being the only member of the expedition to perish. He was buried on a bluff near what is now Sioux City, Iowa.

The other members of the crew were amazingly lucky: they survived dysentery, boils, colic, frostbite, open wounds, snakebites, dislocated limbs, influenza, and starvation. They even survived the medical treatments Lewis administered to them, "thunder pills" (strong laxatives), for example, or bleeding (a catchall treatment for many ailments that probably did more harm than good).

Of all the Plains tribes, it was the Sioux who were the most warlike, and the expedition dreaded them most. As the men camped at the fork of the James and Missouri Rivers news came that some Yankton Sioux were in the area, causing both fear and excitement. A meeting took place on August 30, ten days after the death of Sergeant Floyd, and Lewis delivered a speech that he was to give many times before the journey was over. In it, he told the Indians that the American cities east of the Mississippi were "as numerous as the stars" in the night sky and invited the chiefs to visit "the Great Father" in Washington. He also urged the Indians never to listen to the advice of the "bad birds," the English or French.

It was assumed the meeting went well, but on the following day, the Sioux demanded more gifts—in particular, more "milk of the Great Father," or whiskey. After some discussion, the Yanktons seemed satisfied with the promise of future gifts, but still to be faced upriver were the much fiercer Teton Sioux.

On September 25, the Tetons were encountered near present-day Pierre, South Dakota. The Indians came to inspect the keelboat, then were taken back to shore in a pirogue, which they seized to prevent the whites from returning to their ship. However, expedition members on the keelboat kept the Indians covered with swivel guns, and when twelve more of the expedition members came ashore to help, Chief Black Buffalo quieted his men. That evening, a celebration was held, but it was two nights before the whites could continue their journey.

By October 5, there was frost on the ground, and three days later the expedition encountered a band of Arikaras. Unlike the Sioux, they weren't warlike nomads but lived in round houses made of willow branches plastered with mud and grew crops such as beans, squash, pumpkins, and tobacco. The Arikaras became fascinated by York, Clark's servant, and attempted to rub off the "black

A woodcut by Patrick Goss, a member of the expedition, shows the construction of what was probably Fort Mandan. NORTH WIND PICTURE ARCHIVES.

paint" on his skin. Their attitude toward alcohol was much different from that of the Sioux; they refused it when some was offered, saying that white men gave liquor to Indians to make them behave foolishly.

The following week, the captains had to administer punishment to an insubordinate crew member, Private John Newman. The sentence was seventy-five lashes, and an Arikara observer cried aloud to witness the victim's suffering.

He protested that the Indians never beat even their children. When the captains explained that sometimes it was necessary to set an example, the Indian reluctantly agreed, acknowledging that in his culture, hardened criminals sometimes had to be killed. Newman later was discharged and sent back to St. Louis.

In late October snow began to fall, and the expedition was glad to reach a Mandan village, near Bismarck, North Dakota. The Mandans were farmers too, and had a more sophisticated culture than any of the Plains tribes. A wooded site about three miles downriver from the Indian village was selected as a campsite, and expedition members set about building cabins in which to spend the winter. Two rows of four cabins, each fourteen feet square, were erected to form two sides of a triangle. The triangle was closed on the third side by fortresslike posts; an American flag was hoisted above the compound, and it was named Fort Mandan. Lewis calculated they had traveled 1,600 miles since beginning their journey on May 14.

Indians were not the only people the expedition had contact with at this time. British and French traders and fur trappers were active in the area, and although Lewis and Clark had many conversations with them, animosity was felt on all sides. The British especially resented the activities of the Americans and tried to incite the Indians against them; in turn, Lewis (was he thinking of his father's early death?) sternly warned them to cease and reminded them they were operating on U.S. soil.

The winter was much colder than any of the men, who were mostly from Virginia, Kentucky, and Tennessee, had ever experienced. By mid-December, temperatures dipped to 45 degrees below zero. Yet hunters went out every day to supply the fort with meat, and nearly every day Lewis administered medical treatment not only to his crew but to the Indians, who often sought his advice.

In February 1805, Toussaint Charbonneau, a French Canadian who had lived among the Mandans for several years and had just been hired as an interpreter for the expedition, asked Lewis to assist his young wife, Sacagawea, through a difficult childbirth. Lewis had never anticipated having to act as a midwife and had no suitable medicines in his kit. However, when someone suggested that the crushed rings of a rattlesnake's tail would help, he fetched some that he'd brought along to use as an antidote for snakebite. He watched as two rings were crushed, put in water, and given to the young woman to drink. Within ten minutes, a healthy baby boy was delivered; privately, Lewis doubted the rattles were responsible.

It wasn't the last contact Lewis would have with the interpreter's teenage wife. When he found out she was Shoshone, Lewis realized she would be an important addition to the expedition. The Shoshone tribe lived in the foothills of the Rockies, and the corps hoped to buy saddle horses from them; yet neither George Drouillard, the expedition's main interpreter, or Charbonneau spoke that language. Sacagawea did, so Charbonneau was asked to bring her and his infant son, Jean Baptiste, on the journey.

That journey commenced on April 7, 1805. The keelboat was left behind; the two pirogues and six canoes the men had built over the winter were loaded, and the corps set off. Lewis wrote in his journal: "I could but esteem this moment of my departure as among the most happy of my life." By April 26, the expedition reached the mouth of the Yellowstone; in early May, a sudden snowfall startled everyone. A huge grizzly bear nearly got the best of six hunters, and when it was finally killed the men discovered that eight bullets had passed through it before it fell. On May 19, Lewis reported that Seaman was bitten by a beaver and almost bled to death.

Halfway across Montana, the river unexpectedly forked, and a choice had to be made as to which branch to follow. The northern one was brown and muddy, like the Missouri itself; the southern fork flowed clearly. Lewis explored the north fork, and Clark went down the clear one; both agreed that the true continuation of the Missouri was probably the clear southern one. Lewis named the north branch Maria's River (now known as the Marias), after a cousin of whom he was fond.

When they arrived at the Great Falls of the Missouri, the captains knew they'd made the right choice, because the Mandans had told them they would come to such a place. Lewis called the ten-mile stretch of falls and rapids "the grandest sight I ever beheld." Traveling was extremely difficult, however, inasmuch as the falls meant an eighteen-mile portage around them, which was complicated by rough, cactus-covered terrain, and by the sudden, life-threatening illness of Sacagawea, which required a temporary halt of the journey. The young Indian mother recovered after Lewis treated her with bleeding and quinine.

Lewis decided it was time to test his collapsible canoe. The iron framework was unpacked, and an elk hide was used to cover it. Since there were no evergreen trees nearby from which to gather pitch to caulk the boat, Lewis used a mixture of melted tallow and charcoal; alas, when put in the river *The Experiment* leaked like a sieve! Lewis gave up "all further hope of my favorite boat"; it was taken apart, the frame was buried, and it likely still lies on a bluff above the Missouri somewhere in Montana.

Once again, the travelers came to a branch in the river—but this time there were three forks. After examining each one, Lewis decided that none of the three ought to be considered the true Missouri, and he gave each its own name: the southwest fork became the Jefferson River in honor of the president; the middle fork the Madison, after the secretary of state; and the southeast branch the Gallatin, after the secretary of the treasury. Lewis considered the Three Forks area to be "an essential point in the geography" of the West, for the three rivers joined to form the origin of the true Missouri, 2,500 miles from where it emptied into the Mississippi near St. Charles, Missouri.

In late July, Sacagawea told Lewis the country they were passing through was where she'd been kidnapped from her Shoshone tribe years earlier. Lewis and Clark eagerly awaited their first encounter with her people, from whom they could get horses. Without them, travel across the Rockies, called the Shining Mountains by the Indians because even in summer the topmost peaks were covered with snow, would be difficult if not impossible.

Not only did they find the Shoshones, they found the very band from which Sacagawea had been kidnapped as a child of twelve. At first, the Indians suspected the newcomers were some strange tribe of Indians themselves; Lewis realized it was because their skins were so darkened by the sun they no longer resembled white men—so he quickly raised his sleeve to show that he was indeed white. Sacagawea's brother, Cameahwait, was now chief of the tribe, and even though his people had lost many horses in a recent raid by other Indians, he promised Lewis that he would provide mounts.

The journey over the Rockies took from September until November. Food was in short supply, and often the men were on the verge of starvation, sometimes subsisting on a thin soup made of tree bark, and once they dined on candle wax. Lewis and Clark had hoped to be able to canoe down the tributaries of the great Columbia River, but the waters of the Clearwater and Snake Rivers were rough, and it was often necessary to portage over steep, rocky terrain that was difficult for the horses. On October 16, 1805, the expedition members finally reached the broad Columbia, which had been their aim from the beginning of their journey.

Travel down the Columbia was no easy task either, but by late October sea otters were seen, indicating that the Pacific couldn't be far away. On November 7, 1805, there was rejoicing because it was believed that the ocean had been sighted; the body of water was Gray's Bay, however, twenty miles inland. It was on November 14 or 15 that Lewis finally sighted what he called the "Great South Sea," or the "Western Ocean"—4,133 miles from where his journey had begun at Camp Wood.

A permanent camp was needed, and Lewis found what he considered to be an ideal spot on a high point of wooded land near a marshy area thick with elk that could provide meat. The Clatsop Indians, accustomed to dealing with white men because British traders were active in the Northwest, were friendly and helped the party settle, and soon Fort Clatsop was ready for occupation. It was fifty feet square and consisted of two long structures facing each other and joined on the sides by palisaded walls. A freshwater spring thirty yards away provided drinking water. One building was divided into three rooms to be occupied by the enlisted men; the other consisted of four rooms: one for the captains, one for the Charbonneau family, an orderly room, and a meat-keeping room.

On Christmas Day, a celebration was held. Whiskey rations had long since been used up, but the men provided merriment by singing, dancing, and firing their pistols. The captains distributed half of the remaining tobacco to those who smoked, new handkerchiefs to those who did not. Sacagawea gave Clark a dozen ermine tails, but—tellingly—gave nothing to Lewis, testament to the fact that although she had established a warm feeling toward Clark (who called her "Janey"), she and Lewis never became friendly. Christmas dinner was memorable, but not for its gourmet quality: it consisted of spoiled fish, rotted elk meat, and a few roots.

The winter was a long one. True, it wasn't as cold as it had been at Fort Mandan, but from November until March 1806, there were only twelve days when it didn't rain, and the constant grayness was dispiriting. Mildew rotted clothing and bedding; many men suffered from rheumatism or influenza; infestations of fleas kept everyone miserable.

To combat boredom, the captains tried to keep everyone busy. One job—hated by most of the men—was the chore of making moccasins for the return trip; nevertheless, by March 1806, 338 pairs had been made, or about 10 pairs for each person. Men were sent down to the ocean to make salt for the return trip; other men were sent to buy whale blubber from the Indians; hunting for fresh meat was a regular chore. The captains themselves worked on their journals; Lewis finished his meticulous descriptions of plants and animals while Clark completed the map he'd started at Fort Mandan.

The homeward journey was commenced on March 23, 1806. Travel up the Columbia River was treacherous because now the river was swollen from melted snow. Then, in April, the group was joined by some Nez Percé Indians, who said they knew a quicker and better route to the east. Recrossing the Bitterroot Mountains was hazardous even in June because the snow was still deep,

Charles-Balthazar-Julien-Févret de Saint-Mémin's watercolor portrait of Meriwether Lewis two years before his death. COLLECTION OF THE NEW-YORK HISTORICAL SOCIETY.

feed for horses was limited, and game animals were scarce. Late in the month, however, the expedition arrived back at Lolo Hot Springs near present-day Missoula, Montana, where the men bathed in the soothing water. Lewis compared the water temperature favorably with the hottest springs in Virginia.

The captains divided the men at a point called Traveler's Rest; Lewis and a small party went back to the Great Falls of the Missouri to investigate the Marias River in greater detail, and Clark and the rest of the party explored the Three Forks area again. It would not be until forty days later—August 12—that the two parties were rejoined. Then, travel downstream on the Yellowstone, then the Missouri, was swift, and two days later the expedition arrived back at Fort Mandan, which, in their absence, had been partly destroyed by fire. They rested for three days, then prepared to return to St. Louis on August 17. John Colter was the only man who didn't go back; he requested permission to stay to trap furs and explore. He remained in the Northwest for four more years, becoming the first white man to travel through what is now Yellowstone Park.

The lower Missouri had become a highway for travelers, and on the way home the men were brought up to date on news they'd had no way of hearing in their absence: Alexander Hamilton had been killed in a duel with Aaron Burr. . . . Zebulon Pike had set out to explore the Red River. . . . And since the rest of the world hadn't heard from members of the corps in such a long while, it was assumed they were all dead!

At dawn on September 23, 1806, the expedition arrived at Camp Wood;

the journey had taken two years, four months, and ten days, and covered seven thousand miles. It had indeed been a "voyage of discovery," but ironically, the mission ended in failure—that is, no waterway to the Pacific was discovered. Yet it was a success inasmuch as Lewis proved men could cross the mountains to the sea.

Lewis sold the supplies left from the expedition at an auction for $408.62. When he submitted the expedition's final bill, it totaled $38,722.25—less than what some Americans spend today to buy an automobile. Each soldier in the expedition received 320 acres of land and double pay, or between $10 and $16 for each month served. Those who wished to leave the military were honorably discharged; those who remained were offered choice assignments.

The captains each received 1,600 acres of land and double pay amounting to $1,228. Clark went home to Virginia, where he intended to court the young woman for whom he had named the Judith River in Montana. He eventually freed his black slave and gave him a wagon and a team of six horses; York later established a freight-hauling business in Louisville, Kentucky. Lewis arrived at Locust Hill in time to spend Christmas with his mother, then moved on to Washington on December 28.

The U.S. Congress approved the appointment of Clark as the superintendent of Indian affairs for the Louisiana Territory and made him a brigadier general, which no doubt soothed any feelings about the earlier denial of a captaincy. Jefferson appointed Lewis the first governor of that same territory, and both men took up their new posts in the territorial capital, St. Louis.

Jefferson considered it to be of utmost importance that the journals kept by Lewis and Clark be published as quickly as possible. Other men in the expedition were also eager to publish theirs; Lewis was severely critical, saying that enlisted men weren't adequately qualified to render worthwhile opinions. In March 1807, Lewis found a publisher, C. and A. Conrad of Philadelphia, and a three-volume project was agreed upon that would sell for $31, a hefty sum in those times. However, the task of writing up his journal notes became hopelessly entangled in his responsibilities as governor of the Louisiana Territory, and Lewis never finished the project. The territory was beset by many problems, not the least of which was that a variety of schemers—Indian traders, land speculators, ambitious government officials—made Lewis's job a nightmare. Perhaps the most serious problem of all was that Lewis was not "a people person" and often clashed with those around him.

Lewis's second-in-command, Frederick Bates, who had directed the territory during Lewis's journey to the Northwest, began to undermine Lewis's efforts to govern properly. Lewis also was at a disadvantage because he no longer had the support of Jefferson; a new president, James Madison, had been elected in 1809. Lewis had been a moody man in the best of times, and now the added burdens of his new job caused him to begin drinking heavily.

In order to defend his reputation against growing criticism, Lewis decided to go to Washington. He granted his old friend Clark the right to take care of his personal affairs in his absence, and then on September 9, 1809, he and a half-black servant, John Pernia, set out for the capital. Two days later, in what turned out to be a prophetic move, Lewis prepared his last will and testament.

When Lewis arrived at Fort Pickering on September 15, near what is now Memphis, Tennessee, the commander of the post, Captain Gilbert Russell, realized the famous explorer was in a "state of mental derangement." He learned that Lewis had attempted suicide twice and detained him at the fort for his own safety. Within a week, Lewis seemed improved; his funds were running low, so Russell lent him about one hundred dollars to continue his journey.

On October 10, 1809, Lewis decided to rest at a backwoods inn called Grinder's Stand, about seventy-two miles from Nashville, along a wilderness trail known as the Natchez Trace. Mrs. Grinder, the proprietor, welcomed Lewis and prepared a meal for him. He ate little, but he smoked his pipe for a time as he looked out the doorway toward the west—where he had accomplished so much—and Mrs. Grinder heard him murmur, "What a sweet evening this is!"

Then, about 3 A.M. on October 11, two shots were heard. Mrs. Grinder and her servants were frightened and waited till daylight before hurrying to Lewis's cabin. They found him alive but bleeding from a wound to the head and another in the chest. Among his last words was the lament, "I am no coward but I am so strong. It is so hard to die." He was thirty-five years old; his momentous journey had ended only three years earlier.

Lewis was buried in an unmarked grave near the inn. A friend, Alexander Wilson, visited the site not long after the explorer's death. "He lies buried close by the common path with a few loose [fence] rails thrown over his grave," he noted. "I gave Grinder money to put a post frame around it, to shelter it from the hogs and from the wolves." Not until 1846 was a real marker placed at the site.

Rumors circulated that Lewis had been murdered, yet no firm evidence existed to support such tales. In 1814, when Lewis's journals were finally published, Jefferson himself stated that the death was the result of suicide and asserted that Lewis had always been afflicted by "hypochondriac affections," which today would be called depression. Jefferson—who had been a father to Lewis, just as Lewis had been a son to him—believed the explorer's mental turmoil worsened after he became governor of the Louisiana Territory, when his moods "began to alarm his friends." Clark, upon hearing the news, was especially stricken and declared, "I fear the weight of his mind has overcome him."

Meriwether Lewis is not remembered for his anguished death, however, but for his courageous life. His tenacity and dedication—for he was the principal leader of Jefferson's Corps of Discovery—were responsible for proving that overland travel to the Pacific Ocean was possible. He and Clark cataloged 122 animals previously unknown to Americans and 178 types of new plants. They brought back important information about the languages and customs of more than forty Indian tribes that lived west of the Mississippi. They charted rivers, mountains, and important landmarks to aid future travelers. Whatever his ending, there is no doubt that Meriwether Lewis lived up to his family's motto: To the brave man, everything is done for his country.

James McLaughlin

1842–1923 Indian agent. A native of Canada, McLaughlin came to Minnesota in 1863, and a year later married a woman of mixed Sioux and white ancestry. Entered the Department of Indian Affairs in 1871; became proficient in the Sioux language; sometimes found himself at cross-purposes with white military leaders. Wrote *My Friend the Indian* in 1910, wherein he considered the Battle of the Little Bighorn from the Indians' point of view.

Although there are thousands (approximately thirty thousand) pages of material in the Archives of Assumption Abbey in Richardton, North Dakota, that relate to James McLaughlin, very few of them pertain to his early life. He left a single long, galloping sentence about his origins (a biographer noted it was "truly McLaughlinian," and lived up to its author's penchant for convoluted prose):

"Born in 1842, in the province of Ontario, of both Irish and Scotch ancestry,—an accident of birth the distinction of which I gladly share with some millions of my contemporaries—I arrived in Minnesota in 1863, with two strong, bare hands, and entered into an appren-

ticeship for a career among the Indians by becoming acquainted with many of them and of their mixed bloods at St. Paul, Mendota, Wabasha, Fairbault, and other places in that then frontier state."

Other details about James McLaughlin are now known, having been gleaned from documents, letters to friends, or the tiny notebooks he kept throughout his career. His father, Felix, was born in Ireland in 1807; his mother, Mary Prince, had been born in Scotland a year earlier, then moved to Belfast when she was a child. The young couple met, married, and sailed for Canada the day after their wedding. When the seventh of their ten children was born on February 12, 1842, near the village of Cornwall, Ontario, the busy parents apparently had exhausted their supply of middle

244

names and christened the new baby simply James.

James attended a country school at Avonmore, Ontario, and graduated from the eighth grade in 1857. Since there was no high school nearby where he could pursue further studies, the boy began a three-year apprenticeship as a blacksmith. He was bright and learned more than the mere basics of his trade by also studying the mechanics of sawmills and gristmills.

When he was twenty-one, James left Ontario for the United States—specifically, for Minnesota—where job opportunities were better. (Another young Canadian, four years older than McLaughlin and also named James, had emigrated to Minnesota in 1856 for the same reason. He, too, hadn't been given a middle name, but he created one for himself and became a man the American railroad industry wouldn't forget—James Jerome Hill.)

James McLaughlin arrived in St. Paul on April 13, 1863. He wasn't a tall fellow, only about five feet six inches in height; nevertheless, he probably made an impression on those who saw him step from the train that day. He was well dressed, slender, and had jet black hair, a lean and angular face, and a shrewd look in his dark eyes. He worked for a time in the quartermaster's department at Fort Snelling, near the village of

Mendota, Minnesota, where a certain young lady soon caught his eye.

Marie Louise Buisson was a small, handsome girl of one-quarter Sioux ancestry. Her grandmother was a full-blood member of the Mdewakanton Sioux tribe who had married a Scots fur trader, Duncan Graham. One of her daughters, Mary, married Captain Joseph Buisson, a French trader, and in turn gave birth to a daughter of her own, Marie Louise, on December 8, 1842. From her mother and grandmother, Louise (as she was called by her family) learned the Sioux language and customs, and she also was given an upper-class "finishing school" education at a convent in Prairie du Chien, Wisconsin.

After James McLaughlin and Louise Buisson married on January 29, 1864, they moved to the village of Owatonna in southern Minnesota. A year later James applied for his U.S. citizenship. During the next three years, two daughters, Mary and Clara, were born but died in infancy. James went into partnership in a blacksmith shop with a certain Mike Quiggle, who borrowed a considerable sum of money from him, only to seek the more hospitable climate of California when business got slow. Quiggle never repaid the debt.

James then moved his family to the village of Wabasha, along the Mississippi River downriver from St. Paul, and

James McLaughlin in his later years. THE NEW YORK PUBLIC LIBRARY, SPECIAL COLLECTIONS.

started over in a new partnership with John Hunter. There was little smithing to be done during the winter, however, so he took a job as a traveling salesman. He traveled as far as Iowa, Kansas, and Missouri selling jewelry, watches, tools, and kitchen utensils.

It was an era long before malls or department stores, when frontier folk had little opportunity to purchase the sorts of items McLaughlin was selling, and as a result he did very well for himself. When he set out for another trip in December 1869, he took Louise and their healthy new baby, Harry, with him. Since business was good, he continued the trip into the late spring and was able to buy himself a team and a new wagon.

When he returned to Minnesota in July 1870, McLaughlin took up the smithing trade again, then received a message from home telling him that his mother was seriously ill. Whether he reached her side before she died isn't known; the note he made of the occasion reported merely that "Mother died . . . on Friday AM August 5, 1870."

Back home in Minnesota, McLaughlin spent the next several months supplementing his blacksmith's earnings by hauling water, clerking, and carpentering. He applied for another job as a salesman, this time with a New York firm, but delayed accepting a position because of the birth in November 1870

of Imelda, the only one of his daughters to reach adulthood. It was a delay that changed the course of his life, for a couple of months later he received news that Major William Forbes had been appointed the agent for a new Sioux reservation to be established at Devils Lake in North Dakota, and needed men to staff his agency.

McLaughlin wrote to Forbes in early 1871, informing him that "I am a blacksmith by trade. Can do anything in that line. I have a fair knowledge of most kinds of business. If you . . . have not already [got] another person, I would like to go with you. P.S. I have a very good double rig for such a trip with an extra saddle pony."

Forbes also was Canadian and had come to Minnesota more than thirty years earlier to clerk for John Jacob Astor's American Fur Company. He had learned the Sioux language and for twenty-five years had been involved in trade with the Indians, with whom he built up a relationship of mutual trust. When the Great Sioux Uprising of 1862 turned whites against the Indians and destroyed his trade, Forbes volunteered for service in the Civil War. He returned to Minnesota in 1866, a man in his mid-fifties whose health and spirit seemed to have been broken by his wartime experiences. Forbes languished, awaiting retirement, but when the chance of an appointment as Indian agent in Dakota Territory came along, he felt he'd been given a new lease on life.

When McLaughlin got word in March that Forbes had accepted his application, he tidied up his affairs in Minnesota and got ready to enter the Department of Indian Affairs, never supposing that he was about to embark on a career that would span fifty-two years. Forbes put him in charge of ordering supplies and getting them ready to be taken out to the reservation. Then, in July 1871, with a crew of five men and six teams of oxen, James headed west. The journey took a month, and McLaughlin—a stranger to the Sioux—recalled his welcome: "They were not exactly cordial."

However, one of the chiefs, Tio Waste (Little Fish), knew Forbes well from his days as a trader and was pleased to welcome both white men. Work was immediately begun to make livable the new reservation headquarters, which were located not far from Fort Totten. Some of the more cooperative Indians were put to work cutting logs to build twenty cabins; others put up hay and harvested corn, potatoes, and turnips. And—for the first time—the Indians now had access to the services of a blacksmith. After Forbes obtained some gunsmithing tools, McLaughlin also became a gunsmith, for as Forbes ex-

plained on the purchase order he forwarded to Washington, "The lakes in spring and fall abound here with ducks," and would give the Indians a good source of food. He also pointed out that guns would be a protection "against the hostile bands [who still prowl] around this reservation . . . for the purpose of horse stealing or other depredations."

Under the terms of President Grant's Peace Policy, the method of "civilizing" the Indians embodied a three-pronged approach: they were to be (1) educated to do manual labor, (2) Christianized, and (3) taught how to farm. To accomplish the first two tasks meant obtaining teachers and religious personnel, but ordinary schoolteachers seldom made themselves available for such positions, nor would any Catholics in the United States answer Forbes's call. Finally, the Gray Nuns of Montreal agreed to come (two of Forbes's cousins belonged to the order), and the services of a French priest, Father Reville, were obtained.

In 1873, the U.S. Congress designated five thousand dollars to build a school, and Forbes sent McLaughlin back to St. Paul to buy building materials and hire bricklayers and construction workers. A building forty by sixty feet and two stories high rose quickly, and by July, the cornerstone of St. Michael's School of Manual Labor was laid. In 1874, four nuns arrived from Canada in the midst of a severe November storm. Sister Allard noted in her journal that during the wagon journey through deep snow and against fierce winds to Fort Totten, eighty-five miles north of Jamestown, "the horses were exhausted. . . . We were almost frozen. . . . Mr. James McLaughlin, our driver, took off his fur coat and gave it to Sister [Lajemmerais]. It was done with so much kindness that the favor was accepted."

The school, seven miles from the fort, hadn't yet been completed, so McLaughlin invited the sisters to stay at his home, where Sister Allard said Mrs. McLaughlin "received us with the greatest politeness and kindness." Enrollment at St. Michael's was slow because, true to Forbes's suspicions, the tribal medicine men opposed it. Nevertheless, by early 1875 twenty-nine students were attending regularly.

It wasn't easy to persuade the Sioux—who for centuries had been wandering nomads who followed the buffalo herds across the plains—to learn farming. Many Indians were willing enough to accept blankets, food, and housing, and to have their health needs tended to during the winter, but when spring came they vanished back onto the prairie and subsisted on wild game, as was their custom. The life of homesteaders—plotting off a piece of ground for individual families—was totally foreign to the Indians' approach to life. They had always lived communally as a single large, extended family, with everyone in the tribe sharing whatever food, goods, or possessions were available. Yet by 1875 Forbes was able to write to the *St. Paul Press* that there were "102 families living in good houses, some of them of hewn logs, and floors in all of them . . . with cooking utensils, chairs, tables, crockery."

Forbes realized that a great part of the success of his assignment was due to the untiring efforts of his blacksmith, who had become much more than a mere craftsman. Therefore, when requesting funds for 1875, Forbes asked, "as a matter of justice . . . that he [McLaughlin] be paid $1,200 per annum." (James had been hired at a salary of $60 a month, or $720 yearly.) Forbes pointed out that McLaughlin saw to the "operation of the grist mill, the saw mill, making of bricks. . . . It would be impossible to replace him . . . and I have to acknowledge that I am indebted to him."

With Forbes's permission, McLaughlin wisely made a copy of that document, because his supervisor died suddenly a few months later, in July 1875. McLaughlin submitted his name as a candidate to fill Forbes's position. He had the endorsement of local Catholic priests, of General Henry H. Sibley in St.

Paul, and of other prominent Indian officials, as well as of the Sioux themselves. Alas, on August 4, a stranger, Paul Beckwith, a native of South Bend, Indiana (so young he was sometimes called "the boy"), was appointed.

McLaughlin wasn't the only one who was dismayed when Beckwith arrived on September 10, 1875. The Indians at the Devils Lake reservation were equally disenchanted. Beckwith sensed that he wasn't welcome and attributed his cool reception to McLaughlin. He set about trying to remove him, urging government officials to transfer him southward to the Standing Rock agency near Fort Yates along the Missouri River. Nor did Beckwith endear himself by one of his first acts—the firing of Frank Stone, an employee whose work McLaughlin had found satisfactory.

A war of nerves ensued—or, more accurately, a war of letters. Beckwith wrote letters of complaint to Washington, and McLaughlin wrote follow-up letters defending himself as best he could. Priests at the agency were afraid violence would break out among the Indians if Beckwith remained, and McLaughlin believed that if an impartial investigator were sent to the reservation, the truth regarding Beckwith's ineptness would become obvious. Therefore, he refused to resign his position or agree to a transfer.

Beckwith then took the only action left to him: on April 2, 1876, he fired McLaughlin and ordered him off the premises within three days. Many Indians, thoroughly disgusted with the whole affair, left the reservation and announced they wouldn't return until Beckwith himself was removed and McLaughlin had been reinstated.

Finally, the secretary of the interior in Washington decided that Beckwith must resign and be replaced by McLaughlin, who clearly had the Indians' trust. On June 8, McLaughlin was confirmed by the commissioner of Indian affairs, and on July 2, 1876, Beckwith departed. When McLaughlin took charge, he discovered that Beckwith—no doubt to give his successor a rocky beginning—had let food supplies run so low that the Indians who had remained at the agency were forced to scavenge in the hills for wild turnips in order to survive.

As soon as Beckwith was gone, McLaughlin set about making the Devils Lake reservation a model of agency management. (The Indians called him "the Major," as they had called Forbes, even though McLaughlin, unlike Forbes, had never served in the military.) McLaughlin followed the practices of the last third of the nineteenth century, when it was believed that in order to integrate Indians into society it was necessary to take away their customs, beliefs, and rituals. Like many whites of the time, McLaughlin regarded medicine men in particular as malicious and superstitious, failing to recognize that such men had the welfare of their people at heart. McLaughlin opposed any ceremonial dancing and was largely successful in his efforts to stamp it out; yet today such celebrations are lauded by Indians and whites alike.

Admittedly, it wasn't an easy time to be an Indian agent, especially in Sioux country. McLaughlin took charge of the Devils Lake agency less than a week after the Battle of the Little Bighorn had been fought on a hot afternoon on June 25, 1876, in eastern Montana. Rumors of possible new attacks were heard almost daily, the most serious being the intention of warriors from the Standing Rock agency to seize Fort Totten and clean out its stash of guns and ammunition. (No such attacks materialized.)

Article VIII of the 1867 treaty that established the Devils Lake agency specifically stated that "no goods, provisions, groceries, or other articles . . . [be given] unless it be in the payment of labor performed, or for produce delivered." The aim of such regulations was to encourage individual self-reliance among the Sioux. Therefore, McLaughlin was pleased that by 1880, enough wheat was being produced at Devils Lake to warrant a first-class flour mill on the reserva-

tion. He reported to Washington that the "Indians are highly pleased with it. . . . This will be a great incentive to them in cultivation of larger fields next year."

Working with older Indians often was disappointing, however, and McLaughlin understood that the best way to effect changes in tribal behavior was by educating the young people. He was pleased with the progress of students at St. Michael's, but at one point he almost lost the sisters. Without consulting McLaughlin, the commissioner of Indian affairs in Washington decided St. Michael's ought to be a day school, rather than a boarding school, and cut funding accordingly. McLaughlin strenuously objected to the day-school idea, pointing out that few of his pupils lived close enough to go home at night and return again the next day. The commissioner finally yielded, and the Gray Nuns agreed to stay.

The sisters were happy to teach girls of all ages but refused to take boys past age twelve, who could be rowdy and hard to manage. McLaughlin therefore asked for a teacher just for them, and Father John Apke arrived in 1878 to teach shop classes to young men. As the school grew, new wings were added, one of which became a hospital to serve the Indians' medical needs.

Meanwhile, things were not going so well at the much larger Standing Rock agency to the south, and the government decided to transfer McLaughlin there to see if matters could be improved. Politics in the Indian Bureau delayed his move until September 1881; then McLaughlin and his family boarded a steamboat in Bismarck and headed for Standing Rock. As the Major stepped off the boat, many Indians boarded it for a trip downstream to begin prison sentences at Fort Randall, South Dakota, led by their chief, Sitting Bull. Two years later, the two men would meet again, their relationship destined to be a tragic one.

Part of the trouble at the Standing Rock reservation stemmed from the fact that many of its Indians were veterans of the Battle of the Little Bighorn. Although they'd been victorious over Custer's Seventh Cavalry, proud leaders such as Gall and Crow King deeply resented the position their people now found themselves in as wards of the government. Rain-in-the-Face, a handsome man in the prime of his life, expressed it well when he declared: "The yoke of the Great Father is degrading. . . . I do not want to be treated as an ox or a child. . . . I do not like the men the Great Father sends us. Their tongues are not straight. . . . Flowers grow in their mouths, but their hearts are filled with hate."

Therefore, many Indians waited with curiosity to see what kind of flowers grew out of the mouth of their new agent. A thousand of them gathered at one o'clock on an afternoon shortly after McLaughlin's arrival to hear what he had to say. Among other things, McLaughlin declared he had no objections to the Indians' past mode of life. "But look around you—everywhere," he urged. "In a few years the buffalo will be gone and the footprints of the deer will be seen no more among your valleys." As he had at Devils Lake, he described the benefits of learning to farm. If the earth were treated kindly, he said, "it will blush and blossom with flowers and fruits and grain."

However, McLaughlin was shrewd enough to know the Sioux at Standing Rock couldn't turn themselves into farmers overnight, no more than those at Devils Lake had. After the hard winter of 1882 had caused everyone to be irritable and restless, he announced that a buffalo hunt could be made; furthermore, he said, he would accompany them. On June 10, 1882, two thousand Indians headed west, and McLaughlin followed them on a handsome gray horse given to him by Crow King.

McLaughlin participated in the ritual games that took place before the hunt, enhancing his image in the eyes of his wards. When the hunt began he requested that someone bring him a live buffalo calf to take home to his children. The hunt was hugely successful, but it exhausted McLaughlin so badly that he collapsed into bed that night and slept like a dead man. He never heard the Sioux rise early in the morning to continue their hunt, and he got up to discover himself abandoned. "My tent stood alone," he wrote, "but ranged about it, tied to stakes, were twenty-two buffalo calves!"

McLaughlin took a deep personal interest in the families under his jurisdiction and reported in the spring of 1887 that he'd made a 550-mile trip through the reservation to visit each of its 1,180 families. The experience taught him something about roads too, and he established a requirement that every able-bodied man must work two days per year repairing or building bridges and grading roadbeds. When a government supervisor, O. H. Parker, came to inspect the school at Standing Rock, he discovered that "schools are his chief objects of interest." Parker told his superiors that McLaughlin was a "model Agent. . . . He seems to know every man, woman and child upon his Reservation."

By 1891, ten years after his arrival at Standing Rock, McLaughlin was able to report that even though farming often was precarious due to the nature of the weather on the plains (droughts, hot winds, hailstorms, early frosts), his efforts had resulted in five thousand acres under cultivation and a harvest that

yielded an estimated 5,225 bushels of wheat, 21,000 bushels of oats, 15,150 bushels of corn, 5,000 tons of hay, and many bushels of turnips, rutabagas, beets, carrots, melons, squash, and pumpkins.

The problem of discipline at Standing Rock had usually been handled by soldiers from nearby Fort Yates, but McLaughlin preferred to depend on Indian police, a practice that his mentor, Forbes, had used. Policemen of their own kind were given respect and obedience by the Indians, whereas dependence on white soldiers as enforcers caused ill will. McLaughlin began with a force of twenty and picked Indians who were fearless when it came to maintaining order. Their pay was only eight dollars a month, but the prestige of wearing a uniform and a badge and having permission to shoot the cattle that were to be butchered on "issue days" made up for the meager salary.

In May 1883, Sitting Bull and his followers were transferred from Fort Randall to Standing Rock. McLaughlin no doubt assumed Sitting Bull would be as cooperative as Gall, Crow King, or Rain-in-the-Face, but he quickly learned that was not to be the case. Sitting Bull presented a list of demands (wagons, white man's clothing, horses, oxen), and declared that neither he nor his people intended to participate in any farming activities, at least not during their first year at Standing Rock. McLaughlin was irritated and considered the aging chief to be "pompous, vain, and boastful . . . [because] he has been lionized and pampered by the whites since the battle of the Little Big Horn, I do not wonder at his inflated opinion of himself."

With Sitting Bull's arrival, a chapter began in McLaughlin's career that tainted his otherwise fine reputation. He has been accused by some notable historians, both white and Indian, of being prejudiced against the great Sioux chief (who was a medicine man, not a warrior), while others have maintained it was a matter of two men doomed to confrontation because their aims were so starkly different.

Sitting Bull was the spiritual leader of his people and still hoped for a return of the "old ways." McLaughlin believed those ways were obsolete, that there was no way to turn back history. From the beginning of his work as an Indian agent he had sternly opposed any celebrations or practices that would encourage Indians to believe otherwise. In his book, written twenty years after the medicine man's death, McLaughlin portrayed Sitting Bull in the most unflattering terms: "crafty, avaricious, mendacious, and ambitious . . . possessed all of the faults of an Indian and none of the nobler attributes. . . . I never knew him

to display a single trait that might command admiration or respect." In almost the same breath, however, he grudgingly admitted that Sitting Bull had an "accuracy of judgment, knowledge of men, a student-like disposition to observe natural phenomena, and a deep insight into affairs among Indians [which gave him] a high standing among his people."

Tensions weren't eased when Sitting Bull was deluged with requests for his presence at various public events, nor when he was invited to join Buffalo Bill Cody's "Wild West" show. He did indeed join the show for several months, and to McLaughlin's way of thinking, he came back with an even higher opinion of himself.

Yet there was one thing McLaughlin and Sitting Bull could agree on: they both opposed the Sioux treaty of 1888, which, in essence, offered the Indians terms that didn't favor their long-term interests. McLaughlin helped negotiate a better agreement, and an altered treaty was signed in 1889 that gave the Indians a somewhat better price for the lands they were giving up.

Nevertheless, when the treaty was ratified, Sitting Bull became bitter, and McLaughlin was so concerned that he increased his police force to thirty men because he feared "the Sitting Bull element of malcontents" at Standing Rock.

At about this time, news that an Indian messiah named Wovoka had appeared in Nevada ran like wildfire from agency to agency. Wovoka was predicting that all whites would be expelled from Indian lands. One method of hastening the return of a time when the Indians could live again as they had in the past was the performance of a Ghost Dance, which was immediately forbidden by reservation authorities.

Agents on all reservations—Pine Ridge, Standing Rock, Rosebud, Crow Creek—were alerted to a possible bloody uprising, and when it became known that local tribes intended to ignore the prohibition and participate in a Ghost Dance, the tension became inflammable. McLaughlin recounted his last meeting with Sitting Bull, after which he never again saw the medicine man alive, and his own words lend credence to rumors of his bias.

"'Look here, Sitting Bull,' I began, 'I want to know what you mean by your present conduct and utter disregard of department orders. Your preaching and practicing of this absurd Messiah doctrine is causing a great deal of uneasiness . . . and you should stop it at once.'" Modern conflict-resolution counselors would correctly observe that McLaughlin's mediation skills needed some polishing.

General Nelson Miles called upon Buffalo Bill Cody, an old friend of Sitting Bull's, to help resolve the situation, but McLaughlin asked him to rescind the request because he feared the showman's visit would only make matters worse. A decision was made to arrest Sitting Bull, which resulted not in his arrest but in his death on December 15, 1890, at the hands of the Indian police, specifically Bull Head and Red Tomahawk. Sitting Bull's seventeen-year-old son, Crow Foot, also was killed. Two days later Sitting Bull was buried in a corner of the military cemetery near Fort Yates.

News of the Sioux chief's death created a sensation across the country. He had been the most famous of the Sioux leaders, and newspaper headlines of "Murder!" and "Foul Play!" were followed by demands for an investigation of McLaughlin's conduct. The furor eventually died down, and although McLaughlin said he regretted the violent death of the Sioux chief, he also admitted being glad he was gone.

One of McLaughlin's personal challenges during the 1880s was educating his five children, four sons and a daughter. The older children were ready for college, and a salary of $1,700 a year was no longer adequate. On a visit to Washington, McLaughlin discussed financial matters with his superiors and let them know he intended to resign if his situation didn't improve.

Catholic missions had always supported McLaughlin's efforts on the reservation, but now he got help from an unexpected source—Protestant missionaries, who pledged the sum of $400 to keep McLaughlin at Standing Rock. The Protestants explained their viewpoint in a letter to the commissioner of Indian affairs: "Please regard these [pledges] as a private protest against the . . . government policy of cheap salaries for cheap men for Indian agents."

By 1894, the burdens and challenges of being the agent at Standing Rock had worn down fifty-two-year-old McLaughlin. He had a small income from real estate investments; his sons were established on ranches in South Dakota; he was being mentioned as a candidate for the U.S. Senate; he decided it was a good time to retire. Then he was called to Washington in January 1895 and informed that President Cleveland intended to name him assistant commissioner of Indian affairs. When McLaughlin declined the honor (because he was aware that his appointment could be negated by a future president), the job of inspector of all Indian agencies was offered. McLaughlin accepted it gladly; he believed he fit the job and that it fit him.

For the next twenty-eight years, McLaughlin continued to devote himself to Indian welfare in many more ways than he could have as the head of a single agency. The National Hotel in Washington became his base of operations, though he was mostly on the road, visiting each agency just as he had visited each family on the reservations he had supervised earlier. One of the first inspections McLaughlin made in May 1895 was at his first agency at Devils Lake. He traveled around the agency for four days and was displeased with what he found: children were not in school; homes were not properly furnished; Indians had been swindled in a contract to repair their homes; polygamy once again was practiced. McLaughlin outlined a plan to the agent in charge that required the dismissal of any Indian police or employees who wouldn't commit themselves to vigorous reform.

In February 1906, he inspected the Tongue River agency in Montana, where he spent six days visiting nearly all of its 1,400 Cheyennes. His assessment of the poor conditions he found indicated his understanding of Indian temperament: "The Northern Cheyenne are . . . proud-spirited. . . . They have many noble traits of character and can be led by moral suasion, but will not brook coercion." He pointed out that such people needed an agent with patience and sound judgment; he gave Agent J. C. Clifford high marks for attempting to be the right man for the job.

McLaughlin's responsibilities included inspecting Indian schools; rendering decisions regarding reservation boundaries (as in the case of the Cheyenne, Klamath, and Yakima Indians); establishing grazing rights for sheep and cattle (as among the Navajo and Hopi); and relocating Indian tribes who weren't satisfied with their situation (as when the Brulés requested relocation to the Rosebud agency).

The most important relocation problem was brought about by the desire of Chief Joseph of the Nez Percés to return to his ancestral home in the Wallowa Valley of Oregon. McLaughlin set out on June 11, 1900, to accompany the elderly chief, who was, in McLaughlin's words, a "most amiable and a very pleasant traveling companion. . . . He is quite intelligent and exceedingly shrewd." But many whites had sworn revenge upon the Nez Percés for an uprising in 1877, not to mention the fact that Chief Joseph's own people didn't want to leave their reservation at Lapwai. In McLaughlin's judgment, relocation was not in the best interests of any of the parties, and as a consequence, Chief Joseph died in September 1904 never having achieved his last wish.

In spite of having to refuse Chief Joseph's request, McLaughlin was keenly sensitive to the problems faced by Indians, and during his efforts to re-locate the Mission tribe of California, he eloquently described their problem. "It is here as in all other parts of the country. First the Indian occupied the fertile valleys and rich agricultural lands. But gradually he has been pushed back, until now there is nothing left for him but barren hills. Out of these they endeavor to make a living on land which the white man would not accept as a gracious gift and on which he would starve. . . . They [the Indians] are struggling with conditions which would down many a white man."

When McLaughlin finally located a site that he thought would benefit the Mission tribe, his advice was dismissed, and he remarked bitterly that he "felt keenly the manner in which my selection was ignored—the judgement of a tenderfoot, as one of the Los Angeles papers put it—but I am even more sorry for the poor Indians, whose comfort and prosperity are lessened thereby."

His travels as inspector took him to forty-five states, brought him in contact with all major tribes in the country, and kept him away from his family for long periods; nevertheless, the prairie of the West was always home. His only daughter, Imelda, was married in 1895 but died suddenly in 1899, leaving Mrs. McLaughlin so lonely that Emma Crow King, an orphan girl who had been adopted by the McLaughlins, returned from school to live with her during the Major's extended absences.

McLaughlin was proud of his four sons and had given them a fine upbringing, but he was often disappointed in their conduct. In 1908, he scolded John for his drinking habits, which had resulted in the young man's "squandering money lavishly, thus injuring your reputation in the country." Only a few months later, thirty-five-year-old John died of a broken neck after a fall from a horse. Harry died in 1913; only Charley and Sibley outlived their parents.

It was McLaughlin's nature to be a penny-pincher, and although his sons' spending habits annoyed him considerably, he made several unwise investments himself, particularly in gold and silver mines that never paid off. Nor did the publication of his book, *My Friend the Indian*, become a moneymaker. It appeared in May 1910, and though it sold briskly, his royalties amounted to only eight hundred dollars.

In 1907, the Chicago, Milwaukee, and St. Paul Railroad founded a town in Corson County, South Dakota, and named it McLaughlin in the Major's honor—which, although it didn't provide him with income, was a pleasing recognition. Louise and Sibley soon moved to McLaughlin, and the Major arranged to have his three deceased children reburied there.

In May 1920, Congress passed a law mandating retirement for civil service employees at age seventy. At seventy-eight, McLaughlin was well past the deadline. A month after the law was passed, he received a "Notice of Separation from Service," informing him that his last payday would be in August—but the words "unless you are otherwise advised" were underlined in red. Attached to the letter was a note explaining that steps were being taken to exempt him, and within a few weeks he was notified that he'd been given a two-year extension. McLaughlin was pleased, even though he suffered from the aches and pains of rheumatism. He told a friend that he'd "rather wear out than rust out."

On June 30, 1921, he was honored at Fort Yates with a celebration for fifty years of continuous service in the Department of Indian Affairs. In December 1921, he went home to Avonmore, Ontario, to visit his brother Felix, and returned to Washington with a bad cold. By spring he had recovered enough to spend two weeks helping the Cherokees of North Carolina recover school tax refunds that were due them. Then, while on an inspection trip at the Fort Berthold reservation in upper North Dakota, he injured his back trying to hoist a car out of a mudhole.

Word circulated among his friends that McLaughlin was on his last legs; nevertheless, the eighty-one-year-old agent geared himself up for a final burst of activity. He threw himself into the task of obtaining annuities for the Santee Sioux that were due them from a treaty signed long before, in 1863. After many years of contention, a payment of $386,597.89 was approved, but problems arose when full-blood Santees objected to the enrollement of mixed-blood members of the tribe. McLaughlin immediately set to work reviewing the claims of each tribal member, keeping in mind the wording of the court judgment that "degree of blood has nothing to do with the right of a person to share in the payment of this money."

In the midst of such work, he took time to write to his son Charley regarding Louise's welfare. "I wish you to write me frequently and keep me advised of your Mother's condition. . . . I shall always arrange for the monthly check [for her care] to reach you by the 1st of each month."

After working for a week on the Santee enrollment, McLaughlin rose on the morning of July 28, 1923, feeling more unwell than usual. A friend volunteered to help him, and when she arrived at two o'clock that afternoon the ailing Major asked her to call a doctor, who examined him and wrote out a prescription. When a nurse delivered the medicine two hours later, she discovered that McLaughlin had quietly died. He'd gotten his wish: he'd worn out, not rusted out.

The funeral took place on August 3, in McLaughlin, South Dakota; so many people attended—Indian and white alike—that it was necessary to hold two services. Several of the Indian police who had assisted McLaughlin thirty-two years earlier in the confrontation with Sitting Bull were honor guards: Red Tomahawk, Bear's Ghost, George Flyingby, Otter Robe, Little Soldier, Good Voice Elk, Brown Man, Shoots Walking, and Tall Bull.

McLaughlin's own words are his finest epitaph. In the opening pages of *My Friend the Indian*, he declared, "While I enjoyed and still enjoy the friendship of white men who are very dear to me . . . I hold to nothing more firmly, am proud of nothing so much as of the fact that my red friends of the West have given me the title of friend. . . . It is a small thing to be proud of, some will say, the friendship of an Indian . . . [but] I believe the Indian was a man before outrage and oppression made him a savage."

John Muir

1838–1914 Naturalist, conservationist, writer. Came to America from Scotland as a boy of eleven. In 1867, made a one-thousand-mile hiking trip from Indianapolis to Florida. Was instrumental in making Yosemite Valley into a national park; founder and first president of the Sierra Club.

In The Story of My Boyhood and Youth, *written at the end of his life, John Muir recalled his growing-up years in Scotland. "I was fond of everything that was wild," he wrote, adding, "when I was five or six years old I ran away to the seashore or fields almost every Saturday." In a sense, he remained a wilderness-loving, wandering boy all his life.*

John Muir was born on April 21, 1838, in Dunbar, southeast Scotland, and was his parents' first son. He joined two sisters, Margaret and Sarah, and was called Johnnie as a boy. His mother, the former Anne Gilrye, was the daughter of a prosperous "flesher"—the Scots term for a butcher. Although she had been one of ten children, only she and a sister survived; the others died of tuberculosis, the scourge of that era.

Johnnie's father, Daniel, tall, handsome, and of English and Highland Scots ancestry, had joined the Campbellites, an evangelical Presbyterian sect, when he was a young man. Ever after, he practiced a stern brand of religion, and his sons—Johnnie was soon joined by David and Daniel junior—were often disciplined more severely than their boyhood pranks warranted. When he was grown, Muir told a friend that his mother always "tried to second father's sternness" to make it easier for the children to bear.

After his marriage to Anne Gilrye, Daniel Muir's grain business prospered. Johnnie remembered that once his father played the violin and loved Scots ballads, then gave up music because he concluded it was sinful. He also disapproved of idle talk, and no laughter was permitted at the meal table. Johnnie had to memorize a Bible verse every day; if he recited it incorrectly, he got a "skelping"—a thrashing.

One of Johnnie's earliest companions was his kindhearted grandfather, the retired flesher who lived across the street from the Muir home. Grandfather Gilrye walked with the boy up and down High Street, teaching him how to read signs on buildings, which perhaps was one of the reasons Muir developed such an excellent memory.

Once, Gilrye and his grandson wandered into a hayfield, an occasion Muir recalled vividly in his autobiography: "When we sat down to rest on one of the haycocks I heard a sharp, prickly, stinging cry, and . . . called grandfather's attention to it. He said it was only the wind but I insisted on digging into the hay. . . . We discovered the source of the strange exciting sound—a mother field mouse with half a dozen naked young. . . . No hunter could have been more excited on discovering a bear and her cubs in a wilderness den."

Johnnie was barely three years old when he entered Davel Brae School. As a result of those long walks with Grandfather Gilrye, he was already familiar with his letters and learned quickly—

not that his ability spared him an occasional touch of the taws, a small whip that was often applied to the backsides of little Scots boys. At home, there was even greater discipline, for Daniel Muir had a knack for making "every duty dismal." At the end of his life, Muir said, "I know of nothing more pathetic . . . than a heartbroken child, sobbing itself to sleep after being unjustly punished by a . . . misguided parent."

Johnnie might have hated the skelpings he got, but he never hated learning. At school, he did well in French, English, and Latin grammar. He had classes in history, spelling, arithmetic, and geography. Long before he came to America he was familiar with the work of John James Audubon. On the playground, Johnnie eagerly played a game that required boys to roll down their wool stockings; then playmates lashed them with whips made of coarse knotweed until blood was drawn. The game was over only when a boy cried, "Enough!"

Neighborhood boys also took part in "skootchers"—games of daring forbidden by cautious grown-ups. One such game (today we would call it terroristic) was making guns from old gas pipe, cut-up scraps of lead for bullets, and gunpowder. Another involved digging a hole in the sand on the beach and tamping gunpowder into it around a homemade

The famous nature writer John Burroughs (left) was photographed on a visit to John Muir.
CORBIS-BETTMANN.

fuse, to cause what the boys called an "earthquake."

On the evening of February 18, 1849, John and his brother David were studying their lessons beside the fire at their grandfather's house. Daniel strode into the room with a startling announcement: "Bairns, you needna learn your lessons the nicht, for we're gan to America in the morn!" Without consulting his wife, Daniel had decided to follow a group of Campbellites to the New World.

To America! The boys felt "utterly, blindly glorious" to hear the news, and told their grandfather so. The old man pressed a gold coin into the palm of each of his grandsons and murmured sorrowfully, "Ah, poor laddies, you'll find something else ower the sea. . . . You'll find plenty [of] hard, hard work."

Grandfather Gilrye was so concerned about the future of his daughter's family that he forbade her to go until Daniel had established a suitable home. She remained behind with her youngest son,

Daniel junior, and all but one of her daughters, who now included twins, Mary and Annie. Later, another daughter, Joanna, would be born in America. Only John, Sarah, thirteen, and David, nine, accompanied their father to Glasgow the following morning. The Atlantic crossing took forty-five days, and they arrived in New York on April 5, two weeks before Johnnie's eleventh birthday.

Daniel Muir planned to head for Ontario, Canada, where he intended to become a wheat farmer, but the Campbellites talked him out of it. The weather to the north wasn't suitable, they explained, and the forests were so thick a man could spend a lifetime clearing a few paltry acres for planting. They all planned to settle in the states of Michigan or Wisconsin and urged Daniel to do likewise.

When Daniel arrived in Milwaukee, he met a farmer who had just sold his crop and was returning to Kingston, a small community to the northwest. Arrangements were made for the farmer to go back with a full load—Daniel and his children, plus all the supplies needed to begin farming life.

Before they left Dunbar, Daniel had promised the boys a pony, and one was purchased in Kingston. Johnnie and David named him Jack and loved him dearly. The pony was mild-mannered, and the boys quickly became good rid-ers, but Daniel was annoyed by Jack's habit of nipping the cows on their rumps as he herded them in from pasture. The pony "had the deevil in him," Daniel declared, threatening to shoot him. He sent Johnnie for the rifle, then relented at the last moment; instead, Jack was sold to a neighboring farmer, to the boys' great despair.

The family settled along the Fox River in Marquette County, Wisconsin. Nearby was a lake fed by several glacial springs, and Daniel Muir named his new homestead Fountain Lake Farm. Until a house could be built, Daniel and the children lived in a rude log hut. Johnnie and David were put to work helping hired men clear land while their father and carpenters worked on an eight-room, two-story home that was to be ready when Mrs. Muir and the other children came in November.

When Mrs. Muir arrived, family life was resumed, which meant Johnnie often crept into his mother's arms to seek comfort from his father's wrath. Even when he was grown and living far away, he needed to be "mothered" by an understanding older woman.

Making a farm out of the sort of wilderness Muir had selected was back-breaking work. It meant that Johnnie and David worked long hours, especially during the hot, humid midwestern summers. There was livestock to be cared for, wood to be chopped, fences to be built, crops to be sowed, fields to be harvested. The boys' father did not excuse them even when they were sick; once, Johnnie had to work even though he had the mumps and couldn't swallow any food except milk. When he got pneumonia, no doctor was called; Daniel believed "God and hard work are the best doctors." By the time he was sixteen, Johnnie could outwork most of the hired men—and took secret pleasure in being able to split a better fence rail than his father.

In spite of the hard work, Muir said there was a wonderful advantage to farm life. "One of the greatest is . . . gaining a real knowledge of animals as fellow mortals, learning to respond to them and love them. . . . too often the . . . doctrine is taught that animals have neither mind nor soul, have no rights that we are bound to respect." Beginning in boyhood, Muir always believed otherwise.

Johnnie had loved school in Scotland, but there was no time for it in America. However, he made friends with David Taylor and David Gray, whom he called "the two Davies." As they worked together on a road-building project, the two Davies recited the poetry of Milton and Robert Burns to their younger friend and encouraged him to read the novels of Dickens and Sir Walter Scott. Johnnie knew all too well that his father

thought such stuff was the work of Satan. The boy had always yielded under his father's iron fist, but now the matter of what to read or when to read it caused him to rebel inwardly, though he was not yet ready to rebel outwardly.

In 1855, six years after the family settled at Fountain Lake Farm, Daniel bought a larger piece of land four or five miles to the east and named it Hickory Hill Farm. Johnnie knew exactly what the move would mean: everything would begin "all over again . . . all the stunting, heartbreaking chopping, grubbing, stump-digging, rail-splitting, fence-building, barn-building, house-building, and so forth." Daniel was a tall man, but Johnnie attributed his own modest stature—he grew to be about five feet nine—to the fact that his growth had been stunted by the kind of work he'd done since he was eleven years old. "Heavy jobs . . . earned for me the title 'Runt of the Family,'" he lamented.

In spite of hard work and family tensions, Johnnie began to study mathematics on his own. He had learned basic math as a boy in Scotland, though "without understanding any of it" at the time. Now, he began to review in his mind what he remembered and worked out problems on chips of wood. He moved on to algebra and geometry and developed a keen interest in clocks.

His father had decreed when the family should rise in the morning and when it should go to bed at night, but when Johnnie won permission to rise as early as he wished in order to study before the workday began, he built a clock to wake himself. Soon, he was designing what he called "inventions," including a model of a self-setting sawmill. He also invented thermometers, barometers, waterwheels, door locks, an automatic gadget to feed the cows, and a huge clock to be mounted on the side of the barn. (Daniel forbade it, saying it would attract the neighbors' attention.) Most ingenious of all was an "early-rising machine," a device that could be set for a certain hour, would raise the sleeper's bed to a vertical position—then tip him out!

A neighbor, William Duncan, urged Johnnie to display his peculiar inventions at the Wisconsin State Fair in Madison, saying that any machine shop in the country would be eager to hire a young man with such talent. Of course, Daniel gave his son's endeavors no encouragement whatsoever.

Johnnie had saved the gold coin Grandfather Gilrye had given him in 1849; his mother added another; he had about ten dollars he'd earned raising wheat on a patch of ground his father didn't use. In 1860, twenty-two-year-old John Muir set out for the state fair with two handmade wooden clocks and a thermometer made from an old wash-

board. His life was about to change forever. Around him, the United States was changing too: Abraham Lincoln had just been nominated for the presidency, and the Civil War was only about six months away.

John's inventions were a great success in Madison. On September 25, 1860, the *Wisconsin State Journal* predicted that "few articles will attract as much attention as these products of Mr. Muir's ingenuity." Another newspaper concluded the devices had been made "by a genuine genius." Mrs. Jeanne Carr, the Vermont-born wife of Wisconsin State University professor Ezra Carr, was a judge at the exhibit and later became a second mother to Muir. She suggested a special award be given to the young inventor because the "Committee regard him as a genius in the best sense." When Daniel Muir heard of the public response to his son's inventions, he offered no praise; instead, he urged John to remember that vanity was a sin.

As the result of his sudden fame, John was given the chance to work at a machine shop in Prairie du Chien, one hundred miles west of Madison, where he could learn mechanical drawing and have access to many technical books. He bought some better clothes and began to wear a beard. For a time he felt pleased with his new life, but he soon discovered that foundry work was as unrewarding as farmwork, and he returned to Madison in January 1861. Four months later, the Civil War commenced with the firing on Fort Sumter. When President Lincoln called for seventy-five thousand Union volunteers, eight students from the university enlisted immediately. John Muir wasn't one of them; he was a pacifist even then.

John worked at a variety of jobs in Madison, all the while hoping to earn enough money to enter Wisconsin State University, which had been established in 1848 on the shores of Lake Mendota and now boasted an enrollment of 180 students. When John discovered that a twenty-week program cost only thirty-two dollars, he asked for an interview with the university chancellor. He explained that he "hadn't been to school since leaving Scotland at the age of eleven years. . . . Hearing my story, the kind professor welcomed me to the glorious University—next, it seemed to me, to the Kingdom of Heaven." No one was more pleased to have him on campus than Mrs. Carr and her husband. Some of John's conversations with Dr. Carr were to deeply influence his later theories about how the Ice Age shaped the earth's surface.

John was admitted to the scientific program but never became a regular student. He selected only the courses he thought would be most useful to him,

"particularly chemistry . . . mathematics and physics, a little Greek and Latin, botany and geology." His roommate said Muir became "the most proficient chemical student in [the] college," and in his second year— perhaps because of Mrs. Carr's influence—John became devoted to the study of botany. To pay for his education, he worked summers in nearby grain fields; one winter, he taught school ten miles from Madison for twenty dollars a month.

John had his photograph taken in 1863—the first in his family to do so. He put on his best suit of clothes and trimmed his beard for the occasion. When he sent the picture home to his mother, she and his brothers and sisters all had their pictures taken too. Daniel did not, since he believed pictures of any kind were graven images, nor would he permit any of the photographs to be hung in the house.

In spite of his busy schedule, Muir didn't give up inventing unique contraptions. He built a desk in which all of the books he had to study for the term were arranged; moments after his magic bed set him upright in the morning, the desk pushed up the first book to be read from a rack below, and fifteen minutes later replaced it with another book! His "scholar's desk" is now displayed at the Wisconsin State Historical Society Museum in Madison.

In 1863, it became clear that President Lincoln couldn't maintain the Union army with volunteers, so a bill to draft young men was passed in Congress. John Muir registered, as was required, but the law was so unpopular it caused a riot in New York City in July. Nevertheless, in early 1864, Lincoln called for a second conscription. David Muir had already fled to Canada to avoid the draft, and on March 1, 1864, John decided to "skedaddle" himself. Not only was he a pacifist, he considered himself a Scotsman, not an American, and did not become a U.S. citizen until he was sixty-five years old. Leaving the university without a degree did not concern him, for as he wrote in the conclusion of his autobiography, "I was only leaving . . . Wisconsin University for the University of the Wilderness."

When John's mother learned of a third draft call, she urged her youngest son to flee northward too, and John met young Daniel near Niagara Falls in September 1864. Both brothers worked in the small village of Meaford until the spring of 1865, when the Civil War ended. John then went to Indianapolis, lured there by what he called "the richest forest of deciduous hardwood trees on the continent," where he intended to continue his study of botany.

An accident in March 1867 caused Muir to change his life again. He was working on a new invention when the sharp end of a metal file pierced his right eye. Within moments, sight in the eye faded completely. He managed to get back to his rented room, where vision in the left eye dimmed too. When he was examined by a doctor, the news was better than expected: vision in the eye that had been pierced would return somewhat, while vision in the other eye likely would return to normal.

As Muir recovered from his injury in a darkened room, he realized that working on mechanical devices was not how he wanted to spend the rest of his life. Botany and the study of nature were his first loves, and he made plans for a walking tour. Before setting out, he visited Hickory Hill in the summer of 1867. His father criticized his son's interest in botany, which he called blasphemous, and the visit ended bitterly when Daniel demanded payment for room and board during his son's visit. Father and son didn't speak again until Daniel was on his deathbed.

John began his thousand-mile walk on September 2, 1867; his journey took him through Kentucky, Tennessee, North Carolina, Georgia, and Florida. He kept a "commonplace book" of his observations, which was published after his death as A *Thousand Mile Walk to the Gulf*. "I could have become a millionaire," he later said, "but I chose to become a tramp," and he traveled as lightly as any hobo: in a bag he carried a change of underwear, soap, a towel, a comb, a map, the New Testament, and a copy of Robert Burns's poems.

As he noted the natural wonders about him, Muir began to reject his father's belief that death was something to be dreaded. "We are taught . . . [it] is the arch enemy of life," he reflected, but he now came to believe death and life were an "inseparable unity," and that "death is stingless indeed."

Death soon became more than a philosophical problem because on October 23, 1867, Muir fell seriously ill with malaria in a village on the coast of Florida, and nearly died. He hadn't fully recovered by January 1868, but when he learned a ship was leaving the harbor bound for Cuba, he boarded it. In Havana he studied flowers and plants on the seacoast, then headed to California to visit the Yosemite Valley, about which he'd heard so much from his friends the Carrs.

In the spring of 1868, Muir got his first sight of the Yosemite Valley, four thousand feet above sea level, the best known of the many valleys in the Sierra Nevada range. He decided to stay, and worked at nearby ranches breaking horses, shearing sheep, and running a ferry. When he was offered the chance to take sheep into the Sierras for a local rancher, he accepted gladly. Since his job was only to supervise Billy, the regular herder, he had time to read Shakespeare, do botany, study geology, and make sketches. His mountain experiences further freed Muir from his father's grim view of the world and resulted in a different kind of spiritual experience. He began to feel that he was a "part of all nature, neither old nor young, sick nor well, but immortal."

Muir's observations of the geology of the Sierra Nevadas caused him to speculate in 1869 that glaciers had sculpted Yosemite into its fantastic contours. When his sheepherding job was finished, Muir went to work as a sawmill operator for the owner of the Hutchings Hotel, who recognized early the tourist potential of the valley and had claimed 160 acres of land in it. John also spent as much time as possible hiking in the wilderness. In Hutchings's absence he often guided tourists.

Muir and Hutchings's wife, Elvira, became good friends in the same way that he'd been friends with Professor Carr's wife, but soon a much more exotic damsel became interested in him. Therese Yelverton, the ex-wife of a European nobleman, came to stay at the hotel, planning to write a novel with the Yosemite as its background. She named the hero of her story "Kenmuir," and lovingly described his "intelligent face . . .

open blue eyes . . . and glorious auburn hair."

Muir, however, was far more interested in geology than in romance and explained his theory of glacier sculpting to anyone who would listen. His explanation refuted the popular one advanced by Professor Josiah Whitney of the California Geological Survey, who believed glaciers had nothing whatever to do with Yosemite's formation. Instead, Whitney believed earthquakes had caused Yosemite to develop the way it had; he dismissed Muir as a "mere sheepherder" and an "ignoramus."

In October 1871, however, Muir discovered a "live" glacier in the Sierras and over the next two years found several others. He devised a way to measure the movement of the glacier and proved that it moved toward the coast at the rate of about one inch per day.

In May 1871 an event occurred in Muir's life that he would never forget: Ralph Waldo Emerson, whose poetry and essays he had long admired, visited the Yosemite Valley. John was too shy to approach the frail, elderly poet, and it was Emerson—also a friend of Mrs. Carr—who sought Muir out. Emerson said later that Muir was "more wonderful than Thoreau." The two never met again, but after Emerson's death, a list of the men he most admired was found among his papers—and young John Muir's name had been added to it.

On December 5, 1871, Muir published his first article in the *New York Tribune* about how Yosemite had been formed by glaciers. The article attracted the attention of such men as John Runkle, the president of the Massachusetts Institute of Technology. Runkle was so impressed with Muir's ideas that he suggested he write them up for the Boston Academy of Sciences and even offered him a job at MIT. Muir did indeed quit his job at the sawmill—not to go to MIT, but to devote all of his time to trekking the Sierra Nevada range and gathering more material to support his theory of how glaciers had done their handiwork.

Before long, he was able to earn a modest living writing articles about the animals, trees, flowers, and geology of the Sierra Nevadas—enough money, in fact, to enable him to help with the education of his brother Dan and sister Mary. His parents had finally separated; Daniel had gone to Canada to become a full-time preacher while Anne remained in Wisconsin.

In 1874, when John was thirty-six years old, his loyal friend Jeanne Carr believed it was time for him to give up his monkish life. She introduced him to the family of Dr. John Strentzel of Martinez, California, whose daughter Louie was a quiet, gray-eyed, college-educated young woman whom Mrs. Carr believed could share John's life.

John himself was in no hurry to settle down and continued wandering for three more years, including walking trips to Nevada, Utah, Oregon, Washington, British Columbia, and finally Alaska. Only then was he ready to consider marriage. In 1879, he and Louie became engaged; they were married a year later. In 1881, their first child, Wanda, was born. As a husband, Muir tended to be aloof and inaccessible— but no one ever questioned his devotion to his children.

For the next eight years, John spent much of his time supervising Dr. Strentzel's fruit ranch. He studied how to graft fruit trees to get a maximum yield and wasn't a Scotsman for nothing: he was a tough businessman, and when buyers wouldn't pay a fair price for pears, cherries, or grapes, he refused to sell. Eventually, buyers gave in, and the ranch prospered under his management.

As the years passed, Muir became more concerned about the destruction he noted in the Yosemite Valley. Herds of sheep—he called them "hoofed locusts"—were destroying grass and plants; lumbermen were harvesting the ancient sequoias; miners dug deep into the earth. In his writings, Muir began to call for preservation of the wilderness. He gave a public lecture in Sacramento,

wrote an article to accompany the speech entitled "God's First Temples," and began to work on national conservation legislation. In the 1880s, he worked on two bills to be submitted to Congress, but public opinion was not on his side, and it would be years before such laws were passed.

In August 1885, Muir was struck by a premonition that his father, whom he hadn't seen for nearly twenty years, was near death. Daniel now lived in Kansas City with his favorite daughter, Joanna. John hurried to his sister's home; at first, Daniel didn't recognize his oldest son. When he did, he murmured, "Is this my dear John? . . . Oh, yes, my dear Wanderer." The old man had softened remarkably in his final years, and Muir wrote to Louie, "His last years . . . were full of calm divine light, and he spoke . . . of the cruel mistakes he had made . . . and spoke particularly well of me."

After Muir's daughter Helen was born in 1886, Louie suggested to her husband that part of the ranch ought to be leased and part of it sold, which would give him more time to pursue his writing and research. His sister Margaret and her husband came to help manage the part of the ranch that was kept, freeing Muir from business worries.

Robert Underwood Johnson, who had been one of Muir's longtime admirers, contacted him in 1889. After camping with John in the Yosemite Valley, Johnson became convinced that the area must be made into a national park if it was to be preserved. He pledged to use his magazine, the *Century*, to promote such an idea. Muir agreed; he did the writing and speaking, while Johnson lobbied the U.S. Congress, and on September 30, 1890, a bill creating Yosemite National Park was signed by President Harrison.

However, the state of California retained control of the Yosemite Valley until 1906, and public opinion in California still favored unlimited exploitation of the wilderness. Muir, Robert Johnson, and others gathered to discuss the need for an association to preserve the wonders of places such as Yosemite. So it was that in 1892, the Sierra Club was founded, with John Muir as its first president. Within months of its founding, the club had 182 members; one hundred years later, membership stood at more than half a million.

In 1893, Muir finally decided to make a trip to Europe. In the process he met many famous Americans in the East, Mark Twain among them, and Rudyard Kipling in Britain. He also began a friendship with Henry Osborne, dean of science at Columbia University, with whom he kept up a correspondence to the end of his life. When Muir's ship

docked at Liverpool in July, he took a train for Scotland and revisited his old home in Dunbar, strolling up High Street as he had done as a child with Grandfather Gilrye.

In 1894, Muir's first book, *The Mountains of California*, was published, and it quickly became popular. There were still opponents to conservationism, however, and Muir sought other allies. One of them, Charles Sargent, director of the Arnold Arboretum at Harvard, joined Muir's cause, and in 1896 the U.S. government created the National Forestry Commission, to "recommend the creation of new preserves, and submit a . . . policy for governing them." A year later, the commission recommended thirteen new reserves in eight western states and the creation of two new national parks—at the Grand Canyon and at Mount Rainier.

Harvard University gave Muir an honorary master's degree in 1896. The occasion was remarkable for another of Muir's sudden premonitions of death: on his way east, although he hadn't been notified that his mother was ill, he went first to Wisconsin. There, he discovered Anne Gilrye had suffered a heart attack; she rallied briefly, then died on June 23.

One of Muir's staunchest supporters was President Theodore Roosevelt, who declared after he took office that he

John Muir (right) with President Theodore Roosevelt at Yosemite. CULVER
PICTURES, INC.

intended to resolve the issue of wasteful
use of the nation's resources once and
for all. Muir was asked to guide the president through Yosemite. At the end of
the trip, the man for whom the teddy
bear was named but who also was a
"Rough Rider" declared, "Come and see
me in Washington. I've had the time of
my life!" As the result of the growing
concern about wildlife areas, Mount

Rainier National Park was formally established in 1899, and three years later, Crater Lake National Park in Oregon. Glacier National Park also was created during Muir's lifetime.

While Muir traveled widely—to Finland, Russia, Australia, China, and Japan—Louie made sure Wanda and Helen were properly raised. Helen had always been a sickly child and took many cures in the dry desert air of Arizona, but in 1905, it was Louie herself who became ill with lung cancer. She died on August 6 and was buried on the ranch beside her parents in the shade of a eucalyptus tree. Now, Muir wrote harder than ever. In 1911 *My First Summer in the Sierra* was published, followed in 1912 by *The Yosemite*, a guidebook. In 1913 *The Story of My Boyhood* came out.

The greatest disappointment of Muir's life was his inability to save the Hetch Hetchy River valley, part of the Yosemite National Park, from destruction. Businessmen and politicians in San Francisco were looking for cheap water power and decided the valley should be dammed up and the water piped to the city. The fight to preserve the Hetch Hetchy (an Indian phrase meaning "grassy meadow") was long and bitter, and pitted people with utilitarian interests against preservationists. In 1913, President Woodrow Wilson signed a bill giving San Francisco the right to dam up the valley. Friends believed the loss of the Hetch Hetchy robbed Muir of his will to live.

During much of 1914, Muir was troubled by a persistent cough and finally went to Arizona to stay with Helen, now married and the mother of three sons. His cough became worse; he was taken to Los Angeles by train and entered a hospital. He seemed to recover but died quietly on Christmas Eve. On the table beside him was the manuscript for a new book about Alaska. Muir had once written that death was *heimgang*—a Norse word meaning "home-going"; consequently, many people believed he ought to be buried in Yosemite, to which he'd devoted so much of his life. But although he and his wife had had an unusual marriage—he was gone from home a great deal and was not given to intimacy—he had left instructions that he wished to be laid to rest beside her.

Time magazine called Muir "the real father of conservation," and any map showing locations of national parks or wilderness areas reveals that each of America's fifty states, plus Puerto Rico, has such areas set aside for the enjoyment of all citizens. As Muir reminded the world: "Everybody needs beauty as well as bread, places to play in and pray in, where Nature may heal and cheer and give strength to body and soul alike."

Charlotte Darkey Parkhurst

1812–79 Stagecoach driver. After she was placed in an orphanage by her parents at an early age, Charlotte eventually donned boys' clothing and ran away. She changed her name, learned how to drive a six-hitch team, and earned a living as a stagecoach driver. After the kick of a horse damaged her eye, she wore a black patch over it, thereby earning the nickname "Cockeyed Charley."

Unlike the biographies of other men and women in this volume, the most unique thing about Charlotte Parkhurst's story is that it begins not with her birth, but at her death.

Cockeyed Charley, who often wore a black patch over one eye, was a familiar and respected figure around Watsonville, California, in the last half of the 1800s. Those who knew the old man remembered him from his glory days as a stagecoach driver, and when he died alone in his cabin at age sixty-seven, acquaintances prepared themselves to bury an elderly chap they were sure they knew pretty well. To their astonishment, residents around Watsonville discovered they hadn't really known him at all.

"Cockeyed Charley" Parkhurst—one of the most reputable stagecoach drivers of the turbulent gold rush days—was a woman.

Gradually, certain facts came to light, and now a fairly clear picture has emerged about this unusual and colorful figure, whose story makes Calamity Jane's pale in comparison.

Charlotte Darkey Parkhurst was born in Lebanon, New Hampshire, sometime in 1812. There must have been a serious reversal of fortunes in the Parkhurst family, for when their daughter was still a young child, her parents placed her in an orphanage. No child would have chosen to be there—especially not a strong-willed girl like Charlotte—and as soon as she was old enough to do so, she donned boys' clothing, crawled out a window one night, and ran away. In those times, boys and girls probably ran away from such institutions regularly, and apparently no effort was made to find her and bring her back.

How Charlotte got to Worcester, Massachusetts, will never be known. Perhaps it was by hitching rides on farm wagons with kindly strangers who felt a natural sympathy for a boy who'd been turned out on his own at such a young age. It probably wasn't much of a stretch for Charlotte to call herself Charley, and she was accepted exactly as she presented herself—as a plucky lad who was fending for himself as best he could.

In Worcester, Charley—who dressed as a boy and man the rest of her life—found a job at a stable owned by a certain Ebenezer Balch. Balch was pleased with his new stableboy, who was an eager worker and seemed to have the energy of two. The youngster mucked out stalls and washed down carriages, and when the boy asked if he could learn how to handle a team, Ebenezer willingly set about to teach him.

From the outset, Charley seemed to have a natural gift with horses, and as a teenager could handle a six-horse hitch as well as Ebenezer himself. When Balch decided to purchase an inn, the Franklin House, along with the What Cheer Stables in Providence, Rhode Island, he invited Charley to come along with him.

In Providence, Charley no longer mucked stalls but became one of Balch's most reliable stagecoach drivers, or "whips," as they were called in those days. It was said that some customers inquired ahead of time as to who would be driving the stage on a given day, then arranged their trips accordingly, because they preferred the way Charley drove a team. They claimed the ride was smoother when Charley was "on the box," the seat high above the carriage.

After a time, the routes in Rhode Island became crushingly familiar to Charley, and he decided he needed a change of scenery. He bade Ebenezer good-bye and headed for Georgia, where he once again established a fine reputation as a stagecoach driver. In 1848, after two friends, John Birch and Frank Stevens, established a stagecoach line in California at the height of the gold rush, Charley concluded he needed another change and decided to go west to join them.

Charley could have gone overland, but it was a long and arduous trip, so instead he boarded a steamship in Boston Harbor in 1851. During the trip around the Cape, Charley—now a stocky fellow close to forty years of age—met John Morton, the president of a freight-hauling company in San Francisco. Morton recalled later that Charley was an agreeable companion, had intro-

No photographs or portraits of Charlotte (Charley) Parkhurst are known to exist. This stage-coach, showing passengers both inside and out, is the kind of vehicle Charley would have driven. CORBIS-BETTMANN.

duced himself as a stagecoach driver from the East, and said he intended to take a job with some friends as a driver between Stockton and Mariposa, California. To another traveler who remembered him from that trip, Charley introduced himself as "Charles Clifton," and said that he had traveled in France, England, and Sweden. (The ability to tell a good tale was apparently one of Charley's talents.) When anyone inquired about the black patch that he wore over his left eye, Charley explained that several years before he'd been kicked by a horse, and the eye was so badly damaged that henceforth he'd kept it covered.

Charley's voice was described as very low-pitched, and with his strong, husky build—he was about five feet seven inches tall—he gave no hint of any feminine characteristics. He was fond of chewing tobacco and was a cigar smoker as well. Because he dressed in a heavy jacket, wore trousers with a wide belt that revealed very little about his physique, and always had a hat clamped low over his brow, there was no reason for those who came in contact with him to ever wonder if Charley really was who he represented himself to be.

Charley's disguise was so convincing that occasionally he found it necessary to avoid females, who sometimes assumed he was a good candidate for matrimony. In California, he had to give up a stagecoach run that he'd held for three years because one of his lady passengers seemed determined to become romantically involved.

Instead, Charley stuck to male companions, to drinking and playing poker with the best of them. In 1868, Charley voted in an election in Santa Cruz right along with his cronies—thereby becoming the first woman in the country to do so, more than fifty years before women's suffrage was enacted!

Like many other stagecoach drivers, Charley got held up more than once. One story has it that as Parkhurst lashed his team over some mudholes along a creek bed in Grass Valley, a road agent with a potato sack over his head ordered him to stop the coach. Charley gave his whip a smart flick across the potato sack covering the would-be thief's face, then rolled right on down the road. On another occasion, Charley had to let loose with his shotgun when the Sugarfoot gang tried to stop him; later, Sugarfoot himself was found dead in the ditch.

Charley spent several years on the San Jose to Santa Cruz stagecoach run, often making double trips for double pay when the company was short of drivers. During one such trip he met Anton Roman, the owner of a bookstore in San Francisco, and told him many colorful yarns about the life of a stagecoach driver. Later, Roman repeated the stories to one of his friends, a man named Bret Harte, who included some of their details in the short stories that helped make him a famous American writer.

Stagecoach driving was a tough, demanding job. A change of teams took place at stations fifteen or twenty miles apart, and the time most looked forward to by the whips was the major stop at the end of the day, or after about sixty miles. However, one observer described the fare that awaited both driver and passengers, and didn't give it high marks. "The usual meal is fat ham and eggs, or boiled pork, potatoes, and bread that looks as if were baked in black ashes, while the coffee is the very vilest stuff. . . . They never expect to see their passengers again, so they give them as little as they can and charge as much as possible."

After the railroads came west, there was no need for travelers to put up with such treatment, and with the change in style of travel came the end of a way of life for men like Charley Parkhurst. To support himself, he began to do odd jobs. He worked at a lumber camp in the Santa Cruz Mountains for a time, dabbled in the cattle business—and when he sold 150 head of stock to a Charles Moss, he put the money aside for his retirement. Eventually, Charley bought himself a small place near Watsonville, where he continued to live alone, tending a small flock of chickens, keeping a couple of horses, and growing a few crops such as wheat, turnips, and hay.

His health began to fail, and after suffering for a considerable time with a sore mouth and a swollen tongue, Charley finally consulted a Mr. Plumm, who may (or may not) have been a doctor. Charley took some medicine home with him, but his condition did not improve. He died alone in his cabin on December 19, 1879, twenty-eight years after his arrival in California. When acquaintances discovered his death, the body was removed and taken to nearby Watsonville, where an autopsy was performed. It was only then that the folks who thought they knew old Cockeyed Charley Parkhurst discovered they re-

ally knew nothing about him at all. *Charley was a woman.*

Yet another surprise awaited such acquaintances. In Charley's little cabin, a locked trunk was found, and when it was forced open a baby's red dress was discovered inside. The autopsy also supported the suspicion that not only was Charley a woman, but once had been a mother as well. No one knows now under what circumstances—or when—a pregnancy and birth had occurred; the secret was carried to the grave with Charley.

In his will, Charley left four thousand dollars to young George Harmon, a neighbor boy who had treated him kindly during his final years. On January 24, 1880, the *Providence Journal* of Rhode Island declared that "Charley Parkhust was one of this city's finest drivers. The only people who have any occasion to be disturbed by the career of Charley are gentlemen who have so much to say about 'women's sphere' and the 'weaker vessel.' It is beyond question that one of the soberest, pleasantest, most expert drivers in Rhode Island and one of the most celebrated of the world famous California stage drivers was a woman."

The *Journal* article also revealed that after Charley went to Georgia, he had returned to Rhode Island for a spell and worked for William Hayden, then for

Charles H. Child. "He drove the best team in the stable, six gray horses, exactly matched," the article reported. When an old acquaintance heard of Charley's death, he judged him to have "understood his business; he was pleasant and steady and sober."

Reflecting on the little red dress that had been discovered in the trunk, on January 8, 1880, a writer for the *Watsonville Pajaronian* suggested that perhaps in her early years Charlotte Parkhurst had "loved not wisely, but too well . . . and from that event, dated her strange career."

After the death was reported, a story was told by a Mrs. Clark, whose husband had hired Charley to do some work. One night, as the story went, Charley came home quite inebriated, and Mrs. Clark asked her seventeen-year-old son, Andy, to help him to bed. A while later, the startled boy rushed to tell his mother that Charley wasn't a man at all, but a woman. Helen T. Tarr, Mrs. Clark's granddaughter, related the story and claimed that the family was determined not to give the secret away—and until Charley's death they never did.

Major A. N. Judd, writing about his recollections of Charley in the October 18, 1917, issue of the *Santa Cruz Surf*, testified that part of Parkhurst's "greatness stems from his safety record of never having injured a passenger." It

was the judgment of W. H. Hutchinson that Parkhurst "was a responsible driver who could bring coach and cargo in on time, covering sixty miles a day over roads that were hub-deep in summer's dust, and he did it come hell, high water, or road agents."

Another Rhode Island newspaper stated that Charley had died of a malignant disease and went on to assert rather morbidly that although "she could act and talk like a man," the effort of remaining silent for an entire lifetime about her true identity had "resulted at last in death from cancer of the tongue."

The *San Francisco Chronicle* was more philosophical. "It is useless to waste time in conjectures as to what led the dead to take up the cross of a man's laboring life."

It was inevitable that much speculation would surround the life choice that Charlotte—or Charley—had made. The *Yreka Union* observed that perhaps it was because "she may have been disgusted with the trammels surrounding sex, and concluded to work out her fortune in her own way."

In 1955, a stone was erected by the Pajaro Valley Historical Association to mark Charlotte "Cockeyed Charley" Parkhurst's final resting place in a cemetery near Watsonville. The sum of her life remains as remarkable as when she lived it—and just as mysterious.

Francis Parkman

1823–93 Historian, writer. Phi Beta Kappa graduate of Harvard; love of the outdoors was strengthened by wilderness excursions his wealthy family provided for him. In 1846, he traveled the Oregon Trail; in spite of poor health and near blindness, came to be regarded as the "greatest writer among American historians."

Francis Parkman, named after his father, was born into a world very different from the kind that would fascinate him as a grown man.

It was a silver-spoon sort of life, full of wealth, comfort, and privilege, that welcomed the first child of Francis and Caroline Hall Parkman at his birth on September 16, 1823. The family's fashionable address on Allston Street in a Beacon Hill neighborhood was proof they belonged to the elite of Boston society. One historian noted that there was great family satisfaction in "its pride of learning and its pride of power."

Pride and power came in hefty measure from the baby's grandfather. Samuel Parkman, one of twelve children of a country parson, was a penniless youth when he arrived in Boston. He went to work as an errand boy at the Bunch of Grapes tavern, became involved in shipping and commerce, and ended his days as owner of the *Herald* newspaper, having amassed one of the largest fortunes in early-nineteenth-century America. Francis's father, a Unitarian minister, had been educated in Scotland and became pastor of the New North Church of Boston, where he served for thirty-six years, until shortly before his death in 1852. He was an affable man, famous among his friends for his gift with language. He also suffered from what the family delicately referred to as melancholia; in modern times we call it mental illness, and the minister's tendencies were to affect his son.

Francis's relationship with his mother,

A portrait of the young Francis Parkman from a daguerreotype. CORBIS-BETTMANN.

a descendant of Cotton Mather, was an especially warm one. His youngest sister, Eliza—Lizzie to all her kinfolk—remarked that their mother had "a peculiar tenderness toward him, her eldest child." On his mother's side of the family Francis also was related to two famous American historians, Henry Adams and Peter Chardon Brooks. Francis—the family called him Frank—was idolized by his younger sisters, Caroline, Mary, and Lizzie. His brother John Eliot, eleven years younger, was born in 1834. Neither boy was interested in following their father into the pulpit; John chose a career in the navy, was taken prisoner during the Civil War, and died several years later in an accident.

Frank described his childhood as being "neither healthful or buoyant." He recalled that he was "sensitive and restless, rarely ill, but never robust," which was a cause of concern to his parents. As a consequence, they sent the boy to live at his grandfather Hall's fifty-acre farm on the edge of Five Mile Woods, later called the Middlesex Fells, in West Medford, Massachusetts. He remained there from age eight until he was thirteen. Peter Chardon Hall, his bachelor uncle, also lived at the farm, and being the only child in the household, Frank was more or less given the run of the place. He attended school without much enthusiasm, preferring instead to roam freely about the countryside.

The Fells now is a public park crisscrossed by neatly groomed bridle paths, but in Parkman's day it was a rock-strewn, heavily wooded, pond-filled area only eight miles from the center of Boston, then a city of about thirty or forty thousand. For five happy years, Frank explored this wilderness at will, collecting birds' eggs, trapping squirrels, woodchucks, and snakes, and practicing his marksmanship with a bow and arrow. Many years later he told a friend these childhood experiences caused his thoughts to be "always in the forest . . . waking and sleeping, filling him with vague cravings."

Frank was keenly aware that his parents believed he had a weak constitution, and as he roamed the woods near his grandfather's home, he hoped that he was improving his strength and endurance. It was a time that he resented having interrupted. Therefore, when the Reverend Parkman appeared in a carriage one Saturday afternoon to take his son back to Boston for the weekend, the boy felt quite annoyed. On Sunday, he sulkily followed the family home from his father's sermon at New North Church—and startled passersby with a dead rat that he carried by its tail, dangled at arm's length.

At thirteen, Frank returned to Boston. Samuel Parkman had died, and the family had moved into the old gentleman's gracious, tree-shaded, three-story mansion at 5 Bowdoin Square. Frank began the sort of studies at Thayer's Academy—Greek, Latin, and the classics—that would prepare him to enter Harvard. He didn't spend all of his time hunched over dusty books, however. With his cousins and other boys from the neighborhood, he formed the "Star

Theatre" and gave performances in the coach house behind the mansion. Because of his delicate complexion and high voice, Frank often played girls' parts, such as Katherine in *The Taming of the Shrew*.

One of Frank's instructors at the academy recalled that the boy's English compositions "were especially good. . . . He might have excelled in narrative and descriptive poetry." Parkman remembered one of his lessons from that time: the boys were given "a list of words to which we were required to furnish as many synonyms as possible, distinguishing their various shades of meaning." Parkman considered that this type of wordsmithing was one of "the chief sources of success as I have had in this particular."

When he was about fifteen, Parkman's interest in the natural world was rekindled by a family vacation to the mountains of New Hampshire, and he began to envision certain literary projects, no doubt stimulated by his boyhood love of James Fenimore Cooper's *The Leatherstocking Tales*. Frank also was attracted to the work of the great English poets Byron, Coleridge, and Milton, and was a lover of Shakespeare; all were writers who would later deeply influence his own writing style.

As Parkman got older, his enthusiasms, whether for nature or for education, had a way of running off with him like a wild horse, and the result was that he often overtaxed himself. He apparently shared not only his father's name but Francis senior's tendency toward the sort of mental illness that in Frank's case had overtones of manic-depression. He would be consumed by a manic sort of energy for a period of time, after which he would be plunged into a listless depression. At first, such episodes might have seemed merely a matter of a lively boy's tendency to overdo certain activities; later, they would be recognized as something much more serious.

In 1840, a month before his seventeenth birthday, Frank became a Harvard freshman. He shared quarters for a time with B. A. Gould, who later became a well-known astronomer, then announced that he'd rather room alone. His preference for keeping to himself at least part of the time didn't mean he was a loner or that he disliked companionship; on the contrary, he was popular with fellow students. He belonged to the Hasty Pudding and Chit-Chat Clubs, but in debate he tended to become so enthusiastic that he was unpleasantly belligerent.

And—still obsessed with his frail health—young Parkman continued to press himself in physical activity. At Harvard, he took boxing lessons, rowed, practiced marksmanship, and trekked tirelessly through the swampy woods around Cambridge. Hoping to improve his horseback-riding skills, he took lessons from an ex-circus performer. A college friend noted that Frank always chose "the hardest horses, practiced riding in every form, with or without a saddle or stirrups; [he] could run, leap, jump on a charger at full speed."

At the end of his freshman year in 1841, Parkman decided to take a month-long hiking trip into the wilds of northern New Hampshire and Maine. The White Mountains were a popular tourist retreat of the time, but Parkman didn't intend to be just an ordinary tourist. His aim was to go much deeper into the woods, then canoe up the Magalloway River and proceed toward the Canadian border, a region then known only to Indians or a few white hunters. Frank had started to dream of a career as a writer—imitative of the kind of adventure tales by Cooper and Sir Walter Scott that he'd always admired—and he wanted to be able to write about field, forest, and river from firsthand knowledge. He commented in a journal that he kept of this trip that his "chief object in coming so far was . . . to have a taste of the half-savage kind of life . . . and to see the wilderness where it was as yet uninvaded by the hand of man."

Dan Slade, a Harvard classmate, was his companion. Slade soon became disenchanted with the whole adventure,

complaining crossly at one point, "I wish we had never come." Parkman's response was very different, even though swarms of mosquitoes infested the deep north woods or that clouds of black flies felt like "a blast of red hot sand was beating against our faces." The trip was abandoned when Slade refused to proceed any farther, but in his journal Frank noted prophetically that he hoped the journey was "only the beginning of greater things."

Back at Harvard for his second year (his parents hoped he would become a lawyer), Parkman gave up his secret dreams of becoming a novelist and instead became deeply interested in the early colonial struggle between Britain and France for control of North America. In April 1842, he wrote to Professor Jared Sparks requesting help obtaining proper research materials for further study. He noted in his letter, "I . . . find it difficult to discover authorities sufficiently minute to satisfy me." Sparks was a unique history professor for his time; he was concerned with the history of his own country, rather than with reinterpreting European history, and in particular he stressed the importance of studying original documents rather than depending on the work of others. Something else made Sparks a suitable mentor for Parkman and accounted for the fact that they became lifetime friends: he shared his student's fascination with primitive living and once had dreamed of becoming an explorer in the heart of Africa.

During this time, Parkman—though he was only an eighteen-year-old college sophomore—carefully designed for himself what was to become a lifelong work in American history. Many years later, he recalled the momentous decision in a letter to a friend. "Before the end of my sophomore year my various schemes had crystalized into a plan of writing a story of what was then known as the 'Old French War'—that is, the War that ended in the conquest of Canada. . . . It was not until some years later that I enlarged the plan to include the whole course of the American conflict between France and England, or, in other words, *the history of the American forest;* for this was the light in which I regarded it." Italics have been added to emphasize how the project—which would ultimately make him famous—reflected his childhood infatuation with the magical woods surrounding his grandfather's farm. To the end of his long life, Parkman said he continued to be "haunted with wilderness images day and night."

Frank spent the summer vacation following his sophomore year in 1842 on a trip designed to fit these projected historical interests. From Albany, New York, he and Henry Orne White, another Harvard chum, proceeded northward to the battlefields of the Seven Years' War near Lake George, New York, also the setting of one of his favorite books, James Fenimore Cooper's *The Last of the Mohicans*, then followed the boundaries of Vermont and New Hampsire into Canada, returning by way of Mount Katahdin in Maine. It was in the journal he kept during this trip that Parkman also referred to a feeling of total exhaustion.

It was true the trip was filled with great physical effort, yet what he seemed to suffer from wasn't mere physical exhaustion but rather what he described as a "spiritless" sensation. He admitted the feeling had plagued him for some weeks. He attributed the problem to heart trouble caused by strenuous exercise in the Harvard gym, but more likely it was some sort of emotional exhaustion that overcame him.

A third long journey was undertaken in the summer of 1843; in the course of this one, like the previous excursion, Parkman intended not merely to enjoy the wilderness but to collect historical information for the work that he hoped to commence soon. The notebook he used this time was tiny—measuring only 2 1/4 by 4 inches—yet he packed it with data and observations that he would use later. As always, there was another expectation of such an outing: that it would improve his health. Unfortunately, he was left worse off than before.

So it was that on Sunday morning, November 12, 1843, a month after his twentieth birthday, Parkman's parents escorted him to the Boston docks and put him on the *Nautilus* for a trip to Europe. They urged him to rest rather than complete his senior year at Harvard. His mother was overcome with tears to see him leave. The kind of trip Frank took was called "a grand tour" and was considered to be a rite of passage for wealthy young men during the mid-nineteenth century. As others had done before him, he made stops in Sicily, Italy, Switzerland, France, and England.

Parkman was pleased with his European experiences, which were hardly restful but were crammed with a great deal of activity. Although he'd been raised a Protestant, he became much intrigued by Catholicism, which was so different from the cool, rational faith of his Unitarian ancestors. He arranged to live in a Roman monastery for a week, partly because he wished to gain a more intimate knowledge of Catholic life, which had had such a profound effect on French colonizing efforts in the New World. In his journal, he practiced the type of colorful writing that would one day make him unique among writers of dry history. His description of a visit to a Capuchin monastery, where thousands of mummies were preserved in underground vaults, is as vivid as if it were written yesterday:

> The mummies, each from his niche in the wall, grinned at us diabolically as we passed along. Several large cats, kept there for the benefit of the rats, stared at us with their green eyes, and then tramped off. When we got to the little chapel, the prior put off his coarse Capuchin dress, and arrayed himself in white robes—the curtain was drawn aside from the image of the Virgin behind the altar—the lamps lighted—and the Mass performed.

Frank returned from Europe in June 1844, having been gone more than six months, his health seemingly improved. He gave a commencement oration that demonstrated his skill at evoking a time and place as he recalled for his audience the battlefields around Lake George, where French, English, and Indians had fought and died:

> Blood has been poured out like water over that soil! . . . It is sown thick with bullets and human bones, the relics of many a battle and slaughter. . . . The raven that plucks the farmer's corn once gorged on the dead of France, of England, and a score of forgotten savage tribes.

In another year, he would be troubled again by inner demons, yet in 1845 he was able to make a research trip to Pennsylvania, New York, and Canada to gather historical material about Chief Pontiac of the Ottawa Indians, an ally of the French, who in 1775 had formed a confederacy of Ottawa, Ojibwa, and Potawatomi Indians. When he returned, however, he suffered from "indigestion" and was confined to bed for a lengthy period.

In January 1846, Parkman was able to get his law degree from Harvard due to the dedication of his sisters, particularly Lizzie, who read law texts such as *Blackstone* aloud to him while he rested, with his weak eyes shielded from the light. Later, Lizzie refused a suitor's proposal of marriage, preferring instead to devote the rest of her life to the care of her sickly brother. Since Parkman's mental state continued to be erratic, his father suggested that perhaps a hunting trip was what the young man needed. The Parkman family, as much as Frank himself, seemed to believe that exercise and outdoor life would cure whatever ailed him.

Parkman left Boston on March 28 and headed for St. Louis for a trip to the West. It was his good fortune to meet Pierre Chouteau, the manager of John Jacob Astor's American Fur Company; Thomas Fitzpatrick, the famous trapper and guide; and most importantly, a hunter named Henry Chatillon. Chatillon, who was married to Bear Robe, the daughter of the Sioux chief Bull Bear, had extensive knowledge of the Indians, their language, and their customs, of which Parkman was eager to avail himself. On May 9, twenty-two-year-old Parkman set out with his companions to follow the Oregon Trail.

Although Parkman's fame rests upon his trip along the Oregon Trail, the journal that he kept, which was later published, has been the subject of much controversy. Some critics now believe that he gave a wealthy easterner's distorted view of the "Wild West" and that he had no genuine appreciation of what westward migration really meant in terms of the democratic development of the nation. However, others have considered that his documentation of the West just as it was about to change was invaluable. In any case, he was one of only a few *educated* white men who spent extended time among the Indians in a primitive setting. In some ways, Parkman might have been the least likely candidate for such experiences; he was a patrician, often a snob, and admitted his irritation with the "raw, noisy, western way" of life as he found it. However, he wasn't such an elitist that he couldn't also remark, "The vigorous life of the nation springs from the deep rich soil at the bottom of society."

The trip didn't have the effect that Parkman or his family had hoped for because he was ill most of the time. At Fort Laramie, he came down with a severe case of dysentery that might have been caused by eating contaminated meat. In spite of being ill, and because of his peculiar ability to force himself onward in spite of how he felt, Parkman took advantage of the chance to spend three weeks with the Sioux in their camp in the foothills of the Rockies. There, he was the guest of Big Crow, a warrior whose chest and arms were marked by the scars of the sun dance.

Although he was sweaty and dizzy from dysentery, Parkman took part in buffalo hunts, joined the Sioux as they gorged on fresh buffalo liver after a kill, and witnessed how the women of the tribe skinned the carcasses and made new lodge covers, robes, and clothing. The artifacts that he collected from this journey—a medicine pouch, a warbonnet, a pipe, a bow and arrow—remained hanging on the wall of his study until he died. And of Henry Chatillon, Parkman would write, "I have never, in the city or in the wilderness, met a better man than my true-hearted friend, Henry Chatillon." Parkman was fortunate to have been able to travel the Oregon Trail when he did because only a few years later the Sioux turned fiercely against the intrusion of whites.

Parkman came back from his Oregon adventure in October 1846. The trip that was designed to help him recover his health had done precisely the opposite. His eyesight was bad before he left, and the alkali dust of the plains and the constant glare of the sun made it worse. His insomnia often left him totally sleepless, and he complained of a variety of aches and pains. Modern doctors might suggest that Parkman's physical disorders were at least partly psychological, stemming from his highly emotional, excitable personality. He was only twenty-three years old and ought to have been in the prime of his life, yet he had a long list of physical woes: chronic sleeplessness, indigestion, circulatory disorders, "iron bands" that tightened around his head, and what he called a "whirl" in his brain—in short, the kinds of symptoms ordinarily associated with an ill, elderly person.

For the next two years Parkman was treated by a doctor in New York, who had tended to his older sister Caroline, also a sufferer of nervous disorders; his brother John had similar problems, though not as severe. One aspect of Parkman's treatment was the avoidance of any sort of mental activity. For such a man, the treatment ended up being nearly as bad as the disease, and Parkman spoke of being confined to a "Dungeon of the Spirit." Finally, he began to work in bursts of no longer than ten to fifteen minutes each. Since his eyesight was so poor, he designed a contraption with wire guides to assist his pen across the page. For six months, his output averaged about six lines a day.

Although Parkman referred constantly to "cerebral devils" and "the enemy" that continued to plague him, he was cheered by the success of his account of the trip on the Oregon Trail, which was published in installments in the *Knickerbocker* magazine from 1847 through 1849. Later, a book-length edition was published, illustrated by the western painter Frederic Remington. Frank engaged in a steady correspondence with his cousin, Charles Eliot Norton, and with Ephraim Squier, both of whom had interests similar to his own. These relationships supported him during a dark time. In spite of his health, Parkman was intent upon beginning his masterwork, which he had divided into seven parts:

- *Pioneers of France in the New World*—the settlement of the French Huguenots in Florida and the Carolinas;

- *The Jesuits in North America*—an account of efforts by Jesuits to convert the Huron and Iroquois Indians;

- *La Salle and the Discovery of the Great West*—the exploration by the French of the Great Lakes and Mississippi River valley;

- *The Old Regime in Canada*—the exploitation of Canada for benefit of France;

- *Count Frontenac and the New France under Louis XIV*—examination of the conflict known as King William's War, 1689–97;

- *Montcalm and Wolfe*—an account of the Seven Years' War of 1756–63; and, finally,

- *A Half Century of Conflict*—covering the years 1700–48.

In spite of such grandiose plans and poor health, Parkman's life at this time was surprisingly like the life of an ordinary young man. He was now in his mid-twenties; his friends were falling in love, and so did he—not once but twice. First, with someone known in his journals and letters only as a mysterious "Miss B.," to whom he felt strongly attracted but who seemed a bit too high-spirited for his Puritanical taste. Perhaps that was the reason he became engaged to Catherine Bigelow, the quiet and refined daughter of a Harvard physician, and married her in May 1850. Because of her early death, Catherine has remained a shadowy figure, and little of a personal nature is known about her; nevertheless, Parkman was able to write to the wife of his cousin Samuel, "Looking for peace and rest, I found happiness."

Happiness wasn't destined to be any easier for Parkman to achieve than good health. In spite of becoming the father of a baby girl, named Grace, in 1851, in spite of receiving a comfortable inheritance after his father's death in 1852, and then becoming the father of a son himself in 1853, Parkman was haunted by the return of his "enemy." In addition to his mental and emotional suffering, he was bothered by severe arthritis in one knee, which kept him from hiking in the woods as he once loved to do. His eyesight was a continual problem, and when in the grips of such attacks, he had to be carried about on a litter—in his own words, "like a crate of brittle China."

In all, these chronic mental and physical problems consumed twenty years of Parkman's life. No definite diagnosis was ever made, perhaps because in those days not enough was known about such ailments. One biographer suggested that Parkman, because he came from a wealthy family and never had to work for a living, was able to indulge his symptoms, since "no economic necessity drove him to conquer them." Perhaps there is a grain of truth in such an assessment; that is, vague illnesses were fashionable among many wealthy upper-class English and American Victorians.

By the mid-1850s Parkman had recovered enough to do some research in Montreal, Ottawa, and Quebec. Unforeseen tragedy awaited him at home, however. In 1857, his only son died of scarlet fever. A short time later, Catherine, his wife of eight years, still distraught over her son's death, gave birth to another daughter, Katherine; then his wife also fell into a severe depression, and died in 1858. After her death, his daughters, one only an infant, were cared for by their mother's sisters.

The loss of his wife and only son plunged Parkman into his severest mental collapse. His family feared that he might become truly insane and sent him to Paris for the winter of 1858–59, hoping that he could be helped by the famous brain specialist Dr. Edouard Brown-Sequard. The French physician assured Parkman that he was not insane, yet there was little else he could offer. Parkman did a bit of research in French colonial archives and recovered enough that by July 1863 the first chapters of his seven-book project were completed and published in the *Atlantic* magazine.

Parkman had been deeply stirred by the Civil War; there was no way that he could have served the Union, of course, and he confessed to a friend, "The plight in which I found myself was mortifying. . . . I was doomed to sit an idle looker on." He despised the fact that he was left "holding the pen with the hand that should have grasped the sword." During this time Parkman also fell in love again; however, the young woman he was interested in—Ida Agazziz, the daughter of a famous Harvard scientist—decided to marry a veteran of the war, which must have humiliated Parkman even further.

In spite of such disappointments, Parkman's health began to slowly and steadily improve. He was able to sleep better and took up gardening as a pastime. As with everything else in his life, he pursued this activity with energy and passion, building his own greenhouse, learning how to hybridize plants, and winning more than three hundred awards from the Massachusetts Horticultural Society, even though he often needed to get about in a wheelchair. He published *The Book of Roses*, considered for many years to be the most reliable book on the cultivation of this flower, and served for a year as professor of horticulture at Harvard.

Parkman's efforts to push onward with *France and England in North America* had to be carried out in bits and pieces. Light bothered his sensitive eyes so badly that he kept his north-facing room shuttered except on the grayest of days. He wrote with red pencil on orange-colored paper because it had no glare (though one can imagine it must have been difficult for Lizzie, who acted as his secretary, to decipher afterward).

Parkman realized that the conflict in North America between France and Britain could be written by focusing on the central characters of each phase of the struggle—for example, around Champlain, La Salle, Chief Pontiac, General Wolfe, and so forth. He also perceived that the struggle between the two major European powers was one of "feudal, militant, Catholic" France and "democratic, industrial, Protestant" England. As he viewed it, it was inevitable that England, which was moving boldly into the future rather than clinging to the past, would prevail.

In the first segment of his proposed seven-volume work, Parkman drew extensively on the journals he had made years before, when he was a Harvard student, to re-create the forests and streams that the early French and English explorers encountered on the American continent. As one reads Parkman's work, it seems to the reader that he actually *became* the French explorer Champlain, and that he could see through the dead man's eyes, using his own experiences in the wilderness as a means to do so.

In the second volume, Parkman continued to paint scenes with words. He was the first American historian to bring history alive for readers, which he often did by actualizing the lives—and deaths—of real men. His account of the death of the Jesuit priest Father De Noue in a wintry forest is anything but dryly factual; it possesses the quality of good theater:

> [He] had dug a circular excavation in the snow, and was kneeling in it. . . . His head was bare, his eyes open and turned upwards, and his hands clasped on his breast. His hat and snowshoes lay at his side. The body was leaning slightly forward, resting against the bank of snow . . . and frozen to the hardness of marble.

The second volume of Parkman's life-work, *The Jesuits in North America*, was published in 1867 and the third, *La Salle and the Discovery of the Great West*, in 1869. That year the author was elected an overseer of Harvard. The next volume of Parkman's masterwork didn't appear until 1874, and the other volumes appeared at lengthy intervals, the final one, *A Half Century of Conflict*, appearing in 1892, a year before Parkman's death.

The years between were filled with activity other than writing. Parkman continued to travel in Europe, where he was warmly welcomed by men such as James Russell Lowell, then the American ambassador to the Court of St. James in London, and Henry James, the famous expatriate writer. He was elected a fellow of the Harvard Corporation in 1875, became president of the Massachusetts Historical Society that same year, and developed a new lily, *lilium Parkmanii*, in 1876. His daughters grew up, married, and presented him with grandchildren whom he took time to love more than he had his own children.

In Boston, he counted among his friends the likes of William Dean Howells and Oliver Wendell Holmes. He helped to found St. Botolph's, a men's elite social club, and became its first president. He wrote at length on the issue of suffrage for women, taking the position that women should never be allowed the vote or equal rights with men!

In the years just before his death, Parkman was able to return to a more active life than ever before, making a six-day horseback trip, then a month-long camping expedition to Canada. His final summer was spent at his beloved cottage on Jamaica Pond, just outside Boston, where he was ably looked after by faithful Lizzie, while he worked on revisions of his previous writings.

In September 1893, with a new century just around the corner, Parkman celebrated his seventieth birthday. A couple of weeks later he went out for a row on the pond, after which he was struck by severe abdominal pain, probably caused by a ruptured appendix. Peritonitis set in, and he died on November 8 after a three-day illness. One of Parkman's final acts was to reread his favorite work by Byron, *Childe Harold's Pilgrimage*, and his last words were to describe a dream he'd just had about killing a bear—a dream that perhaps came out of his longtime love of the wilderness.

Professor John Fiske, a fellow historian, paid tribute to Parkman by referring to his seven-part masterpiece on the early colonial wars: "Of all American historians he is the most deeply and peculiarly American. The book . . . clearly belongs . . . with the works of Herodotus, Thucydides, and Gibbon."

Years before, at one of the most stressful times in his life, Parkman wrote to his cousin-in-law, Mary Parkman, "In *achievement* I expect to fail, but I shall never recoil from endeavor, and I shall go through life, hoping little from this world, yet despairing of nothing."

In his will, Parkman left his journals to the Massachusetts Historical Society, and the maps and sketches he'd made went to Harvard. Little attention was paid to his journals, which were a treasure trove of information that one early biographer unaccountably dismissed as "extraordinarily scanty," perhaps because of their extremely small size. After 1904, the journals were seldom re-

Francis Parkman near the end of his life. STOCK MONTAGE.

ferred to again, and it wasn't until the mid-1950s that they were appreciated for their true worth.

Of all of Parkman's writing, perhaps his work on the French explorer René-Robert La Salle is the most remarkable for its insight and psychological depth. One of the reasons Parkman was so fascinated by the French explorer was because La Salle, too, suffered from mental "demons." Parkman wrote of the explorer: "It is easy to reckon up his defects, but . . . one must follow on his track through the vast scene of his interminable journeyings, those thousands of weary miles of forest, marsh, and river, where, again and again, in the bitterness of baffled striving, the untiring pilgrim pushed onward towards the goals which he was never to attain."

Parkman concluded his portrait of La Salle with words that described not only the Frenchman, but his own deepest self: "Serious in all things, incapable of the lighter pleasures, incapable of repose, finding no joy but in the pursuit of great designs, too shy for society and too reserved for popularity. . . smothering emotions which he could not utter . . . he contained in his own complex and painful nature the chief springs of his triumphs, his failures, and his death." One must admire the courage and fortitude with which Parkman dealt with his unusual problems, and his prose—as alive as when he first composed it—is his most enduring monument.

John Wesley Powell

1834–1902 Explorer, geologist. Losing an arm during the Civil War didn't prevent Powell from pursuing an interest in exploration and geology. He became one of a new breed of mountain man: he didn't go west searching for furs or gold; he went seeking information about the land. He made two major forays into the Grand Canyon, wrote *Exploration of the Colorado River and Its Tributaries* in 1875, and was a founder of the National Geographic Society in 1888.

John Wesley Powell has been called the greatest explorer-hero since the days of John Charles Frémont. Like Frémont, he had an intense interest in the political side of exploration and was concerned not merely with opening the West for settlement but in making sure the natural resources of the area would be used wisely.

His beginnings at Mount Morris, New York, on March 24, 1834, held some hints that he might become exactly the sort of man he did. His father, Joseph, a devout Methodist, had grown up in Shrewsbury, England; his mother, the former Mary Dean, came from Hull; the couple emigrated to America in 1830 with two young daughters, Martha and Mary. A son was born after their arrival but died soon after; when a fourth child, another son, arrived he was named after John Wesley, the founder of Methodism.

As a small boy, Wes (as the family called him) spent much of his time helping run the family's backcountry farm, while Joseph, an itinerant preacher, rode the circuit and supplemented his income doing tailoring for local folk. In 1841, the family moved west to Jackson, Ohio. Their welcome in the community was not enthusiastic because slavery was becoming an issue of fierce controversy and Joseph was a staunch abolitionist. As a result, Wes got a taste of how difficult the life of a reformer could be (an experience he'd have again as a grown man). He regularly got into fights at school, often getting the worst of them, until finally when he was nine his parents put his education in the hands of a neighbor, a fellow abolitionist named George Crookham.

Crookham, six feet tall and weighing three hundred pounds (called a "gentle giant" by one biographer), was considered an eccentric in the community because he chose not to work at a regular job. Instead, he built a two-room log cabin as a schoolhouse-laboratory, where he indulged his interest in natural science along with tutoring a few students. Most of Crookham's pupils were adults; Wes was one of the few youngsters among them, but because of his curiosity and intelligence he became one of the tutor's favorites.

During the next four years, the boy went on many field trips with Crookham and learned how to conduct the kind of laboratory experiments most young people of the day only read about. As his knowledge grew, Wes learned how to look beneath the surface of things for their deeper meanings. He no doubt would have continued his education with Crookham, but local ruffians burned the tutor's cabin to the ground, destroying his library, manuscripts, and science collection—perhaps because they'd discovered he was active in the Underground Railway, which helped slaves escape to the North.

A few years later, the family, which now numbered eight children, moved again, this time to a small farm in Walworth County, Illinois. Here, Wes came of age. He was eager to get a college education, but when he declined to study for the ministry as his father wished, Joseph refused to help him. Wes went out on his own and at eighteen got his first job, as a teacher in southern Wisconsin at a salary of fourteen dollars a month. From there he went on to teach in the Illinois villages of Clinton, Decatur, and Hennepin, and along the way took college classes whenever he could, including some at Oberlin in Ohio.

When he had time, Wes took field trips and made a long journey across Michigan to collect specimens of plants and minerals. On that occasion, he tracked down an uncle on his mother's side of the family, John Dean, who had emigrated from England after Joseph and Mary, but whom they had not seen in twenty-five years. He also made long trips down the Ohio, Illinois, and Des Moines Rivers, and followed the Mississippi from St. Paul, Minnesota, to New Orleans. Such journeys—along with the fact that he'd collected and cataloged six thousand plants for his herbarium—enhanced his reputation among his peers, and Wes was elected secretary of the Illinois Natural History Society. In 1860 he was named principal of the public schools of Hennepin.

Twenty-seven-year-old Wes wasn't

Joseph Powell's son for nothing; he answered Lincoln's first call for Civil War volunteers, enlisting on April 14, 1861, two days after the firing on Fort Sumter. A clerk in the Twentieth Illinois Infantry noted a few pertinent details about Private Powell in his records: "height 5'6 1/2" tall, light complected, gray eyes, auburn hair." Powell took his military career as seriously as he took his scientific field trips; he was promoted steadily and made captain by November.

He purchased books on military engineering and developed enough expertise to supervise the construction of Union fortifications at Cape Girardeau, Missouri. As a result, he met General Ulysses S. Grant, and their friendship became personal enough that the general allowed Wes a special furlough to travel back to Detroit to marry his cousin Emma Dean, the daughter of that long-lost uncle whom he'd located five years earlier. After his marriage on November 28, 1861, Powell was appointed commander of the Second Illinois Artillery. He was a firm disciplinarian, and the soldiers in his command—which now included his youngest brother, Walter— were ready when called to action at Shiloh in April 1862.

In that battle, Powell and his men made a stand in the center of the advancing Confederate troops in a peach orchard nicknamed the "Hornet's Nest"

and were able to hold the enemy off long enough for Grant to regroup his forces. On Sunday, April 6, a minié ball shattered Powell's right arm. He was taken behind the lines, where the arm was amputated two inches below the elbow. Emma was present during the operation because Grant had given her a special pass to accompany her husband whenever possible.

In spite of the loss of his arm, Powell continued on active duty, took part in the siege of Vicksburg in 1863 under General "Black Jack" Logan, and rose to the rank of major, then to brevet lieutenant colonel. ("Brevet" meant the promotion was made on the battlefield and lasted only for the term of service.) Perhaps worse than losing his arm was participating in Sherman's campaign against Atlanta, where he saw his brother captured by the Confederates. Later, when Walter attempted to escape from a southern prison and was recaptured, he suffered a temporary mental breakdown. After he was returned to the Union side in a prisoner swap, Walter was discharged from the service, but he never seemed to completely recover his emotional balance.

When Wes himself was discharged in January 1865, he went back to teaching in Illinois. As a wounded Civil War veteran (henceforth, he was always addressed as "Major"), Powell was invited to run for political office but declined. Instead, he accepted a job as professor of natural history at Illinois Wesleyan College in Wheaton, where he taught a wide variety of courses: botany, zoology, anatomy, entomology, and geology. Whenever possible, he duplicated the teaching method he'd learned from Crookham so long before, taking his students out to the field or into the laboratory for practical experience. Although this was a customary practice in most European universities, it was an innovation in a conservative midwestern American college.

But it was not Powell's nature to be satisfied with such a secure and modest life, even though it was what his father insisted was best, considering his disability. The Major's real wish was to go west—specifically, to explore the Rocky Mountains. He knew Lincoln's Homestead Act of 1862 would change the nature of the land beyond the Mississippi, luring thousands of settlers to the Far West, as it had already drawn them to the Midwest states of Kansas, Nebraska, and Missouri.

Powell was eager to see the country before such inevitable changes occurred, and he devised a plan to facilitate such an adventure. He transferred to Illinois Normal University, where he set to work persuading that institution, in collaboration with Illinois Wesleyan and the Illi-

nois Natural History Society, to support his proposal to establish a natural-history museum in Bloomington. He traveled to Springfield to lobby state legislators and obtained a grant of $1,500. He was appointed the new museum's first curator, then was given permission to use $500 of the grant to fund a trip to the Rockies, where he intended to collect plant, animal, and mineral specimens.

The allotted sum wasn't adequate to do the job properly, so Powell obtained extra financial backing from the Chicago Academy of Science and the Union Pacific Railroad. He went to Washington to get the support of Grant (then acting as U.S. secretary of war), which consisted of permission to buy rations at a reduced cost from army outposts in the West, as well as the use of a military escort from Fort Laramie to the Rockies. Joseph Henry of the Smithsonian gave Powell advice, as well as certain instruments to be used in exploration. For the rest of his needs, Powell dipped into his own pocket.

Now it was time to select the personnel who would make the journey west with him. Emma, who'd already shared an adventurous life with her husband, was included in the party, as was Powell's brother-in-law, Almon H. Thompson. Thompson also was a teacher and soon became a fine explorer in his own right, as well as the chief mapmaker for what came to be called "the Powell Surveys." Other party members included college students, amateur naturalists, and fellow teachers.

Military officials had advised Powell to steer clear of Dakota Territory, where Indians who were increasingly resentful of intrusion by whites might be a danger, so the explorers left Council Bluffs, Iowa, on June 1, 1867, and headed across the plains toward Denver, where they intended to join a wagon train at Fort McPherson. While in Denver, Powell met William Byers, publisher of the *Rocky Mountain News*, who gave the team the kind of publicity that would eventually make Powell's name famous.

The group left Denver on a little-used and difficult trail over the Rampart Range and camped in Bergen's Park for a month, making collections of specimens. They began an ascent of Pikes Peak on the morning of July 27, and it was believed at the time that Emma Powell was the first woman to have climbed to the top. (Later research documented that in 1858 a certain Julia Holmes, a spunky Kansas girl, actually was the first white woman to have done so.)

The explorers spent three weeks in South Park before heading back to Denver, where the group disbanded. Powell and his wife stayed another two months, exploring the Grand River, and it was during this time that Powell de-cided to explore the Grand to its junction with the Colorado River, a journey that would mark the beginning of his greatest work as a western explorer.

Two of Powell's major talents were his organizational skill and his ability to generate enthusiasm and excitement in others, and after his return to Bloomington he lectured widely to as many audiences as would invite him to speak. When he went to Washington, he solicited more help from Grant, this time for enough supplies to outfit a party of twenty-five whose aim it would be to explore the Colorado River. Again, Joseph Henry of the Smithsonian enthusiastically supported Powell's plans.

In 1868, the team once again departed from Denver; once again, Emma Powell was included (although some of the men came to regard her as "bossy"). The team numbered only twenty-one and included Byers, the newspaper editor, and Powell's brother Walter, who had recovered enough from his Civil War experiences to participate. Powell established his headquarters along the Grand River and spent three months collecting specimens and whatever fossils could be found. He also hiked the Colorado and the Gore Ranges of the Rockies, the highest peak of which was Mount Lincoln at 14,300 feet.

In August, the camp was visited by some sightseers—but they were much

An engraving depicts the start of Powell's expedition from Green River Station. NORTH WIND PICTURE ARCHIVES.

more important than casual summer tourists. The Speaker of the U.S. House of Representatives, Schuyler Colfax (soon to be Grant's vice president) was among them; Samuel Bowles, editor of the *Springfield* (Mass.) *Republican*, one of the country's most influential papers, and correspondents from two Chicago newspapers also were present. Bowles was greatly impressed by Powell, describing him as "enthusiastic, resolute, a gallant leader"; such friendships advanced Powell's growing reputation.

On August 20, 1868, the party set out

to climb Long's Peak, and three days later they reached the top. They crossed the Continental Divide via the Berthoud-Bridger Trail and moved downstream to the White River, 150 miles from where it joined the Green. Then F. M. Bishop, who had been sent back for supplies, became lost for five weeks, and one of the mountaineers, Gus Lanken, deserted the party, taking a mule and supplies with him. One member of the group carved into a tree words for all the world to see: "Gus Lanken is a mule thief . . . this 14th day of September 1868."

In the White River valley, Powell and his men built three log cabins to be used as headquarters for a winter exploration of the Colorado River. The Major reviewed what was already known about the area from earlier explorers, such as Captain J. W. Gunnison's work for the Pacific Railroad in 1853, Lieutenant Warren's map of 1857, and J. C. Ives's 1861 account of his descent into the Grand Canyon near Diamond Creek. He also listened closely to the stories of the Ute Indians, whose legends described how travelers had vanished in the turbulent rapids of the White River.

In the spring, floods forced the team members out of their cabins; supplies ran short; tempers began to flare; by March 1869 it seemed best to abandon exploration for the time being. While Emma took time to visit her family in Detroit, Powell went to Chicago to arrange with a boatbuilder to construct four special craft for a descent down the Colorado River. Three of the boats, each twenty-one feet long, were built of oak and had watertight compartments at either end to assure buoyancy. The fourth was a smaller craft, only sixteen feet, and made of pine; it would be used as a pilot boat to lead the others. Before he loaded his boats on a railroad car and headed west, Powell tested each one on Lake Michigan to make sure it was seaworthy.

Again, it was Powell's responsibility to supply a large part of the finances for the trip himself, and again he sought the support of universities and railroads. His group of explorers was an eclectic one: his brother Walter again was included, as was Andrew Hall, a young Indian fighter; George Bradley, a former army sergeant whom Powell had met at Bridger's Fort in 1868; and an English sportsman, Frank Goodman. (This time, Emma remained at home.) Critics have faulted Powell for not taking with him any "real" scientists, but no doubt such men would have expected to be paid, while Powell's companions worked for little or nothing.

Powell met his team at Green River Station in Wyoming Territory on May 11, 1869, and they spent several days teaching themselves how to handle the boats.

Then food supplies were gotten together, tools stowed on board, and at noon on May 24 the men shoved off from the riverbank and began their voyage to explore the Colorado River and its main tributary, the Green.

At that time, the whole Colorado River system had been written off as a "profitless locality," but now its waters are more precious than gold. The Little Colorado River begins as a mere trickle high in the Never-Summer Mountains northwest of Denver; its major tributary, the Green River, comes down from the Wind River Range in Wyoming. When the two rivers combine with other, smaller tributaries to form the Colorado, it drains water from seven states—Wyoming, Utah, Colorado, Arizona, New Mexico, Nevada, and California—on its way to the Pacific. Today, that water is used to grow fruit and vegetable crops in New Mexico and Arizona, fill swimming pools in California, and water golf courses in Nevada.

Powell took the lead in the lightest boat, which he named the Emma Dean, after his wife; next came the *Kitty Clyde's Sister*, carrying Walter Powell and George Bradley; then the *Maid of the Canyon*, with Andrew Hall and William Hawkins; in the rear came the *No Name*, with the Howland brothers, Oramel and Seneca, and the English-man. After making eight miles on their first day, the team ran aground, which would give them a taste of the hardships that lay ahead.

When no word came from the adventurers after a few weeks, articles in newspapers around the country reported the men had been killed in the rapids of the upper Green River. An opportunist named Risdon was able to make himself briefly famous when he claimed to be the only survivor of the accident. The truth was, no one really knew much about what the adventurers were facing. Yes, old Jim Bridger, the famous scout and hunter, had crossed the plateau above the river and knew something of its wildness; John Charles Frémont had explored a portion of it; General William Ashley saw parts of the river when he descended it in a bullboat (buffalo hides stretched over a green willow frame)—but no one had yet traveled the length of the Colorado. Among other things, no one knew how the river could drop a vertical mile during its 900-mile journey—when, by comparison, the Mississippi dropped only 1,670 feet in 2,560 miles.

Contrary to news reports, the adventurers were anything but dead. On either side of them, canyon walls rose as much as 2,000 feet straight up as they passed through Flaming Gorge, Horseshoe Canyon, Kingfisher Canyon, and Red

Canyon. Sometimes it was necessary to let the boats down the rapids by a method called "lining." A rope was tied to the bow, or front, of the boat, and another to the stern, or back. Next, the bow line was taken downriver, below the rapids, and tied securely to a tree or rock. Then several men on shore held on to the stern line, letting the rope out slowly as the boat was lowered down the rapids. When the men could no longer hold the craft against the pull of the water, they let go of the rope, then hurried below to pull the boat in with the bow line. If the rapids were too rough for lining, the boats had to be unloaded and portaged around the whitewater. The team was put on notice it was not the first to travel on this section of the river; painted on a rock in midstream was a reminder: "Ashley 1825."

Powell made it a point to climb up out of the canyons to inspect the plateaus above. When he viewed the Canyon of Lodore from 2,000 feet, he wrote of his impression: "The sun is going down, and the shadows are settling in the canyon. The vermillion gleams and roseate hues, blending with the green and gray tones, are slowly changing to somber brown. . . . Black shadows are creeping over them below. Now 'tis a black portal to a region of gloom."

On June 7, 1869, the first serious accident occurred. As usual, Powell was traveling in the lead, and he noticed a bad falls ahead. He gestured frantically to the boats behind, but neither the Howland brothers nor Goodman noticed in time to avoid shooting over the falls, where boulders were scattered like enormous land mines. The *No Name*, which carried some of Powell's instruments, broke in half. The men were pitched out; the Howlands made it to a small island downstream, while the Englishman was able to cling to a rock until he was rescued. The explorers gave the rapids the name they deserved: "Disaster Falls."

Fortunately, part of the boat was found the next day, and Powell's barometers were rescued, as well as a keg of whiskey the Howland boys had sneaked on board. The next accident involved an empty boat: the *Maid of the Canyon* slipped away from the men one day, then shot down the rapids alone; happily, she was rescued undamaged. Thirty-seven days after their departure from the banks of the Green River, the team arrived in the Uinta Valley near the spot where Father Sylvestre Escalante, a Spanish priest, had crossed in 1776. The men hiked out to the Ute Indian agency for supplies and took time to send their first letters home. Here, the Englishman decided he'd had enough. "Frank Goodman. . . has concluded not to go on with the party, saying he has seen danger enough," Powell noted in his journal.

The journey continued on July 6, but two days later Powell got himself trapped on a rock ledge and was unable to move either down or up. He clung to the cliff face with his one hand (readers are apt to forget this adventurer had only one arm!) and later recalled his predicament: "It is sixty or eighty feet to the foot of the precipice. If I lose my hold I shall fall to the bottom, and then roll over the bench, and tumble still farther down the cliff." He called out to ex-sergeant Bradley, who was above him.

"At this instant it occurs to Bradley to take off his drawers [long underwear], which he does, and swings them down to me. I hug close to the rock, let go with my hand, seize the dangling legs, and with his assistance, I am enabled to gain the top." Powell often retold the story to his audiences, where it got laughs—perhaps because the idea of a bare-bottomed Bradley seemed humorous; at the time, neither Bradley nor Powell was amused.

By July 17, the men reached the junction of the Grand River, having traveled 538 miles from their starting point. They took time to caulk their boats and make new oars before proceeding to Glen Canyon, where they sighted a ruined cliff-dwelling two hundred feet above. The three-story structure had stood undisturbed for centuries, and Powell was so struck by its beauty that an interest in Indian culture was kindled in him that lasted the rest of his life.

In early August 1869, the men reached the Little Colorado River, the beginning of the Grand Canyon. Powell noted the importance of the moment: "We are now ready to start on our way down the Great Unknown. . . . We have but a month's rations remaining. The flour has been resifted through a mosquito-net sieve; the spoiled bacon has been dried." Then they began their plunge down the canyon. Cataracts swamped the boats. There was no time for the leisurely hikes or observations that Powell had enjoyed earlier. Often there was no foothold along the sheer canyon walls; the travelers were obliged to go forward in spite of themselves. On August 27, the men encountered a series of deadly rapids that descended eighteen to twenty feet, and it seemed impossible to go any farther. The Howland brothers and fellow explorer Bill Dunn decided to quit and left the next day to hike out to some Mormon settlements seventy-five miles to the north.

Powell himself was uncertain. "Is it safe to go on?" he asked in his journal. But he "could not bear to leave the exploration unfinished . . . having already almost accomplished it." Powell took the measure of the men who remained;

they agreed to continue in the two craft that were left. Bradley took his boat first and vanished in the foaming white water. Powell's heart sank, and he tersely recorded his sense of doom: "Bradley is gone." But moments later the young ex-sergeant emerged, man and boat still intact, and waved his hat in triumph. Powell, on shore, watched anxiously as the second boat went down, tumbling like a wood chip through the rapids; then it too emerged safely.

Three days later the men came to a bend in the river where they met a Mormon father fishing with his two grown sons and an Indian boy. The fishermen were surprised because they'd been alerted by Mormon authorities to keep a watch for debris—pieces of broken boat, clothing, equipment—that would indicate the crew had perished somewhere upstream. Powell and the men who'd stuck with him had survived the mighty Colorado. The same could not be said for the three who had given up the trip. The Howland brothers and Bill Dunn never reached their destination at the Mormon settlements; they were ambushed by Shivwits Indians and lay dead on a plateau above the canyon.

When Powell returned from the journey, he was a national hero. Newspapers were eager to publish the story of his great adventure, and the unfortunate deaths of his three companions only enhanced public interest. In the autumn and winter of 1869, Powell lectured extensively and became an even more polished public performer. He wrote an account of his journey that appeared in *New Tracks in North America,* and again critics pointed out that Powell's work was more descriptive than it was scientific. That was due partly to a mishap: Powell had accidentally given the Howland brothers *both* sets of technical notes he'd made, and the material was lost when the men were massacred.

Powell's fame was sufficient to wring an appropriation of ten thousand dollars out of the U.S. Congress to fund a "Geographical and Topographical Survey of the Colorado River of the West." No salary came with the stipend, but Powell continued to hold on to his professorship at Illinois Normal, and a year later he headed for a second major exploration of the Grand Canyon.

Powell ordered three new boats and spent a year preparing for the second expedition, which had three aims: first, and most importantly, to properly map the river; second, to find a way to more easily bring supplies downriver so his party wouldn't find themselves on the brink of starvation as it had before; and third, to find out what had happened to his three companions. After gaining the confidence of the Shivwits Indians, Powell learned that the Howlands and Dunn had been killed when they were mistaken for some white prospectors who had murdered a woman from the tribe. This meeting was important not only because it settled the fate of the three men but because it promoted Powell's growing interest in the Indians themselves, their culture, and the unhappy circumstances—namely, attacks by the warlike Apaches—that had forced them out of their homes and into the mountains, where survival was difficult.

Powell made only part of the 1871–72 river trip himself; rather, his brother-in-law and second-in-command, A. H. Thompson, took charge. The party also included seventeen-year-old Frederick Dellenbaugh, who in spite of his youth had already studied art in Paris and painted the first impressions of the Grand Canyon. Also present was a photographer, James Fennemore from Salt Lake City. It was during this trip, after ten childless years, that the Major and Emma became the parents of a baby girl born in early September 1871. She would be their only child.

The three new boats that Powell ordered were improved over the first ones; these had watertight compartments amidship as well as at either end, which increased storage space and also added broadside strength. Just before departing on May 22, 1871, Powell lashed a

chair to the middle deck of the *Emma Dean* and made observations from this makeshift crow's nest. In February 1872, Powell returned to Washington, and in his absence Thompson conducted some of the most important parts of the exploration, discovering an until-then unknown river that was named the Escalante, and an unknown mountain range they called the Henry Mountains.

When Powell rejoined the expedition in the summer, it was to find that the water was running much higher than the year before, making travel even more hazardous than it had been on the first trip. When the party reached Kanab Canyon, Powell decided to end the expedition, even though data for the lower reaches of the Grand Canyon were still more meager than he would have liked. It was not his nature to back away from a challenge, but this time it probably saved the lives of some or all of his men.

Perhaps the most famous of Powell's contributions to knowledge of the area related to his understanding of the relationship of the Colorado River to the Uinta Mountains. He had posed a question to himself and now was able to answer it: "Why did not the stream turn around this great obstruction [the mountains], rather than pass through it? The answer is that the river had the right of way; in other words it was running ere the mountains were formed . . .

before the formations were folded, so as to make a mountain range. . . . The river preserved its level, but mountains were lifted up."

When Powell's first major report, *The Exploration of the Colorado River and Its Tributaries*, was published in 1875, it quickly sold out. One unintended but important outcome of the trip was his developing interest in the science not merely of geology but of man. He had encountered many tribes in his exploration—the Paiutes, Shivwits, and Utes—and established friendly relationships with their members because he was more respectful of their customs than were some of his contemporaries. Whenever possible, he avoided the use of an army escort when he went into the wilderness; he blamed the military aspects of such travel for many of the problems that whites had with Indians.

Powell became as interested in Indian languages as he was in plants and minerals, and he learned to speak more than one of the languages of the plateaus. In 1877, after consultation with Professor William Whitney of Yale, the country's foremost philologist, Powell published *Introduction to the Study of Indian Languages*, which became a standard text for use in the collection of tribal vocabularies. In 1879, the Smithsonian Institution founded its Bureau of Ethnology, designed to study native cul-

John Wesley Powell with Tau-Gu, Great Chief of the Paiutes. CULVER PICTURES, INC. PHOTOGRAPH BY JOHN K. HILLERS.

tures, and Powell served as its director for twenty-three years.

Powell became so expert in Indian problems that in 1873 he was appointed a special commissioner to investigate the various tribes and make suggestions concerning their future. He went to Utah with the painter Thomas Moran, spent several months studying the Indians and their problems, and attended a council in Salt Lake City in August of that year.

Most of the impoverished tribes agreed to move to reservations, partly because of the encouragement of the man they called Kapurats, or One-Arm-Off.

What Powell had witnessed as he visited the various tribes aroused his reformer's zeal, and he went to Washington to report personally on the fraudulent treatment Indians received at the hands of various agents. The result was a series of investigations that led to an exposé of wrongdoing and the resignation of the secretary of the interior, Columbus Delano.

Among Powell's suggestions regarding Indian welfare was that they should not be merely "fed with flour and beef, to be supplied with blankets from the Government bounty . . . but that a reservation should be a school of industry and a home for these unfortunate people." He established an eight-point program for what should take place on a reservation, and among the most important were:

1. All bounties (provisions) should be used to promote work.
2. Reservations should be irrigated, and Indians taught how to farm.
3. Reservations should have a medical clinic.
4. Schools should be established on each reservation.

Of course, Powell had just as many ideas about how whites should use the West, and in 1878 his most famous work, *Report on the Lands of the Arid Regions of the United States*, illuminated a problem that had been ignored by the "boom or bust" promoters of western settlements. Powell pointed out that due to its aridity, the West was not suited to the type of farming operations that were familiar in the East. He recommended irrigation practices similar to the kind he'd observed in the Mormon colonies, with water rights being inherent for each piece of land that was sold.

Not surprisingly, Powell's recommendation of a program of irrigation that included grazing districts, dams, reservoirs, and mountain catch-basins for water collection wasn't well received by many westerners. His plan threatened large timber, mining, and railroad interests, not to mention wealthy corporate cattlemen; consequently, his proposals were brushed aside. Powell was persistent, however, and in 1881 he became director of the U.S. Geological Survey, a government agency that had originally served mainly as a tool of the mining industry. It was Powell's conviction that government science ought to serve all of the people, and he expanded the bureau's activities.

When a serious drought hit the West in the 1880s—just as Powell predicted it would—Senator "Big Bill" Stewart of Nevada pushed a resolution through

Congress giving Powell permission to do a survey of potential dam sites. Stewart expected the former explorer to do a quick study, then step aside to let developers take over. The senator obviously didn't know that Powell had a reformer's heart, but the Major quickly made it clear he took a different view of what his job ought to be.

"I think it would be almost a criminal act to . . . allow thousands and hundreds of thousands of people to establish homes where they cannot maintain themselves," he wrote. Rather than a quick survey, Powell began to map irrigable lands in the entire public domain, a project that would take at least ten years to complete. Land sales in the region were suspended indefinitely. Senator Stewart was outraged; he called for a series of investigations, during which he lambasted Powell for mismanagement of government funds and spread ugly rumors about the Major's private life.

Powell ignored the harassment and presented himself before the congressional hearings as a professional who expected to be treated like one. His dealings in Washington had usually been pleasant, but this time he was bucking a national trend. There was no hunger in the country for farsighted planning; rather, there was hunger only for cheap, available land—land *right now*, that is.

In 1891, Powell's budget was slashed from $720,000 to $325,000, and his survey was terminated. Three years later, on May 4, 1894, the Major resigned his position as director of the U.S. Geological Survey.

Throughout his life, the regenerated nerves in the stump of Powell's amputated right arm had caused him considerable pain and prevented him from wearing an artificial limb. Now, surgery was recommended, and a few days after his resignation, he entered Johns Hopkins Hospital. The surgery was successful, but not long afterward Powell developed heart disease and withdrew from public life.

For the next eight years, the Major spent his days quietly organizing wilderness excursions for others, writing letters, and working on his philosophical essays. (His published books and articles total over 250.) In 1901, he made a trip to Cuba and Jamaica to study the languages of Arawak and Carib Indians and came home more exhausted than he wanted to admit. His spirits brightened in June 1902, however, when President Theodore Roosevelt signed a bill creating the U.S. Bureau of Reclamation, which would fund dams to be built by the government in the West, thereby guaranteeing that water—the liquid gold of the region Powell knew so well—would be used wisely.

Powell had long been a close friend of Alexander Graham Bell, and in September 1902 the famous inventor hurried to the Powells' vacation cottage in Maine after hearing the Major was ill. He arrived a few hours too late; sixty-eight-year-old John Wesley Powell died early on the evening of September 23, his wife and daughter at his side. After funeral services at the National Museum in Washington, he was buried at Arlington National Cemetery with full military honors. A scientist to the end, Powell willed his brain to the Smithsonian, where it now rests in an old-fashioned specimen jar in a dusty back corridor. Today, if we eat apples from Washington, peaches from California, or cantaloupes from Arizona, we are enjoying the literal fruits of John Wesley Powell's explorations of the Colorado River system and of his recommendations about irrigation. Glen Canyon was dammed up in 1963, and the resulting body of water,

Lake Powell, was named in the Major's honor. That tribute might strike him as a bit ironic, however, because the very things he warned about have come to pass: the water resources of the West have been overused and continue to be.

Powell gained fame as an adventurous explorer, and rightly so, yet it was his philosophy of man that made him truly remarkable in a time when Indians were deprived of their lands, then despised for being a burden to the white man. Powell understood the Indian as few of his peers did because Crookham had taught him long ago that one must look beneath the surface of things in order to truly understand them.

"Man's opinions are the children of his own reasoning," Powell wrote, "and he loves his offspring. When I stand before a sacred fire in an Indian village and listen to the red man's philosophy, no anger stirs in my blood. I love him as one of my kind."

Frederic Remington

1861–1909 Artist, writer. After finishing his second year at the Yale School of Fine Arts, Remington took a trip to Montana Territory. There, around a campfire near the Yellowstone River, an old-timer told him that the Old West as it had existed was dying. Remington—who hadn't yet committed himself wholeheartedly to a career as an artist—made up his mind to capture such scenes as still were left. Critics and historians paid him the ultimate tribute: "His Indians are Indians; his Apache is an Apache; his Sioux is a Sioux."

The world that Frederic Remington painted has vanished. The shoulder-high prairie grass has been turned under, and corn or wheat stands in its place. The buffalo herds are gone; Indians no longer live in skin lodges; longhorn cattle aren't herded by men on horseback. Yet we still can catch a glimpse of those days because of the paintings of a man who came from a comfortable upper-class home in the distinctly unwestern state of New York.

Frederic Sackrider Remington, his parents' only child, was born on the fourth day of October 1861, in the home of his paternal grandparents in Canton, New York, not far from the Canadian border in the northern part of the state. Five years before his son was born, Seth

Remington became a partner in the *Plaindealer*, the newspaper that served the area for more than a century. Seth, who could trace his ancestry back to the archdeacon of Lockington, England, was a tall, lean young man of passionate convictions, and nothing affected him more deeply than the Civil War, which had begun on April 12, a few months before Frederic's birth. When his son was only two months old, Seth—whom many compared in appearance to General George Armstrong Custer—left the newspaper to recruit a military unit that became a part of the famed Eleventh New York Cavalry.

Rather than remain with her parents-in-law while her husband fought for the Union, Clara Remington moved back across town with her infant son and settled in her own parents' home. Grandfather Sackrider, who owned a hardware store, doted on his daughter's little boy and was an ideal surrogate father in Seth's absence. Clara believed that she observed artistic talent in the boy when he was only two or three years old, and no doubt he was praised for his childish scribbles.

Seth Remington served with distinction in the Civil War and was greatly admired by his men, who called him "brave and dashy." He returned to Canton when Frederic was four years old and was addressed ever after as "Colonel." After having seen the wider world, Seth found his old hometown not quite to his liking, so he took a job at a larger newspaper in Bloomington, Illinois. Clara was unhappy in the Midwest, however, and after a year the family moved back to Canton, where Seth repurchased an interest in his former paper.

Returning to Canton—still a cozy village where everyone knew everyone else—carried certain benefits for young Frederic. As the only son of a prominent war hero, he too was accorded certain privileges—so much so that he became a pain in the neck to some village residents. He was a hyperactive boy, enjoyed hunting, fishing, and camping with his chums, and was the first to test the waters of the nearby Grasse River each spring. Cowboys and Indians was a favorite game, and since Remington knew he couldn't actually scalp one of his playmates, he settled for cutting off the boy's hair with a pair of sewing scissors. Little girls thought he was dreadful, and more than one parent did too—especially after Frederic painted Alice Pettibone's pet cat bright green.

The Colonel was concerned about his son's grades in school, which bordered on disgraceful. The boy wouldn't tend to his lessons if he could find something more exciting to do, and his deficiency in math meant he'd have trouble getting into West Point, as was the Colonel's fondest wish.

In August 1869, half of Canton's business district, including the offices of the *Plaindealer*, was destroyed by fire. The newspaper was rebuilt but burned down again a year later. When Seth was appointed a collector of customs in the larger village of Ogdensburg, eighteen miles away, the family moved again. Frederic (who'd been nicknamed Puffy because of his stout size) was popular with his new chums and just as dreaded by the local girls. In spite of his pranks, however, the boy was never scolded or harassed by his parents. Seth, in particular, was endlessly tolerant of his only child and, as was the fashion of the time, addressed the boy as a miniature adult who could be reasoned with. Seth was a lover of fine horses, shared that love with the boy on a man-to-man basis, and admired his son's sketches of the animals.

Becoming thirteen ushered in a change of focus for Frederic: his parents decided to place him in a military school, the Episcopal Institute, at Rock Point, Vermont. It wasn't his hyperactive behavior that caused them to make such a decision; rather, the educational opportunities in Ogdensburg weren't the kind that would prepare a boy for West Point, which, in spite of Frederic's grades, was still what Seth had in mind for his son. Taking leave from home for the first time can be hard for some boys, but it apparently was easy for Frederic, who was as confident as a teenager as he'd been as a toddler.

The institute was set in magnificent surroundings on a bluff above Lake Champlain, facing the Adirondacks across the water. In August 1875, Remington took his place among fifty other boys and got his first formal art instruction from the headmaster himself, the Reverend Theodore Hopkins. Art class appealed to Frederic, but he also had to study subjects he hated— German, algebra, and public speaking. Since discipline was strict (it certainly wasn't enforced at home), Frederic earned his share of demerits, which were paid off at the rate of five lashes per demerit. Worst of all, he later explained, was that he had been raised to eat heartily, and the portions doled out in the mess hall never filled him up. The boy indignantly wrote home to say he was "always hungry," and finally decided he'd had enough. He ran away.

After conferring with his parents, Frederic agreed to return to the institute, accept his punishment for running off, and finish out the term—but he extracted a promise from his father that he could transfer to a different school the following year.

That summer, when his parents went on a lengthy trip, Frederic stayed at his maternal grandparents' home on Miner Street in Canton, where he'd spent so much time as a child. He was happy there, and was given the chance to do mostly what he wanted, when he wanted—including eating. Perhaps it isn't surprising that it also was the summer of his first large drawing. The boy used everything he'd learned in the Reverend Hopkins's art class, then created a three-by-four-foot composition of a Roman soldier guarding a barbarian captive that he titled *The Chained Gaul*. His grandparents were delighted with it and hung it in the hallway.

The following year, Frederic attended Highland Military Academy in Worcester, Massachusetts. By this time, his nickname was Bud, and English turned out to be his best subject. Even though his enthusiasm for military discipline was lukewarm, he stayed at the academy for two years. One of the things that distinguished him was his physical strength, as cadet Julian Wilder of Maine discovered. He suffered a broken shoulder blade, a broken collarbone, and a dislocated arm in a "friendly" wrestling game with Frederic. Remington cheerfully described himself as having "a good many [an advantage over his peers] on muscle. My hair is short and stiff, and I am about five feet eight inches and weigh about one hundred and eighty pounds. There is nothing poetical about me."

Frederic may not have liked military discipline, yet he was as popular with the other boys as he'd been in Canton or Ogdensburg. He was breezy, irreverent, and seemed to be a genuinely happy person. He gleefully gave away the impudent cartoons that he drew of officers and teachers at the academy and was often asked to illustrate the pages of other students' diaries or journals. The drawings were amusing and energetic but otherwise gave no hint of the artist's future talent.

When he was sixteen and about to leave military school, Frederic confided his life plans to his uncle Horace Sackrider in a letter. "I never intend to do any great amount of labor," he admitted. "I have but one short life and do not aspire to wealth nor fame in a degree which could only be obtained by an extraordinary effort on my part." Instead, he intended to continue working on his art and ultimately to enter Cornell College, where he wanted to study both art and journalism.

Cornell had no art department, however, so Frederic opted to enroll in the Yale School of Fine Arts. His family was somewhat dismayed by his insistence that he aimed to pursue an art career; in those days, art was regarded as a pleasant pastime best suited to young ladies. In addition, he didn't seem to have any unusual ability, though everyone admitted he drew horses rather well. Serious art students would have chosen to go to Europe, still the center of the art world in that era, but that might have been out of the question for Frederic, whose parents were comfortably well-off but not wealthy.

In 1878, when Frederic began his art training, he was one of thirty students, twenty-three of whom were women. The young ladies rated separate, well-lighted classrooms on the upper floor of the art building; the seven men were confined to a gloomy basement. Frederic was the only first-year student among them and often worked entirely alone. He drew from plaster casts of famous works such as Praxiteles' dancing faun and detested the exercises as much as he'd loathed military school. Once again, he took pleasure in making cartoons or caricatures of the people and situations around him. His first published illustration—a cartoon of a bruised and bandaged football player—appeared in the *Yale Courant* on November 12, 1878.

When Frederic went home in August 1879 to attend the county fair, he discovered that his parents' neighbors, the DeForests, were entertaining two young houseguests, William Caten and his sister Eva, both of whom were students at St. Lawrence University. Frederic and William were the same age, while Eva, nineteen, was two years older. Eva—who liked to be called Missie—was a small, friendly girl, very much accustomed to the teasing banter of boys. Soon, Frederic was calling on her every day.

When Frederic returned to school in the fall, he was still the only male in his class. Second-year studies were rather technical, and—still being a hyperactive sort—he found himself bored. He enthusiastically accepted an invitation to try out for the Yale football team and was on the winning side in a game against Pennsylvania. The second game was with Harvard, and again Frederic's team emerged victorious. When Seth Remington attended the final game of the sea-

son on November 28, 1879, he brought a doctor with him. Frederic assumed his father feared for his son's safety on the playing field and never imagined that it was because Seth was concerned about his own health.

When Frederic went home at Christmas, however, he realized that his father was desperately ill. For the next two months, he watched the man he admired above all others die slowly of tuberculosis. On the afternoon of February 18, 1880, the forty-six-year-old Colonel died with his wife and son at his side. The local newspaper remarked that "the men most needed seem to be those first appointed to death."

The loss of his father was a severe blow to eighteen-year-old Frederic. However, his father's will provided well for him, and the young man didn't need to make an immediate decision about his future. One thing he knew, however: he wouldn't return to Yale. He got a job as a clerk in a local store but quit after a few days; he was convinced he was destined for something out of the ordinary.

Frederic and his mother returned to Canton, and once again moved in with the Sackriders. An uncle living in Albany got Frederic a job as a clerk for Alonzo Cornell, the governor of New York, at the handsome salary of seventy dollars a month. For a time, Mrs. Remington came to keep house for her son, but the arrangement didn't last long. They were far too much alike—"stubborn" best describes the disposition of each—and she returned home to her parents.

The thing that held Frederic in Albany wasn't the charm of his job, it was the charm of Missie Caten, who lived forty miles away in the village of Gloversville. In August 1880, having decided that he wanted to marry her, Frederic composed a letter to the young lady's father on the governor's official stationery, declaring that he felt "warranted now in asking whether or not you will consent to an engagement between us."

The answer was swift in coming: *No.* Mr. Caten pointed out that his wife was dying, that he needed Missie at home to care for her younger brothers and sisters, and that in any case Frederic was far too young at eighteen to think of anything as serious as marriage.

Never before had Frederic Remington been denied his heart's desire. He still felt the loss of his father, and now he'd been told he couldn't marry the girl he loved. There seemed to be no reason to stay in Albany; in fact, there was no reason to stay in New York. He quit his job as the governor's clerk, which he hadn't liked in the first place. He continued to sketch in a halfhearted fashion, but when the family urged him to return to art school at Yale, he refused. His instructors there, Professors Weir and Niemeyer, had already implied that he lacked the necessary talent to succeed as an academic painter.

Remington spent the summer of 1881 back in Canton, amusing himself with old friends, hunting and fishing, and going on camping trips. His uncle arranged another job for him, this time with the New York State Insurance Department. Although it was considered a splendid opportunity, Frederic knew it would be just another desk job that he'd quickly despise. He also knew he ought to agree to at least try it, but he asked his family for the chance to first take a vacation to Montana Territory.

The magic of the West had been a popular topic during his college years, and Frederic, like his friends, had read of the adventures of Lewis and Clark, who brought back tales of glory from their famous expedition, of the painter George Catlin, the first artist to record the appearance and habits of the Indians, and of writers like Francis Parkman, who captured in words the lure of the Oregon Trail. For a robust, energetic fellow like Frederic, it must have seemed the ideal place to be. When he left New York in August 1881, the local newspaper noted that Canton's favorite young man intended "to make a trial of life on a ranche." Twenty-four years later, in an article in *Collier's* magazine, Remington described what would be the turning point in his life. He bought himself a horse and was sleeping out in the open as he traveled along, when he chanced upon the camp of an elderly wagon freighter. The old chap was a former New Yorker himself, who had come west at an early age.

"'And now,' said he, 'there is no more West,'" Remington quoted the old man as saying. "'In a few years the railroad will come along the Yellowstone and a poor man can not make a living at all.'"

Those words caused Remington to reflect that "the wild riders and the vacant lands were about to vanish forever. . . . I saw the living, breathing end of three American centuries of smoke and dust and sweat." Indeed, the West that Remington saw that year *was* changing: Custer and his Seventh Cavalry had been wiped out five years earlier; Crazy Horse was murdered in 1877 at Fort Robinson; white men swarmed through the Black Hills, once the sacred Pa Sapa of the Sioux; a transcontinental railroad would soon connect the East and West Coasts. Remington witnessed something else in 1881: the slaughter of one million buffalo in Wyoming and Montana by five thousand hired white hunters who had come out by train expressly for that purpose. Buffalo lay "dying on the prairie so thick that one could hardly see the ground," Remington wrote.

Remington decided to "try to record some facts" of what he saw going on around him. At this point in his life, he was still dabbling in art and had brought no sketching materials with him. Nevertheless, he mailed *Harper's Weekly* a rough little sketch that he'd done on common wrapping paper. The magazine's art director was intrigued by the sketch—especially by its Wyoming postmark—and passed it on to an experienced illustrator to be redrawn. When Frederic returned to New York in October, he made an appointment with an editor at *Harper's* to talk about the illustration. The sketch was indeed purchased, and the redrawn version was published in February 1882.

A career as an illustrator was not yet to be; after all, Frederic had made a deal: a Montana vacation in exchange for his agreement to go take a job as an insurance actuary. He lived up to his part of the bargain, but although he wrote home that he liked his work and was diligent, other employees remember that he spent a lot of time sketching rather than tending to his calculations. Not surprisingly, he was soon out of a job again.

Frederic bided his time; according to his father's will, he would come into his full inheritance on his twenty-first birthday. When that happened he knew exactly what he intended to do: go west again. As soon as he got access to the money, he went to Peabody, Kansas, where a former college chum, Robert Camp, lived on a nine-thousand-head sheep ranch. The "sheep craze" had begun in 1879, when prices climbed from a dollar a head to five dollars. Ranchers expected the price to go as high as ten and were bedazzled by visions of wealth. Camp offered to advise his friend on how to get started, and Frederic plunked down $3,400 of his inherited money on a piece of property.

When Frederic—who had always enjoyed the finer things of life—inspected his friend's ranch, it dawned on him that he might have made a terrible mistake. The Kansas landscape was bleak and treeless; Camp's ranch house was no more than a hovel; ranch work was backbreaking; the sheep smelled awful. But like it or not, he was in the sheep business.

The spring was a cold one, but it was lambing time, one of the most arduous phases of any sheep rancher's life, and Frederic found himself carrying cans of milk out to the prairie to care for needy lambs early every morning and the last thing at night. He traded his eastern clothes for frontier duds, acquired another quarter section of land, built another sheep shed, and increased his investment to $7,750. He bought himself a part-Thoroughbred mare, "a beautiful light gold-dust color, with a Naples-yellow mane and tail" (then lost her in a card game), participated in boxing matches, did a small amount of sketching—in short, he had a wonderful time. His hardworking Kansas neighbors were annoyed and nicknamed him a "hot sister"—a playboy.

Remington apparently believed his ranch would be successful even if he neglected it. There was grumbling from home when he asked his uncle to wire another large sum of money, which raised his total investment to $9,000, the end of his inheritance. Due to his inattention, the whole ranching venture turned sour; in February 1884, he auctioned off his sheep, horses, and land, recovering all but $2,000 of his investment. Getting into—and out of—sheep ranching took only ten short months. Years later, when Remington was wealthy and well known, folks in Kansas who'd been so disgusted with his antics said they "couldn't believe it was him."

When Frederic returned to Canton, it was to discover that his old love, Eva Caten, had been freed from her family duties as the result of her father's remarriage. Remington proposed immediately, and this time there were no objections. Frederic bought a home in Kansas City, where he'd invested as a "silent partner" in a saloon, and where he also intended to begin an iron-brokerage business.

Eva and Frederic Remington photographed in the year of their marriage, 1884. FREDERIC REMINGTON ART MUSEUM, OGDENSBURG, NEW YORK.

The couple were married on October 1, 1884, three days before Remington's twenty-third birthday, and headed for their new home without pausing for a honeymoon.

Eva quickly discovered that Kansas was not New York. Manners were coarse; her new husband's friends were not to her liking; there seemed to be no iron-brokerage business. Instead, her new husband spent hours sketching,

and it distressed her that many of the pictures were of the inside of pool halls or saloons. After two months, Eva had had enough; at Christmastime, she packed and went home.

Remington's Kansas City friends thought his response to his wife's departure was on odd one: he didn't fret or take to drink; rather, he took even more earnestly to sketching. Soon, he was experimenting with oils and watercolors.

He bought his art supplies from W. W. Findlay's store and gave Findlay three paintings with the request that he try to sell them. One buyer took all three pieces for $150; Frederic's cut was $100.

Once again, he began to submit his work to *Harper's Weekly*, this time with accompanying text. Both were purchased, though the art was redrawn by a staff artist and the text rewritten by an editor. In August 1885, when no more paintings had been sold at Findlay's, and no more work was accepted by *Harper's*, Remington paid fifty dollars for a flea-bitten mare and rode off to Arizona. With no wife, no home, and no job, there was nothing to do but paint and sketch. Lonesomeness finally got the best of him, though; he wrote to Missie, asking her to stick with him while he gave his chances as an illustrator one last try. She agreed, and he headed home.

What happened next is the stuff legends are made of. At last, Frederic Remington was the right man in the right place at the right time. When he began making the rounds of magazine art departments in October 1885 to show the best of his western scenes, the nation was coming to the realization that the West was indeed the most American thing about America. Among other things, the horse—a creature of courage and mystique—was widely celebrated, and if there was one thing Remington knew from mane to tail, it was a horse.

Remington got a call from Henry Harper himself and when they met made a deep impression on the publisher of the most sophisticated magazine in the country. To Harper, Frederic was a young man who seemed larger than life, who exuded a western openness and charm, and who could draw action scenes that evoked the real thing. The publisher realized that Remington's drawings were crude and unpolished but purchased two sketches for seventy-five dollars each, enough money to keep Frederic afloat for the short term. The long-term problem was that there were five thousand illustrators in New York looking for work, and the only thing Remington knew how to paint were rough scenes from the West. Finally, in March 1886, Uncle Horace agreed to pay five dollars a month for lessons at the Art Students' League.

Also at the League at that time was another artist-writer, the naturalist Ernest Thompson Seton, and portrait painter Charles Dana Gibson. The League was different from the art school at Yale, inasmuch as the students were instructors as well as students. Remington learned easily and quickly from his contemporaries, experimented for the first time with india-ink washes, and soon sold two more pieces to *Harper's*. Classes ended in May and were the last formal training Remington would have. He believed he knew enough now to go it alone.

Three days after his last class at the League, the twenty-four-year-old Remington was on a train headed for New Mexico on an assignment for *Harper's*. The magazine wanted to do some pieces on Geronimo's struggles against encroachment on his lands by the whites, and the efforts of General Nelson Miles (who had subdued the Nez Percés under Chief Joseph in 1877) to resolve the crisis.

Remington was a brash, self-important young fellow, but the general saw that he could be of use. Miles had been criticized for his handling of the campaign against Geronimo, but someone like Remington could focus the public's attention on the positive aspects of the struggle. Miles made sure that Remington met the right men, such as General George Forsyth and Lieutenant Powhatan Clarke, and saw that he was permitted to go on military missions if he wished.

Remington used a camera to photograph scenes for later use and learned how to develop his own film. He also made quick sketches, adding "color notes" to refresh his memory when the sketches were expanded into full illustrations: "The middle ground is streaked with yellow greens, deeper greens and yellows all cold while the foreground is blue and red. . . . Any water settled on the plains is yellow ocher and gamboge." He noted that the "shiny glitter of the sun on the white ground . . . makes a reflected light on the belly of a horse . . . shaddows [*sic*] of horses should be a cool carmine & Blue."

Remington's new series of sketches began appearing in *Harper's* in July, and with his flair for journalistic description, he also supplied material that editors at the magazine refined. But as rosy as his career was, he soon encountered a dilemma: there simply wasn't enough western work at one magazine to keep him fully employed. He began to search for other publishers who could use his material and was published in *St. Nicholas*, a well-known children's magazine of the day, and also in an outdoor magazine.

In his first year as a commerical artist, twenty-five of Remington's illustrations appeared in newspapers, magazines, and books. He earned $1,200, a handsome sum in 1886, considering that a schoolteacher made $500, a factory worker earned $600, and a minister was paid $750. He paid only $8 a month for his apartment; he repaid a loan from his mother at the rate of $5 per month; he and Missie spent the remainder of their income on fine clothes, good food, and entertainment.

Other artists began to criticize Remington for working from photographs and claimed that his perspective wasn't accurate. He also was faulted for the gait of his horses; artists who had been trained in European art schools depicted horses with their limbs extended front and back, so that they resembled cats leaping through the air. Edward Muybridge called such a gait the "zenith of absurdity" and in a series of timed photographs was able to show the correct position of a horse's legs in a gallop—exactly as Remington had been painting them all along!

Now it was time to branch into the world of fine art. At the Exhibition of the American Water-Color Society in February 1887, Remington's work was hung next to that of a former instructor at the Art Students' League; better yet, it sold for $85. He also entered a juried exhibit of the National Academy of Design, where his work was displayed with the likes of that of the famous Winslow Homer.

Harper's sent him on a sketching trip to Canada, which gave Frederic a chance to study the "horse tribes" of the Blackfoot and Crow Indians. Now his drawings for *Harper's* occupied a full page and sometimes were used for the covers as well. Having had his watercolors exhibited, Remington also was determined to become proficient in oils. As his income stabilized, the Remingtons moved into a more expensive apartment, close enough to Central Park that Frederic could indulge his favorite pastime of riding horseback for an hour every afternoon.

In 1887, Theodore Roosevelt suggested that Remington was the ideal artist to illustrate his book, *Ranch Life and the Hunting Trail*, which also appeared as a serial in *Century* magazine. There were to be a total of eighty-three illustrations, and they made Frederic a star in the world of commercial illustration. He was envied by some of his contemporaries, but his admirers pointed out that Remington was successful because he drew the soldiers, miners, Indians, and cowboys of the West "as he saw them," not as sanitized figures who were spruced up for public consumption as painters had done in the past. His supporters also pointed out that "action was at the bottom of everything Remington recorded," which set him quite apart from an artist such as George Catlin (whose biography also appears in this volume).

In March 1888, Remington—only twenty-six years old—entered a full-color oil painting, *Return of a Blackfoot War Party*, in an exhibition and placed on it the price of $1,000, four times what most painters new to the art world were bold enough to ask. The *New York*

Return of a Blackfoot War Party, Frederic Remington's famous painting of 1888. FREDERIC REMINGTON ART MUSEUM, OGDENSBURG, NEW YORK. ANSCHUTZ COLLECTION. PHOTOGRAPH BY MILMOE.

Herald granted that he would someday be "listed among our great American painters," but another newspaper criticized Remington's Indians as "caricatures" and complained that their faces were too dark. The painting was indeed sold, not for what Remington was asking, but for $250; later, however, a similar piece of his work sold for $155,000 in Los Angeles.

Remington, who'd been his mother's darling as a boy, was outraged when she decided to remarry in 1888, and he attempted to argue her out of it. The two were still as stubborn as mules, and Clara Remington followed through with her plans to wed Orris Levis, a hotel owner. Her son couldn't forgive her for not remaining true to his father's memory and never spoke to her again.

Remington now had more work than he could handle. He painted seven days a week, finishing a piece every two or three days. He was commissioned to make other trips to the West, where he photographed and sketched Comanche,

Kiowa, and Cheyenne Indians. He got a contract to do more than four hundred illustrations for Longfellow's *The Song of Hiawatha*, his largest commission to date, did several illustrations for a book by naturalist John Muir, and was described by his peers as the most talked-about artist in the country. He was only twenty-seven years old, yet his income was fifteen times that of the average American wage earner. He had told Uncle Horace that he didn't care if he ever was rich, but now he was.

Remington still was eager to be recognized as a fine arts painter and entered a large oil, *The Last Lull in the Fight*, in the Paris International Exposition in 1889, where it won a second-place medal, a remarkable distinction for so young a painter. He was commissioned by industrialist Edward Converse to do a four-by-seven-foot painting called *A Dash for the Timber*. But he was never too busy to indulge his favorite pastimes: eating heartily (six pork chops for breakfast wasn't unusual) and drinking more brandy than was good for him. The result was that soon he weighed a very portly 230 pounds.

Missie was often left at home while her energetic husband worked or attended various parties and functions, and she was understandably unhappy. When she decided that she wanted a home worthy of their new station in life, Remington did not object. They bought a three-acre estate in New Rochelle, thirty minutes from downtown New York City, which provided opportunities for duck shooting, sailing, and horseback riding. At last Remington had the kind of studio he'd always dreamed of—thirteen by twenty-two feet, with a good north light. Missie wanted to call the place Cozeyo (Cozy-O), but Remington named it Endion, an Ojibwa Indian word meaning "place where I live."

At Remington's suggestion, Owen Wister, the popular author of *The Virginian*, wrote an essay, "The Evolution of the Cowpuncher," which Remington then illustrated. The publication of the article in September 1895 was the first serious effort to mythologize the American cowboy, establishing a point of view that continues to this day in films, novels, and song. Wister regretted that his friendship with Remington seemed to cool after their collaboration and wondered if he had somehow offended the artist, but that wasn't the case. Instead, Remington was about to embark on a brand-new artistic passion.

When a friend, the playwright Augustus Thomas, commented to Remington that he had "a sculptor's degree of vision"—that is, that he saw things in three-dimensional terms—it was enough to persuade the artist, who had been painting hard for ten years, to try his hand at sculpture. Remington ordered a modeling stand, tools, and modeling wax, then built a twelve-inch armature-and-wire skeleton to support the piece he intended to create.

No one had ever before constructed a three-dimensional cowboy on a bucking horse, but even though he was a novice at the craft, Remington tackled the project with his usual intensity. He worked for five months but encountered mechanical problems he couldn't resolve. When a professional sculptor, Frederick Ruckstuhl, moved into a studio nearby to work on a mammoth statue for a park in Harrisburg, Pennsylvania, Remington visited every afternoon to observe the proceedings. As he watched the other artist work, he understood how to solve his own problem. He went home, abandoned his twelve-inch model, built a new twenty-four-inch skeleton, and *The Bronco Buster*, the most famous piece of western sculpture ever produced, was the result. A painter friend exclaimed, "Is there anything that man can't do?"

The work was cast in bronze by the Henri-Bonnard foundry in New York City and was copyrighted on October 1, 1895, three days before Remington's thirty-fourth birthday. A copy was displayed in the window of Tiffany's jewelry store and received a full-page treatment in the October issue of *Harper's*. American es-

The Bonnard casting of Remington's *The Bronco Buster*. FREDERIC REMINGTON ART MUSEUM, OGDENSBURG, NEW YORK.

sayist William Dean Howells noted that the piece was "a wonder in every way"; the *New York Times* said it "revealed Mr. Remington in a new and unexpected light"; and one of Remington's biographers believed that the artist had hit "a home run in his first time at bat, in a new kind of ballgame." Only twenty-four editions of *The Bronco Buster* were made and sold at $250 each; each is now priceless.

Remington was intoxicated with the new medium and wrote to Wister to say of the finished bronze product that "all other forms of art are trivialities. . . . It dont decay, the moth dont steal [it], the rust and the idiot cannot harm it." Yet he continued to produce illustrations; he did some for a story by Rudyard Kipling, then began to write and illustrate his own books, beginning with *Pony Tracks* in 1895, still his best-known work, and ending with *The Way of an Indian* in 1906.

Remington was sensitive about his work and wanted nothing to be preserved that didn't live up to his own stern critical judgment. A note in his diary for February 8, 1907, revealed that he "burned every old canvas in the house today . . . about 75." The destroyed pieces had been illustrations in *Collier's* magazine, and among them were many that collectors would be delighted to own today. In 1908, he again went on a burning spree, destroying another twenty-seven pieces, among them the whole *Explorer* series of ten paintings.

After living at his New Rochelle estate for nearly twenty years, Remington bought a fifty-acre farm near Ridgefield, Connecticut, and designed a house even more to his liking. It had a studio so large that it could accommodate a man on horseback. He supervised the move himself, which someone described as being like transporting a whole Wild West show that included costumes and artifacts, not to mention an extensive

library. In May 1909, he and Eva were ensconced in their new home, which friends called "Remington Village."

Remington exhibited several paintings at Knoedler's gallery in New York in December 1909. Reviews were excellent and sales were good. One reviewer called the works "among the best Remington has done," then went on to observe that in "all of Remington's pictures, the shadow of death seems not far away."

On December 22, 1909, as he took the morning train into New York from the fine new home where he'd lived for only seven months, Remington experienced the kind of stomach pains he'd complained of earlier in the month. He blamed his discomfort on constipation and took a powerful laxative—precisely what one should avoid if there is any possibility of appendicitis. He returned on the noon train in even greater misery; a local doctor was called, who sent for a consultant from nearby Danbury, Connecticut.

The following day, as a winter storm raged outside, it was decided that emergency surgery was necessary, and the kitchen table was scrubbed down. Water was put to boil; the patient was helped onto the table; a nurse administered ether. Remington had gotten so stout that making a proper incision was difficult. When the surgeon finally entered the abdominal cavity it was to discover that the appendix had burst and peritonitis had set in; the prognosis was gloomy. The infection was cleaned up as well as possible, a drain was inserted before the wound was closed, and the patient was given morphine for his pain.

Remington rallied enough to enjoy opening presents on Christmas morning, then sank into a coma about midday. Early on December 26, as snow continued to swirl beyond the windows, Frederic Remington died at age forty-eight. Because of the weather, the funeral was small and simple. He was buried in Canton, where a small headstone carried only his name, plus the date of his birth and death, but not the fitting epitaph he'd once suggested for himself: "He Knew the Horse."

Frederic Remington left behind a remarkable body of work: 2,739 drawings and paintings that appeared in 142 books and countless magazines; illustrations and text for 8 of his own books; and 25 pieces of bronze sculpture. When Eva died nine years later, she bequeathed all of her husband's unsold paintings to the Ogdensburg Public Library.

When he was sixteen, Remington had confided to his uncle Horace: "I have but one short life and do not aspire to wealth nor fame in a degree which could only be obtained by an extraordinary effort on my part." His prophecy about a short life was fulfilled, but once he committed himself to art, his efforts to capture the West were indeed extraordinary and preserved a glimpse of those times and those people for us who came after.

Sacagawea (Bird Woman)

1788?–1884 Guide, interpreter. Was captured as a child from her Shoshone tribe by Hidatsa warriors. Later married Toussaint Charbonneau, an interpreter. When her husband was hired by Lewis and Clark, they requested that Sacagawea accompany him because she spoke the language of the Shoshones, from whom they hoped to buy horses for the last half of their expedition.

Sacagawea was born among folk who didn't record dates in a formal way, but calculated guesses place her birth date in 1788 or 1789, and the location as eastern Idaho, near the present-day town of Salmon. She was the daughter of a Shoshone chief and was called Bo-i-naiv—Grass Maiden—by her people.

If destiny had not intervened in this Indian girl's life, she probably would have married the man her father had promised her to when she was only an infant in a cradleboard. She would have shared the nomadic, hunting-gathering ways of her kin, then vanished from history without a trace.

But fate *did* intervene. When Bo-i-naiv was ten or eleven years old, she traveled east across the Rocky Mountains with her tribe into an area known as "the Three Forks," where three small rivers empty into the Missouri. It was a favorite summer campground for the Shoshones, but this particular year they were attacked by Hidatsa warriors. Sacagawea later told Captain Meriwether Lewis that she had been berry picking with other girls and was captured as she tried to escape across a river. Another girl, slightly older than Bo-i-naiv, was captured at the same time.

The Hidatsas gave the younger girl the name we remember her by: Sacagawea, or Bird Woman. Some historians have spelled it with a j, but many linguists now believe a soft *g* sound more accurately represents the correct Indian pronunciation (Sah-cawg-a-way-ah). When she was about fourteen years old, Sacagawea became the wife of Toussaint Charbonneau, a French Canadian trader and interpreter many years older than she, who had lived among various Indian tribes for several years. At the same time, the older girl also was taken in marriage by the trader. It was said that he won both girls from the Hidatsas in a gambling game.

Marriage in that time and place was *à la façon du pays*—"in the fashion of the country"—which meant nothing more complicated than a man and woman simply living together. Some men had more than one wife, and Charbonneau already had one from the Mandan tribe. He wasn't highly respected by either whites or Indians and had been given various nicknames, among them Forest Bear and Chief of the Little Village.

In November 1804, Sacagawea and her husband's other Shoshone wife, identified by Chief Poor Wolf of the Hidatsas as Otter Woman, were living with Charbonneau near what now is Bismarck, North Dakota. That autumn, something unusual happened along the Missouri River that aroused great curiosity among the Indians: a large party of white men, commanded by Meriwether Lewis and William Clark, had arrived from downstream and were building themselves cabins in which to spend the winter. It was whispered that when the ice melted, these men in-

tended to continue their travels upriver to the Great Water, far beyond the Shining Mountain, the Rockies.

The Indians, who were accustomed to seeing white traders traveling singly or in pairs through their country, observed the many newcomers from the river bluffs, then went down to get a closer look at the camp. Sacagawea and Otter Woman must have been among the sightseers, because on November 11, Lewis made a journal entry indicating that two Indian girls whom he had been told were the wives of "a Mr. Chaubonie" were among the visitors.

Chief Poor Wolf described Sacagawea as being about sixteen years old at this time and remembered that Otter Woman, two or three years older, was the mother of a little boy, Toussaint junior. What he didn't mention was that Sacagawea herself was pregnant, and on February 11, 1805, she began what turned out to be a long and arduous labor. Lewis and Clark had brought with them a variety of medicines but understandably never expected to encounter childbirth problems among their all-male crew. They had nothing to offer the suffering young woman.

Finally, one of Charbonneau's fellow French Canadians, René Jussome (sometimes spelled Jessaume), suggested that a bit of rattlesnake rattle, crushed and washed down with water, might assist the birth. He might have made this suggestion because the Shoshones were also called the Snake Indians, referring to their home country along the Snake River. Lewis happened to have a rattle with him and offered it to Jussome. Lewis wrote that Jussome snapped two rings off the rattle, which he then broke "into small pieces with the fingers, and added to a small quantity of water. . . . I was informed that [Sacagawea] had not taken it ten minutes before she brought forth." The child, a healthy boy, was named Jean Baptiste, then nicknamed Pompy, a Shoshone word meaning "leader," and often applied to a firstborn son.

Lewis and Clark had already employed Jussome as an interpreter. Charbonneau, they discovered, could make himself understood among the Indians who lived along the river, where much of the expedition's traveling would be done, and hired him as well. No sooner had the forty-six-year-old Frenchman been hired, however, than he objected to certain tasks that were assigned to him, and the expedition leaders discharged him.

Part of the expedition would require the use of horses, and when Lewis and Clark learned that Shoshone tribes living near the Rocky Mountains kept horses and would probably be willing to sell them, they realized they needed

someone who spoke that language too. Although Lewis considered Charbonneau to be a "man of no peculiar [particular] merit," when it became known that the Frenchman's youngest wife was Shoshone, both Lewis and Clark knew she would be a valuable asset. Later, when Charbonneau apologized for his behavior and asked to be hired back, the expedition leaders quickly agreed—but only on the condition that his youngest wife accompany him. So, as Chief Poor Wolf recalled, "they took Sacagawea and her French husband and left Otter Woman with us."

The expedition left its winter quarters at Fort Mandan on Sunday afternoon, April 7, 1805. In addition to Charbonneau, his seventeen-year-old wife, and their two-month-old baby, the Corps of Discovery—as President Jefferson had named the exploratory force—consisted of Jussome, three sergeants, twenty-three privates (one of whom was John Colter, who would become famous as the first white man to discover what is now Yellowstone National Park), and the corps captains, Meriwether Lewis and William Clark. Also included was York, Clark's black servant, who sometimes let curious Indians attempt to rub off his "black paint." Seaman (some historians insist the dog's name was Scannon), Lewis's 140-pound Newfoundland dog, also was a member of the expedi-

This statue of Sacagawea and her son was dedicated by women's suffrage leader Susan B. Anthony at Oregon's Lewis and Clark Exposition in 1905. BENJAMIN GIFFORD COLLECTION, OREGON HISTORICAL SOCIETY.

tion. Many of the team were somewhat in awe of Captain Lewis, an aloof, brooding man, but Captain Clark, red-haired, blue-eyed, and always cheerful, became popular among whites and Indians alike.

It has been a durable myth that the young Indian mother, her infant son strapped in a cradleboard on her back, unerringly led Lewis and Clark to their destination on the Pacific Coast. The reality was that it was *water*—mostly the Missouri River and its tributaries—that dictated the early travel, and later it was the Columbia River. The expedition's possessions were carried in six small canoes, plus two large pirogues (a type of boat used by French voyageurs), each equipped with a sail.

Only five weeks into the expedition, Sacagawea (whom Clark often called "Janey") showed the kind of stuff she was made of. On May 14, as she was seated in the rear of one of the pirogues on the Missouri, a sudden gust of wind filled its sail and keeled the vessel over, knocking much of its cargo—medicines, books, instruments, the captains' journals—into the water.

Charbonneau, who was described as "the worst steersman of the party," panicked and had to be threatened with a pistol before he took hold of the rudder and did his job. Meanwhile, his young wife calmly leaned out of the boat and collected whatever she could reach. Some of the material—medicine, for example—was ruined, but in two days everything else that she recovered had been dried and repacked. In his journal, Lewis described Sacagawea's conduct as "equal in fortitude and resolution with any person on board at the time of the accident."

On June 10, while the group camped near the mouth of the Marias River in Montana, Sacagawea suddenly became ill. At the turn of the century, bleeding was a customary treatment for many diseases, and she was bled twice. Four days later, she became even sicker and was treated with what might have been quinine. The following day, her condition worsened but she refused to take any medicine. Lewis was concerned not only for Sacagawea but for her four-month-old baby, who would die if anything happened to his mother.

Near the camp was a mineral spring, and Lewis, who took care of the medical needs of the expedition's members, decided to remain there while he doctored his patient with sulfur water. In a few days, Sacagawea was able to drink some rich soup made of buffalo meat and had improved enough to walk along the river a little each morning. When Charbonneau foolishly allowed her to eat too much dried fish and Indian breadfruit, however, she became ill again, and Clark noted grimly, "If she dies, it will be the fault of her husband."

By June 24, Sacagawea had recovered from her ordeal. Four days later, the expedition was caught during a severe rainstorm in a dry gully that rapidly filled with floodwater. Sacagawea snatched her son from his cradleboard and with Clark's help was able to scramble up the rocky hillside to safety. Behind them, the gully filled to a depth of fifteen feet; a severe hailstorm followed, one stone measuring seven inches across, and in the confusion Clark lost his compass. Luckily, it was found a few days later, buried in the mud.

The journey around the Great Falls of the Missouri, near the present-day city of Great Falls, Montana, took a month. In the third week of July, after they'd passed through what the expedition called the Gates of the Mountains while being driven nearly insane by hordes of mosquitoes, it was Clark's turn to fall ill. His health wasn't improved by having to rescue Charbonneau, who couldn't swim, when the interpreter was nearly swept away by the swift current while crossing a stream.

Sacagawea soon recognized the country they were passing through and told the expedition leaders they were nearing the area of "the Three Forks." When they arrived, Sacagawea pointed out to Lewis where she'd been captured as a child. In his journal, Lewis observed, "I cannot discover that she shews immotion of sorrow in recollecting this event, or of joy in being restored to her native country," and concluded that she was not an emotional person. He soon discovered otherwise.

Lewis and Clark named the three rivers that fed into the Missouri the Jefferson, the Madison, and the Gallatin after President Jefferson and two of his cabinet members. About this time, the corps members witnessed Charbonneau strike his young wife; he received an angry scolding from Clark, who refused to tolerate such behavior.

For the first four months of their journey, the expedition hadn't encountered a single Indian. True, footprints had been found along the edges of rivers . . . occasionally, smoke could be seen rising from distant signal fires . . . sometimes, remnants of deserted camps had been discovered—but the Indians themselves remained as elusive as phantoms. This concerned Lewis and Clark, who were eager to make contact with the mountain tribes that could supply them with the necessary horses to make the journey over the Rockies.

In the second week of August, Clark was unable to walk far due to a carbuncle on his ankle, so Lewis left him behind while he went on ahead with a smaller party to scout the area around the Continental Divide near Lemhi Pass,

Alfred Russell's painting of Sacagawea guiding the Lewis and Clark expedition. CORBIS-BETTMANN.

which now marks the border between Montana and Idaho. They came upon two women and a little girl; the younger woman fled in terror, while the older one and the child cowered, heads bent, apparently expecting to be killed or captured. After Clark assured the woman that she was in no danger, she led him to her people's camp, four miles away. Lewis told the Indians that his party was traveling with a Shoshone girl, a way of indicating the expedition's peaceful mission, but he realized that in order to win the Indians' full trust he would also have to supply meat, for they were in desperate need of food. Lewis's men, who were armed with rifles in contrast to the bows and arrows of the Indians, were able to quickly bring down a deer; the meat-starved natives devoured it raw.

Meanwhile, Clark proceeded slowly up the Beaverhead River with the rest of the expedition, including Sacagawea. In his journal, Clark said that when he rejoined Lewis, Sacagawea exclaimed in sign language, "This is my tribe!" and danced with joy.

Later, in a conference held in a circular tent made of willows, Lewis and Clark were greeted by the head chief, Cameahwait. Ceremonial pipe smoking commenced, and soon Sacagawea was sent for to act as an interpreter. "She came into the tent, sat down . . . when, in the person of Cameahwait, she recognized her brother," wrote Clark. "She instantly jumped up, and . . . embraced him, throwing over him her blanket . . . weeping profusely."

Cameahwait also was moved, "though not to the same degree," and Sacagawea later gave him a small bit of sugar as a gift. After composing herself, she continued to interpret, though "she was frequently interrupted by her tears." When the conference ended, Sacagawea learned that most of her family were now dead, including her oldest sister, who'd left behind a small boy. Sacagawea pledged to take the child as her own, as was the custom among her people.

If Sacagawea had indicated that she wanted to end her journey at that point and remain with her tribe, the leaders of the expedition could not have forced her to continue. She was even approached by the man to whom she had been betrothed as a child, but since she was now the mother of another man's child, he didn't press his case. It was Sacagawea's decision to continue with the expedition, so her brother Cameahwait drew rough maps for Lewis and Clark that indicated how the Lemhi River flowed into the Salmon, the Salmon into the Snake, the Snake into the Columbia, and finally, the Columbia into the Pacific Ocean. He also warned that the rivers were rough and difficult to navigate.

When Sacagawea learned that her people were planning to break camp and head for buffalo country, she relayed the news to Charbonneau, who delayed passing the information on to Lewis and Clark. When he finally did, both captains immediately became alarmed because they knew what it meant: if the Shoshones left with their horses, the expedition would be doomed.

Lewis hastily approached the Indians and reminded them of their promise to supply horses. Cameahwait said that it was only because of extreme hunger that his people needed to move on and promised the expedition leaders twenty animals in addition to nine others that had been agreed upon earlier. The expedition leaders even persuaded Charbonneau to get a pony for Sacagawea!

Weather can be capricious in the high

mountains of the Northwest, and two inches of snow fell in the first week of September. A few days later, the expedition ran into a band of Flathead Indians, who supplied them with eleven more horses. The severe shortage of meat continued to be a desperate problem, and one journal entry noted, "We were obliged to kill a second colt for our supper . . . for there is no living creature in these mountains except a few small pheasants." When the expedition encountered a friendly band of Nez Percés, they bought several dogs as a future source of meat—but it was said Sacagawea never felt hungry enough to eat such fare; she made do with whatever roots and berries she could find.

In October the expedition leaders decided to begin traveling by boat once again, and several canoes were built. Travel in rivers that were so full of rapids was no easy task; canoes were constantly damaged, which meant precious time spent making repairs. How did Sacagawea and her baby fare during this period? No one can be sure, because between August 27 and October 13, 1805, no mention is made of her in the expedition's journals.

Travel down the Columbia was dangerous and time-consuming; at one point the river dropped sixty feet in only two miles. But when the fog lifted on November 7, 1805, the expedition got its first glimpse of the Pacific Ocean, twenty miles away. Lewis and Clark had fulfilled Thomas Jefferson's twenty-year dream of finding an overland route to the west coast of the continent.

The Corps of Discovery spent the winter on the coast. There was an ample supply of meat and fish to be had, and also wapatoo, a root favored by the local Indians, which when roasted had an agreeable potatolike taste. When an elk was killed, Sacagawea smashed its shank bones into fine pieces, then boiled them in water. Later, the pint of grease she skimmed off was described by Clark as being "superior to tallow" for oiling boots and guns.

The worst aspect of wintering in the upper Northwest was the weather: day after day, it was cold, gray, and rainy. The expedition members were tormented by severe infestations of fleas; several men had colds; one man was bedridden with a back injury due to felling trees. Nevertheless, eight cabins, each about sixteen by thirty feet, were built and surrounded by a stockade. The camp, near present-day Astoria, Oregon, was named Fort Clatsop, in recognition of the help given to the explorers by the Clatsop tribe.

Christmas Day, 1805, was spent in a cheerful celebration, during which Sacagawea presented Clark the gift of two dozen ermine tails. The expedition's holiday feast would strike modern readers as grossly unappetizing: the main course was elk meat that had begun to rot due to an unexpected spurt of warm weather.

Early in the new year, 1806, some of the men decided to travel down to the ocean's edge to obtain whale blubber from the coastal Indians, and Sacagawea asked Clark if she could go along. It was the first request she'd made during the entire journey, and she was gladly included. No one recorded what she thought about her first close-up view of the Great Water, something no man or woman of her tribe had ever seen.

The expedition remained at Fort Clatsop until the equinoctial winds melted the snow at higher elevations, then set out on their return trip on Sunday, March 23. On the way home, Lewis suffered what must have struck him as a dreadful loss: his faithful companion Seaman was stolen by Indians. Three armed men were sent in pursuit of the thieves, who panicked and—no doubt to Lewis's immense relief—turned the dog loose.

When the expedition reached the Yellowstone, Clark named a tall, spectacular rock formation on the south side of the river Pompey's Pillar in honor of Sacagawea's son, now almost seventeen months old, of whom he'd grown exceptionally fond, often calling him "my boy Pomp." Clark inscribed his own signature on the rock and dated it July 25, 1806. It is now preserved by an iron grating to protect it from tourists' probing fingers.

Once they were on the Yellowstone, boat travel downstream was swift. On August 14, 1806, the travelers reached the Hidatsa village near Fort Mandan that had been their starting point a year and a half earlier. Charbonneau was no longer needed as an interpreter and was paid the sum of $500.33 for his services.

Captain Clark also wished to repay Sacagawea for her part in the expedition and asked permission to take her boy with him to St. Louis, where he could be educated, promising "to raise him as my own child." But it was common for Indian children to nurse at their mother's breast until they were at least three years old, and Sacagawea refused to part with her son. However, she agreed to bring him to St. Louis in a year and to place him in Clark's custody. She kept her word, and records show that for a time she also lived in St. Louis.

Later, Charbonneau served as interpreter for other expeditions, but there is no record that Sacagawea ever accompanied him again. She continued to live with Charbonneau for almost twenty years. There has been a suggestion that Otter Woman died during this time, and soon Charbonneau took another wife, a Hidatsa girl named Eagle, with whom

Sacagawea had a friendly relationship. But she became resentful when the Frenchman took yet another young wife, a Ute girl, and after receiving a beating when she told him of her displeasure, Sacagawea ran away.

Now began a life of wandering for Bird Woman, and she became known by other names, among them Porivo, or Lost Woman. It was said she later married into the Comanche tribe, lived with them for many years, and had other children, only two of whom survived. Eventually, she also lived among the Apaches and Nez Percés, and was reported to have traveled as far west as California. At about seventy years of age, Sacagawea was described as "not dark in looks . . . a woman full of brightness and smartness . . . handsome, as many Shoshone women are." Charbonneau was last seen in 1839, when, at eighty-one years of age, he appeared at the Department of Indian Affairs in St. Louis, asking to be paid for his services as an interpreter among the Mandans.

Jean Baptiste, no longer called Pompy, grew up educated in the ways of the white man. In 1823, when he was eighteen, he was befriended by Prince Paul of Württemberg, Germany, who was traveling in the American West. The prince took Baptiste back to Europe, where he lived for the next six years and learned to speak several languages.

After he returned to America, Baptiste served as the mayor of San Luis Rey in California. When gold was discovered in Montana, he set out to make his fortune. He never reached the gold fields but died in Oregon at the age of sixty-one.

At long last, Sacagawea rejoined her own people on the Wind River reservation in Wyoming, where she lived with relatives, one of whom was her dead sister's son, Bazil, whom she'd promised to adopt so many years earlier. She died peacefully in her sleep on April 9, 1884, at nearly one hundred years of age. The Reverend John Roberts, a missionary on the reservation, said, "She walked alone [without assistance] and was bright to the last." Roberts added that Sacagawea was buried "with her face toward the dawn on the sunny side of the Rocky Mountains," which seems fitting, for she had been the daughter of a mountain tribe.

Everything modern readers know about Sacagawea comes not from Bird Woman herself but from others who had met her or believed they knew something important about her. Sacagawea left no written documents or testimonials about what *she* thought of her adventurous life. Although she has been celebrated in stories and in film, one biographer believes that, in truth, Sacagawea remains "the girl nobody knows."

Nancy Ward

1738–1822 Cherokee leader, peacemaker. Because of her bravery in a battle against the Creeks, she was called "Beloved Woman" by her tribe. She also was a loyal friend of the whites, known by many as the "Cherokee Pocahontas." Said to be commanding in appearance, with piercing black eyes, she was instrumental in saving the life of a white woman who was about to be burned at the stake.

The Cherokee Indians had no written language in Nancy Ward's time, and their stories and histories were handed down orally from generation to generation. However, the unakas, or white people, who knew Nancy—traders, settlers, soldiers, and government agents—preserved enough information in letters, reports, and diaries that historians have been able to develop what seems to be an accurate picture of this unusual woman.

James Robertson, an agent for the Overhill band of Cherokees in North Carolina, remembered Nancy Ward as a "queenly and commanding" woman. Thomas Nuttall, a well-known colonial botanist who visited the Cherokees in 1819, described her as "tall, erect, and beautiful, with a prominent nose, regular features, clear complexion, long, silken black hair, large piercing black eyes and an imperious air." However, that recollection must have been given to him by someone who knew Nancy Ward in her youth, for in 1819 she would have been a woman past eighty years of age.

According to the remembered history of the Ani-Yunwiya, or the Principal People, as the Cherokees called themselves, Nanye'hi was born about 1738 in the village of Chota. (The precise month and day of her birth have not come down via the oral tradition.) Chota, in the present-day state of Georgia, was the capital village of the Cherokees and was sometimes called the "Mother

A 1992 painting by Troy Anderson, a Cherokee artist, shows *The Trail of Tears* as Cherokees were forcibly removed to Arkansas and Oklahoma.

Town" or the "City of Refuge," where those who were pursued by enemies or misfortune knew they could find protection, just as children are protected in the circle of their mother's arms.

There were seven clans among the Cherokees: the People of the Wolf, the People of the Deer, the People of the Bird, the Paint People, the Long Hair People, the Wild Potato People, and the Blue People. The infant girl born in 1738 was the first child of Tame Doe, a sister of the great Cherokee chief Attakullaculla, and belonged to the largest of the clans, the People of the Wolf.

The baby's father was Sir Francis Ward, an English officer, who gave his daughter the English name Nancy, by which she was known to the whites, who found it easier to pronounce than Nanye'hi. Legend tells that the child's birth was a difficult one and that finally the midwives had to consult an *adawehi*, or medicine man, who gave them advice that guaranteed the baby's safe delivery.

As a little one, Nanye'hi was sometimes called Wild Rose, for it was said that her skin was as darkly pink and soft as the wild rose that grew in that part of the country. Later, she was joined by a brother, Long Fellow. In those times, the Cherokees roamed south of the Ohio River, beyond the Tennessee River, then deep into the headwaters of the Coosa, Savannah, and Tugaloo Rivers. It was a rich and beautiful country, the heart of which lay at the edge of the Great Smoky Mountains. Now, that area is where the states of Tennessee, Georgia, and North and South Carolina come together.

Tame Doe had learned enough of the English language from her husband to be able to raise her daughter to speak both tongues, which set Nanye'hi apart early in her life and made her a special sort of girl. Although she was part white, among most tribes—Cherokee or otherwise—such a person was considered to be all Indian. It's likely that Nanye'hi never had to endure the kind of ostracism that was sometimes visited upon such children in white society, where a child such as Wild Rose was derogatorily referred to as a "half-breed" and looked down upon.

Although there is no written record of Nanye'hi's girlhood, no doubt she grew up learning the customary "woman's work" of her tribe: how to pound corn into flour, tan deerskins and make garments, preserve meat by drying it, and gather fruits, nuts, and berries from the woods. She also would have learned how to take care of a garden filled with corn, peas, beans, squash, and pumpkin, because the Cherokees had already adopted many of the habits of the whites.

In her early teens, as Nanye'hi grew into a tall, handsome young woman, she probably attracted the attention of young men in her tribe, many of whom she'd known throughout her childhood. Soon, one in particular began to appeal to her more than any of the others. He was Kingfisher, not much older than she, and a member of the Deer clan.

Kingfisher was skilled in the art of warfare and hunting; he knew how to fish, and he made it clear to Nanye'hi that he was ready to start a home of his own. The young couple found ways to spend time alone together, and soon they agreed to marry. Nanye'hi was only about fourteen or fifteen, but it was customary for Cherokee girls to wed early.

The bridal pair were dressed by their kinfolk in garments of white deerskin elaborately decorated with quills, beads, and feathers. The groom's head was shaved, except for a crown lock to which a few turkey feathers were attached; the bride's hair was drawn smoothly to the top of her head, where it was fastened with a silver clasp. The couple exchanged the kinds of gifts that were traditional among the Cherokees: Kingfisher gave his bride a haunch of venison (deer meat) and a blanket, a sign that he would provide well for her and any children to be born; Nanye'hi gave her new husband an ear of corn and a blanket, a pledge that she would be a good wife, keep a fine garden, and be a good homemaker. The ceremony was followed by joyous feasting and laughter, for the people of the Wolf clan and those of the Deer clan had been joined, thereby strengthening the bonds of the entire Cherokee nation.

Two children were born to Nanye'hi, a boy whose childhood name was Short Fellow but who later earned the name Five Killer in battle, and a girl who was given the English name Catherine. When her children were still very small, an event took place that forever changed Nanye'hi's role among her tribespeople. Unlike the practice of most other tribes, Cherokee women sometimes accompanied their men into battle, so in 1755, when war was called against the Creeks, longtime enemies of Nanye'hi's people, she went with Kingfisher to fight at Taliwa, near the present town of Dahlonega, Georgia. Unfortunately, Kingfisher was shot and killed, whereupon Nanye'hi seized his weapon and used it as fiercely as any warrior. The other Cherokees, inspired by the example of the seventeen-year-old girl, were victorious over the Creeks.

After the tribe returned to Chota they held a special ceremony to honor Nanye'hi's great courage. From that moment on, the young Indian widow was called *Ghigau*, meaning "Beloved Woman," a title that was bestowed only upon the bravest of women. Beginning at that moment, Nanye'hi was allowed to attend all of the highest council meetings and to make her voice heard when it pleased her to do so.

Nanye'hi grieved for Kingfisher, but eventually her heart was healed. In time, Bryant Ward (some historians believe he was Sir Francis's nephew) became her new love. Young Ward had also been widowed, and his son was being raised in Ireland by his grandparents. On September 18, 1756, when Nanye'hi was about eighteen, the couple were married in the white man's way at Fort Loudoun, according to the rituals of the Church of England, and the date was officially recorded.

In her new marriage, Beloved Woman gave birth to another boy and a girl; again, the boy was given a Cherokee name, Little Fellow, and the girl was given the English name Elizabeth, which was shortened to Betsy. Once more, life was good; Nanye'hi's garden was full of vegetables and also a little tobacco to be used for ceremonial purposes. Bryant bought several pigs, which meant the family didn't need to depend as heavily on hunting wild game in the surrounding forests.

By the time Nanye'hi was a mature woman in her mid-thirties, with her children growing tall and strong around her, rumors of increasing conflict among the whites were often heard in the Cherokee village. All of the whites were under the rule of the English king, but now some of them—called Patriots—wanted to be free, while others—called Loyalists—wanted to remain faithful to the British Crown.

This change in allegiance presented a problem for the Indians too: Which side should they support? Should it be the British, who were determined to exercise control over the colonists, or the colonists, who were determined to direct their own lives?

The colonists' struggle for self-determination against the British was something the Cherokees could understand, yet it presented them with a problem. It was a traditional belief among all Indian tribes that *no one* owned the land. Rather, people could freely use it for whatever they needed, but the land itself belonged only to the Great Spirit. The *unakas*—both colonists and British—believed that it could be owned, a point of view that was des-

tined to cause problems for the Indians no matter which set of white men got the upper hand in the coming conflict.

The Cherokees' predicament was complicated by something that had happened almost without their noticing it: they had become accustomed to bartering or trading for goods such as blankets and cloth, pots and pans, axes and knives, dye and beads, guns and powder. They had only one thing to trade, however, the thing the colonists wanted most: land. To make matters worse, when parties of whites came to talk about exchanging goods for land, they usually brought another powerful tool to make sure they got a good deal for themselves—whiskey.

During such visits, Indians were encouraged to eat, drink, and have a good time, then were asked to put their marks on pieces of paper called treaties. It often wasn't until much later that the Cherokees (and other tribes as well) realized what they'd signed away. Even more disturbing to the Indians' way of thinking was that small parcels of land were taken without any fair exchange at all. White settlers, accompanied by their women and children, simply came with wagons and livestock, cleared a place in the forest, marked it with stakes at four corners, and spoke of "owning" what they'd taken.

One of King George's representatives,

Alexander Cameron, gave his opinion in 1768 of such goings-on: "No nation was ever infested with such a set of villains and horse thieves. A trader will invent and tell a thousand lies; and stir up trouble against all other white persons." It was in that same year that Chief Oconostota believed he'd taken steps to put an end to the whites' encroachment. He traded away one hundred square miles of land, then declared that he'd given the white men enough to live on so they wouldn't constantly crave more. Little did he guess that such a trade only whetted the appetite of the *unakas*.

In the spring of 1775, after the Battle of Bunker Hill had been fought and Paul Revere had made his famous ride, the Cherokees met with the Transylvania Company at the headwaters of the Tennessee River at a place called Sycamore Shoals. A treaty with the British in 1763 had guaranteed that the land west of the Appalachians would be reserved as hunting grounds for the Indians, but white settlers kept coming—and coming. (Among them was Daniel Boone, who had already begun to carve the Wilderness Road across the Cumberland Mountains and down into the bluegrass country.)

The *unakas* weren't the only problem the Cherokees had to contend with. They'd recently suffered heavy losses in battles against the Chickasaws, who were well supplied with guns and ammunition they'd gotten from the British. When agents from the Transylvania Company offered the Cherokees ten thousand English pounds in the form of goods and guns in exchange for additional land, the temptation to accept it was irresistible. Not everyone in the council believed it was wise to trade land for such goods, but at last Nancy Ward agreed with the old chiefs, her uncle Attakullaculla and Oconostota, who said it was necessary to have guns in order to make a stand against their old enemies, the Chickasaws.

Beloved Woman's cousin, Dragging Canoe, wanted guns too, but he didn't want to trade land for them. Instead, he wanted to get them to make war against the whites themselves, rather than against the Chickasaws, and to permanently drive the *unakas* out of the country. Such action would align the Cherokees with the British, which many Indians did not want to do. As a consequence, the Indians were as divided among themselves as the colonists were in their own struggle to be free.

Nevertheless, after a long trading session in which whiskey was abundant, a deal was finally agreed upon. Vast acres of what eventually became the states of Kentucky and Tennessee—land which Shawnees and Iroquois also hunted on—were traded away to the Transylvania

Company. Dragging Canoe bitterly opposed the exchange. He predicted that the area would become "a dark and bloody ground," and for a time it did indeed.

As the Indians' struggle against the whites became more intense, Nanye'hi warned her husband that he might not be safe among her people. It was a hard thing for Bryant Ward to understand; after all, hadn't he lived peacefully among the Cherokees for many years? Wasn't he the father of Little Fellow and Betsy? Hadn't he cared for his stepchildren as if they were his own? Ward protested that his life couldn't possibly be in genuine danger, that it was only her woman's imagination that made Nanye'hi say such a thing. Beloved Woman was insistent; she explained that the Cherokees were determined to seek revenge against the whites and might not be too particular about which whites they killed.

She urged Bryant to return to South Carolina, where he'd lived before they were married, and they arranged to meet there whenever possible. Bryant resisted but finally followed his wife's advice. Sometime later, Nanye'hi was surprised to find a stranger on her doorstep who looked surprisingly like the husband she'd just sent into exile, except that this man's hair was very red. His introduced himself as Jack Ward

and told her that he was Bryant's son from Ireland. He had come to America hoping to locate his father. The young man stayed with Nancy for several weeks and eventually married Katie McDaniel, whose mother was Cherokee and whose father was Scottish.

Nancy Ward hoped it wouldn't be necessary to make war on white settlers. She believed it was possible to persuade them to leave peacefully. (Of course, history proved she was grievously mistaken.) Cornstalk, chief of the Shawnees, harbored no illusions of peace and adopted Dragging Canoe's point of view; he urged war against the settlers.

In May 1776, a great council meeting was held in Chota and was attended not only by Cherokees from the surrounding area but by representatives of the Iroquois, Mohawk, Delaware, Ottawa, Shawnee, and Mingo tribes. Also present at the council was Henry Stuart, one of the agents of the English king, who promised to provide one hundred horses loaded with ammunition from the king's stores in Florida and who urged the Indians to support the whites who were loyal to the Crown.

Cornstalk said that now, while the whites were fighting each other, would be a good time to redress some of the Cherokees' grievances. When other chiefs wanted a further explanation of how the war between the whites could be an opportunity for the Indians, Beloved Woman offered a different perspective. Until the English came, she said, Cherokees had relied on themselves and had no need to trade. But they had grown accustomed to the easier way of relying on the white man's goods, and now it was too late to undo the habit. The only solution was to try the path of peace. Yet she agreed that if war came, the Cherokees ought to side with the British.

The call for war was loud, much to the satisfaction of such warriors as Dragging Canoe and his sympathizers, Doublehead, Bloody Fellow, and Raven. Beloved Woman knew that war would not solve the Cherokees' problems. In this she had the support of the older chiefs, Attakullaculla and Oconostota. The men and women of Chota were divided as to the wisdom of pursuing war, but women's opinions didn't carry as much weight as did those of the men, and the supporters of Nanye'hi weren't able to prevail.

At the time, traders Jarrett Williams, Isaac Thomas, and William Fawling lived in an American settlement not far from Chota. As the first step in their plans, Dragging Canoe and his followers captured the traders and seized their goods. The three men were held prisoner in a stockade while battle plans were made to raid the American settle-ments near the Holston River and along the Virginia border. July 20, 1776, was the date chosen for the attack.

As a woman of high honor, it was Beloved Woman's duty to prepare a special ceremonial potion called "the black drink" for the warriors, and she did so reluctantly. Water was fetched from the river; a kettle was set to boil over a fire. Then, dressed in her official white deerskin raiments, Nancy Ward threw into the boiling water the leaves of *yaupon*, or holly, which had been collected from a sacred place in the mountains.

After the warriors partook of the brew, a war dance was commenced. Nancy Ward, however, was deeply troubled by what was about to happen. While the others were occupied with the war dance, she hurried to the stockade under the cover of darkness. She threw a rope over the wall and called to the three captives inside, urging them to escape. When they climbed over the wall, she explained that very soon a party of seven hundred Cherokee warriors would be sent to attack settlers along the Holston and Nolichucky Rivers and that the whites must be warned of the danger they were in.

At first, the three men suspected they were being led into some sort of trap, but Nancy Ward explained that if she had to take sides, it would be with the Americans. One of the traders, William

Fawling, who was part Cherokee himself, took her at her word and convinced his companions to do the same.

The Cherokee raids took place exactly as the warriors planned, but the settlers had been warned in time to seek safety in nearby military forts. Although they'd abandoned their homes, they'd taken most of their possessions with them. Finding the cabins empty, with very little remaining to be carried away as booty, was a great disappointment to the Cherokees. Dragging Canoe had been seriously wounded by a rifle ball that passed through both legs, but he was pleased that at least some captives had been taken. One of them, Mrs. Lydia Bean, had been captured as she tried to get her dairy cows to safety when the Cherokees swooped down on her homestead.

The fate of such women usually was slavery, but this time the warriors—bitterly disappointed not to have seized more goods in the raid—planned a very different end for Lydia Bean. They decided that she should be tied to a stake and burned alive. By the time Nancy Ward realized what was about to happen, she had scarcely enough time to put on her ceremonial white deerskin garments, throw her swansdown cape across her shoulders, and take up her swan's wing fan before running to the site of the execution.

Nanye'hi exercised all the power she had as a *Ghigau*. She scolded the warriors and told them they were about to do violence to the Great Spirit. She used the swan's wing as a scepter, leveling it first at the warrior who was about to set ablaze the pile of wood at Mrs. Bean's feet, then directing it at the terrified Mrs. Bean. Reluctantly, the warrior dropped his torch to the ground. Then Nancy ordered the woman to be untied. She protected Mrs. Bean with her snowy cape as they both hurried away to Nancy Ward's home.

Lydia Bean was the wife of William Bean, a captain in the settlers' militia who had been the first settler in the Watauga region. The Beans' son Russell was the first white child born in what later became the state of Tennessee. After recovering from the shock of her ordeal, Mrs. Bean looked about her and was impressed at how well her Cherokee benefactress lived. The home was well furnished and tidily kept; furthermore, Nancy Ward was a fine companion.

The two women became well acquainted as the weeks passed and Nancy Ward tried to figure out a way to get Mrs. Bean safely back to her family. One of the things the women discussed was cows. Yes, *cows!* Nancy wanted to know why Mrs. Bean did not flee to the fort to save herself, rather than take the time to drive her cows—who were notoriously slow, poky beasts—to a safe place. It was because of the cows' milk, Mrs. Bean explained, which was a healthy drink for children and adults alike. In addition, the milk that cows produced could be made into such things as butter and cheese, which could be traded for things a family needed. It all sounded quite foreign to the Cherokees' way of life; not only were Indians unaccustomed to drinking milk, but cows needed constant attention. Just the same, Nancy Ward listened attentively.

When she'd had time to think it over, Nancy decided cows would be a worthwhile acquisition for the women of her tribe. After all, the Cherokees already raised corn, which would give the animals plenty of feed, and fine pasturelands lay all about Chota. While Mrs. Bean remained a captive, Nancy got some cows and let the white woman teach her and the other village women how to care for them.

In December 1780, almost four years after Lydia Bean was returned safely to her family, militiamen from the white settlements battled the Indians at Chickamauga in Georgia. (More than eighty years later, Chickamauga would become a famous Civil War battlefield as whites fought against whites.) Dragging Canoe, who had recovered from his serious leg injuries, fought

bravely. As the Americans waited for reinforcements, Nancy Ward decided to try once more to act as a peacemaker.

On Christmas Day, she rode to meet Colonel Arthur Campbell. She told the colonel that her people were tired; more importantly, many among them longed for peace, even though Dragging Canoe and his followers wanted to fight the *unakas* to the end. The colonel admitted that his own men were starving and were living only on the nuts and berries they could scavenge from the woods. As a gesture of goodwill, Nancy Ward supplied the Americans with a few head of her precious cattle, which they butchered and ate. But the colonel had never promised Nancy that the Americans would behave as charitably, and a few days later militiamen burned the village of Chota and four other smaller Indian camps.

Nancy Ward and her family were captured, along with many other Cherokees. Thomas Jefferson, who was governor of Virginia at the time, told Colonel Campbell in February 1781 that the Wards were to be treated in whatever way Nancy herself believed they should be. Eventually Nancy Ward returned to Chota and the Indian villages were rebuilt.

But matters between whites and Cherokees were by no means settled. Among the Cherokees, there still were those who wanted peace but just as many who wanted war; the same was true among the whites. Colonel William Fleming of the militia reported to Jefferson that continued aggression against the Cherokees would cause them to attack the settlers more bitterly than ever. "The burning of their huts and destruction of their corn, will, I fear, make the whole Nation Our irreconcilable Enemies," he wrote.

On the Indian side, however, Cherokees such as Raven were determined to follow the path of war. Raven made a treaty with the British in which they agreed to pay him for any colonial captives and their horses that were brought to them. Raven captured John Martin, a militia leader, and four others, and threatened to kill them, but again Nancy Ward interceded and saved their lives.

Finally, on July 10, 1781, a treaty council was held on Long Island on the Holston River, and Captain John Sevier declared that he wanted peace with the Cherokees; the only reason he kept fighting, he said, was to protect his own people. Nancy Ward attended the council meeting, dressed in her ceremonial white deerskin dress and swansdown cape. It was unusual for an Indian woman to speak up at a meeting with white men, but on this occasion Nancy Ward did exactly that. Partly as the result of her speech, the impulse of the whites to demand more land in return for peace

was—for the moment—put aside. A treaty was signed which made no other demands on the Cherokees than that they remain peaceful. This enabled the Americans to send their troops off to fight with George Washington against General Cornwallis in the final battle of the War for Independence, after which the British surrendered in October 1781.

But the hunger of the white man for land hadn't been quenched, merely dampened temporarily. More treaties were made and broken, and in November 1785, a new council was called to take place along the Keowee River in South Carolina. It lasted ten days and was signed by twenty-seven Indian chiefs. Nancy Ward hoped fervently that this time it would be honored by each side.

In the meantime, both of Nancy's daughters married white men. Betsy married John Martin, the militiaman whose life Nancy had saved, who then became an agent employed by North Carolina to deal with the Cherokees. Betsy went to live on a fine estate on the south side of the Hiwasse River. Catherine married John Walker. Nancy's sons, Five Killer and Little Fellow, married Cherokee women, became chiefs, and lived near their mother in Chota. Between 1804 and 1816, however, the Cherokees gave up more land in Georgia, Tennessee, and Kentucky, and the population of Chota dwindled until it was scarcely more than a ghost town.

Five Killer fought with the Americans against the British in the War of 1812, and the Cherokees believed that such actions on the part of their warriors would guarantee them the right to stay on their ancestral lands. Andrew Jackson was not sympathetic to Indian claims, however, and the Cherokees found themselves facing the end of life as they had known it.

The U.S. policy regarding Indians' rights called for their removal from land that was coveted by whites. Many Cherokees went to Arkansas, as directed by the government, then to Oklahoma. For a long while, Nancy Ward remained where she was and continued to be respected by Indians and whites alike. When the Cherokees called a council in May 1817 to discuss drawing up their own constitution, Nancy—by then a woman of almost eighty years—was too frail to attend. However, she had someone carry her walking stick to the meeting, a symbol of her presence, and with it she relayed a message. This time, Nanye'hi warned her people not to make any more treaties with the whites because too many had been dishonored in the past. "Your mothers, your sisters ask . . . you not to part with any more of our lands. . . . Keep it for our growing children, for it

was the good will of our Creator to place us here."

But such a hopeful outcome was not to be the fate of the Cherokees, no matter how hard Nancy Ward had worked nor how patient she had been. Piece by piece, the Indians either traded away their lands or saw them taken by force. In the Hiwasse Purchase of 1819, the Cherokees lost the valley of the Little Tennessee River and with it the village of Chota. They moved south and built new towns. Nancy Ward herself settled along the Ocoee River, where she established an inn. Then, as hunting grounds and game became ever more scarce, the Cherokees depended more and more on agriculture to sustain themselves.

The year before Nancy Ward died, one of her tribesmen, Sequoya, invented a system of writing Cherokee words down on paper, and by 1825 the Indians had their own newspaper. But time was running out. On December 29, 1835, the U.S. government drew up a removal treaty, and a year later President Andrew Jackson announced that the treaty was binding on *all* Cherokees. During the next two years, two thousand Cherokees journeyed west to Arkansas or Oklahoma.

However, the majority of Indians refused to leave their land, whereupon the government removed them forcibly in 1838. Cherokees were dragged from their homes, locked in stockades, then driven like a herd of cattle toward the west. Their possessions had to be left behind; they traveled with only the clothes on their backs. By March 1839, the forced march was over, but three thousand exiles had died along the way from disease, exposure, or starvation. The Cherokees called the journey *nunna-da-ult-sun-yo*, or "the trail where the People cried." The whites called it "the Trail of Tears."

Perhaps it is just as well that Beloved Woman didn't live to see what became of her peacemaking efforts or what happened to the Ani-Yunwiya, the Principal People. She died in 1822 at approximately eighty-four years of age. She was buried near Benton, Tennessee.

Those who were present at her death said they saw rise from her body a pale light, about the same color as the swans-down cape Beloved Woman had worn with such distinction. They said the light turned in small circles, passed through the door, then lingered for a time in front of the house. When the light rose higher in the air, observers were sure it assumed the shape of a swan with wings outspread and were equally certain that it flew toward the spot where the village of Chota, the City of Refuge, once stood.

Marcus and Narcissa Whitman

1802–47; 1808–47 Missionaries. Whitman was practicing medicine in New York when he heard a lecture describing the need for missionaries in Oregon. Only married couples were sought; he proposed to a new acquaintance, Narcissa Prentiss, who as a girl had committed herself to work with "the heathen." They joined their lives and dreams, and headed west.

Just as his distant relative Abraham Lincoln was born in a log cabin, so too was Marcus Whitman. The third son of Beza and Alice Whitman came into the world on September 4, 1802, in the village of Rushville, New York. Two years earlier, his parents' second son had died, no doubt making the new baby especially welcome.

Beza Whitman was a tanner, currier, and shoemaker, and when he built a new frame home for his growing family he made it large enough to serve as a "public house," adding tavern keeping to his other trades. His wife, Alice, was described as strong-willed, but her lack of a "good profession of godliness" later deeply troubled her third son.

Beza Whitman died at age thirty-seven,

leaving Alice to raise their five children alone. Marcus, age eight, was sent to live with his uncle Freedom and aunt Sally in Plainfield, Massachusetts, while his twelve-year-old brother, Augustus, stayed home to help their mother. Marcus's grandfather also lived with Freedom and Sally Whitman; he was an intimidating old chap whose blind left eye didn't track with the right one, but he was a devoted Christian, and saw that Marcus became one too. Religious training in those days was rigorous: the sabbath began at noon on Saturday and lasted until Sunday evening. A "good" boy learned not to run or skip during that time and refrained from smiling, which was considered impious.

Marcus lived in Massachusetts for ten years, returning home only once, when

Marcus Whitman around the time of his appointment as a missionary in Oregon.

he was thirteen years old. His mother had married a man named Calvin Loomis, and the boy discovered he now had two half brothers. The three-week visit began unhappily, for when Marcus arrived his mother didn't recognize him, causing the boy to burst into tears.

Back in Plainfield, Marcus continued to attend a school founded by Moses Hallock, his grandfather's third cousin. The school, conducted in Hallock's home, was remarkable: of its 300 graduates, 132 went on to attend either Williams, Amherst, or Harvard College. Fifty of those students entered the ministry, as Marcus yearned to do himself.

When Marcus graduated at age eighteen, however, he returned home to help at the tannery and tavern, now run by his stepfather. He earned extra money teaching school and joined the Congregational church. For four years, he continued to dream of becoming a preacher, but getting educated for the ministry was a costly undertaking. Marcus knew that training for medicine would be easier: one simply began "to ride with the doctor" and learned the art in an on-the-job fashion.

On March 14, 1808, when Marcus was still a boy of five and hadn't yet lost his father, Judge Stephen Prentiss and his wife, Clarissa, of Prattsburg in western New York also welcomed a third child

into the world. She was the first daughter in a family that eventually included four boys and five girls. Her father was a man of influence: he had built the Presbyterian parsonage, among many other buildings in town, and operated a sawmill, gristmill, and distillery. He greatly enjoyed the title of "Judge," even though it was the result of a single brief term as an associate justice. Mrs. Prentiss was as imposing as her husband; acquaintances said she "possessed . . . a great weight of Christian character."

Narcissa was the family favorite, which seems to have caused no envy among her siblings, perhaps because she had such a cheerful disposition. She was a great help to her mother in raising the younger children and became noted for her beautiful singing voice. Narcissa attended her first revival meeting when she was eleven, and at age sixteen, after reading a biography of Harriet Boardman, a missionary to India, decided that's how she wanted to spend her own life.

Narcissa received more education than most girls of her day and studied for a time in Troy, New York, at an Episcopal school for girls run by Mrs. Emma Willard, the author of the stirring hymn "Rocked in the Cradle of the Deep." When she returned to Prattsburg, Narcissa enrolled at the

Franklin Academy, of which her father was a founder and trustee. There, she pursued the missionary dreams she'd set for herself.

In making her decision, Narcissa participated in a growing passion in the United States to rescue the Indians from their state of "savage wildness," a movement that was a romantic mixture of Puritanism and Jeffersonian democracy. The famous historian Lewis Mumford remarked that "pioneering is romanticism in action," and folk such as Narcissa and Marcus—whether they were Episcopal, Presbyterian, Methodist, or Catholic—were caught up in a desire to be pioneers of religious salvation.

At the Franklin Academy, Narcissa's dreams became peculiarly entangled with those of a certain Henry Harmon Spalding. Henry was the illegitimate son of a woman from Wheeler, a village not far from Prattsburg. At age fifteen, Henry had been thrown out of his mother's house by a man she had married; homeless, the boy wandered down the road toward Prattsburg. He was taken in by a kindly schoolmaster, Ezra Rice, who also took it upon himself to educate the boy. He sent the young man to the new, coeducational institution, the Franklin Academy.

Perhaps it was inevitable that a penniless, brooding young man with a dark past would fall in love with the blue-eyed, golden-haired daughter of a well-to-do family. Henry shared the same aspirations about missionary work that Narcissa did; yet when he put his love for her into words, she rejected him. Until Narcissa died, he never forgave her. Henry later found a new love in the person of Eliza Hart, a plain girl who also shared his dream of becoming a missionary. They were married in September 1833, and afterward Henry entered a seminary in Cincinnati. Neither he nor Narcissa guessed they would yet play pivotal roles in each other's lives.

In Rushville, Marcus began to ride the countryside with Dr. Ira Bryant and learn the art of medicine. He also taught Sunday school and gave temperance lectures. But there was a limit to what could be learned from old Dr. Bryant, who knew nothing about modern anesthesia or the science of infection, so in 1825—having finally saved enough money—Whitman enrolled in medical school in Fairfield, New York. The college offered the type of courses that a man who intended to practice frontier medicine would need, and Marcus graduated in 1832.

Whitman settled in Wheeler and started a medical practice. His soul remained filled with longing, however; preaching or mission work still called to him. When Marcus attended a lecture by the Reverend Samuel Parker, the Presbyterian minister spoke of the need for physician-missionaries in far-off Oregon; Marcus quickly realized it was the perfect opportunity to pursue his dream.

Dr. Parker had been searching for young men exactly like Marcus to present as candidates to the church's American Board of Foreign Missions, and he happily wrote to his wife, "Dr. Whitman, of Wheeler . . . has agreed to offer himself to the Board to go beyond the mountains." At a separate lecture, Parker met a young schoolteacher who wished to serve, and inquired of mission officials, "Are females wanted? A Miss Narcissa Prentiss . . . is very anxious to go to the heathen. . . . She will offer herself if needed."

Marcus, now thirty-two years old, wasted no time making his interest in Oregon known to the board, but he was informed that married missionaries were preferred. Unknown to him, Narcissa also was petitioning the board. She too was discouraged by its insistence that unmarried persons weren't being recruited.

The date of the couple's first meeting isn't known, but when it came about they must have discussed their mutual dreams. Some people regarded Marcus as a country bumpkin; they called his

Narcissa Whitman. CORBIS-BETTMANN.

dress careless and his manners crude, but Narcissa must have thought otherwise. The fact that she was twenty-seven, old enough to be considered an old maid, might have influenced her opinion.

In January 1835, Whitman accepted his appointment by the board. He learned more about Narcissa from Dr. Parker and proposed marriage in February 1835; in March, Narcissa herself was accepted as a missionary. However, it was believed that crossing the Rockies might be too rigorous for a white woman, a problem for which Dr. Parker had a solution: together, he and

Marcus would make the overland trip to Oregon, and if they decided a woman could, indeed, make the journey, Narcissa would go on the second trip—as Marcus's bride.

Dr. Parker and Whitman left St. Louis on April 8, 1835. St. Louis was a rowdy, sprawling city with much activity going on, most of it based on the fur trade. A beaver skin that could be gotten for a few trinkets from Indians up the Missouri fetched up to six dollars in the city, and a cup of whiskey could be traded for a buffalo robe worth even more. Whitman looked upon the commercial hustle and bustle with a disgust that was reinforced after he lost his wallet containing seven dollars even before the trip began.

Parker and Whitman joined Lucien Fontanelle's fur brigade—not to trap furs, but to take advantage of the experience and protection of men familiar with the country through which they intended to travel. Their presence wasn't appreciated by the rough-and-tumble trappers—that is, not until Whitman's medical skills proved valuable when, on June 10, 1835, he diagnosed a case of cholera in the brigade. Travel came to a temporary halt while he treated the sick—Fontanelle among them—and thereafter everyone was more congenial.

At the Green River rendezvous in Wyoming (a rendezvous was an annual gathering of mountain men, where news, furs, and other goods were exchanged), Whitman performed his famous operation on Jim Bridger, the well-known trapper and guide. Bridger had received a wound about three years earlier, and an arrowhead had buried itself deep in the flesh of his hip, where it hooked itself into the bone. The surgery was performed without anesthesia and was an ordeal for patient and doctor alike. As a result of their meeting, Whitman and Bridger became friends, and later Bridger sent his oldest part-Indian child to be schooled at the Whitmans' mission in Oregon.

Whitman not only treated the needs of trappers and traders; he also collected as much data as possible about the Indians and their language and customs, to be used on the second trip he planned to make with Narcissa. He also knew it would be important to have someone with him who spoke the Indians' language, so when he turned back for home, he took two young Nez Percé boys with him: Tackitonitis, whom he called Richard, and Ais, whom he called John.

Rather than go on to cross the Rockies with Parker, Whitman—apparently satisfied that the trip would be safe for his bride—returned to New York. He went first to Rushville to say farewell to his mother, then hurried on to see the young woman who had agreed to marry him.

Marcus and Narcissa decided that it would be essential to have at least one other married couple travel with them, so an urgent hunt was conducted to find others willing to serve in the West. A couple named Powell seemed likely; then they became parents, eliminating them from consideration. No one can be sure how Marcus learned from the mission board that a certain young couple had just accepted a job ministering to the Osage Indians in Missouri, but when he heard about them, he must have thought, *If only I could persuade them to go to Oregon instead!*

Whitman knew timing was critical because if travel couldn't be commenced by early spring, they'd never be able to make proper connections with a fur brigade in St. Louis. The agreement of the young man and his wife was essential, so he spared no effort tracking them down. On February 14, 1836, he was able to persuade the young couple—Henry and Eliza Spalding—to agree to go to Oregon instead. Whitman could not have known that Spalding once called Narcissa a frivolous woman with poor judgment, vowing never to serve at the same mission as she.

Before anything further happened, there had to be a wedding. Marcus and Narcissa were married on the evening of February 18, 1836. The bride's dress was of black bombazine; her attendants also wore black; in Narcissa's trousseau were dresses of brightly colored material, which she'd been told appealed to Indians, and a pair of stout leather boots crafted by Marcus's older brother, Augustus. Richard and John, the Nez Percé boys, proudly attended the ceremony. The closing hymn was one of Narcissa's favorites, and her clear soprano voice floated above the gathering: "Let me hasten/Far in heathen lands to dwell!"

The Whitmans and Spaldings boarded the *Chariton* in St. Louis and headed upstream to Liberty, Missouri, to commence an overland journey that the *St. Louis Observer* declared would be "fraught with peril." Part of the peril would stem from the fact that it soon became obvious that Whitman and Spalding were uncomfortable with each other—a problem that, according to many observers, was mostly Spalding's fault. However, there now were others to share the adventure: the board had recruited young Dr. Benedict Satterlee and his twenty-three-year-old wife, Martha, and young Emmeline Palmer, whose fiancé would soon join her.

The *Chariton* reached Liberty in April 1836; the overland journey of nearly two thousand miles lay before the group. The first third of it would be across the

An unidentified artist portrayed the Whitman group at prayer during their long journey. CORBIS-BETTMANN.

plains of Kansas and Nebraska; next, they would cross the Shining Mountains—the Rockies—followed by a crossing of the desert portion of Idaho. Along the way were only five outposts manned by whites: Fort Leavenworth, the Otoe Indian Agency, Fort William, Fort Hall, and Snake Fort.

Before the group departed, a young carpenter came upriver; he too had just been appointed, and his practical skills were welcome. Samuel Allis arrived to marry Emmeline Palmer, but the adventure was marred by tragedy as well: Martha Satterlee died, probably of tuberculosis.

The plains were broad and untraveled in those times; there was as yet no Oregon Trail; no Mormon Trail had been carved out. The famous "Pathfinder," John Charles Frémont, had yet to work his mapmaker's magic. There were only grass and sky as far as one could see. Thomas Fitzpatrick led the fur brigade and chafed at having to slow his schedule to match the pace of a gaggle of missioners with a cumbersome wagon and assorted pack animals, livestock, and milk cows. Narcissa soon learned to thrive on buffalo meat, remarking in a letter that "I never saw anything like it to satisfy hunger. . . . We have meat and tea in the morn, and tea and meat at noon."

In May, Eliza and Narcissa discovered how odd it was to be the object of Indians' curiosity. They had never seen a white woman before and came to peep into the missioners' tent, then to laugh, as if what they saw was highly amusing. By July 6 the party arrived at the Green River rendezvous in Wyoming, where Marcus and Narcissa met dashing Joe Meek. Like Jim Bridger, Meek also would send the Whitmans a half-Indian child to be cared for.

The group reached Fort Hall, in the heart of Blackfoot country, on the morning of August 3, 1836. Perhaps it was about this time that Narcissa realized she was pregnant. The Snake River country was hot and miserable to travel across; pasture and water were scarce. At a river crossing, Marcus decided the wagon must be lightened, and Narcissa's little trunk was cast aside. "Farewell little trunk," she wrote wistfully. "I thank thee for thy faithful services. . . . I have been cheered by thy presence so long." Late in August, the group decided to split in two parts—the Whitmans in one, the Spaldings in the other. Was the split necessary because of continuing differences between Marcus and Henry? No one can now be sure.

The Whitmans were welcomed at Fort Vancouver by Dr. John McLoughlin, chief agent for Britain's Hudson's Bay Company. Towering six feet four inches, wearing a mane of shoulder-length white hair, McLoughlin was widely respected by Americans, British, and Indians alike. He treated Marcus and Narcissa to a bountiful breakfast of ripe melons, fresh salmon, potatoes, bread, butter, and tea. Supper that evening was as fine as any back home—pork, potatoes, beets, cabbage, turnips, more bread, and tea. Best of all, they could sit on *real* chairs again! When the Spaldings arrived a day later, McLoughlin complimented the ladies on being the first white women ever to cross the Rocky Mountains. He also suggested they remain at Fort Vancouver until their husbands had selected mission sites.

In retrospect, many historians agree that it would have been wise if the two families had agreed to settle at a single location, but both were determined to be independent of the other. The Nez Percé Indians had expressed an interest in being Christianized and professed to look forward to having white missionaries among them; they were disappointed when Whitman decided to locate his mission in Cayuse country. The Nez Percé warned that the Cayuses were treacherous folk, that Whitman would regret settling among them, but the doctor would not be dissuaded. Spalding, however, agreed to settle on Lapwai

A sketch of Marcus Whitman's mission at Waiilatpu. It included a working farm, a gristmill, and a blacksmith's shop. WASHINGTON STATE HISTORICAL SOCIETY.

Creek, ten miles above the mouth of the Clearwater River, and became the missionary the Nez Percés wanted.

The spot Whitman picked was called by its Indian name, Waiilatpu, "the place of rye grass." A branch of the Walla Walla River bent to the southeast below the Whitman house, and on the opposite bank was a line of timber and groves of cottonwood trees. Narcissa had been given the gift of a small dog and arrived at her new home eager to fulfill a lifelong dream.

The Whitman home wasn't completed by the time of her arrival, however, since it truly had to be built from scratch—that is, the trees cut down, the lumber hand-sawed. Yet she could see that the house would be ample when finished, thirty by thirty-six feet. The Cayuse Indians' sullen welcome didn't match the warm one the Nez Percés reportedly gave the Spaldings. Narcissa wrote of the Cayuse chief, Tilaukait (his name was spelled several different ways), "His heart is . . . full of all manner of hypocrisy, deceit and guile." We do not know, however, what Tilaukait himself thought about white men settling in one of his tribe's favorite haunts.

The Whitmans' first wedding anniversary passed. The little dog Narcissa had been given was joined by a cat. The young couple worked fiercely hard getting their mission established. Then, on the evening of Narcissa's birthday, March 14, 1837, there was another special birth to celebrate: the Whitmans' only child, Alice Clarissa, was born. As happy as she was, Narcissa had cause to realize how much there was to be faced with no woman to turn to—no mother, no sister, no neighbor's wife. Had the relationship between the Whitmans and Spaldings been more congenial, Eliza might have offered reassurance, but she was about to have a child herself and soon gave birth to a daughter, also named Eliza.

When Methodist missionary Jason Lee—who in 1833 had established the first mission in Oregon along the Willamette River—visited the Whitman and Spalding operations in April 1837, he lamented that the two Presbyterians couldn't work closely with each other. "It was a rather rash measure to put themselves so entirely into the hands of the Indians," he noted prophetically. Lee was amazed to discover that both Whitman and Spalding used the lash to

punish Indians; he realized that such treatment was bound to breed ill will among such proud people. He also wondered at the Presbyterians' solution to Indian hunger: teach them agriculture. Lee believed that raising cattle, rather than hunting, was a much more efficient way of teaching the Indians how to supply food for their families.

During his visit, Lee also reported news that stunned the Presbyterians: he intended to dramatically expand the Methodist mission. He included the rumor that Catholics were interested in missioning in the Northwest. Lee had obtained the grand sum of forty thousand dollars from the Methodist Missionary Society, and his plans called for five new ministers, a doctor, four teachers, two carpenters, a blacksmith, a cabinetmaker, and two farmers.

Lee's success in obtaining such riches temporarily brought Whitman and Spalding together and galvanized them into action. They were determined that *their* missions would be as outstanding. Spalding promptly wrote a letter to David Greene at the Presbyterian mission board in Boston, describing his and Whitman's plans for expansion, and Whitman signed it. Spalding's letter requested—"demanded" might be a better term—"30 ordained ministers, 30 farmers, 30 school teachers, 10 physicians, and 10 mechanics. . . .You have only to make the request known and the men and the money are at your command." Among other things, the list included a request for five hundred yards of fabric, books, slates, and pencils, not to mention saws, axes, adzes, candlesticks, chisels, and cowbells.

The letter had a disastrous effect on the cautious men of the board, who feared a commercialization of what was supposed to be a Christian undertaking in Oregon. The board had worries of its own: it was concerned about the U.S. economic crisis of 1837, and members were aghast at the recklessness of the missionaries' plans.

David Greene's answer was candid: "You are quite mistaken, Dear Brethren, when you assert . . . that the Board have only to make their wants known and funds and men will be furnished without delay." He closed by saying a small part of what was requested would be forthcoming, then advised the missioners to rely on the power of prayer.

The likely truth is that neither the Whitmans nor the Spaldings ever imagined how demanding their life as missionaries would be. The two women not only had to be wives and mothers, but cooks, seamstresses, housekeepers, organizers of religious worship, schoolteachers, and social workers to the Indians they'd come to serve. The men also were challenged beyond what they might have anticipated: they had to learn farming, carpentering, and husbandry; they had to preach, minister, and learn a new language. Whitman worked hardest of all, because he also was in constant demand for medical services. Most disheartening, each family—isolated at its own site—was handicapped in different ways: Whitman had the best land but the fewest and least cooperative Indians, while 180 miles away, Spalding had the poorest land but the greatest number of Indians willing to be Christianized.

In 1839, some of the missionaries that Whitman and Spalding requested finally arrived: four married couples—the Eells, Smiths, Walkers, and Grays—plus a young bachelor, Cornelius Rogers. The company was welcome, yet it proved no easier for these folk to cooperate among themselves than it had been for the Whitmans and Spaldings. Gray was determined to have his own mission among the Flathead Indians, then grumpily agreed to become Spalding's assistant. The Walkers and Eells settled to the north, at Tshimakain, while the Smiths went to Kamiah. However, with six white women about, Narcissa organized the Columbia Maternal Association, and on September 3, 1838, Eliza Spalding became its first president.

As Jason Lee had reported, Catholic missionaries were indeed bound for Oregon. The only reason they hadn't come earlier was the same handicap that plagued Presbyterians: lack of funds. In October 1838, forty-three-year-old Jesuit Father François Blanchet celebrated the first Catholic mass in the region and was joined later by Father Demers. Eventually, the priests were joined by six French nuns, who were able to minister to the "orphans of the forest" with the sort of enthusiasm that the overworked wives of the Protestant missioners couldn't match.

Protestant and Catholic friction had a long history in the United States, and the arrival of the Jesuits was naturally upsetting to the Protestant missioners who had arrived first. The priests nearly always wore their cassocks and relished their name, "the Black Robes"; Protestant misssionaries, on the other hand, sometimes couldn't be distinguished by their dress from traders or trappers. Then, for whatever reason, many Indians seemed more beguiled by Catholicism, perhaps because its mysticism appealed to their superstitious natures, whereas Protestantism—not far removed from its Puritan roots—was in many ways an unpleasantly stern faith.

In spite of such distractions, however, life seemed good for the Whitmans. Marcus planted about twenty-five acres of corn, peas, beans, squash, carrots, and onions; a few apple trees had been started. The mission barnyard held oxen, cows, pigs, and chickens. A larger house was on its way to completion. Best of all, two-year-old Alice was healthy and a great comfort to her lonely mother. Little more could be asked.

All that changed on the afternoon of June 23, 1839, when Alice wandered out of the yard and drowned in the river that ran close by the Whitman home. She was buried in a coffin built by her heartbroken father. The Reverend Henry Spalding came from Lapwai to conduct the funeral. He chose a passage from II Kings 4:26: "Is it well with thee? Is it well with thy husband? Is it well with the child?" The words seem intentionally cruel and are considered by some to be testimony of the grudge Spalding still carried against Narcissa.

The Whitmans' difficulties with Henry Spalding caused dissension in the entire Protestant community in Oregon. A year and a half after Alice's drowning, Narcissa wrote to her parents, asking them to keep the letter secret, asserting that Spalding "never ought to have come. My husband has suffered more from him in consequence of his wicked jealousy, and his great pique toward me, than can be known in this world. . . . It has nearly broken up the mission."

Narcissa also found fault with herself: "I see myself to be the most unfit for the place I occupy on heathen ground. I wonder [why] I was ever permitted to come." The problem between the missionaries had a more dangerous consequence: the Indians observed how bitterly the whites were pitted against each other and used the rift to their own advantage.

At the annual meeting of the Oregon Mission in June 1841, it was announced that the Smiths had decided to leave mission work. Soon young Cornelius Rogers went downriver, married the daughter of a Methodist missionary, and became an interpreter. Then a quarrel erupted when Spalding learned that many of the group had sent letters about him to the mission board in Boston.

Missionary work was increasingly complicated by the fact that of all people in the world to minister to, Indians perhaps were the least likely to accept it. They were proud, independent people, not used to being ordered about, much less whipped; they had cherished their own customs for many generations. The missioners thought of them as "lazy," but it was mostly a matter of understanding the world in very different terms. The Indians—in their unique ways—provided well for their families, but they definitely were disinclined toward the type of farmwork both Whitman and Spalding demanded. Whitman eventually came to the conclusion that trying to make farmers out of

Indians was hopeless, but even at the end of a long life, Spalding stubbornly insisted otherwise.

Part of the difficulty the Whitmans had with the Cayuse Indians originated not with themselves, but with the Reverend Samuel Parker. Parker had promised the Indians payment for their lands, but of course the Whitmans had no money, and the board did not advance them sufficient funds for such payments. One way the Indians had of bringing up the subject was to let their livestock into Whitman's unfenced fields; when Marcus reacted angrily, Chief Tilaukait took pains to remind him of the debt that still was owed.

The pain of Narcissa's loss of little Alice must have been eased when fur trapper Joe Meek, on his own after the American Fur Company disbanded, asked her to take his half-Indian daughter, Helen, into her home. Narcissa agreed and before long also took in Jim Bridger's half-Indian child, Mary Ann, as well as the son of a white man and a Cree woman whom she named David Malin, in remembrance of an old classmate at the Franklin Academy.

In May 1842, eighteen covered wagons belonging to Pennsylvania emigrants gathered at Independence, Missouri, in preparation for a trip to Oregon. Fifty-two persons were men more than eighteen years of age; the rest were women and children. They were escorted part of the way by the same Tom Fitzpatrick who had escorted the Whitmans and Spaldings. When the travelers arrived at the Whitman mission in September, they were impressed to find a spacious house, a building to house travelers, a blacksmith shop, a gristmill, and well-tended fields.

The emigrants also brought mail, and a letter from Boston informed Whitman that the board intended to recall Spalding from mission work, that he must "return by the first direct and suitable opportunity." In addition, Whitman was ordered to take over the northern mission at Lapwai and to vacate the one at Waiilatpu. It was a decision that neither missionary expected and which both refused to accept.

Whitman suggested that he travel east to present an argument to the board. After debating the issue, Spalding agreed. Marcus set out on October 3, 1842, accompanied by the family's little dog, Trapper, and Asa Lovejoy, a young lawyer from Massachusetts who'd recently arrived in Oregon. A durable myth grew up around this famous journey, that Whitman rode to Washington with a grand scheme to save Oregon from the British.

However, Marcus's aim seems to have been rather modest. He wrote that it was " to get funds for founding schools, and have good people come along as settlers and teachers." Of course, more American settlers would naturally favor American over British claims in the Northwest, yet that doesn't seem to have been uppermost in Whitman's mind. As Narcissa noted, "He goes . . . in the cause of Christ in this land."

Whitman covered the four-hundred-mile distance to Fort Hall in ten short days; then, perhaps because he was worried about bad weather, he turned to the southwest, toward Santa Fe, which added a thousand miles to his journey. Even so, Whitman and Lovejoy were exposed to severe storms, and ever after Marcus bore vertical red frostbite scars on his cheeks. During one especially bad siege, loyal Trapper was sacrificed to the stew pot. In Santa Fe, Lovejoy— although he was six years younger than Whitman—decided he couldn't keep up the pace, and Marcus traveled on alone.

Whitman didn't go straight to the board but made a brief stop in Washington. He met with the secretary of the treasury and the secretary of war, and outlined an idea for government posts that could supply settlers headed west and would facilitate mail delivery. On March 29, 1843, newspaperman Horace Greeley met Whitman in New York, calling him "the roughest man we have seen this many a day—too poor, in fact, to get any better wardrobe," referring, no doubt, to the fact that the bearded Whitman was still dressed in greasy leather leggings and a coat trimmed with buffalo hair.

In Boston, Whitman met with the Board of Foreign Missions and learned that a vote had already been taken regarding Spalding's dismissal and his own transfer to Lapwai. The following day, Whitman returned for another meeting, having bathed and gotten a new suit of clothes. He was finally able to persuade the board to let him stay at Waiilatpu and to retain Spalding at least temporarily.

Before heading back to Oregon, Marcus visited his mother and was aggrieved to find that she was still a tough-minded pragmatist who put little faith in the power of prayer. He took pleasure, though, in the impression he made on his nephew, twelve-year-old Perrin Whitman. The boy, son of Whitman's brother Samuel, begged to travel back to Oregon with his uncle, and when Marcus left Rushville on May 31, 1843, Perrin rode at his side.

Shortly after Whitman had departed for the East, Narcissa was badly frightened when someone—she believed it was Tilaukait himself—broke into her home in the middle of the night. She took the two half-Indian girls with her to the Methodist mission at Willamette and made arrangements for little David

Malin to be cared for at Fort Walla Walla. In her absence, the mission's gristmill was burned, windows in the house were smashed, farm equipment was destroyed. Narcissa probably would have been even more alarmed if she'd known that rumors were circulating among the Indians that Marcus had gone to Washington to ask for soldiers to subdue them, causing them to become even more resentful.

Whitman returned to Waiilatpu on October 10, 1843; his six-thousand-mile journey had taken a full year. His family of informally adopted children soon increased; in addition to David Malin and the half-Indian girls, there now were Perrin Whitman and two motherless white girls age six and thirteen. When Mrs. Henry Sager, an emigrant mother, requested on her deathbed that the Whitmans take her brood of seven ranging in age from five months to fourteen years, they also were added to the household. To the end of her life, Catherine Sager remembered "Mother" and "Father" Whitman with devotion. Also living at the mission were the Looney and Littlejohn families, and a young French Canadian bachelor. In all, twenty-six people lived in the main house and another twelve in the smaller one nearby.

On October 25, 1844, Narcissa wrote, "They have just begun to arrive," *they* being fifteen hundred new settlers. For years, the board had refused to send emigrants, so it must have gratified Whitman to see them now coming on their own. It was Narcissa's fondest dream that her sister Jane might come on one of the trains, but that was never to be.

Whitman's dreams now began to take a different turn; rather than ministering exclusively to the Indians' spiritual needs, he foresaw "an Academy and College" in the Northwest, and his plans for rebuilding Waiilatpu were shaped around the idea that it should serve as a supply station to aid white settlers.

At Lapwai, Henry Spalding's concerns were quite different: he was aware of the growing animosity among both Nez Percé and Cayuse tribes, now fostered by the presence of Tom Hill, an educated Delaware Indian who had once worked with Kit Carson. Hill spoke fluent English as well as Nez Percé, was possessed by a fiendish hatred of whites, and was doing his own kind of preaching. He warned his brethren what the influx of white men meant, offering as proof what had already happened to many eastern tribes. Chief Tilaukait, more than any other, listened thoughtfully.

In 1846, the number of emigrants to Oregon dropped off. True, they were still arriving, but most continued on for California, perhaps attracted by the bet-

ter weather. But the year also had a plus: Congress approved a treaty with the British that set the U.S.-Canada border at the forty-ninth parallel, making the slogan "Fifty-four-forty or Fight" obsolete and ending twenty-eight years of joint occupancy in the Northwest. A year later, the number of emigrants reached four or five thousand, giving Whitman great satisfaction. The effect on the Cayuses was understandably quite the opposite.

Suddenly, Chief Tilaukait declared he had no objection to the building of a Catholic mission near Waiilatpu and said ominously that he had decided "to send the doctor away." Friends urged the Whitmans to leave, but their interest in the welfare of new emigrants kept Marcus and Narcissa in place. It was to be a fatal decision.

In October 1847 the tense situation was worsened by the outbreak of measles and dysentery, carried into the country by one of the emigrant trains. The stricken Indians, knowing nothing of immunity, observed that white folk who caught such diseases nearly always recovered, whereas Indians usually died. Two of Tilaukait's young sons died, and when an emigrant child at Waiilatpu also died, Narcissa accepted it as a blessing, hoping the Indians would see that whites weren't always spared. Friendly Indians told the Whitmans that another rumor was being passed from village to village—that the missionaries had released poison into the air. Still, the Whitmans remained where they were.

On the cold, gray morning of Monday, November 29, 1847, Marcus Whitman rose early. When Narcissa finally rose too, the older children noted she had been crying. Catherine Sager recalled that Marcus had returned from a trip late the evening before and that he and Narcissa then talked deep into the night about the Indians' increasing hostility.

In late morning, a terrible message was delivered to the mission: another of Tilaukait's sons had died. Whitman followed the news bearer into the November gloom to officiate at the funeral. He probably took his life in his hands, for the Cayuses were a superstitious tribe and had been known to kill their own medicine men when "good medicine" wasn't forthcoming.

It was late before Marcus came home, and about two o'clock the large household sat down for its midday meal. Afterward, Narcissa prepared a bath for Elizabeth Sager, then was shocked to discover Tilaukait standing in her kitchen. He was accompanied by Tomahas, one of the most sullen of the Cayuses, and they demanded to speak to the doctor. There is no precise record of what was said, but Tilaukait had rendered a verdict, and now Tomahas carried it out—by bringing a tomahawk crashing down across the head of Marcus Whitman.

Young John Sager, seated nearby, reached for a weapon but was killed instantly. Whitman, already tomahawked, was shot as well. Children shrieked and scrambled for cover; the men working in the mission yard—Marsh, Gilliland, Saunders, and Hoffman—were also tomahawked or shot by other Indians. During Narcissa's efforts to rescue her husband she was struck by rifle fire coming through a window, yet was able to herd the children upstairs. Later, when the Indians tempted everyone downstairs with the promise of safety, Narcissa was shot again and thrown into the muddy yard. In all, eleven people lost their lives that November afternoon; Narcissa Whitman was the only woman among the dead.

Afterward, the Indians made captives of the remaining women and children. On Tuesday, November 30, one of the survivors of the massacre tried to bury the dead in a shallow grave, but a few days later wolves scattered bones and bodies about, and they had to be buried again.

Eventually, five of the assassins gave themselves up, among them Tilaukait and Tomahas, and a trial began in Oregon City on May 22, 1850. When asked why he had

Narcissa Whitman nurses a sick Indian. NORTH WIND PICTURE ARCHIVES.

surrendered, Tilaukait replied, "Did not your missionaries teach us that Christ died to save his people? So die we to save our people." All five were hanged on Monday, June 3. Joe Meek, now a sheriff, carried out the sentence. His daughter Helen, who had been cared for so well by the Whitmans, died of measles shortly after the massacre.

Jane Prentiss, Narcissa's beloved

younger sister, had begged someone for an explanation of what had happened to the mission dreams of her sister and brother-in-law. The Reverend H. K. W. Perkins, who had become acquainted with Narcissa during her stay at the Methodist mission during Marcus's year-long absence, tried to provide an explanation in a letter dated October 19, 1849.

"I should say, unhesitatingly, that both [Narcissa] and her husband were out of their proper sphere," he wrote. He was quick to praise their good intentions but noted that Marcus could never "parley" with the Indians and demanded yes-or-no answers to any matter. Narcissa, whose heart was sympathetic toward the Indians, nevertheless was "considered haughty" by them. "She loved company, society . . . & ought always to have enjoyed it. The self-denial that took her away from it was suicidal," he said. This might have been what Narcissa herself began to suspect.

Perkins shrewdly pointed out that the Whitmans were never able to make the Indians' interests paramount; rather, those interests were secondary to their own—a harsh judgment, but perhaps an accurate one. In Perkins's view, the Indians held the Whitmans responsible for the arrival of so many emigrant trains, for being advocates of white men, not of Indians. He noted that the Indians' own desire was simply to keep "their lands, their homes, the graves of their fathers, their rich hunting grounds & horse ranges. . . . The result could have hardly been otherwise than it was."

Perhaps Marcus Whitman himself had foreseen what was inevitable. Shortly before the massacre, he had confided to his adversary, Henry Spalding, that in death he might do more for Oregon than he ever could in life. So it was: after the massacre, Congress quickly passed a law declaring Oregon a territory, with all the privileges of one.

The Whitmans' story is perhaps one of the most compelling in the history of the American West. Nowhere else were the lines drawn so sharply between the interests of Indians and whites; nowhere else was the mixture of human frailty and human idealism on both sides so vividly dramatized.

Further Reading

Andrist, R. K. *The Long Death: The Last Days of the Plains Indians.* New York: Macmillan Company, 1964.

Andrist, R. K. *To the Pacific with Lewis and Clark.* New York: American Heritage Publishing Co., Inc., 1967.

Goetzmann, W. H., and W. N. Goetzmann. *The West of the Imagination.* New York: W.W. Norton & Company, 1986.

Hicks, J. D., G. E. Mowry, R. E. Burke. *A History of American Democracy.* Boston: Houghton Mifflin Company, 1966.

Morgan, T. *Wilderness at Dawn: The Settling of the North American Continent.* New York: Simon & Schuster, 1993.

Neider, C. *The Great West.* New York: Bonanza Books, 1958.

Rawling, G. *The Pathfinders: The History of America's First Westerners.* New York: Macmillan Company, 1964.

Riegel, R. E., and R. G. Athearn. *America Moves West.* Fifth Ed. New York: Holt, Rinehart and Winston, 1971.

Schmitt, M.F., and D. Brown. *The Settlers' West: With 300 Rare Photographs.* New York: Bonanza Books, 1982.

Unruh, J. D., Jr. *The Plains Across: The Overland Emigrants and the Trans-Mississippi West, 1840-1860.* Urbana, Illinois: University of Illinois Press, 1982.

DANIEL BOONE

Elliott, L. *The Long Hunter: A New Life of Daniel Boone.* New York: Reader's Digest Press, 1976.

Faragher, J. M. *Daniel Boone: The Life and Legend of an American Pioneer.* New York: Henry Holt & Company, 1992.

Lawlor, L. *Daniel Boone.* (Juvenile) Niles, Illinois: Albert Whitman Press & Co., 1989.

Lofaro, M. A. *The Life and Adventures of Daniel Boone.* Lexington: University Press of Kentucky, 1986.

JAMES BOWIE

Baugh, V. E. *Rendezvous at the Alamo: Highlights in the Lives of Bowie, Crockett, and Travis.* New York: Pageant Press, Inc., 1960.

Garst, S. *James Bowie*. (Juvenile) New York: Julian Messner, 1955.

Hopewell, C. *James Bowie: Texas Fighting Man*. Austin, Texas: Eakin Press, 1994.

JIM BRIDGER

Alter, J. C. *Jim Bridger*. Norman, Oklahoma: University of Oklahoma Press, 1925.

Caesar, G. *King of the Mountain Men: The Life of Jim Bridger*. New York: E.P. Dutton, 1961.

Locke, R. F. *The American West*. New York: Hawthorn Books, Inc., 1971.

MARY JANE CANNARY (CALAMITY JANE)

Burke, M. C. *Life and Adventures of Calamity Jane: By Herself*. Fairfield, Washington: Galleon Press, 1986.

Faber, D. *Calamity Jane: Her Life and Her Legend*. Boston: Houghton Mifflin Company, 1992.

Mueller, E. C. *Calamity Jane*. Laramie, Wyoming: Jelm Mountain Press, 1981.

KIT CARSON

Burdett, Charles. *The Life of Kit Carson*. New York: Grosset & Dunlap, 1902.

Gerson, Noel B. *Kit Carson: Folk Hero and Man*. New York: Doubleday & Company, Inc. , 1964.

Vestal, Stanley. *Kit Carson: The Happy Warrior of the Old West, a Biography*. Boston & New York: Houghton Mifflin Company, 1928.

GEORGE CATLIN

McCracken, H. *George Catlin and the Old Frontier*. New York: Dial Press, 1959.

Plate, R. *Palatte and Tomahawk: The Story of George Catlin*. New York: David McKay Company, Inc., 1962.

Rockwell, A. *Paintbrush & Peacepipe: The Story of George Catlin*. (Juvenile) New York: Atheneum, 1971.

Ross, M. *George Catlin*. Norman, Oklahoma: University of Oklahoma Press, 1958.

JOHN CHAPMAN (JOHNNY APPLESEED)

Glines, W. M. *Johnny Appleseed, by One Who Knew Him*. Columbus, Ohio: F.J. Heer Printing Co., 1922.

Hunt, M. L. *Better Known as Johnny Appleseed*. New York: J.B. Lippincott Co., 1950.

Lawlor, L. *The Real Johnny Appleseed*. (Juvenile) Morton Grove, Illinois: Albert Whitman & Company, 1995.

Price, R. *Johnny Appleseed: Man and Myth*. Bloomington, Indiana: Indiana University Press, 1954.

WILLIAM CLARK

Ambrose, S. E. *Undaunted Courage: Meriwether Lewis, Thomas Jefferson, and the Opening of the American West*. New York: Simon & Schuster, 1996.

Blumberg, R. *The Incredible Journey of Lewis & Clark*. (Juvenile) New York: Lothrop, Lee & Shepard, 1987.

Clark, W. *The Field Notes of Captain William Clark, 1803–1805*. New Haven, Connecticut: Yale University Press, 1964.

Peterson, D., and M. Coburn. *Meriwether Lewis and William Clark: Soldiers, Explorers, and Partners in History*. (Juvenile) Chicago: Children's Press, 1988.

WILLIAM CODY (BUFFALO BILL)

Rosa, J. G., and R. May. *Buffalo Bill and His Wild West: A Pictorial Biography*. Lawrence, Kansas: University of Kansas Press, 1989.

Russell, D. *The Lives and Legends of Buffalo Bill.* Norman, Oklahoma: University of Oklahoma Press, 1960.

Sell, H. B., and V. Weybright. *Buffalo Bill and the Wild West.* New York: Oxford University Press, 1955.

Yost, N. S. *Buffalo Bill: His Family, Friends, Fame, Failures, and Fortunes.* Chicago: Swallow Press Inc., 1979.

CRAZY HORSE

Ambrose, S. E. *Crazy Horse and Custer: The Parallel Lives of Two American Warriors.* New York: Doubleday & Co., Inc., 1975.

Hassrick, R. B. *The Sioux: Life and Customs of a Warrior Society.* Norman, Oklahoma: University of Oklahoma Press, 1964.

St. George, J. *Crazy Horse.* (Juvenile) New York: G.P. Putnam's Sons, 1994.

Sandoz, M. *Crazy Horse: The Strange Man of the Oglalas.* Lincoln, Nebraska: University of Nebraska Press, 1942.

DAVY CROCKETT

Hauck, R. B. *Davy Crockett: A Handbook.* Lincoln: University of Nebraska Press, 1982.

Kilgore, D. *How Did Davy Die?* College Station: Texas A & M University Press, 1973.

Lofaro, M. A. *Davy Crockett: The Man, the Legends, the Legacy, 1786–1986.* Knoxville: University of Tennessee Press, 1985.

Shackford, J. A. *David Crockett: The Man and the Legend.* Chapel Hill: University of North Carolina Press, 1986.

GEORGE ARMSTRONG CUSTER

Ambrose, S. E. *Crazy Horse and Custer: The Parallel Lives of Two American Warriors.* New York: Doubleday & Co., Inc., 1975.

Custer, George Armstrong. *My Life on the Plains: Or, Personal Experiences with Indians.* Introduction by E. I. Stewart. Norman, Oklahoma: University of Oklahoma Press, 1962.

Utley, R. M. *Cavalier in Buckskin: George Armstrong Custer and the Western Military Frontier.* Norman: University of Oklahoma Press, 1988.

Recommended Video: "Son of the Morning Star," 1991, Republic Pictures Home Video, 12636 Beatrice Street, Los Angeles, CA 90066-0930. Taken from the novel of the same name by Evan S. Connell.

JOHN DEERE

Aldrich, D. *The Story of John Deere.* (Privately printed) C.C. Webber, 1942.

Broehl, W. G., Jr. *John Deere's Company: A History of Deere & Company and Its Times.* New York: Doubleday & Company, Inc., 1984.

Collins, D. R. *Pioneer Plowmaker: A Story About John Deere.* Minneapolis: Carolrhoda Books, Inc., 1990.

GEORGE BIRD GRINNELL

Grinnell, G. B. *The Fighting Cheyennes.* Norman, Oklahoma: University of Oklahoma Press, 1956.

Parsons, C. *George Bird Grinnell: A Biographical Sketch.* New York: University Press of America, 1992.

Reiger, J. F. *The Passing of the West: Selected Papers of George Bird Grinnell.* New York: Winchester Press, 1972.

JAMES J. HILL

Holbrook, S. H. *James J. Hill: A Great Life in Brief.* New York: Alfred A. Knopf, 1955.

Martin, A. *James J. Hill: The Opening of the Northwest.* New York: Oxford University Press, 1976.

Pyle, J. G. *The Life of James J. Hill.* Vol. I & II. New York: Doubleday, Page and Company, 1917.

SAM HOUSTON

Braider, D. *Solitary Star: A Biography of Sam Houston.* New York: G.P. Putnam's Sons, 1974.

Carter, A. R. *Last Stand at the Alamo.* (Juvenile) New York: Franklin Watts, 1990.

De Bruhl, M. *Sword of San Jacinto: A Life of Sam Houston.* New York: Random House, 1993.

Williams, J. H. *Sam Houston: A Biography of the Father of Texas.* New York: Simon & Schuster, 1993.

MERIWETHER LEWIS

Andrist, R. K. *Lewis and Clark.* New York: American Heritage Publishing Co., Inc., 1967.

Bakeless, J. E. *Lewis and Clark: Partners in Discovery.* New York: William Morrow & Company, 1947.

Dillon, R. *Meriwether Lewis: A Biography.* New York: Coward-McCann, 1965.

Peterson, D., and M. Coburn. *Meriwether Lewis and William Clark: Soldiers, Explorers, and Partners in History.* (Juvenile) Chicago: Children's Press, 1988.

JAMES McLAUGHLIN

McLaughlin, J. *My Friend, the Indian.* Seattle, Washington: Superior Publishing Company, 1970.

Pfaller, L. L. *James McLaughlin: The Man with the Indian Heart.* New York: Vantage Press, 1978.

JOHN MUIR

Melham, T. *John Muir's Wild America.* Washington, D.C.: National Geographic Society, 1976.

Muir, J. *The Story of My Boyhood and Youth.* Madison: University of Wisconsin Press, 1965.

Naden, C. J., and R. Blue. *John Muir: Saving the Wilderness.* (Juvenile) Brookfield, Connecticut: Millbrook Press, 1992.

Tolan, S. *John Muir: Naturalist, Writer, and Guardian of the North American Wilderness.* (Juvenile) Milwaukee: Gareth Stevens Children's Books, 1990.

Wilkins, T. *John Muir: Apostle of Nature.* Norman, Oklahoma: University of Oklahoma Press, 1995.

CHARLOTTE DARKEY PARKHURST

MacDonald, C. *Cockeyed Charley Parkhurst: The West's Most Unusual Whip.* Palmer Lake, Colorado: Filter Press, 1973.

Reinstedt, R. A. *One-Eyed Charley, the California Whip.* Carmel, California: Ghost Town Publications, c1990.

FRANCIS PARKMAN

Doughty, H. *Francis Parkman.* New York: Macmillan Company, 1962.

Jacobs, W. R. L. *Francis Parkman, Historian as Hero: The Formative Years.* Austin: University of Texas Press, 1991.

Wade, M. *Francis Parkman: Heroic Historian.* New York: Viking Press, 1942.

Wade, M. *The Journals of Francis Parkman.* Vol. I & II. New York: Harper & Brothers, 1947.

JOHN WESLEY POWELL

Darrah, W. C. *Powell of the Colorado.* Princeton, New Jersey: Princeton University Press, 1951.

Goetzmann, W. H. *Exploration and Empire: The Explorer and the Scientist in the Winning of the American West.* New York: Alfred A. Knopf, 1966.

Powell, J. W. *Exploration of the Colorado River.* Chicago: University of Chicago Press, 1957.

Terrell, J. U. *The Man Who Rediscovered America: A Biography of John Wesley Powell.* New York: Weybright and Talley, 1969.

U.S. Department of the Interior Geological Survey: *John Wesley Powell's Exploration of the Colorado River.* Washington, D.C.: U.S. Government Printing Office, 1975.

FREDERIC REMINGTON

McCracken, H. *Frederic Remington: Artist of the Old West.* New York: J.B. Lippincott Company, 1947.

Remington, F. *Pony Tracks.* Norman, Oklahoma: University of Oklahoma Press, 1961.

Remington, F. *Frederic Remington's Own Outdoors.* New York: Dial Press, 1964.

Samuels, P., and H. Samuels. *Frederic Remington: A Biography.* New York: Doubleday & Company, Inc., 1982.

SACAGAWEA (BIRD WOMAN)

Bryant, M. F. *Sacajawea: A Native American Heroine.* (Juvenile) Billings, Montana: Council for Indian Education, 1989.

Clark, E. E., and M. Edmonds. *Sacagawea of the Lewis and Clark Expedition.* Berkeley: University of California Press, 1979.

Frazier, N. L. *Sacajawea: The Girl Nobody Knows.* (Juvenile) New York: David McKay Company, Inc., 1967.

Howard, H. P. *Sacajawea.* Norman, Oklahoma: University of Oklahoma Press, 1971.

NANCY WARD

Ellington, C. J. *Beloved Mother: The Story of Nancy Ward.* Johnson City, Tennessee: Overmountain Press, 1994.

Felton, H. W. *Nancy Ward, Cherokee.* New York: Dodd, Mead, & Company, 1975.

Gilbert, J. *The Trail of Tears Across Missouri.* Columbia, Missouri: University of Missouri Press, 1996.

Tucker, N. *Nancy Ward, Ghigau of the Cherokees.* Georgia Historical Quarterly, June 1969.

MARCUS AND NARCISSA WHITMAN

Cranston, P. *To Heaven on Horseback: The Romantic Story of Narcissa Whitman.* (Juvenile) New York: Julian Messner, 1952.

Drury, C. M. *Marcus Whitman, M.D.: Pioneer and Martyr.* Caldwell, Idaho: Caxton Publishers, Ltd., 1937.

Eaton, J. *Narcissa Whitman: Pioneer of Oregon.* New York: Harcourt, Brace & World, Inc., 1941.

Jones, N. *The Great Command: The Story of Marcus and Narcissa Whitman and the Oregon Country Pioneers.* Boston: Little, Brown and Company, 1959.

Index